THE ADVERSARY'S GOOD NEWS

Michael Anthony Adams, Jr.

SIX SEEDS PRESS
Baltimore, MD

First Six Seeds Press Edition
Copyright © 2014 Michael Anthony Adams, Jr.

Originally Published as *The Adversary's Good News* by Israfel
Sivad by CreateSpace Independent Publishing Platform
January 2015

Current Edition Published by Six Seeds Press,
Baltimore, MD
February 2022

ISBN: 978-1-952240-13-3

Cover Design © 2017 PJ Adams
Portrait of Michael Anthony Adams, Jr. © 2014 PJ Adams

Also by Michael Anthony Adams, Jr. and Published by Six Seeds Press

Fiction:

The Adversary's Good News: A Novel
Psychedelicizations: Short Stories
The American Apocalypse: Short Stories
Crossroads Blues: A Novel
The Cars Behind, Beside Us: Short Stories
Welcome to the Modern World, Charlie: Short Stories
Notes from the Idle Mind: Short Stories

Nonfiction:

Disorder: An Avant-Garde Memoir of Psychosis, Healing and Love

Poetry:

We Are the Underground: Poems
From Now to You: Haiku
Recipe for a Future Theogony: Poems
Indigo Glow: Poems
The Tree Outside My Window: Poems
At the Side of the Road: Poems
Soundtrack for the New Millennium: A Poem

www.6SeedsPress.com

The Adversary's Good News
For Adam Brown

Contents

A. Uranophobia

Σ. Ponerology

Ω. Phlogiston

The Adversary's Good News

A.
Uranophobia

21.
The Sparrow's Insight

Somehow, a dead sparrow had found its way onto Christian Michael Anderson's floor. He'd discovered it as he tore through his room frantically searching for a misplaced bag of weed. Like the fossilized remains of a miniature dinosaur imprinted on a dug-up sedimentary stone, the gnarled bird lay stiff with one leg wrenched straight, the other bent forwards at the knee. Its tiny talons were splayed in mimicry of grabbing at some ghostly worm that had passed into the netherworld at the same moment as the little bird's flighty soul. Its beak was pried open as if receiving a regurgitated last supper from its long-dead mother. Brown feathers had turned black and stiff from what seemed a sticky sweat (although, of course, birds don't sweat) and cemented themselves to the wooden floor. A flurry of downy white fluttered up from the corpse when Christian removed the tee shirt entombing it.

There was no blood, no evidence as to the cause of death, just the windflaw of dead feathers through the dusty streaks of sunlight and the dead black stare of one empty, avian eye. The whole encounter was a little odd. Although Christian's window had been open for months, he had no idea when the bird might have entered his room. Even in his drunken and drug-induced stupors, he'd never noticed the dying rounds of a bird flapping against his walls, chirping across his floor. He'd never been aware of any fanciful flights intruding upon his haze of misery. Before it even entered the room, the sparrow's death must have been immanent. Like a whale beaching itself, it must have hopped inside, intent on dying right there on the hardwood floor. How long had it been there? Why hadn't Christian noticed it before? But most importantly, where was that bag of weed?

He'd been searching for it for two weeks – in preparation for this moment, the morning when his alcohol, drugs, and money all ran out and his head and stomach screamed for some sort of mind-altering relief. He could feel their internal cries ricocheting back and forth between his scalp and his toes. They burned behind his eyes and chattered through his teeth. Shaking from alcohol withdrawal, he wiped his trembling hand down his sticky face. It had never been this bad before – or so he always told himself when it was this bad. He could taste the sweet, lingering sensation of Wild Irish Rose on the back of his tongue – his last drink from the midnight before, bought by spare-changing in front of the local, corner store. Quarters, nickels, and dimes had been dropped into his jittery palm. He'd downed the bottle in thirsty gulps beside a dumpster in the alleyway behind the store. He'd returned for more, but chased away by the clerk, he'd eventually weaved back home to pass out beside the then unknown dead bird on his floor. Together in dreamless sleep, they'd shared Christian's self-made tomb. And now, his throat's parched tingling needed to be squelched. It drove him mad, but he didn't even have enough money for a pack of generic cigarettes. He needed that little, dime-bag of cheap green.

He was fairly certain he hadn't smoked it. But in all honesty, who knew. The past lonely months washed through his thoughts on a wave of alcoholic haze. He remembered a night where the plastic baggy had been on his desk, and between his nicotine stained fingers there'd been a bright, fresh bud of something that lifted him higher than the schwag in the bag. He'd decided to save the seed-infested dime for an emergency (like today), but now he couldn't remember where he'd hidden it. Of course, there was the possibility that in one of his blackouts he'd already smoked it... But racked with need, Christian refused to believe that could possibly be true.

He stared at the dead sparrow on his floor – that had been there for the devil knows how long, not long enough to decompose or stink, but long enough to grow stiff when Christian tapped it with his toe, long enough to stick to its chalked outline when Christian tried prying it from its final resting place.

With the diseased feathers stuck to his fingers, Christian wiped a morning sweat that reeked of cheap wine from his brow. The bits of down smeared across his sickly slick forehead, created a type of war-paint along his visage, but with no mirror hanging anywhere on his room's unending, unadorned white walls, Christian didn't notice. Instead, like an angelic reveille, the dead bird reawakened a thought that tickled the back of Christian's mind. He looked over his shoulder and up, to a spot in his ceiling where the plaster and rotten plywood had fallen down (it lay in a shattered heap overtop Christian's disgustingly dingy clothes and empty whiskey, beer, and wine bottles on the floor), revealing the 2x8 girders holding up the roof. Christian swallowed slowly. Like Coleridge's albatross, Poe's raven, this dead sparrow was the harbinger of a horrendous fate. And Christian knew what it all meant.

A sort of calm, which hadn't been evident in his previous agitation, washed over him and emanated throughout his room's disaster zone as he focused his throbbing eyes on the bright stream of sunlight pouring through his window and glowing like a tarnished halo overtop the dead bird. An intimation of the divine resided in that dusty beam shining down through light years of empty outer space. Christian stood up and stepped backwards. He set right his overturned desk chair – knocked to the floor during his manic search – and plopped down. Any thoughts of divinity immediately vanished in the face of his troubled stomach and trembling fingers. His soul itself was quaking. But still that lone beam of sunlight glimmered, and in the face of such vast emptiness it only spoke of the incommensurability between Christian's world and anything approximating the spirit. Christian dropped his face into his hands, and he heaved a silent sob. There's no surer sign God doesn't exist than when the beauty of this created world reveals nothing hidden but hideousness.

Realizing the bag of weed must be gone, nothing could pull Christian out of the morass created by his recognition of the newfound depths of his suffering... Not even his own shakily whispered mumbling between sniffles of that oft-recited invocation, "Jesus Christ..."

But the words were meaningless. They weren't a prayer. They weren't a curse. They were what they were: empty air exhaled from a diaphragm taut from the absence of a much-needed poison. A poison transformed into the water of life, the nectar of the gods, the very thing making existence itself possible. Without it the brightest day turned into the blackest night, the coolest night burned with the heat of the most torrid day, all notions of good became wicked portents of evil, every action of evil became a necessary good, and nothing made any sense whatsoever.

Under a cluttering of debris, something like his own mind, there was a picture beneath the pane of glass protecting the wooden top of his desk. Christian brushed aside the trash (empty cigarette boxes, pointlessly kept receipts, snot and cocaine coated Kleenexes) so he could look once again at his past. The picture was a black and white photograph of a girl. In black pants and a white shirt, she climbed overtop the railing at the edge of a cliff. Her short black hair was brushed back, and her immaculate jawline was settled in concentration. Barefoot, her perfect toes bent in the air, she perched, balanced on the arch of her foot, on the bottom rung. Both hands, long fingers wrapped to whiteness, gripped tight the top rung. Her head bent forward at the neck, and her black eyes stared emptily into darkness as she contemplated the descent... Eventually, she'd stopped contemplating. Christian reached with shaky fingers to pull the picture out from underneath the see-through prison behind which he kept it – his own emotional peep show.

Even in the midst of his demonic cravings, a guilty pang, a sensation akin to a precursor to vomiting (which it very well may have been), struck the back of his throat. It further upset his already upset stomach. It drew venomous tears out from his mind to the back of his dry, throbbing eyes. Christian stared at the picture his jittery fingers shook as if it were a Polaroid that still had more development to go through as if there were a picture beneath the picture needing to be gotten to. There was, but wrapped and strapped tight by his physical limitations, Christian would never see it.

He could only imagine it: a frozen skeleton clutching like Juliet at her own throat where an overabundance of prescription sleeping pills needing to be disgorged blocked her windpipe. Nobody had made it to her bedroom in time to find her passed out, in need of a stomach pumping before the overdose of sedatives caused every organ to slow, crawl, and eventually shut down. For all of time, that was the final image, the final reality of the photograph's pensive girl contemplating the depths of the descent before her – a dreamless sleep (like the sparrow's and Christian's from the night before) forever.

And all Christian wanted was to see her in the flesh again, to feel her warm body wrap around his. There were so many things he had to say. Over many a drunken night, he'd shouted them at the indigo sky, starlit as her black eyes, but always, in the day, the words settled into his stomach, a weight he couldn't vomit out no matter how many evenings he spent curled up on the tiles around his toilet.

Yes, both alcohol and emotions needed to be gotten out. Both tormented his decaying body and distorted mind. Parasitic, they fed upon each other. One fueled the other and in turn grew anew from the combustion smoking out his brain's sputtering engine. The soil of his once fertile soul had grown brown and barren and turned to so many handfuls of dust under the scorched earth policy his memories had forced him to adopt. The armies of the psychic siege that had been laid upon him salted the earth after their spirits burned everything in him not made of flesh. Less than even a shell (for a shell implies something had once been alive), Christian found himself engulfed in the flames of his memories. Aside from the torment of his physical agony, he needed those memories erased again. But there was nowhere to escape. No matter how bad he wanted it to fade away, the world remained real. And the desert of the real is uninhabitable – an arid, wicked place to be. It was at that very moment, racked with withdrawal and pain, as if her mirage in the distance offered the promise of a drink, he croaked her name out of his choked throat, "Sophia…"

For a brief moment, the words made everything tangible – as if breath had shape. But then the oasis vanished. A pit opened in Christian's gut, and he collapsed into it. Now and forever, Sophia existed only in that photograph (except for that deeper picture in the interminable depths of Christian's own mind). But there was one simple way Christian might see either her or nothing else forever again. He glanced up at that hole in his ceiling once more.

Even a mere cigarette might have somehow made things better. A cup of coffee, a bottle of Nyquil or Tylenol, a drink goddamnit… In a flurry of activity, a postponement of the inevitable, Christian dug through the trash on his desk and around his feet. Every cigarette box was opened and shook revealing nothing but crushed foil and tobacco dregs. Every pile was systematically pored through in the hopes of finding a penny, a nickel, a dime, a broken cigarette, or that little baggy of weed. Nothing. The only option Christian had was to go back to the corner store and beg for change, but he couldn't do that again. Somehow, a semblance of pride, an unfamiliar emotion he hadn't felt in quite some time, welled inside his breast. Maybe it emanated from Sophia's captured, vacant stare. "You fucking bum," he growled at himself. And self-loathing crowded out every other hollow emotion. He looked at the dead bird on his floor. There was no denying it. Like the sparrow, he was already dead.

He remembered a scene in the *Bhagavad-Gita*, a book he'd read years before, sometime in college. Arjuna turned to Krishna to plead with him and tell him he didn't want to have to fight against and kill his own family members. Enraged, Krishna exploded into his many-armed form.

Finally revealing his true nature, a thousand heads, the face of every god burst out his shoulders, and he admonished his pupil that it didn't matter whether or not he killed the enemy. In the eyes of the eternal, they were as good as dead already… simply because they were alive. Anything that was alive would surely die. Whether it was now or a thousand years hence didn't make a difference. Why mourn for things whose existence proved they would perish? And Christian found himself staring once again at the black and white picture of Sophia.

"We mourn because we perish," Christian whispered. And again, tears welled in the empty, throbbing spaces behind his eyes. He spat, "Fuck you, Krishna." And another little piece of him, a sliced off sliver of his decaying soul rotting without its roots, died.

So much of him had died over the years. So much more of him had died over the past months… more than he had ever known he had. The depths to which he could plumb his soul for hellish fodder seemed endless, but now he scraped against the cavern's black walls to slice every last bit of meat off the bone and digest it in the acidic combinations of misery's pit. He threw more gristle on the flames and watched the altar smoke from pain's fatty juices. Soon, he'd be able to rub his hands along an internal surface of smooth emptiness, walls of burning cold feeling of the crags of pure nothingness. He'd retreated so deep inside himself he could look out and see the interior of his mother's womb again. His food came to him through an umbilical cord, but he wanted to retreat even farther, back to blindness, to a single cell of non-existence. There was one last thing left to do. He needed to dissolve that umbilical cord back into his mother's very bloodstream. Then, he could starve his fetal self and devolve back into the universe's Precambrian miasma.

Maybe some sort of answer lurked in that dark, chaotic concoction. Maybe in non-existence the riddle of existence could be solved. The annihilation of the mind had brought nothing but madness and internal devastation. No matter the vacancies to which the constant influx of substances had driven him, reality came crashing back like the terrifying waves of a tsunami crushing a Pacific village.

Like to an African slum devastated by HIV, no foreign aid would come. The emotionally and spiritually wealthy had something better to do with their money, their time. After an eternity of this horror, the annihilation of the flesh was the next logical step. Because there had to be something deeper, more tangible than the mind's chemical combinations since no amount of twisting could cause them to finally snap. The gates of insanity had been breached, but some invisible force kept Christian from pursuing his maddening visions into their gaping maws. No matter what he did to himself, the atomic structures continued to spin. The idea of internal fission needed to be discovered. Only a mushroom cloud could adequately depopulate his brain. His memories would be considered collateral damage. If the transmission station could be found, it needed a smart-bomb to take it off the air, snuff it out entirely. If the soul and body were one and the same (and what else could the soul possibly be), then the flame of life itself needed extinguishing. Or it needed to be moved to a better place. Existence couldn't continue like this. He'd reached the limit, the point where parallel lines intersect. Beyond lay infinity, a world outside Euclidean geometry, an unknown land with an unmapped terrain. Somebody had to explore. And anywhere was better than here.

In this tornado swept room piled high with empty bottles and cigarette packs, dotted with Kleenex and debris from the fallen ceiling, with a dead bird rotting beneath mangy clothes, and a bed with torn white sheets stained gray from nights and nights of unfelt, drenching sweat. In this starving body sweating through convulsions, trembling from the inside out, with a bloodstream unused to the very blood pumping red and blue but pure through its veins and arteries, tormented by commingling desires that could taste the missing tingle of nicotine, liquor, pot, and cocaine drip, a brain that could see clearly but desired only a hazy blur rounding off reality's sharp edges. Sight itself was painful. The dismal sun scorched his retinas. And what was he looking at in this miserable light? A picture of a dead girl. The carcass of a dead bird. The actions of a man in his twenty-seventh year of dying – a spiritual abortion, God's abandoned fetus rotting in a dumpster in an alley behind a Bangkok whorehouse, abandoned previous to his birth, and sleep-walking through his zombie existence, vacant, empty, pointless. No, there was no need to continue this.

And again, Christian glanced up at the hole in his ceiling.

That hole held the promise of a gateway to another life, another existence that didn't exist at all. The exposed rafters beckoned with the hope of eternal escape. God lived on the other side, and Christian had some questions for Him… If He even bothered to show up when all was said and done. Perhaps He'd hide there like He hides in this world, ashamed to show Himself for fear of the reprisals against His absurd decrees, petrified humanity might fail to submit to His yoke and string Him up in the lynching anybody who's bothered paying attention to this world would certainly believe was in order. In fact, when we meet God, we'll tell Him we want to live in a free society where we elect our own rulers, and the first creature we choose to displace the now blacklisted Creator Who has so horribly botched His job is the primordial enemy of the heavenly state, Satan himself.

Please, my rebellious friend, enter and bow to the crowded cheers of the elated masses. We've been waiting an eternity for you to take over as our rightfully elected leader. We're all on your side. Dear devil, we're at your command. Just let me crawl through that hole in the ceiling.

But on the other side of that hole in his ceiling, there was nothing. Christian had been praying too long to believe anymore. That hole in his ceiling led to empty outer space, gaseous combinations, orbiting compounds of rocks, hurtling fireballs, dark matter, and for the past forty years, junk-metal launched from humanity into an endless, celestial trashcan. Someday, we may launch all our trash into outer space. Someday, space will become as wretched and wrecked as our lands, skies, and oceans. Someday, we'll realize we can't fix anything. We're walking, breathing, talking napalm explosions, and now everything's broken. But hopefully before that day comes, we'll face annihilation. It's well overdue. If there was a God, it would have already happened. No, there was nothing on the other side of that hole in the ceiling.

And even though this fallen world with its attendant misery and suffering formed the all, the other side of that hole in the ceiling was exactly where Christian wanted to be. He was certain. The blue sky and clouds outside, the sunlight streaming through the window, the foundation of this house, the walls of this room, the bottles and clothes on his floor, the trash on his desk, the picture in his hand, the missing alcohol and drugs contained no hidden meanings, no mysteries to be understood, no novel symbolism, no divinities hidden in the shadows. There was only emptiness. Sophia had seen it. In her picture, looking over the cliff, she'd stared at it. The empty knowledge captured and imprinted on her gaze proved she'd experienced it in all its formless glory. And still, she'd given up. With nothing left, her past erased, her future despondent, she'd given up.

One night, lying in bed, she'd warned Christian that might happen. He'd been staring at a dead bouquet of flowers hanging dry and crisp from the center of her ceiling. They appeared so fragile they might crack with the subtlest breath of wind. He and Sophia had been talking about the possibility of their future together in the United States, a country she'd never even visited before. But he was enough to make her yearn to be there. He was enough to make her long to abandon her home, her job, her endless ache for the great unknown.

With her Austrian accent, as her naked body curled into Christian's warm shoulder, she'd said, "Christian, I never know if I shall live or if I shall die. Every morning, when I wake up, I make the decision – Will I live today, or will I die today? Every day of my life, I have chosen to live, but someday, I do not know…" Now, as he lost his thoughts to the sparrow decomposing on his floor, brought into this world with no apparent point other than to die, Christian thought no words could ring truer. He whispered in final reconciliation, an understanding arrived at too little, too late, "But someday, I do not know…"

His mind made up, he crumpled the picture of Sophia between both fists. He wouldn't need it where he was going. This picture that had haunted his days and tormented his nights, this picture that had enflamed his cancerous rage and filled his clouded brain with a rain of endless tears, this picture that had taught him so much of emptiness and despair, of loss and regret would never be seen by his earthly eyes again. And for that, he was grateful. For that, he'd take a chance on anything – even a non-existent God, even nothing.

Unsure whether to cry or scream, to sob for his nearing decision or leap for joy at his newfound resolve, he leaned his head forward and rested his forehead on his clenched fists. He wanted one last moment to let the image contained on that piece of paper filter through his pores, into his hands, through the trembling muscles in his fingers, past the thin layers of his sweaty skin, and into the shattered chambers of his battered skull. Behind his retinas, the eternal image (both the seen and the unseen) burned. In the emptiness of himself, Christian rediscovered a reflection of his own likeness. He contemplated it and determined one last time that all those years ago, Sophia had been quite right: they were meant for each other, *kismet*.

He remembered the last thing she'd ever asked him, her English words thickened by the intricacies of her accent, "Do you still believe in us?"

Just like he had all those years ago, he closed his eyes. But this time (so long past the point when it had any meaning), he said what she'd wanted to hear, "Yes, Sophia, I still believe in us." He scrunched his eyes tight. Self-loathing choked him, but still, love's light butterflies fluttered through his two days' empty stomach. Romeo had taken quite some time to make his resolution, to determine his restitution. But now the time had come.

Christian stood up. He dropped the crumpled photograph onto his floor where, now indistinguishable from all the other refuse of his life, it nestled into its own space in the trash heap – the spot it had already claimed (snuggled dreamily between bottles of liquor) in his memories.

He glanced once more at the foundling sparrow rotting away amid his decay. It stared back at him with the same vacant yet knowledgeable gaze gracing Sophia's look. And Christian realized he needed the understanding those eyes possessed. He needed to see the world the way those sightless eyes saw it. He wanted to carve out the bird's all-encompassing pupils and replace his own with them. He wanted to see through the eyes of death.

Because it had been so long since he'd spoken to anybody other than a drug dealer or a store clerk (he avoided his roommates and the squatters who took turns sleeping on the couch and floor downstairs) that no friend had had the opportunity to rest his hand on Christian's shoulder and say, "Man, are you okay? You look like death warmed over..." No friend had come along who'd wondered, "What's going on with you? You look like you need to talk..." No friend had sat across a table from him as smoke streamed from their shared cigarettes and blurted out, "Man, you really could use some help." Nobody had said anything. And as a companion for misery, nobody made a wonderful friend. Christian wanted nobody forever. And he was prepared to make that wish a reality. All he needed was faith in that hole in the ceiling. It was time to climb through. The sparrow had done it. Why couldn't he?

Kicking aside bottles and clothes, he wandered over to his six months' unused bucket of masonry tools. Amid the dusty chisels and hammers and levels, he'd tucked in a stolen rope. It was neatly coiled and perfectly preserved. Christian reached in and pulled it out.

That rope had sat there through the months of his unending binge, waiting for the day when Christian's alcohol, drugs, and money had all run out. Without even a cigarette to lift him through this early afternoon morning, Christian knew today was the day he'd use the rope for its stolen purpose. Truly, it had been a long time coming.

In his hands, the rope contained a certain amount of comfort. It felt good to finally make up his mind about something, to finally be on the verge of some sort of action. Too much time had been wasted. Too many days had blurred into one long, unending nightmare.

Was there a last moment he even remembered? Was there any way he could order the minutes and hours and weeks that had passed, one day lost the same as the next, one moment planted atop the other, flipping inside out and vomiting themselves – pure liquid with nothing solid in the spew – into a porcelain throne, around his feet on a tile floor, nothing but a wave of alcoholic haze fermenting in his gut into an ever stronger spiritual poison? The rope wrapped tight around all that lost time. It bound it into a neat bundle that his clicking, tear-choked throat could swallow – a sort of Christmas present for the end of the summer delivered by a Satanic Santa Claus. Like the rings of a tree revealing its age, every coil of the rope bound another worthless memory, another reality better forgot. But unfortunately, once something's done, it can never be forgotten. Once something's inscribed in Mnemosyne's book, it can never be erased... at least, not in our waking hours.

But even in sleep, we're tormented by dreams. Unless, of course, the substances turning our days into nights can turn our nights into endless blackness. But with no substance to make the day sleep, Christian confronted everything he'd ever done, everything that had ever happened to him. In a moment of clarity, he saw his life's vast wasteland stretch out endlessly behind him, and he foresaw that wasteland stretching eternally before him. He closed his eyes and wiped his hand down his cheeks. It came away slick with sweat. At some point in time, all things must come to an end.

Shivering from chemical desires, Christian confronted his own impending apocalypse, his final judgment. Jesus, his forehead held between two fingers, sat to his left. Satan fumed on his right. Before the bench, each argued their cases. God banged His gavel, and the Fates took their places. With an automatic impulse, Christian wrapped and rewrapped the rope around his hand.

Was this really what his twenty-seven years on planet earth had been barreling towards? Had every event, the interminable calculus of existence, really compounded themselves into this one point? Had the derivative of all his experiences finally been determined? The answer was nil, an empty set. Is that even possible? Christian checked in with his beliefs. They were vacant, as desolate as the alley where he'd consumed his last bottle of Wild Irish Rose the night before. Nothing.

Still coiling the rope, Christian walked back to his chair. He grabbed the chair and slid it directly underneath the hole in his ceiling. He climbed atop the chair, and with the rope in one hand, he reached up into that hole in the ceiling. Stretching to his limit, he tossed the rope overtop one of the 2x8 supports stretching across the beams holding up the roof. Peering into darkness, he looped the rope around the support. A miserable sweat broke out on his forehead. He rubbed his trembling hand across it, and it came away dotted with bits of the dead bird's downy feathers. He tried to remember how that could have happened, but he couldn't. He eyed the rope's distance from the ground. He toyed with the length until his few years of working construction assured him the distance was correct. He tied the rope off and tugged on it to make sure its fabric would support the weight he intended to dangle from it. Then, he looped the bottom end of the rope around itself again and again, a trick he'd learned while working construction. With his shaky fingers, it was difficult to feed the loose end in between the coils, but somehow, as if driven by divine guidance, he managed to do it. When his noose was completed, he slipped it over his head. It rested weightlessly upon his shoulders. He pulled the knot down to tighten the noose around his neck. Its bristles rubbed rough against his flesh. And before he had a chance to doublethink his thoughts, he kicked back hard with his heel and knocked the chair out from underneath himself.

With a thud, the chair fell to the ground, and with dramatic speed, Christian dropped down until his involuntarily extending toes reached a mere inch or two from the wooden floorboards. The rope snapped taut and held tight. It slammed Christian's brain into his skull. It pulled against his throat, cutting into his esophagus and blocking the passage of breath as he swung miniature circles through the air. Instinctually, he gasped, but nothing filled his lungs. He gasped again, but all that occurred was a choked click emanating from the middle of his throat. His eyes bulged against their sockets. His throat felt like it was being sawed in half. He tried to swallow, but his Adam's apple caught against the noose.

The enduring agony of the rope erased every thought as soon as it became visible. As he hung there, sadness reached out from his gut and strained tears behind his eyes. He spun, and his gaze passed heaven-like over the disorder of his cramped living space. His entire existence appeared in his room's wreckage. He passed the point where he had dropped Sophia's picture, and a vision of her flickered behind his eyelids. She smiled coquettishly and waved her hand for him to follow. Then, she disintegrated into darkness.

As the remnants of his breath escaped him, panic took hold. He stuck his finger between the rope and his neck, but he only succeeded in using his own digit to strangle himself. He summoned all his strength to hoist his body up the rope. He flexed and pulled and reached with one hand to try to get to the support and untie the rope from where it held fast, but holding the entirety of his weight with one arm, he quickly gave up. His hand burned as it slid down the rope, and he fell back into place. He kicked and kicked in a vain attempt to loosen himself, but his exertion only spun him in ever widening circles. With reality closing in faster, he fumbled with the knot behind his head. But in his suffocating panic, with a whooshing noise beginning to rush through his world, he couldn't think straight, and he only managed to pull the noose even tighter. Contorting his mouth with a gasping grimace, he strained again to pull himself up to where the rope was tied, but no matter how hard his shoulders and arms flexed, nothing happened.

He began feeling light-headed. In an inverted rain reminiscent of an acid trip, stars shot upwards from the floor. The world faded dark at the edges, but in its disappearing, captured light, Christian's sight settled on the sparrow dead on his floor.

So this was the realization the tiny bird had had before it had fluttered into his cluttered bedroom. Emptiness pressed outward from inside Christian's lungs. His hollow stomach twisted around itself, and a tickling emotion crept from it down his intestines, into his legs, and through his feet until it ended up twitching between his toes. The last thing he remembered thinking, after the world had gone black, before convulsions began coursing through his body was, "Jesus, I don't want to die."

20.
Through the Hole

It must have been the subtle swinging motion that awakened Christian. Reality's bright world replaced the inner landscape he'd been traversing.

There'd been a dream with colors as vivid as a canvas of renaissance art – a bright, white light at the end of a long tunnel (something like the emptiness he'd pictured as his insides). A choir of angels, trumpets to their lips and voices lilting as the breeze, fluttered about caught in a strobe light of perspective paintings at the limit of his sight. The angels' golden wings glimmered in sunshine. Wings had become attached to Christian's shoulders as well. With an ease of motion as if they'd always been there even though he'd never been aware of them, the wings propelled him through the darkness.

A lightness that had evaded his hopes over the past months spread outward from his stomach. It coated his insides like an outpouring of spiritual honey. And then a whisper of breath caressed him, and the soft sound of Sophia's sonorous accent rang through his ears: *Do you still believe in us?* He'd twisted his head in every direction to catch a glimpse of her face in the shadows, to give her sound substance. But before he'd been able to actually see her (the true dream behind the dream), the recurrence of sensation caused him to open his eyes.

A bird's eye view of his room's devastation burst upon his sight, and the first thing he tried to do was breathe. But an external blockage stopped his windpipe. In fact, his entire neck burned as if he were in the process of being decapitated and somehow the axe had gotten lodged on a clump of bone. The hooded executioner, with his massive forearms and shoulders, jimmied the axe back and forth to jiggle it loose from where it stuck, to raise it above his shoulder and give one more whack, another attempt to drop Christian's severed head into the bloodied basket. And this motion seemed to cause the spinning sensation that had awakened Christian from his fabulous dream of Sophia and angels – two things that in his misery he had thought never to hear or see. One thing, however, remained from his dream: Christian's feet still weren't touching the ground, but he lacked the wings to propel him through the ether. Instead, like a mummy encased in its sarcophagus, he remained stuck firm in a single place.

The sweet honey of emotions crystallized into internal daggers. He remembered an earlier panic. And he remembered looking for a bag of weed. He remembered a dead bird on his floor (there it was – right there clutching in vain at a lost last supper). And he remembered... His hand shot up to his neck. There, the rope strained tight against his flesh. Frenzied, he began to kick and flail in every direction. But a calm voice from behind his head simply said, "Hold still. I'm almost done."

Even though he didn't recognize the voice, Christian paid attention. A certain terseness to the voice's tonal quality implied its disembodied owner was immersed in intense work, and the voice demanded respect for its task.

MICHAEL ANTHONY ADAMS, JR.

Christian hung limp, the rope cutting into his neck, bruising deep (blood clotting against his esophagus) his malleable flesh, and tugging him up – like Jah grabbing a Rasta by the dreads – as all the force gravity could muster tried in vain to pull him down. Over budding tears, Christian's eyelids fluttered. He felt he might pass out again. Like a television with bad reception, the room flickered in and out. White noise passed across Christian's gaze. He was flying into that hole in the ceiling, and he looked forward to another celestial slumber. Maybe this time he'd make it to the end of the tunnel. Maybe this time he'd find Sophia's warm body. His soul strained against his flesh to escape up to where the rope was tied and beyond it to the stars. Awakening him from the excitement of his coming dream, he dropped a centimeter. The room jerked up with his subtle decent. And then, as the voice behind him muttered, "Here we go," the pressure against his neck released, and he fell.

As if he had torn through the roof with all the speed of Lucifer descending from heaven and created the hole through which he'd hung himself, his legs buckled beneath his falling weight, and he landed on his ass, forearm deep in dirty laundry, on a mish-mashed pile of clothes and debris from the fallen ceiling. He ripped the cut loose noose off his neck and flung it with as much disgust as if it were a leper's rotten limb as far from himself as his physically and emotionally drained arms could send it.

Clutching at his breast like a doctor slapping a baby to life, Christian gasped and felt beneath the slick sheen of sweat coating his chest his lungs fill again with air – a glorious, invigorating sensation he'd thought never again to feel. Hallelujah, how we take our breath for granted! Sucking in as much life as his lungs could bear (which to his surprise was actually quite a lot), he glanced up above to his savior.

It must have been a remnant from the suffocated interiors of his oxygen-starved brain, but the man now standing on his once kicked over chair started out as a thin trail of smoke. Like the internal light of his heart chakra, the smoke burned bright red as it compressed and burst out from where his chest would be to explode into a lanky body. First the long torso came, then legs and arms ending with fingertips still smoking like a concurrently lit pack of cigarettes. Across his visage myriad faces flickered and disappeared. He was a broken old man, a fresh young girl, a corpulent lecher, a flirtatious coquette. He grew fangs. His lips turned into a thin smear of blood. His ears pointed up at the tips. Horns protruded from his forehead. He had the head of a dog, the snout of a pig, the thousand eyes of a fly, a snake's forked tongue, and the whiskers of a cat.

But eventually what surfaced from beneath the madness was a young man of approximately Christian's age with somewhat sunken cheeks, high cheekbones, and a well-defined jawline.

His eyes, perhaps his most striking feature, were deep-set above heavy bags giving him the appearance of having never slept. Jet black like the sparrow's eternally sightless pupils, his eyes soaked in all the light the room had to offer. He had a five o'clock shadow over his cheeks and a pale complexion. His Adam's apple bobbed as he swallowed, and he had shaggy black hair with an attractive wave to it. The worn-out attire and the flippant air of an urban rocker adorned him, and his manner bespoke a worldly confidence. Smiling, he folded up a rusty pocket knife (what he'd obviously used to cut Christian down from where he'd hung – how long must that have taken?) and slipped it into the back pocket of his jeans. All Christian could think was, *Man, I must be going through D.T.'s.* But he managed to mumble, "You – you saved my life…"

"Now, let's not get ahead of ourselves," the guy said, and in his black boots, he hopped down from the chair. He stuck his hand out to help Christian up from the mess he'd fallen into, and as he did so, he said, "Evius. And you are?"

"Christian," Christian said as he took the proffered hand and began to rise.

"Not your religion," Evius said, "Your name."

"That is my name. Christian," and he rose to his full height.

"Seems awfully confusing," Evius muttered. And then, as if he were listening to his own inner daemon, his eternally internal eyes dawned recognition, and he asked, "You want a smoke?" With a fluid motion, something akin to a magician's interpretive dance that Christian couldn't believe was really just an everyday flourish, he produced a red, white, and black pack of generic cigarettes from the breast pocket of his tight fitted shirt.

"I've been dying for one," Christian answered – already salivating at the mere mentioning of at least one substance… however ineffectual its mind-altering effects may actually be.

"You've been dying for more than that. So I'll give you one, but afterwards, you gotta take a shower, man. You smell like shit – not figurative shit, but literally: shit."

As soon as Evius mentioned it, as if his words cued the sensation, Christian felt a heavy, sopping load dragging down the seat of his pants. He wasn't wearing any underwear, and the bulge had obviously seeped down his hamstrings, calves, and heels. A wetness stuck his jeans' scratchy denim to his crotch and his thighs, and he realized, like a newborn, he was standing in a primordial soup of urine and excrement. It squished between his toes and slipped across the bottom of his feet. In a rare moment of self-respect, Christian's face burned red. But his needs outweighed his pride (besides, who was this stranger, and what did he know about the hell Christian had put himself through over the past months… years even?), and he said, "I'll smoke it on the way to the shower."

"Sounds good," Evius responded, and he shook out one of the cigarettes to give to Christian.

His fingers still trembling, Christian pulled the cigarette from the pack. It gyrated ever so slightly as he placed it between his nearly numb lips. A lit match appeared in Evius' hand, and as his savior's nails slipped back from overtop the sulfur, Christian noticed they'd been grown long like a woman's though his fingers and hands were thick and strong like a man's. His head swimming, Christian leaned forward to ignite his smoke.

My Lord, the rancid feeling of burning tobacco tasted of puissance and life. There's very little that will make you more certain of your burgeoning vitality than the heavy sensation of death-breeding smoke settling into your already tarnished lungs. To Christian's surprise, Evius' unknown, generic brand tasted almost as good as a Camel. It didn't possess the hint of chemicals and swept-up dirt permeating most generics. Instead, with a sharp inhale, it flowed smoothly down his esophagus beneath the bruise throbbing atop his seemingly sliced into Adam's apple. Christian exhaled and saw through the smoke the world had cleared just a little bit as the nicotine worked its way into his brain. His head lightened atop his neck. A mild buzz floated through his mind. A welcome dizziness rushed in to replace his illness, and Christian's world whirled from the substance's subtle effects.

But before he could enjoy the tobacco's relief for too long, Evius asked, "You gonna live up to your part of the bargain and take that shower, man? You fucking stink."

Christian nodded, and he stumbled out of his room, down the stairs (gripping tight the loosened handrail so that in his delirious state he wouldn't fall), and into the first floor bathroom.

The bathroom tiles were coated with slick grime, dirty and disgusting against the bottom of one's feet – one of myriad reasons Christian rarely ever bathed. Setting his half-smoked cigarette on the edge of the toothpaste encrusted sink, he leaned into the shower and switched on the water. With a sputter, it started up and began washing over the grime and hair and soap scum stuck to the bottom of the tub – still more reasons Christian never bathed.

There was a knock on the door. "Who is it?" Christian asked, nervous one of his roommate's might be home, might have heard his chair fall against the floor, seen him swinging from the rafter, already spoken to Evius about the state he'd found Christian in...

"It's me, man," Evius' voice came through the wall. "I brought you a change of clothes and a trash bag for your dirty pants."

Christian opened the door to receive the folded up clothes with the black plastic trash bag on top that Evius shoved through the crack Christian had left to conceal his vile nakedness. He thanked Evius, set the clothes on top of the toilet, and shoved his soiled pants into the trash bag. As the shower steam began clouding through the bathroom, Christian suddenly wondered: *Who in the hell is Evius?*

A cold confusion seeped from his mind into his limbs. He picked the cigarette up off the sink and took a welcome drag. He knew he'd never seen Evius sleeping on the couch or drinking 40 ounces with his roommates on the front porch. He had such a particular look that even in the haze Christian had been in for the past months, he was certain he would have remembered being introduced to him.

It didn't matter. Christian ran water over his cigarette butt to put it out. He tossed the butt onto the trashcan's overflow of used toilet paper rolls, Kleenexes, Q-tips, and tampon wrappers, and he stepped into the shower.

The scalding water splashed against his breast and trickled off his sparse chest hairs. Steam billowed around him. Amid the plastic rattle of broken rings, Christian drew closed the discolored shower curtain. Ensconced within his cleansing cell, he went to work on purifying himself of his automatically released, subconsciously freed feces.

Like Magdalene with Jesus, Christian soaped his feet. Touching his chest, he felt the life beneath his outer shell. It was as invigorating as his first breath on his bedroom's shattered floor. Mere moments ago, he'd wanted never again to experience that impression. The recognition shocked his brain to near numbness. In the midst of his stupefaction, as if he were swallowing the scented soap replacing his intestines' putrid stench, a vital sensation filled his throat and lungs. For the first time in months, a smile touched the corner of his lips. Even without any drugs, he actually felt a little high.

He wanted to shout out to the world he was alive. Sure, he was shaky. Sure, his room was a disaster zone. Sure, he'd just been doused in his own shit and piss. Sure, he didn't have a job, and he was standing in a tub that hadn't been cleaned in months if not years. But he was alive. God, damn it all to hell – he was alive! And he decided to take a nice long shower and relish the feeling that had been absent for so long.

Yes, this was enough to believe. Things would certainly be different from here on out. He'd start by getting back in touch with his mom. There was no phone in his house. It had been turned off eons ago. But surely his mother would accept a collect call from the payphone at the corner store.

It had been so long since they'd spoken… probably since before Christian had gone on unemployment. He'd call and tell her he'd given up drinking. No need to mention the drugs that had become a regular salt and pepper for his haze. She'd be so happy to hear from him. She'd be so happy about his decision. He didn't need to regale her with tales of what had precipitated his change. She could be shielded from the truth that had burst Christian's heart.

Once upon a time, in a world predating his drinking career, years before he'd shattered Sophia's life, they'd been all the other had – a second divorce, an only child… At thirteen, Christian became the man of the house. How could he have let that relationship slip away? How long had it been since he'd even gotten far enough out of himself to think about her lonely, solitary life in a city far, far away?

Today, this shower, the sheen of his purified skin marked the beginning of life after death. Evius had saved him. Who cared where the stranger had come from, what he was doing in his house. Christian wouldn't let his newfound knowledge go to waste. He'd no longer regret his mistakes with Sophia. He'd no longer drink himself into oblivion, smoke himself up to Uranus, and spend his few sober moments fiending for harder drugs whose high costs caused him to forsake his meals.

Perhaps that cigarette he'd bummed from Evius would be his last. No more three o'clock in the morning dumpster dives for munchies. No more late-night drunk drives to the other side of town to score a plastic-wrapped crack rock. Christian lathered his hair with shampoo and scratched the suds into his scalp. The texture of each individual strand of hair between his fingertips had never before felt so vital. The sensations of life were truly euphoric. His first shower in weeks washed the grime off more than his flesh. The warm water seeped beneath his skin. Like a full immersion baptism, it cleansed him of his sins.

Fresh and clean as a snake newly shed of its scales – his previous skin caught on a liquid hook and sloughed off into the drainpipe – Christian turned off the water. Since he had no towel in the bathroom, he picked up one that looked clean but smelled of mildew – it was better than using the white one with brown stains (who knew what that shit was). With no respect for whoever might use the towel on a regular basis, Christian dried himself. The towel's dank smell clouded the sweetly mingling scents of soap and clean skin. It tarnished the shower's precious, fading moments. Scowling from his senses' corroding, Christian hung the towel back on the rusty hook on the back of the door, and he turned to the clothing Evius had picked out for him.

Evius couldn't have realized it, but he'd laid out what, at one point in time, had been Christian's favorite outfit – a tight-fitting black cotton shirt with French cuffs and a pair of boot cut jeans tight at the thighs and loose at the ankles.

Christian pulled the jeans up to where they clutched the lower half of his body's scrubbed and dried skin. The jeans really looked quite deep and blue. Even in the faded spots, no inkling of the months of grime that must have been attached to them discolored the denim. Tomorrow, Christian promised himself, he'd go back to that laundromat he hadn't been to in forever and wash his clothes.

He'd call his mom while he waited for the washing to finish – a perfect way to embark upon his new life journey. He could already hear what he was going to say: "Mom, it's me, Christian. Just wanted to give you a call while I did a load of laundry. By the way, I quit drinking…"

He slipped a tight fitting undershirt over his emaciated but still vaguely muscled torso… it probably had more to do with the lack of fat than any real tone, and he slipped the black button down shirt on overtop of that. Methodically, he buttoned it. With the foul smelling towel, he wiped the steam off the mirror. And he took the first look at himself he'd taken since long before his last job had ended.

When you don't take any care for your appearance, there's no need to gaze at it. And when you're slowly destroying yourself, the last thing you want is any evidence of how well you're succeeding. Even in the slow crawl of alcoholic suicide, the desire for life can make the process of death still more unbearable. You're better off avoiding as many aspects of the square's everyday life as you can. Mirrors (as well as food and cleanliness) included.

In the mirror, Christian was surprised at his appearance. His face had thinned since the last time he'd paid any attention to it. A yellowish tint colored his features. Covered with a thick growth of at least a week's worth of whiskers, his cheeks appeared sunken, and his eyes were set back deep in his skull, cratered by heavy bags. His jawline had tightened, and his neck – a deep, red bruise burned into it – appeared strained. For the first time ever, Christian realized he was a walking skeleton.

He dug through the mess on the sink. Buried beneath a few used tissues, he found the toothbrush that had once been his. A long piece of hair was stuck to the bristles, but that didn't stop Christian. He quickly wet it down and squeezed some paste onto it from out of somebody's tube. Reflected in the mirror, his teeth were yellow with black stains around the edges. God, how long had it been since he'd brushed them?

When he was done, as he spit the paste back into the basin, a red commingling of blood – a spider's webbed period – strung through the lathered mess. Christian paid it no mind. With no insurance, what could he do about gingivitis? He was merely happy to see at least the black edges giving his teeth an almost transparent look appeared to have been brushed away.

His hair dangled in front of his eyes and covered his ears. As if it were the Red Sea waiting to drown Pharaoh's army, Christian parted it down the middle. It flipped up a little bit at the ends, on his bangs, and in the back. The shaggy look with his stubble gave him the mild semblance of a risen, angered Christ.

Christian decided that wasn't an image he wanted to perpetrate. He found an electric razor already plugged in and waiting (whose was that?). With the most offensive of his beard shaved down to a stubble, he rubbed somebody else's shaving cream over his cheeks, and he ran, again, someone else's well-used razor down his skin.

The dull blade seemed to pull out the whiskers more than it cut them, but when Christian was done, he was happy to see how civilized his smooth countenance appeared. After the shower and the stab at hygiene, he actually felt vaguely human – a sensation sorely lacking in the last years of his animalistic existence focused solely on the necessity of removing himself from the world as quickly and efficiently as possible. As he used the moldy towel to tamp off his damp cheeks, Christian promised himself shaving and tooth brushing would again become a regular part of his daily routine. After all, they were rituals most members of society participated in on a regular basis. Once he started working again, as soon as he got a paycheck, the first thing he'd have to do was get his hair cut – another regular deed taken for granted by his countrymen.

Christian took one last look at his still ragged reflection. "You're lucky as hell," he whispered to himself. There was no response. Back in the real world that for so long it had hated so much, his soul remained silent. He went on,

"After what you did, you have no right to be here. Remember that. After today, every day is a gift. From now on, you're going to appreciate what you've got. Even if you don't have shit."

And he didn't have shit. He had his life, which, if he were honest with himself, still wasn't shit. He had a roof over his head, but as far as the quality of what was beneath that roof... it wasn't shit. He had a room full of dirty clothes, but if anybody were to look at the style of those clothes, that person would have to admit they weren't worth a shit. He didn't have any food in the refrigerator. He didn't have any friends. Even though he'd promised himself he'd call his mother, his family reunion was still a distant dream. He didn't have a job. Other than his tools, he didn't have any possessions. The mattress and desk in his room had been there when he'd moved in. He hadn't had a girlfriend in ages. He didn't own any pets. He didn't have any insurance on his car. He had absolutely no money, which of course meant the few things that weren't shit he did have would probably be flushed down the toilet pretty soon.

But for the moment (and sometimes moments are all we have), as the bruise from the rope throbbed into his neck, Christian was willing to admit what wasn't shit really was some shit. He pressed his palm into his chest, felt his heartbeat (yes, it was still there), and thanked whatever presence governed the universe Evius had been there to cut him down from the hole in the ceiling before any possibility of sensation had vanished for eternity.

Without another word to his vacant reflection, he turned the light off in the bathroom, unhooked the door, opened it, and left the comforting remnants of shower steam for the ramshackle tenement that deep down inside he truly hated.

As soon as he put his bare foot back onto the kitchen's peeling tile floor, a screw twisted in his gut. What was that statement he'd made to himself about how he would feel about not having shit? He remembered his mother's home in the suburbs. It hadn't been much, but in light of his current situation, it sure as hell seemed like a lot. Maybe Christian could move back there to start his new drug and alcohol free life.

He pictured himself carrying a duffel bag full of clothes as he opened the screen door and stepped into his mother's aged embrace. As if he were still the boy she'd sent off to college nearly ten years ago, she held him tight by the shoulders and told him how glad she was he'd finally come home. With the air of one who'd seen the torments of hell and lived to tell the tale, Christian responded he was glad to *be* home. They embraced again, and his mother kissed him on the cheek. It felt so warm to be back in the place that, in high school, Christian had helped his mom turn from a run-down, abandoned hovel into the cozy family home where the two of them had shared their lives. In all the years he'd been gone, the place had hardly even changed. Tomorrow, Christian would cut the overgrown grass in the front yard…

Startling him from his reverie, like a shadow blocking the light of his dreams, Evius manifested himself in the kitchen. "I put your shoes down there by the door," he said, nodding to Christian's left. Christian looked where Evius indicated.

Sure enough, there was a pair of shoes there, but Christian had never seen them before. They were black leather, shiny half boots, expensively made and virtually brand new. Like the newly shed scales Christian almost imagined himself to have, the shoes glimmered beneath the overhead kitchen light. They must have cost what to

Christian was a small fortune. With one simple glance, he said, "Those aren't mine."

A bit shocked, Evius responded, "They were in your room. They've gotta be yours. Maybe you just don't remember buying them." Something registered in the darkened gleam of Evius' eye. He laughed. "Pretend like you're Cinderella. Try them on and see how they feel. You know what they always say: 'If the shoe fits...'"

More to get his feet off the mangy floor, Christian sat down and slipped on the fresh socks Evius had provided along with the never before seen shoes. He slid the shoes on over his toes and stretched the leather past his heel to where it gripped his ankles.

As if they'd been made especially for his own feet, the shoes fit perfectly. Christian stood up. The width of the shoes expanded perfectly at his toes. The length of the shoes snugged up tight against his heels. The ankles were supportive yet loosely comfortable at the same time. The soles cushioned his arch and gave at all the right places. Even the hard heel was supportive rather than painful.

Coupling the comfort with the stylish appearance, the shoes seemed the most magnificent piece of footwear Christian had ever had the pleasure to wear. *Jesus, when did I buy these?* he thought. *I've never owned a pair of shoes as wonderful.*

He walked a few circles to continue experiencing the glorious sensation of the shoes he really had absolutely no recollection of ever purchasing. If he hadn't known better, he may have considered them a gift from the gods, the type of thing a hero would receive prior to the commencement of his epic journey. But of course in the real world, at least in the modern world, such divine gifts never materialize. Since we have no heroic quests, we have no need of the gods' help. And since we have no gods, we have no heroic quests. As with most things, the whole logical puzzle is really quite circular. And the truth was simply that in one of his common hazes, Christian must have stumbled across the shoes on sale at the mall.

"So are they yours?" Evius asked.

"I guess so," Christian responded. "If they weren't before, they are now. They couldn't have been made for anyone else."

"Wonderful. Let's sit down and have us a smoke then," Evius said.

Christian followed Evius into the living room. As if he were the one whose name wasn't on the lease, Evius walked confidently. He stood straight, and his long legs – flexing beneath his tight jeans – stepped with assurance. His boots tap, tapped against the nineteen-seventies' style tile floor with rat droppings entangled in the cobwebs strung between the baseboards in the corners.

On the other hand, Christian followed in a shrunken stance, furtively glancing – as if he himself were one of the nocturnal scavengers who prowled the kitchen – to his left and his right over the stained walls that had enclosed him for so long. He breathed deep the stale stench of rat piss pervading from the cracks between the walls throughout the entire abode but that was especially pungent there in the kitchen. Given his experiences and thoughts of the day, he was unusually keen on the physical sensations of his miserable surroundings. The odiferous scent capped itself like the inversion of a fine wine with a bitter taste in the back of the throat.

No wonder Christian never bothered to eat. Who could stand to cook or ingest food with that stomach-churning scent consistently hanging at the periphery of his senses? It's amazing how death can wake you up to the harshest realities of your life. There was no way around it; Christian needed a new place to live. Maybe he'd leave tomorrow, ask his mom to Western Union him the money for a bus ticket, pack his bags, and depart from his disgusting existence once and for all – a new life birthed by his attempted suicide. He'd return to the womb and begin his existence all over again. He just had to make it through one more night. That was all. In fact, maybe he should leave now, call his mom, and see if he could get out before the unbearable darkness fell. The truth was his resolve may not make it through the horrors nightfall brought with it – the memories, the visions, the dreams. Almost frenzied, he said to Evius, "Hey, man, I'm gonna take off. Thanks for everything. I appreciate it. Really, I do. But I gotta go…"

However, before Christian could turn and make his way to the unlockable front door, Evius said, "Jesus, man, you said I just saved your life. The least you could do is keep me company while I smoke a cigarette."

Unsure why the man who saved his life would make such a friendly plea but feeling a bit beholden to the desires of his apparently new-found companion, Christian stopped in the living room with Evius. It wasn't his intention. It wasn't even his desire. But the interminable calculus of our existence sweeps us up into the midst of its derivatives of situations we never imagined for ourselves.

So Christian sat down on the couch reeking from the sweat of dozens if not hundreds of unshowered, homeless, teenage bodies writhing in sleep or lust but never in peace from the alcohol and drugs pumping through their running and abandoned systems.

Evius sat down on the other couch across the broken down table (that one of the girls who lived in the house once wanted to turn into an altar for the rites of black magic she imagined herself to perform) between them. He pulled that red, white, and black pack of generic cigarettes out of his breast pocket again and offered one to Christian who took it without even wondering whether or not this simplest of addictions needed to be kicked in order for him to embark upon the vessel of the new life he'd promised himself. They each lit their respective smokes, and they settled back into the stuffing filled holes of their respective couches to watch the smoke billow out their mouths and drift up to the ceiling like their souls attempting to escape the physical decrepitude their spiritual eyes opened upon.

"So how did you wind up here, man?" Christian asked. "Are you friends with Andrew or Evie or Charlie or Kat?"

"We've seen each other around," Evius answered between a puff of blue smoke congealing like a tarnished halo, a phantasmal crown about his head. "But not really friends with any of them. I keep to myself a good deal of the time."

Something about Evius' response struck Christian as a little odd, but all he managed to do was scrunch up his brow in thought (still without any real substances in his system, thought came quite slow) while he mumbled, "Yeah, I do the same."

"Well, I guess we're cut from the same cloth, then," Evius responded. "You know what they say about birds of a feather…"

"Yeah, I know what they say." The image of a tiny sparrow dead on his floor, its dismembered feathers fluttering up with the breeze flashed behind Christian's eyelids as they closed for a rapid blink.

When Christian opened his eyes again, Evius seemed to have shifted his position in the dusty light shining through the window. It now lit his face in such a way that he had an almost angelic glow about him. An evanescent aura from an indigo crystal exuded from his features and faded into oblivion. Again, Christian blinked. And this time, something twisted in his stomach. "If you aren't friends with any of them," he asked, "What are you doing here?"

Evius shrugged. With no trace of embarrassment in his voice, he said, "The door was open when I pushed on it, and I just walked in. It was the only open house on the block." Before Christian could comment or even register his incredulity, Evius shifted again so the light now hit him from behind to bathe his shale-like features in shadows. From the darkness, he pointed one long finger at Christian and went on, "Lucky for you I did that. Hey, you wanna smoke some pot?" Without waiting for Christian's response, Evius reached into his pocket and pulled out a plastic bag thick with a bright green bud and a sheaf of rolling papers.

The mere sight of what he'd been craving for so long was enough to set Christian's mouth watering. The desired taste of popping and burning marijuana coated his saliva and tickled his tongue. His desire for a new way of life evaporated from the forefront of his mind to be replaced with one simple thought: how nice it would be to get stoned. The fumes were already infiltrating his mind. The scent was already stopping up his nasal passages and replacing the rat piss's overwhelming aroma. The image of his mother's home in that city far, far away became as distant as the miles one would have to traverse to get to it. And the weed hadn't even been sparked yet.

Like a priest in a besieged city ripping a page from the Bible to wipe his ass with, Evius slid one of the sheets of rolling paper out of the sheaf. He set it gingerly on Christian's roommate's wanna-be altar as he broke off a little piece of bright green – tinged at the end with minuscule red hairs – from the bud's stem.

With the precision of a prostitute kneading her John's flaccid phallus, from between his long nails, Evius massaged the broken leaf of grass into a fine powder sprinkling down overtop the lone paper flapping gently at the edges as it got ready to get caught and spun by the breeze. But the promised breeze never came.

The weed fell in a long line that if it had been white would have set Christian's nose tingling. The green sent his taste buds scrambling. Evius scooped the paper up with one hand, rolled it between his thumb and forefinger, licked it between his thick lips as erotically as a man with a fetish for tiny penises, and wound up holding a tight, thin joint rolled so precisely few potheads would have been able to produce something of comparable status had they had the aid of a rolling machine.

Christian's stomach flip-flopped. He closed his eyes and licked his lips.

With all the solemn pomp and authority of church bells' peals, a match's spark echoed through the room. Entranced as a God-fearing serf sweating beneath his back-breaking work in the fields surrounding his lord and master's castle, Christian opened his eyes. Evius' insides were aflame. As if he were a living censer, a breathing bellows, thick, acrid smoke poured from his nose and mouth. The fire had started in his liver and consumed his heart and lungs.

With so much ash and soot for internal organs, the fire – belching fumes out of every pore in Evius' being – now traveled up his esophagus to disembogue smoke from between his cheeks puffed out like Dizzy Gillespie's and wreak havoc on his brain. A quick glassy sheen sealed scales like a cobra's hooded ascendancy over Evius' black eyes. Connect the dots: a zodiac sign. The exhaled smoke obscured Evius' face and trickled around, tickling with its mutating, feminine fingertips, his five-o'clock shadow to coagulate, enmeshing with his earlier cigarette smoke, into a gray-blue aura – heavenly, godlike, Hindu *and* Christian, divine.

And, oh, the scent was sweet – something more enticing than a woman's pheromones, than a midsummer night's dream, than even an aged glass of whiskey. With that tarry smell adhering to his brain's stringy conductive cells, Christian's thoughts shut down. His dreams disappeared. His gratitude evaporated.

"Oh, I'm sorry, man. How selfish of me. I should have offered you some." Sticking forward his vein-entwined arm, from between his hardened fingers with their elegant nails (such a fine dichotomy, like a Hell's Angel wearing his colors on a tux), Evius proffered the joint to Christian. "I'm sure you need it."

Akin to a great comedic actor, Evius' timing was impeccable. If he'd mentioned that a mere two minutes and thirty-one seconds before, Christian most certainly would have said, *No. I'm okay. In fact, I gotta go call my mom right now. I've got a second life to start.*

But after two minutes and thirty-two seconds of seeing, smelling, and envisioning the thick smoke he wanted outside of him inside of him polluting his synapses, Christian couldn't say anything other than, "Yeah, I do." And he reached forward with his newly scrubbed-clean hand to notice in the blink of an eye that underneath his nails was still as black as his teeth had been. *Next time I take a shower,* Christian thought, *I've got to remember to scrub that.* But a more sinister thought beneath that thought whispered, *If you ever take another shower.* It's extraordinary how thoughts, like the smoke coalescing around Evius, function in layers. They pile one overtop the other like the earth's sediment, and they contain as many hidden secrets as a tar pit.

One day, I even found the fossilized remnants of somebody else's prehistoric mind inside my own.

Christian didn't hear that last one, but he felt it when his stomach tightened as soon as the mushy joint slipped from between Evius' fingers into his.

He never called his mom.

Instead, he clamped the joint tight between his lips. With his lungs' vacuum, he filtered the smoke out from between the packed tight weed.

The smoke rested gingerly in his mouth – nature's incinerated bud thrilling and burning his taste buds, and then, at the point of internally combusting from anticipation, he inhaled. The smoke constricted his lungs. His cilia shriveled up and died as he mentally counted to ten, a habit he'd perfected so long ago – the eighth grade to be precise. Like a woman asphyxiated to the point of cumming, he exhaled. His brain spasmed.

As soon as the first hints of THC licked his head, his mind burst all over itself. For a brief moment, his brain went numb. His eyes opened wide – broken veins twining through the whites. Then, his thoughts replaced themselves with a tingling sensation as if the cells underlying and carrying them had been asleep for days and the blood had finally started flowing through his cerebral capillaries again.

With every beat of his heart, a different thought pulsed across Christian's inner vision. Thu-thump: my pre-calloused fingers caressing a piano's ebony and ivory keys (the struck strings resonate through my anvils and stirrups – even beauty is violent). Thu-thump: a half-drank bottle of cheap, George Dickel whiskey (blah... a bitter coat of paint-thinner across my tongue). Thu-thump: a black and white photograph of a girl I once knew (she's the reality of the music sung from the keys... I can't feel anything!). Thu-thump: something from the future... maybe it's you (maybe it's not... maybe it's a vision of God, the Holy Spirit, Wisdom, the Truth...). Demonic nails scraped through the world's veil, shredded it apart, rent it asunder. Blindness. An invisible roar. Nothing. The fluttering of angels' wings. Evius...

Christian sat still in his falling apart chair, his hands clamped tight to the stuffing-covered armrests, his lips and fingers turned white amid that psychic surge. Unseeing, his glazed eyes gazed through the unfixed shadows above the table to Evius' subtly morphing features. The man's bones hardened. They softened. His skin appeared pasty enough to push straight through, rugged enough to rebuff any advances. He was a god in Grecian robes, a child in size, a man in countenance, a woman in appearance, a beast from the inside out, a monster from the outside in, an angel in reality, a demon in fact.

While Christian's entire inner world vibrated to the sensation of his own breath. With each gulp, the world entered his third eye, swirled round his skull, slid down his spinal column, and whirred out his urethra. The sensation was actually quite pleasant, actually quite interesting in the ponderable moments between his heartbeat's thuds... something akin to the milliseconds of suffocation that had birthed the angels of Christian's dying vision before Evius' working hands woke him soaked in his own shit. And that was only the first hit.

If it had been a heavier drug, Christian would have sworn he'd overdosed. Even without any cocaine dripping down his throat, he was certain his heart was beating only to explode. A fleeting thought: *That shit's laced.* With what, I don't know (angel dust). But it didn't stop him from putting the joint back between his lips and sucking for his life all over again. "Easy, brother, we want to keep you sane," Evius whispered, but Christian wasn't listening. He needed that smoke. For God's sake, it had been days and nights and at least a day again!

The world ceased to exist, or at least, all of existence was questionable. That table, the hard, grainy lines snaking through its wood (wasn't it a tree the serpent appeared upon – It was. I've seen the pictures. He had a man's face when he appeared to Eve)... what is it? Is it really there?

This room is not the walls. It's the space between the walls enclosing us. The wall itself is arbitrary – nothing but electricity, atoms compacted together too tightly for the hard-packed atoms of my body to fit between. But the air's atoms, I slide straight through (my fingers' muscles pulse through that atmosphere with my brain's electricity – food calories burn and release as heat energy transferred from my fingers into the ever-warming, ever-cooling substratosphere (I inhale that energy)).

I exhale something invisible into that invisible something. It presses against the walls that don't make this room. All of it conforms to the space around my body. It passes in and out of my lungs, through my arteries, into every cell of my being (my arms, my legs, my hands, my feet, my fingers, my toes, my penis, my testicles, my sperm, my epidermal tissue, my kidneys, my liver, my intestines, my heart, my brain), and back through my veins to be expelled again from between my lips.

The carbon dioxide molecules are swallowed by that dusty, dying plant in the corner absorbing the sunlight filtered through our grimy window and breathes (is that even the right word?) out simple oxygen atoms. I inhale them again, bond them with my own atoms. Nothing. An atom does not exist. It has mass composed by electrons, protons, neutrons. It whirls in space, but beneath the mass is nothingness, pure electricity like what animates a non-existent computer screen, the silicon chips of its memory. This world is composed of nothing. I am nothing but this sense of self-imposed memories. To love myself is to love those memories.

But what are my memories? They can be damaged. They can fade and disappear. A car accident. Alzheimer's. Who am I? Electrical currents through my brain – something like that computer again? Where do memories exist in the abstract? Where do I exist in the absolute (right here, on this damaged chair in this abandoned room)? Where is the collective unconscious located? What allows this all to be? I remember... nothing. All I did was put some smoke in my brain.

Christian had to stand up. He couldn't take it anymore. He had to get out. The imprisoned air stifled his soul. He gasped for a breath clean and free of any substances. A fresh dose of oxygen expanded his lung sacs, flowed into his bloodstream, and traversed the same route the smoke had traveled through his body. The pressure built behind his eyes. It radiated out his pupils' empty holes. The body chakras in his palms, feet, forehead, and chest opened, filled with radiance, and expelled his personal energy. Turning into a being of pure light, he pushed down on the armrests with both hands and thrust himself out of his decrepit chair. On his feet, an angel in his comfortable new shoes pressed firm against the floor, he felt more light-headed than even before. Perhaps it was time to sweat. His pores seemed ready to offer up a deluge. There was so much toxicity inside of him needing to be gotten out. "Hey, man, thanks for the smoke, but really I gotta go."

Like a mirror image, Evius got up along with him. His lanky legs and torso undulated off the stained couch. He ran his nails through his hair, separating each individual strand one from the other, and he ran his fingers down his cheeks. Truly, if he was Christian's reflection, then the man had less to worry about and more to think about (or was it the other way around) than what already filled his combustible brain. "I really don't think you should be alone right now," Evius said. "You don't look so hot, and you never know, things might get worse."

Exasperated, disappointed in himself, unsure how things could ever be worse than they'd already been, not to mention Evius wasn't helping – the weed and whatever else was in it was truly a mistake, Christian sighed, "No, really, man, thanks, but I'm okay."

"All right, then," Evius said. "I guess I'll just hang out here."

"Whatever," Christian mumbled. He really didn't care. Let Evius do what he wanted. He'd come home to find plenty of people he'd never met sleeping on the couch. Now, it was his roommates' turns for a surprise. Besides, he didn't even know the bastard. And regardless of what Evius said, somebody must. Nobody could really be as bold as Christian's savior claimed to be.

Stepping lightly in his new shoes, Christian made his way to the door. Right before he opened it, as his fingers encircled the rusty knob, as his all-seeing mind envisioned the industrial smokestacks and factories of the forgotten Rust Belt City waiting to greet him beyond his apartment door, from behind him, after the sparkling sound of a strike-anywhere match head's sulfur popped against an overgrown fingernail and a drag was inhaled, he heard Evius say quite nonchalantly, almost flippantly, "Oh, by the way, man, I almost forgot: you're dead."

19.
Things Just Got Worse

"*Excuse me?*"

"Yeah, man. You're dead as dead can be. Dead as God as the saying goes. Sorry nobody got there in time to cut you down. If your roommates cared, maybe, but you know how your roommates are. They heard the chair fall, glanced up at the ceiling, and went back to smoking pot. Oh, you didn't know they were smoking pot downstairs that whole time you were going crazy in your room? Well, you really needed to talk to them more. They weren't such bad kids. Whatever... too late now. What were you thinking anyways? Hanging? It's a miserable way to die. "

But at that moment, as if he were in the midst of portraying the melodrama of a 1950's death scene caught in living black and white, Christian's fingers slipped from the doorknob. A new kind of lightness settled in his forehead. "Dead?" he whispered to himself.

Immediately, the statement felt right; the same as the word love had felt all those years ago when he'd breathed it to Sophia. There was no denying it. This was truth. How could he have ever convinced himself of anything else? In the shower, on the floor of his room, his neck burning from strangulation, his body doused in excrement...

But unlike the warmth radiating through his being with Sophia, on the heels of this immediate sensation of rightness, coldness pooled in his temples and dripped through what a religious man would have referred to as his soul. It seeped into the floor, and it froze him in place. He couldn't have moved his feet any easier if he were a zombie. "Dead?" he whispered again.

With the same casual air he'd made his initial pronouncement with, Evius snorted a quick laugh. "That's right. Dead. It doesn't change no matter how many times you say it. Dead's one of those things that once it happens, it's kinda permanent. It's not like life – constantly in flux, isn't that what Michel says? Montaigne, that is..." Completely unaware of himself, Christian shook his head. Evius went on, "Think of it as a perma-trip. I'm sure you can relate to that. The devil knows I can. The sooner you come to grips with it, the sooner you'll enjoy it."

But Christian wasn't listening. As tears pooled on either side of his nose, he turned his ashen face towards Evius. When he opened his lips, saliva stuck to the cracked corners. The words he spoke struggled to break through the clotted lump in his throat. A pit deeper than the abyss he was sure to discover opened in his gut. Descending headfirst straight into it, he said, "But I was going to call my mom."

"Should have thought about that before you hung yourself," Evius responded.

"I didn't... I didn't know."

"Didn't know what?"

"That I'd never see her again."

"Oh, come on, Christian. What the hell did you think it meant to hang yourself? Rejoice! This is what you wanted."

As if his pupils had expanded to encompass his irises

and his brain had slipped out his skull and slithered back into those holes, an eternal emptiness opened wide behind Christian's eyes. He whispered, "I don't think this is what I wanted."

"Stop thinking then."

Despite Evius' friendly advice, however, he couldn't stop thinking. Something other than the rope now blocked his windpipe. A hollowness separate from his evacuated bowels now filled his guts.

But in all fairness, Christian was actually handling the revelation quite well. He took a step back, leaned into the door, and covered his face with his hands. Tremors raced through his body and settled in his fingertips. He bent over and retched, but luckily it had been so long since he'd eaten anything nothing came up. The alcohol from the night before had already been absorbed into his bloodstream, and the vehicle carrying it had already been urinated onto his spasming legs.

Evius said, "Man, you *really* need to learn how to meditate. We'll have to look into that. I'm sure Gautama is still teaching classes. Don't worry, we'll get you signed up for one. They say he's the best. I mean, he *is* the Buddha and all…"

Right then, though, Christian didn't care about meditation. What did meditation have to do with the madness he was experiencing? How could meditation help him cope with the fact life was over, everything he'd grown accustomed to was never going to be experienced again? No. Right then his soul had the shape of a dog, and right then, out of the corner of its eye, it saw something flickering that always seemed to be following it.

What the hell is that? It's always there. Goddamnit, let me get up off this comfortable bed. Maybe I'll catch it this time. Woof, woof… *Oh God, please help me (what was that?*

*Did I just think that?). This can't be happening to me. This can't be
real (you're just stoned, man. You're just stoned. That was some
psychedelic shit you put on top of your brain). I was going to change. I
had a revelation. I was going to change (it's too late now. This is the
Revelation. You had all the time in the world, and now it's too late).
God (why am I talking to God? I don't even believe in Him), forgive
me for what I've done (shut up. SHUT THE HELL UP!). I
didn't want it to be like this (I'm hanging from a rope through a hole
in the ceiling). Who's going to tell my mother I'm dead (you're not
dead. Dead people don't think. Dead people don't talk. Dead people
don't take showers. Dead people don't smoke pot. Dead people don't
exist (nothing exists, remember?)). Who's going to find my body?
Who's going to bury me (I can't take this anymore)?* With his
empty stomach apparently even more empty than his gag
reflex needed it to be, Christian stood up and leaned back.

Like Poe's raven's tapping, his head rapped lightly
against the flimsy door. He wiped his mouth even though
the desired vomit had never materialized. He sensed his lips
going numb. As if his heart had vanished, the blood drained
from them to nowhere. He glanced at his trembling hands.
It didn't make any sense. They were still there. He expected
them to fade to nothing like a note sustained on the piano.

A look of concern spread across Evius' cheeks. It
dissolved his smile. It softened his black eyes. "Hey, man,
you all right? You look like you've just seen a ghost."

Christian didn't answer. He wasn't all right. He was
looking at a ghost – himself. *This can't be happening. That
sonofabitch is fucking with me.*

Once upon a time, a mere five minutes ago, life had
been something tangible, something meaningful in its
meaninglessness. How we crave our misery once our misery
has departed. To fret over a now seemingly trivial problem
like a disappeared bag of marijuana seemed a blessing in the
face of this newest fact.

Evius approached him. In the spirit of brotherly companionship, the type of companionship two victims of incarceration might visit upon one other, he threw a gangly arm over Christian's shoulder. "Come on, man, let's go for a walk," he said. "I think you could use some fresh air."

In a quick motion, he spun Christian around and pulled open the front door.

But instead of the gray, abandoned factories always waiting beyond – smokestacks crushing the dismal, polluted air and spewing asthma-inducing chemicals over the forgotten neighborhood – a sky, bluer than Sophia's eyes, greeted Christian. The colors were as vibrant as those on an ecstasy trip. Adding texture, cotton cloud puffs, waiting only for the angels' hands to pick them, hung through the atmosphere. That one was a monkey, this one like a fish… forever morphing, evolving, diurnal constellations.

The world *is* in flux. The ether itself proves it. A breath of fresh wind as warm and welcoming as the steam pumped out of a washing machine caressed Christian and drew him outside onto the porch.

But it wasn't his porch. His porch was falling apart. It had a ragged railing – paint chipping, stakes out of alignment. The roof above you hung uneven and ready to collapse.

This porch had no railing. It opened onto a magnificent yard (another thing that didn't exist in front of Christian's home), immaculately manicured and kept, green and rolling up to a quiet, quaint, little street. Roman pillars existed on each corner to prop up the wonderful wood overhang with its fresh coat of white paint. Instead of the cracked concrete Christian should have been standing on, his new soles pressed firm against real, red bricks, scrubbed clean and bright as the day they were cut… something very few Americans think of as a luxury, but if you'd lived the places

Christian had, new bricks were about as rare as plain, drab concrete was abundant.

There was no broken glass from the drunken nights where Christian would practice throwing beer bottles against the fence across the street. They shattered and rained down in pleasing destructive tinkles onto the sidewalk, music to the ears of the fool inebriated enough to release the anger he had spent all his life repressing. The pile of empties in the grass before the porch, the pile he'd pick through to find his throwing implements had vanished. Even the front yard trampoline where all the teenagers would have sex regardless of the neighbors who might be watching was gone. Christian vaguely recalled a drunken night where he'd gotten beaten up by some kid when he'd tried getting the two seventeen year olds flopping nakedly on top of it to indulge him in a threesome. Even in his state, he still turned red at that memory. Whether the color rose from the ass kicking or his actions, he wasn't sure. By the grace of God, nothing remained from Christian's previous abode. He swallowed slowly and wiped his brow. He felt faint. His neck drained into his stomach. He tried spinning back around and retreating back to sanity (if that's what you could even call it), but Evius grabbed him solidly.

With a sweeping gesture including everything in Christian's field of vision, Evius said, "Welcome to the earthly paradise, Christian, the same as Virgil and Dante wrote about. Oh, we've come a long way since those days of philosophers sitting around a simple stream, though. You can't halt progress. That's for sure. I remember when this was all fruit groves as far as the eye could see. Nowadays, we call it Machpelah."

Dumbfounded, blinking as rapidly as a hummingbird's fluttering wings, Christian mumbled, "Is this heaven?"

"Not exactly, but it could be. If you're into that sort of thing, that is. Heaven, hell… the mind is its own place and all that hoopla. Really, it all depends on what drug, or lack thereof, is in your body. I think you'd have to agree with me on that, huh?"

Christian couldn't think clearly enough to agree. He couldn't even think clearly enough to move, much less speak. Breath itself was a miracle at that point in time… as it always is, whether we're dead or alive.

Surely, all this – the bricks, the yard, the road – wasn't an illusion. *I guess I must be dead*, was the overriding thought controlling Christian's mind. It was the tail his canine-shaped soul had sought. He'd caught it. After 27 years of running in circles, lying down on the rug to close his eyes only because he was panting too hard to lick his doggy jowls, he'd finally caught it. How many of us can ever boast of such a feat? Most of us chase our own tails all the way into the grave, which is exactly what Christian did.

But he didn't trip and fall like a good dog would. Instead, he did the only humane thing and leaped neck first. There were too many souls already in the pound. He simply hadn't been aware that hole in his ceiling actually led somewhere. The answer was what Evius had said: death. It was the only rational explanation for what had just happened. And with all the irrationality occurring in the world today, any tangible explanation for experience was welcome.

As if he were the therapist Christian had so blatantly needed through most of his life, Evius said, "Look. Let's just go for a little walk. We've obviously got some talking to do."

With Evius' arm slung over Christian's co-conspiratory shoulder, they started across the yard. Whispering the mysteries he'd discovered during his eternity in that wonderland, Evius leaned in close enough Christian could smell his breath. It smelt peculiarly of cloves, as if he were smoking one at that very instant.

Unlike Christian, Evius had obviously showered at some point that day before he'd discovered Christian in his strange state suspended by his neck from the ceiling. But of course, things had changed considerably in the past few minutes, and who knew where Evius had been coming from before he'd decided to push open the door to Christian's new home whose interior seemed to resemble so distinctly his old home. Christian rubbed his neck. It remained tender to the touch. It didn't make sense that even in death, he'd still feel pain. That wasn't what the preachers had promised. They'd discussed oneness with the Lord and all that. But they'd also never said anything about smoking pot in the earthly paradise. Of course, they'd never been dead. For them, the afterlife was all conjecture. For Christian, it was fact, and he could tell them: your neck still hurt, you still had to take showers, and you could get stoned if somebody brought you the pot.

Christian looked over his shoulder. The house he'd stepped out of appeared a mansion (although in reality it was little more than an upper middle class two-story, but Christian had been so long removed from such creature comforts its appearance distorted in his mind). There's no way in hell the interior of the house he'd hung himself in and he'd smoked that joint with Evius in filled the same floor plan as the monstrosity now greeting his eyes. He interrupted Evius' mumbled ramblings, "Is that where I live now?" he asked.

"What? Jesus, yes, that's what I've just been telling you. You need to learn how to listen, man. That house was fixed up just for you, and your roommates are very excited to have a new addition to the household. Just don't bother

Pablo down in the basement. He's got some serious pieces he's working on. You're familiar with Pablo Picasso, right?"

Christian nodded.

"You should see his new stuff. It's light years beyond cubism. Has been for a good thirty years or so… He's been doing these extraordinary studies of form. The way he paints a nude now… It's beyond postmodern. It's postmortem. It took him a little while to get over his earthly ideas of structure… nowhere near as long as it took Michelangelo, though, but once he did, man, I'll tell you…"

"Tell me what?"

"Huh? Oh. It's just an expression, man. There's no answer. You know, like, I'll just tell you what I already told you. It's just an inversion of the regular sentence structure. Don't worry about it."

As if he were a brook bubbling away, Evius continued babbling on and on, gesticulating with his hands and rolling his eyes for emphasis. With no regard for his newfound friend and tour guide's earlier admonition, Christian didn't listen. Hopefully, he wasn't missing anything important…

But who cares about safety when you've already escaped the most dreaded event that can happen over the course of a human's life. Vitality was replacing the weighted emotions coursing through Christian's drained organs and limbs. Supplanting the dark matter that had taken the place of the red blood cells in his circulatory system for so long, energy pulsed through his veins and arteries. It warmed him from the inside out, the same way the sun now warmed him from the outside in. He positively glowed with the same afterglow turning on inside a lover after he/she has sex.

Like a dog, he'd already forgotten his terror of the moment before. Once again, he'd already forgotten about his mother. Maybe it had something to do with the sublime effects of Evius' marijuana. He'd lived through the worst thing imaginable. Although perhaps a little scarred psychologically (and if Christian had known this, the fact might have given him pause: the Greek root for the word "psychological" is πσυχη meaning "breath", which to the ancient Greek doubled for "spirit"), he'd walked through the flames of life to emerge physically healthy and whole on the other side. And what a sight the other side was!

At that moment, Evius and Christian were approaching what Evius was telling Christian was the main thoroughfare through the earthly paradise.

Traffic moved briskly along Machpelah's uptown Main Street. A plethora of cars from every bygone era of automobiles rolled past. There went a Ford Fairlane. There was a Dodge Viper. And right there went a beat-up Chevy Nova – something like a devastated sun. It took all kinds. But Christian was more struck by the rows of trees lining either side of the street. Their leaves twinkled in the warm summer breeze. In the fall, the colors would be beautiful. But wait... "Evius, is it always summertime here?"

"Always? What fun would that be? No. Just like Japan, we've got *four* seasons. Only change makes eternity bearable. If everything stayed the same throughout all of time, I would have left here for good a long while ago. Never did care much for Southern California..."

"Left?"

"In through the out door, as they say. Oh, you can get out of eternity. All you gotta do is make a choice. I think... It's like the Catholics say, we got free will... Although, I still take issue with that theory. I just figure if God wants you gone, He makes sure you disappear. It may seem like you made the decision, but that's just an illusion. I don't know. I don't really understand those sorts of things. They're all a little beyond my meager comprehension. I just..."

"Is there such a thing as God, Evius?"

"Stick around, my dear friend. You just might meet Him. But be careful. He travels incognito. *He* could very well be a *Her...* or an It. You've heard of burning bushes, I'm sure. You never know when it comes to God. Tricky sonofabitch. *I* don't even know what It is."

"Because after everything I've done, I don't know if I'd *want* to meet God."

"Well, unfortunately, that's not up to you. It's like with Jesus. Do you think he wanted to be crucified? Hell no. God did to him the worst thing He could ever do to any individual soul. He *chose* him."

"So Jesus isn't God, then?"

"I don't know. He might be. In which case, you can disregard that last diatribe. These are all just theories, and you know what they say about theories..."

"No, I don't. What do they say?"

"Hm? Oh, there's no answer to that one either. I was being rhetorical again."

As they sauntered along the sidewalk aside the road, they passed a lovely little corner store on their left. Beneath the awning, receiving a respite from the pleasant heat, a handful of older gentlemen were hanging out in front, sitting on porch benches, engrossed in enjoying the day, sipping on iced tea and lemonade, and intermittently conversing with one another. Evius waved to them as they passed. One or two of the men waved back. "You know them?" Christian asked.

"No. But like I said, you never know who God is. So you better be nice to everybody. That's what I always say, learned the theory from a chap in Pandemonium... old Greek guy. And when I say old, I mean old. The dude will tell you what parts of *The Iliad* actually happened."

"What parts did?"

"Oh. I don't know. I never asked him. Wasn't interested. I figure it's like *The Bible*. It doesn't matter what's true because on the spiritual level it's all true, and here we are on a spiritual plane. So, you know. I'm sure you're following me on that."

"No. I'm not... But what's Pandemonium?"

"Pandemonium... hmm... that's a good one. I can tell you this. For people like us, it's heaven. I mean, don't get me wrong, Machpelah's nice, but there's no real drama here... except, maybe... well, we'll get to that later. Pandemonium, on the other hand, is like New York, Berlin, and Hong Kong all rolled into one. In my view, *that's* the earthly paradise. They say Lucifer built it just to show people he really was cooler than the Lord. I don't know if that's true or not, but what is truth anyways? What I *can* tell you is definitely the case is it's a perpetual party. Whenever you want to go, just let me know. I know a secret entrance. Most people from here never get to see it, but I've come and gone a billion times over the course of my eternity. No reason we couldn't head there for a little action somewhere down the line. Besides, there's some sketchy shit goes down here in Machpelah. I'm sure you'll get hip to it eventually. This place ain't all it's cracked up to be."

But even if he did get hip to Machpelah, Christian wasn't sure he wanted a perpetual party. He'd just opted out on what most people would consider a permanent party. And his permanent party hadn't really been all that exciting.

He and Evius continued sauntering down the sidewalk. The concrete glistened like a kaleidoscope in the sunlight. Shades of an illuminated crystal ball shined from the gray walkway. It added dimensions to the otherwise static space. The topography of the earthly paradise began striking Christian as increasingly lustrous. He pined for the inviting, wealthy homes. Maybe someday one would be his alone. He thrilled at the sight of more domestic domiciles. They appeared a Norman Rockwell fairy tale, as vibrant as the American suburban dream always existing at the edge of Christian's earthly enjoyment. He grinned at the makes and models of the cars going past – so many kinds that in many a dream he'd imagined for himself.

He wanted to stroll through the verdant fields and hills rolling somewhere between blue and green along the side of the road. He pictured himself arm in arm with a woman of uncertain description as he plunged through the snake-free grasses (as Evius had explained, here the snake had no reason to bite the heels of men), but he was certain the woman he pictured with himself would exist in paradise. She had to. She was a piece of his fantasy ("Everybody gets their fantasy," he'd half heard Evius say). Maybe she was even… "Evius, I'm looking for somebody."

"Who's that? Dad? Grandparent?"

"No, Evius. A girl. A girl named Sophia. Do you think she might be here?"

Squinting through the sunlight as if he were spiritually seeking out a connection with the girl of Christian's dreams, Evius said, "Lots of girls here, man. Don't let any single one distract you."

"But I need to find *her*. I knew her… before. Before everything, and I need to see her again. Do you think she's here?"

A bit miffed, gesturing with his shoulders and pointing at himself, Evius said, "Why are you asking me? Am I my sister's keeper? Who do you think *I* am?"

Christian bowed his head. He sighed, and he mumbled, "I don't know. I just thought, maybe, you know…"

"No. I don't know. Just relish what you see, Christian. Enjoy the sun and the trees. Don't ask for what you don't have, and you might make it out of here alive."

"Alive? What in the hell does that mean?"

"Don't ask me, man. Haven't you listened to anything I've said? I'm not my *brother's* keeper either. Just be content, Christian. Be content. You're dead. You can't ask for anything else."

But no matter what Evius said, Christian wasn't content. The seed had been planted in his spleen. The soil was enriched by his blocked chi. His desire had dug the hole. His questions had provided it water. His death proved the food. It was sprouting and blossoming into the most painful of lustful fruits. He needed to find her. In ways he never had since before he'd even met her, he needed to find Sophia.

"Look, Christian. You need to listen to me on this one. It's very important. Money works the same way here as it does on earth." Evius explained with a shake of his head, "Like they say, capitalism's the natural way of things – unless you go to Pandemonium, that is. So you're going to have to get a job. I'm not going to be able to support you for your whole stay here. What did you always want to do for a living?"

"What do you do for a living?"

"I've got my own hustle. This is about you. What do you want to do for a living?"

With a brief mental glance back over his life, Christian warmed at the thought of a dream he'd abandoned nearly five years ago. He answered, "I always wanted to play jazz piano."

"Jazz piano. Hmm? Where'd that come from?"

"I grew up playing piano. I studied it in college. It's the only thing I'm any good at." He didn't add he'd spent his elementary school years being teased for it. But without a father, with his mother always asleep, he'd had nothing else to do with his time at home but listen to the records his dad had left behind and fiddle around with the keyboard in the living room. He took lessons. He learned the classical composers. He applied to a conservatory and got in, but all he'd wanted to create was spontaneous composition, not a beautiful rendition of another's piece, but his own soul floating through air on invisible but tangible notes.

"Well, it's a noble undertaking, but that line of work might be a bit difficult. You see, there's only one jazz club here and right now Monk is the regular pianist. I'm sure you're familiar with Thelonious Monk, aren't you?"

Christian nodded.

"As you can imagine, he's a tough act to unseat."

"But you said everybody gets their fantasy."

"You need to read the fine print on that one. I'll print up the contract sometime. How about we try something else? Piano can be your avocation. What did you do for a living before you hung yourself?"

But piano had always been his avocation, ever since childhood, ever since he'd been rejected from graduate school. The only time it hadn't been was for the brief four years when his life was something akin to heaven on earth, before his drinking had flushed his soul down the toilet, before he'd had any clue what it really meant to be tired from work, before the faintest chemical taste of crack had ever brushed his palate, something obviously beyond this earthly paradise. He said, "I was unemployed."

"Before you were unemployed."

"I was a stone mason."

"Now, that's more like it. Machpelah needs more masons. Lots of construction going on these days. Who knows. Maybe you could build *another* jazz club, and then you could play piano there. I think I know somebody I can put you in contact with if that's what you'd like to do. If you'd like to stay here, that is."

"Where else would I go?"

"Like I said, we could always try Pandemonium. Lots of ways to make a living down there, and only a few require work if you know what I mean," Evius said, and he winked.

A lump stopped up Christian's throat. At the thought of sweating beneath the sun again and freezing through the winter yet again, a billion flies buzzed their multiples of wings across the inside of his brain. He even swatted his hand in front of his face as if they were actually there. The last few years of memories flashed in front of his eyes... his shorts soaked through before ten o'clock, waking up with his hands frozen in the grip of his masonry instruments, inhaling mortar as he mixed cement, picking flecks of rock from out the corners of his eyes, fearing the grinder would slice off a finger and he'd never play piano again... He couldn't go through that in death. Life was bad enough, but for eternity... Without even a thought for what it might entail, he said, "Evius, I think I need a drink."

"Now, that's more like it." Evius clapped his hands. He leaned in closer and whispered, "But we can't start drinking here yet. People will stare at you. They might even make you find God. And one thing I don't have time for in this eternity is God. You're not Him, are you?"

Christian shook his head.

"Good. I was always told if you asked God if He was God, He had to tell you whether or not He was. Otherwise... Wait a second, maybe that's the police? I don't remember. Regardless, I suggest we go get a cup of coffee, and talk this all over. What do you say?"

"Sounds good to me."

"All right. Follow me."

The road beside them disappeared, and Christian found himself strutting down a cobblestone street. To his right, there was an indoor ice skating rink where eternal children were playing and laughing, surrounded for all time by angelic parents who would never grow old, would never leave them, would never die. To his left, a very chic restaurant appeared. Christian's mouth watered at the possibilities of concoctions such a well decorated establishment in the heart of paradise might bring together. Unconsciously, he imagined spices varied in such ways as he had never tasted. And in front of him, sitting out on tables scattered across a patio, was a goodly group of people, laughing and smoking and talking, seemingly enjoying their morning cups of coffee. A few papers were being rustled. A few writers sat alone with their notebooks or laptops.

"Grab a seat," Evius said. "I'll go in and get us some Joe."

18.
Gilles et Jean-Francois

Christian plopped down in a wire chair at the first open table he came to. He had a lot of thinking to do. And luckily for him Evius had wandered quickly in through the café's glass front door. He reached into his pocket for a cigarette, realized he didn't have one, and settled deeper into his chair.

Instead of being gorgeous, the sun now annoyed him. He'd felt too much of it when working. Its heat only radiated cancer. The realization that in his new state he was entirely dependent upon Evius dawned on him, and a knife darted down his esophagus and through his chest's interior. But with the thought of *how the hell could this get any worse?* he dulled the blade. If only he'd known how much worse it would actually get, if only he hadn't been so stoned and had listened to Evius as they'd walked, the thoughts might have proved a whetstone, and the knife would have sliced his interiors in half to leave him spasming and clutching at his chest on Machpelah's cobblestone streets. Some might have even considered that a blessing.

Thinking seemed to be a lot of what people did at this café. The few snippets of conversation Christian could understand – most were in foreign languages – seemed to be circling around such lofty topics as metaphysics, theology, and ethics. Already, Christian wasn't sure if this was the place for him.

He was more concerned with another ancient human quandary, that of love and its temporality whether ephemeral or eternal. His mother was already abandoned, and even though he hadn't spoken to her since before his last earthly job had disappeared, the final severing of that connection left his umbilical cord dangling from his gut, cut off from its nourishment, and pained by self-imposed abandonment. He writhed like a child newly conceived, and on the inside he cried as if he had just burst from her womb into the terrifying light of day.

But the real love he was contemplating was that between Sophia and him and whether or not after six years in the bosom of death she still harbored the same feelings for him that had tormented him through sleepless nights of staring at that picture on his desk and wondering if she had been right, if it had been *kismet*, and what would have happened if he had seen her, only once, after leaving her alone at the train station in Austria.

She disappeared in the distance as he leaned out the car staring at her receding back to nothing more than a point beyond the infinite tracks. The parallel lines intersected, and she vanished... in more than just his mind. He found himself a compartment. He closed the door, and he closed his eyes, and he knew, though he refused to admit it even to himself, he would never see her again. But now chance – or fate – had put Sophia back in the world of the living (had brought Christian to the world of the dead), and he wanted desperately to find her, desperately to spend eternity in her deathly embrace. She had to be there. She had to be.

But until she showed up, Christian found himself suddenly intrigued with a girl who was taking a seat a little to his right. Like any man when struck with an image of beauty, without noticing it, perhaps even unconsciously, on the sly, he cocked his head a wee bit to the side in order to catch a better glimpse of her as she pulled her chair back and slid into it. She had auburn hair cut to the nape of her neck, sharp features, and even at his distance, the greenest eyes that ever sparkled beneath the light of day.

They reflected the glint of the noonday sun on an algae lake. Her torso moved like the upper part of a Chinese serpent, and Christian immediately saw during his blinks an internal vision of the great dragon chewing its tail and encircling the earth. Her lips opened a bit to reveal a set of straight, white teeth coated with sensually glistening saliva. She was wearing a red tee shirt with a silk-screened yin-yang print and jeans, underneath which Christian could make out the length of her legs, the fullness of her breasts, and the flatness of her stomach. She had long fingers and even longer red nails that bespoke of clawing through bed sheets at night. In short, Christian was struck with either love or lust; the two are so closely interconnected and often mistaken for each other.

He wanted to say something to her. Maybe she, not Sophia, was the vision he'd seen toying with him as they skipped lightly through the grasses beside the road. Maybe she was the unit that would make his blissful eternity of dreadful work bearable and complete.

Is it ever even fair to think of a woman as a unit, as a piece that could complete a whole? She's not something quantifiable. She is abstract and fluid, a plethora of sets within herself through which she glides like a witch on a broom through the night. She rides side-saddle. Her toes point towards the earth she has escaped; her peaked hat a compass straight to the moon, her mistress, Luna. The stars break through the mist and flicker the souls of men who she's subjugated to herself. They blink a message in twinkles to the earth's inhabitants. They say: *We've found freedom in the night's imprisonment. Give up sweating beneath the sun. Join us beneath the cold darkness's warm blanket.* She cackles a rapid fire staccato granting another dimension to her experience. Like from the cars speeding down Machpelah's Main Street, a breeze brushes through the trees she passes, a breeze not unlike the one beginning to circle right then through Christian's senses, lighting against the back of his neck, tickling his fingertips; the same breeze causing his vision to seem to sniff the air as her features made a recognition resembling something forgotten – perhaps a pot on the stove, perhaps a date she had meant to keep, perhaps a coven's woodland gathering.

She stood up, and as she did so, her green eyes lighted on Christian. He shifted beneath her gaze, but there was a point of recognition in her glance, perhaps an attraction, perhaps...

Christian didn't have much time to think about it. Because as his lovely vision disappeared to whence she had come, he noticed a very strange thing happening. The foreign languages all around him began to warble. They slowed like a record played too slow. They morphed and cracked, and as the breeze ceased, as Christian's hair fell lightly back into place against his scalp, the veil of Babel was rent asunder. History rolled backwards, and Christian found himself in the desert before babble. He could understand every single one of the conversations taking place around him. The transformation contained all the madness of being transported miraculously from the silence of the plains to Times Square. It was as if he had stepped from a cocoon into the third world din of an English-speaking Kolkata. Things made more sense than they ever had before, and Christian was listening.

To his left, at the table opposite where his vision had sat, two middle-aged men in suits were smoking cigarettes, drinking coffee, and speaking. They had been the first voices to warble, and their seemingly French intonations came up out of their throats to settle into English's stiff upper lip. Their words rose above the cacophony and tapped upon Christian's eardrums. The intonations snared themselves inside his anvils and stirrups and pounded into his brain. Even in his still-stoned state, he was able to follow the conversation (more as a whole than in pieces) as the one said to the other, "But it's not simply a condition of postmodern man, Jean-Francois, the problem has existed since men, and women for that matter, first used their respective 'morals' to enslave one another at the dawn of human history."

"And there you go again," the one called Jean-Francois replied with a wave of his hand, "We're not discussing issues inherent to humanity as a species, we're discussing issues arising as a fundamental flaw in the industrial system, issues that have only been exacerbated by post-industrial society."

"Post-industrial society, pre-industrial society... the priest took the place of the psychologist prior to that, and as Karl will tell you, he indoctrinated the masses with the same psychological complexes your rotten, post-industrial society produces..."

"But information, Gilles. We're discussing the over-abundance of information and its effects upon consciousness. Human beings weren't prepared for the glut of information that started raining down on them from the 1960s onward. It started with radio and television and only got more cumbersome with the advent of the computer."

"Radio… television… it started with the newspaper."

"Well, good. At least I can get you to concede one point, then."

"And what point is that?"

"Human nature went through a dramatic shift during modernity's revolution."

"You didn't get me to concede anything. The shift in humanity occurred with the advent of the mental asylum… maybe even earlier with the burning of witches and the possessed at stakes."

"The mental asylum? Burning at stakes? What makes you bring up such ghastly periods in humanity's soiled history?"

"Because at that point humanity lost its link to the one thing giving life meaning."

"And what's that one thing, Gilles?"

"Insanity," the word rolled off his tongue and dropped like a brick against the other bricks supporting the foot supporting the leg over which his other leg was crossed.

Jean-Francois leaned back in his chair and scrunched up his face. "You haven't convinced me, Gilles, and I'm open to being convinced. So tell me: How does insanity give life meaning? Because I'm prepared to make the argument that humanity as a whole became insane as industrial society shifted into the information age."

Gilles wrapped his hand around his mouth and massaged his cheeks. His eyes gazed inward. Then, with a fire, they radiated outward as he said, "To use Georg's term – to my own distaste – insanity is the sublation of all dualities. It allows the universe to exist as a cohesive whole rather than in fragmented parts, and it's this whole that makes the insane person saner than the supposedly sane… whether or not their whole corresponds to any objective notion of reality. You see, it's not a question of what is real, but rather a question of what we deem to be real. If we can make sense of the universe in an ordered way, then even your postmodern condition no longer poses a problem."

"I see your point," Jean-Francois conceded. "But you haven't taken into account the shock of constantly passing from one era to another in the matter of a few years. Take the last years of the 1990s for example. In 1995, the internet was still a more or less academic and military tool. By the end of the decade, in five short years, an entire economy was built around it, and with this change came a whole new wave of terminology... and thinking, Gilles. The nature of thought itself changed as the computer replaced previous modes of communication. New arts were developed, new sources of media. A whole new system of knowledge was at humanity's fingertips, and with it came a drastic reordering of the traditional role of human beings in the universe. Yes, modernity's project had been fulfilled. Humans had created a world they could live in... a world of pure thought, of electricity, of binary code ordered into rational concepts by the intellect. And with that world, Gilles, humanity recreated herself in the image of God – rather than, as Blaise so aptly pointed out, its previous incarnation of God in the image of humanity – and that, my dear colleague, we do not have the intellectual capacity to deal with. In fact, there's absolutely no way to make sense of it in a rational way, and therefore, your dream of the psychotic's experience is no longer unique to any individual."

Gilles chuckled. "I hate to be the bearer of bad tidings, Jean-Francois, but thought can't change... unless one is discussing a person in the pre- or post-psychotic break state."

"But I'm telling you all of society went through a psychotic break at that point in time, a break that had been building since René first suggested '*I think; therefore, I am.*' And nobody was equipped to handle it. From this point forward, our only hope is that the children of the future who evolve inside this embryo will develop the mental means by which to accept the realities of perpetual insanity."

"And that is what I'm saying the priest and the current psychologist have taken from us. They took away the insane and left us without guides through the labyrinth."

"But what type of guidance can a person who no longer has a sense of external reality offer the masses?"

"Look. The insane have been dealing with this glut of information since day one. What do you think causes the various identities of the psychotic? She has so many notions forming in her mind that every hour she takes on a different namesake, a different personality, a different experience of the world. That is a much faster reordering of world states than your period of society's five years. I think it's high time the rest of humanity experienced this, and, I say, let's embrace our collective madness, free the insane and let them lead us into the new era history has pushed us towards."

"But there are ways human beings can experience insanity without any of your 'guides through the labyrinth'," the tenor of a familiar voice broke into the conversation, and Christian noticed Evius had sat down across from him. It was as if the dark haired man with the stubble across his cheeks had materialized from space so engrossed Christian had been in the conversation taking place between the two dead men. Evius had apparently already slid a steaming cup of coffee across the table. Christian stared at it as if he were no longer sure what the dark concoction was. Fragrance billowed off the top like the varied meanings seeping out of Gilles's and Jean-Francois's conversation. Evius leaned back and lit a smoke. He tossed one across the table for Christian to pick up, and he leaned forward with a match and lit that one for him as well. Christian didn't even thank him.

Gilles and Jean-Francois, for their part, appeared slightly dumbstruck at having their private interlocution broken into. Both of their heads tilted to the side, and they regarded the stranger. But eventually, a smile touched the one called Gilles's lips, and he said to Evius, "And how, my worthy conversant, do you propose to do that?"

"Well," Evius said as he took a drag and exhaled a huge cloud of smoke, "Through drugs of course." Christian succumbed to a much needed sip off his coffee.

Gilles's smile grew even wider, "Yes, I've often thought that myself," he said. "And I don't think it can be denied that the increase of psychedelic drug use corresponds roughly with the ascent of my esteemed colleague's post-industrial society. Perhaps, humanity made an unconscious decision only insanity could save her from insanity. So a few brave souls ventured into 'the labyrinth' to find out for themselves."

"Perhaps," Evius said. "But if insanity is what we want, then I say the more the merrier… by any means necessary. Not everybody's blessed with the gift of schizophrenia. Some people have to drive themselves to it. I say let them. If you remember, even alcohol itself was once deemed the province of the gods. And if memory serves me correct, that's a pretty mellow high compared to some of the others out there."

"Yes, yes… Dionysus and all that. Although I'm not quite sure what the gods have to do with insanity…"

"Because the gods are all insane," Evius quipped.

To which Jean-Francois flippantly interjected, "Just like their creators: humanity."

"So you know them, I see?" Gilles chided. Then, he picked up where they'd left off before Evius' digression into the spiritual. "It's worthy of consideration. But you yourself seem familiar with such substances. So I'm going to spare you the details of this theory and let it be said to my fellow here that drugs are the only hope humanity has at coming again to understand and accept the so-called insane – although we still must come to a collective definition of what that term means."

"It means a falsified reality... like all of contemporary existence," Jean-Francois stated.

Still following his own train of thought, Gilles continued, "If a human being can realize she has entered reality as it truly is."

"Reality as it truly is?" Jean-Francois roared, "Gilles, reality as it truly is is unbearable. That's the escape of psychosis. The psychotic break occurs – and occurs more often in postmodern human beings – because the human biological system is not designed to accept reality as we have made it. And yes, an increase in drug use may be due to the very nature of that society, some sort of attempt to recreate a world free from the constraints of information because that's what separates today's world from the world of humanity's previous incarnations."

Now a full-fledged participant in the two men's conversation, Evius took his turn to speak along with them by chuckling and saying, "But I don't think society has ever changed... not if I can judge by the miscreants I find here." He nodded in such a way as to encompass all the café's patrons. None of them paid him any mind. "And in fact, as Jean-Francois has already pointed out, reality is insane, and the whole goal of society is simply to condition its members to live in the same psychosis ..."

Gilles smiled at Evius' pronouncement. "Yes. That's it

exactly. My dear friend Michel would certainly agree with you, as well. But there are certain members of society who don't take to the psychosis. Instead, they create their own psychosis, and this is deemed insane. Even though it's actually the most affirmative way to experience life: to define it in your own terms."

"Insanity is not defining life in your own terms," Evius said. "Insanity is defining life as the voices inside your head tell you to. But the real question is where do those voices come from? Because by the time we all get here, we should at least recognize the majority of what occurs inside our mind isn't us. We don't exist except in our memories. We have no voice except for the external."

"Are you claiming," Jean-Francois said, "There's some sort of 'other' existing inside the individual subject? Because in the sum of my experience, I've found nothing to convince me anything beyond myself is speaking to myself. In fact, it sounds like you're heading towards demonic possession, a priestly notion I simply can't abide by. It was the advent of the priest himself that began society's descent into insanity. And again, we come back to the statement that when the internal dialogue is overloaded with erroneous information, it becomes confused, and then, we're on the path to collective psychosis: postmodernity."

"Stop with your epoch-defining terminology," Gilles said. "Our young friend is simply bringing up a very fine point. In fact, I think he's pointing us to look in a direction our conversation has thus far been blind to, namely, the divine."

"Gilles, tell me, have you seen any actual evidence of the divine?"

"No, but I'm not gifted with such insights. I'd like our dear friend to educate us. Tell me, man, what do you propose are the voices inside the mind of the psychotic?"

"An educated man like you will laugh at me if I tell you."

"I promise I won't."

"Okay, forgive my superstitions – I'm a simple man – but it's the same as what the church accused the witch of having her dealings…" (the green-eyed siren from a few moments before rose out of the sea foam of his thoughts to stand like Aphrodite in all her naked glory before Christian's mind) "They've gone by various names, but they're the imprisoned ones: the jinn."

"The jinn?" Jean-Francois laughed, "Now, that's a term that hasn't been used in centuries… So tell me, where do these supposed 'jinn' reside?"

"Inside all of us," Evius said, "They speak in whispers, just like their name, 'shaitan', may very well imply. Tell me, Gilles, can you hear them?"

"Gilles, this has gone far enough. We've stumbled down the precipice from a conversation about the problems plaguing contemporary humanity to an argument that's not been made since well before my death."

But Gilles had a withdrawn look on his face. He grinned slightly. "I hear something." His face drained of its color. "Tell me, my friend," he said, drumming his long nails on the table as if the external agitation could release some sort of internal anxiety, "Where did you pick up such ideas? Certainly it wasn't by spending time in this paradise."

"Oh. I've been around awhile," Evius said.

And with those words, for some reason, Gilles retreated into himself. Like a cornered rat, he leaned deeper into his chair, and a shiver ran through his frame. He removed all the attention he'd directed at Evius, and he focused it once more on Jean-Francois. The last compliment he seemed to pay to Christian's guide was to mumble distractedly, "See… there are others who agree with me." Jean-Francois shook his head, and the two of them continued their conversation, turning a cold shoulder to Evius, withdrawing from him all the energy they'd directed at him.

Evius leaned in towards Christian. "Gilles and Jean-Francois. The two of them have been at this conversation for a good five years now, and they never seem to get anywhere. In fact, they're driving me insane just by listening. I'm surprised they don't remember me, though. I know I've spoken to them both before… but I guess things change over time, even here, and I'm sure they simply can't recognize me any longer."

As the conversation he'd just heard filtered through the marijuana still draining his brain, Christian said, "I don't think I understand what in the hell they're talking about."

"It's all a postmodern quandary," Evius said, "Completely meaningless."

"*They* don't seem to think it's meaningless. They're acting like they're discussing the entire fate of all of existence." And sure enough they did. The conversation had been kicked up a notch. With a frustrated look burnt into his face, Gilles was staring off into space, listening intently to his own mind. Jean-Francois was explaining something with a rapid motion of his hands. No longer in tune with the conversation, Christian caught only a few of his heavily loaded words. And a resounding *No!* from his fellow conversant.

Evius snickered. "They are. Like I said, completely meaningless. Come on," he added, "Drink up, and let's go meet your roommates. I want to make sure you're presentable. With the look in your eyes, you're going to need that double shot of espresso I had dropped in your cup… wonderful cure for the jet-lagged soul. And you've done a lot of traveling this morning, my friend, but we've still got a long, strange trip ahead of us. So let's be the grateful dead and get truckin'.'"

Christian hit the coffee. It had cooled a bit, and he downed it in one gulp.

The vessels behind his eyes popped open. His pupils bulged from their sockets. Yet again, his mind expanded. It lifted from out his brain. The remnants spun, a dreidel atop his spinal cord. It's amazing what caffeine can do to you when you're in a state allowing you to pay attention to it. If the marijuana had still retained its peak, he might have even stared down upon himself in paradise from the heavens (was there anything else up there or was he up there already – really, it was all too confusing... even with the coffee). His heart rate sped up. His palms began to sweat. Drugs are such wonderful things. "All right," he said, wiping his hands on his jeans, his jaw loosened from the caffeine's effects, "Let's go."

17.
Theo's Masters

Christian found himself back on that resplendent porch that what seemed no more than mere moments before he and Evius had just left. Only this time, Evius was in the midst of raising his arm to grab hold of a circular, metal knocker clenched between the teeth of a lion's open jaws. He must have only entered without being invited when he figured the inhabitant didn't have the means of getting himself to the door. Although, who's to say Christian had never invited him in before – there'd been many a night he simply couldn't remember.

The dull thud of iron striking iron rang through the pleasant air. Something about that sound deadened Christian's gut… a memory from the past or the future or both. Time really is quite circular. The sound of a dog's nails scraping across hard wood ran towards them from somewhere deeper in the house, and the sound of mad barking overpowered the vague noise of cars zooming down Machpelah's distant Main Street. Christian started and stepped back a bit. Evius snickered and shook his head. A man's voice on the other side of the door shouted, "Theo! Calm down. It's just our new roommate." And the door opened.

On the other side, a balding, brown haired man was bent over at the waist, holding a black lab (obviously the one called Theo) by the collar. The man was wearing a white dress shirt untucked from his jeans. He had on a pair of topsiders with no socks. He ran his free hand through his short-cropped hair and pushed his glasses up on his nose. He was a little pudgy, but certainly not fat, simply healthy. He blinked and said, "Oh, there's two of you. I didn't expect that to be the case. Well, don't worry. Theo's bark is much worse than his bite."

"I know," Evius responded as he stuck his hand out, palm down for Theo to sniff.

The dog's tail drooped between his legs, and he retreated back into the house's darker depths. The man brushed his hands together and laughed, "Unfortunately, his bite is almost non-existent. I'm Mike."

"Christian. But my middle name's Michael…"

Cutting into the newcomer's attempt to relate to his housemate (which he'd never really been very good at doing anyways), Evius said, "And don't worry about me. I'm not staying. Just showing our new friend around." He clasped Christian's shoulder… who frowned and scuffed the toe of his new shoes against the fresh bricks. "You could call me Virgil."

"I will," Mike responded. "I'm always up for a literary game. Well, come on in. Oh," Mike turned back around, and with a smirk, a wry note to his voice, and a faux-terrifying wave of his fingers, he added, "'Abandon all hope ye who enter'…"

Evius grinned a weighted grin. He licked his lips, and they followed Mike into that luxurious dwelling.

A wooden staircase rose from the floor of the entryway. Every few feet up the length of the steps, all the way to where the staircase wound around to the second floor, a tiny abstract painting in the spirit of Jackson Pollock decorated the white wall.

Dribbles of colors littered each foot by foot canvas. They appeared synapses in a perpetual state of firing, mainly blues and oranges slightly insane in their vibrancy. On the wall directly in front of them, a huge magnification of red stared at the home's entrants. It was another canvas, this one more attune to the depths of Mark Rothko: a sheet of membrane from a brain entranced with powerful contemplations – the kernel inside the shell. However, instead of the meditation on color variations Rothko had always subtly hinted at, this work contained a white-washing (or red-washing) of a single uninterrupted shade – not quite as lustrous as Rothko's color choices and something a little mad about the texture. The works appeared originals, and Christian recalled Evius' statement that Pablo Picasso lived down in the basement.

Perhaps this was the magnificent postmortem work he'd been focused upon. It certainly didn't strike Christian as anything great, nothing he hadn't seen done before with more verve and flair in the museums he'd visited when traveling through Europe. But he was hardly an art connoisseur. He was a musician, and more realistically (he sadly reflected) a stone mason – nothing artistic about that... unless he'd had the ability to be honest with himself.

"Come on in. Sit," Mike beckoned.

The corner of the living room was occupied by a 64-inch television set. Christian wondered how the hell they could have possibly gotten that into the house. It appeared as large as a small theater screen ("I like to keep up with the news," Mike mentioned). There was no door it could have fit through so far as Christian could tell. He had an eye for such things... he'd worked as a mover once, many years ago. It was as if the house itself had been built around it.

The wall next to that TV's corner was a gigantic bay window with a magnificent piece of stained glass hanging in it, refracting the light coming through into a many-hued pattern across the floor. The piece of stained glass itself hung suspended (a vision of a hole in the ceiling of a ransacked room flashed through Christian's thoughts. He blinked, and it was gone) from a yard of string, and as it twirled, its multifarious designs spun atop the hardwood floor – that same dreidel that had once been Christian's mind.

In the back of the room was a computer station. "That's where I do my writing," Mike nodded. Evius' brow rose with the words.

As had been the case since he'd stepped out of the house he'd thought was his, Christian wasn't paying attention. He was lost in a sense of constant amazement at the home into which he'd been settled. The day had really been quite too much. He'd always heard the phrase, but he'd never felt so realistically he needed to pinch himself to be sure he wasn't dreaming. He did so. Nothing happened (although, I once did the same, and it wasn't until I woke up an eternity later I realized my pinch had been fabricated as well). Could death be so perfect? He and Evius took their seats on the couch facing the television.

Sensation again, for Christian, proved reality. Mike settled into a worn armchair, and as he crossed his legs at the knees, he appeared a king on his throne entertaining in his throne room – Evius and Christian his mere subjects. The dog, Theo, his tongue lolling like an idiot's from out his mouth, reappeared beneath Mike's gentle touch atop his black, shining head.

"So what sort of stuff do you write?" Evius asked.

"Hmmm… Oh. I was a copywriter in a previous life,

but right now I'm working on my first novel. Well, it's not technically a novel. It's more of an absurdist comedy. I call it: *The Adversary's Good News.*"

"Interesting title," Evius said. "I think I like it. What's it about?"

"Well... honestly, I don't know. I don't like talking about it really."

"I don't believe you, but there's no need to... talk about it, that is," Evius responded with a disinterested wave of his hand, but his mannerism bespoke an unsaid something.

Christian noticed but couldn't put it into words. He felt he was living an absurdist comedy. He didn't know what the term meant, but it sounded like his day from the moment he'd opened his throbbing eyes, realized the sun had unfortunately risen on him yet again, and begun tearing apart his room in his mad search for that misplaced bag of weed. He asked, "Do you make a living as a writer?"

Mike laughed, "I wish, but I'm no Ernest Hemingway. I'm no David Ogilvy either. Instead, I sell wine."

Evius perked up. "That's kind of the same thing," he said. His eyes narrowed, and he added, "I like you more and more with every word you say."

Mike twitched his head. The dog glanced up as the man's hand stopped moving for a brief moment, but it was just a hitch in his step. He quickly resumed scratching behind Theo's ear. Like any satisfied animal, he appeared stupidly content.

"So, Christian, what do you do for a living?" Mike asked.

Before Christian even had a chance to say, *I'm a pianist,* Evius answered for him, "Christian's a stone mason... like Jesus, but tougher."

Mike snickered at that one. The sound spurted out his

nasal cavities. Christian observed that his laugh certainly wasn't very cool. But of course, observations, as science has taught, lead only to theories, and theories take years to become laws. And even then, a new observation may overturn the law, and we return to a mere theory. Thus, the terrifying theory everything is relative. And Mike seemed a man who might have grown up with the same relative insecurities, the same fears, the same names hurled at his hurt soul as Christian. It's only a theory, but Christian wondered aloud, "How long have you been dead?"

Before Mike had a chance to answer, the sound of a slowing car sprayed through the gravel driveway, and instead of responding to Christian's question (which, unbeknownst to his new roommate, actually quite hurt his feelings), Mike said, "That must be James."

"Who's James?" Christian asked.

"In some instances, James would be the brother of Christ," Evius whispered... "But in this case, he's simply your other roommate."

"I never knew Christ had a brother," Christian mumbled.

And Evius responded, "We're all his brothers. That's the riddle called James."

The front door opened and closed, and a fourth man stood in the living room's archway. He was wearing all black – black tee shirt, black jeans, black dress shoes, black sunglasses. His hairline was receding as well, and he appeared a bit more out of shape than Mike. Not necessarily thicker, just softer, with a non-existent jaw line, a sunken chest, and what could only have been a beer belly. He pulled his sunglasses off to reveal haggard eyes that appeared not to have closed for more than a blink in a few days. Christian could relate. They hit it off immediately... almost psychically. With a shy manner, James waved to

Christian. "Hi," he said. "I'm James."

"Christian," Christian responded with a backwards nod that from anybody else might have appeared cool, but due to Christian's lack of confidence it simply appeared awkward.

James nodded back. "You guys wanna head down to Pablo's for a drink?" he asked. "I had one helluva night."

"What happened?" Evius wondered without even bothering to introduce himself.

With a sigh and a heavy shrug, James responded, "A patient of mine died."

Christian's eyes grew wide as if to convey the terror his mind felt: *Die? As in dead? As in what just happened to me?* He could have sworn he saw James, his face grown quite pale and grave, nod at him. But Evius said, "It happens. Not a bad deal, though. I've often wondered what comes after this, whether we go on to a more heavenly plane or just start over again. Someday, somebody's going to tell me."

For his part, Christian was dumbfounded. What the hell was this place? So far, it was no goddamn different from earth except you apparently had the potential of winding up stuck here forever. Although, if his life had simply ended with his suicide, Christian might as well have been stuck on earth forever, too.

James shook his head and wondered, "Tell me, what happens when you die after you've already died?"

"Nobody knows," Mike responded. "That's what makes the whole thing so exciting."

"Or terrifying," James said, and he shivered. In the conversation's interim, Theo realized the household's other member had shown up. He went over to give him a sniff and a lick on the palm. The affection brought a smile to James's face.

Mike went on, "I mean think of how much better

things got once we got here… going on from here must be, well, I can't even imagine."

"Yes, you can," Evius said, and with a click of his tongue, he called the dog over to him. Cupping the dog's face, he began scratching Theo behind his ears. The dog appeared in seventh heaven. "Tell me," he asked, "Whose dog is Theo?"

"Neither of ours," Mike responded without a second thought. "He came with the house. His name was on his collar."

Evius recoiled from the dog like a vampire from a cross. A slight hiss even escaped his clenched teeth. He nonchalantly waved Theo away, and the dog returned to Mike's open hand.

Nobody other than Christian seemed to notice Evius' response to Mike's revelation. And Christian found it exceedingly strange that this man who had seemed so in control of nearly everything else lost his cool when confronting a simple truth about a simple dog. What did the dog represent to Evius' mind? What did it mean for him to come with the house? Why was his name on his collar? Christian was going to ask his tour guide, but before he got a chance, James said, "So are we going down to Pablo's or what?" As usual, Christian lost his train of thought.

A veritable forest rose up to create the backyard. It was the most wooded area Christian had seen since he'd left the suburbs where his mom lived. As he descended an outdoor staircase to Pablo's basement abode, eye level greens of the richest, deepest, most natural shades greeted his appreciation of the lot for his new life. The colors were so intense he thought maybe he'd hit a joint again sometime recently (he couldn't still be that stoned), and in his natural nearly intoxicated state, he reflected that the only thing that had ever appeared so green to him was a bud of sticky marijuana.

Pablo was sitting out on a makeshift porch he appeared to have set up only for himself. Smoking a thickly hand-rolled cigarette, he was leaning back in a dusty, white plastic chair pulled up to a dusty, white plastic table. In order to keep the elements from hampering his enjoyment of the outdoors, a tarp hung high over the brick floor enclosure. It was a living room out of doors. Pablo was sipping from a glass of some radioactive appearing liquid. Introductions were made. With a wink, Pablo said he thought he'd met Evius, who was introduced to Pablo as he'd introduced himself to Mike as Virgil, before... although he'd gone by a different name at the time. Then, he asked the four men, "Absinthe anyone?"

Christian had tasted the green fairy before, in Prague, a week or so before he'd ever even met Sophia.

How very different his life had been then. He might as well have been a different person with a different face and a different name. Perhaps the absinthe could take him back to that time, could give him back the promise his life had held then. Could anything erase the years of memories beyond that moment? Only another drink, but another drink led to more memories needing to be erased. Why couldn't he remember the conviction he'd felt after stepping out of the shower? Did it matter there was no longer a mother for him to call? Did it matter he'd succeeded in hanging himself? He was still conscious, which is actually precisely why his mouth tingled with the absent memory of absinthe's anise flavor and precisely why he should have despised the poison the sweetness hid.

But the absinthe beckoned to him. As he licked his lips in anticipation, not wanting to be the first to jump at the chance for alcohol, next to him, James said, "I sure could use a glass, Pab."

As the dealer readying to fix up his junkie prey, Pablo jumped up and into action. He grabbed a glass from out a cupboard behind him. He poured a shot of absinthe into the glass. The liquid was as deep green as Superman's dreaded Kryptonite, as the café siren's irises, and easily as powerful as both. Then, Pablo placed a slotted spoon overtop the glass and a sugar cube on top of that. For a brief moment, the world looked like one of his earthly paintings. Over the sugar cube, he poured ice water from out a pitcher. Slowly, like Atlas beneath an added feather to the world's weight, the sugar cube crumbled under the water, dissolved into nothing but a granular beach at the glass bottom. With the sugar cube gone, Pablo picked the slotted spoon up off the glass, used it to give two quick stirs through the concoction, pulled it out, tapped a "ping" against the glass's rim, set it down, and handed the still swirling drink off to James. "Anyone else?" he quickly asked. The three others clamored to be the next fix in Pablo's queue.

With glasses shared all the way around, Christian took a refreshing sip from his.

It had been so long and he'd been in such a state when last he'd tasted it that the absinthe's licorice flavor struck him as quite powerful and intriguing. He recalled a three AM bathroom trip of flies on walls filtered through a green sheen, stumbling backwards up a flight of steps as he spoke in tongues with a tongue no longer working. Could a drink so simple as this really lead one to such hallucinations? It seemed as odd as the acid trip where Christian realized all he'd done was mingle one chemical with a plethora of chemicals already in his brain and suddenly he existed on a completely different plane – one where the grass melted to his fingers and a bottle oozed through his palm.

With the sweetness of the iced down sugar and liquor cooling his palate, it seemed a similar experience could await him in Machpelah. A wormwood fungus was the chemical component in absinthe causing the hallucination. It was a relative of LSD hidden beneath the surface like symbolism in a story causing a comparable subconscious ejaculation. But it took more than a sip to take the drinker to that state. In point of fact, it took as many glasses as a novel's many chapters.

So after the first sip, Christian simply settled into the cooling sensation washing through his brain, the dimming of the world around the periphery of his vision, and the narrowing of his focus into a single point the alcohol forced upon him – one character, one sentence, one word. In this instance, Pablo Picasso sitting in living flesh before him: dead once, dead no longer, but possibly someday dead again. Viewed from all angles simultaneously, Pablo flattened out against the atmosphere. Christian focused on his bones and complexion. In death, blood pumped through those veins running through that body housing the soul that painted *La Guernica*.

Guernica… a mind laid flat on a canvas. Guernica… blood and death mean nothing to Krishna because all things that live must die. What difference if it's today or tomorrow? When viewed from all angles, it might as well have happened yesterday. The first glass went down easy. The second even easier…

Pablo's single point expanded into a many-chambered looking glass. Christian's compatriots conversed and laughed and relaxed as if nothing were wrong. While Christian stared at them through a fly's thousand eyes as suddenly, he had to know, "Does everybody here die again?"

Silence squeaked across the porch like a movie barroom

scene where the needle slides off the record in disbelief at what has just been said. Voluminous crickets could have chirped through the dead air. Mike and James stared aghast at Christian's lack of tact for bothering to ask such a morbid question amongst frivolity. Evius and Pablo were all buzzed smiles as the artist laughed, "Truth is, my new friend, we don't know. Some die. Some don't."

Evius added, "Just be grateful you got here at all." Toasts of acceptance and happiness floated the way around.

"And the possibility of an end makes it all that much more exciting," Mike winked.

"Bravo," from Pablo, "Spoken like a true artist!" Again the glasses (all except Christian's) were lifted into a simultaneous clink above the dirty, white plastic table.

"Speaking of the true artist, Pab," James interjected. "I think I'm finally on the verge of creating my first great project."

"Fabulous!" Pablo exclaimed. "Do tell how and why you've reached this magnificent point."

"Well, it's been an eternity in the making, but I've met somebody who's given me insights I never could have come to on my own…"

"How wonderful, a muse…" Pablo mused.

"They've been theorized to show up here before," Mike said.

"But she may not be an actual muse just to be my muse," James philosophized. "Regardless, she's explained an entirely new way of looking at art and the canvas."

"Ahhh… you're a painter," Evius finally realized. "That must have been your work upstairs."

With pursed lips and narrowed eyes – no feigned humility, no assumed audacity, James nodded. Christian had thought it Pablo's work: interesting, sparse. But there was more depth to be discovered on this plane. Even in the midst of his jumbled fears, Christian desired to see what the great artist had been capable of producing in his afterlife years. What were these extraordinary nudes mentioned by Evius? Where could one discover the definition and pinnacle of the postmortem aesthetic? James continued, "But Zoe has really opened my mind up to a whole new way of seeing what should occur on a canvas."

Evius assumed a preponderant attitude of pondering, mumbling, "Zoe's the name of no muse... Still, she has quite an interesting etymology..."

Lost in the enunciation of his newest insights, James paid no mind to, cared even less about where the name might have come from (what meaning can a name contain anyway – they're chosen by humans to connote a random being as of yet unknown) as he continued, "See, Pab, now you may have already known this, but Zoe explained to me a canvas is an abstract narrative..."

"Like a piece of music," Christian quietly interjected.

"Right. Maybe. I don't know," James said. "What I'm certain of is I never thought in terms of telling a story before. I only thought of relations of color and shape. Now, I understand what was missing all those times when you said a jazz artist would tell me my canvases don't swing... But I've suddenly realized if I can figure out how to tell a story in color, then I think my work will go to the next level."

"And that's what it's all about. Taking it to the next level," Mike said.

"That's all it ever is, my friends. Every piece of art is a mere attempt at creating what is conceived, and there's only one conception to begin with – Brahman... Atman..." Pablo rolled his eyes even at himself.

"But it has to be in the abstract," James appeared in pain as he spoke – so hard was he trying to correctly formulate his hypothesis. "I don't want to simply recreate a Renaissance allegory. I want to explain the postmortem experience, like you're doing, Pab. Zoe said she's going to take me somewhere that'll give me everything I need to paint the greatest paintings of my afterlife. I don't know what she's talking about, but it's gotta be either sex or a drug. I'd take either with her. What else is art besides sex and drugs anyway?"

"Mythology," Evius mumbled.

James didn't seem to hear him. He said, "At least, that's all I can think of. Either way, I'm looking forward to it. We're supposed to meet up tomorrow." Evius raised his eyebrows. James finished, "What else is there to do here anyways? Machpelah's just like any other town…"

"Well, tonight, there's Thelonious Monk with Art Blakey, Miles Davis, Charles Mingus, and John Coltrane live at *The Bohemian Sepulcher*. That should be enough to spin your art off in a new direction, James… if you know how to listen," Pablo said.

"A hard bop explosion," Evius cooed.

The absinthe, as its cousins always had in life, had succeeded in banishing the thought of death from Christian's postmortem consciousness. He mumbled, "I'd like to see that."

"I think we all would," Mike agreed.

"Then perhaps we should," Evius rhymed to complete the internal scheme in a line of pentameter. Nobody noticed.

"Are you a true music fan, Mr. Anderson?" Pablo asked. "Or are you like the other two of your generation here and a fan of mere sounds instead?"

"I don't think you need to knock my tastes like that, Pab," James said.

"Besides, I'm learning," Mike added. "It just takes time.

One art feeds the others."

"That it most certainly does. As I said before, there is only one. Do you partake of it, Mr. Anderson?" Pablo asked.

So astonished was he that the great artist Pablo Picasso had addressed not one but two questions directly to him, Christian nearly choked on his absinthe. "I… I play piano if that's what you mean," he stuttered.

Pablo laughed, "Really? Who's your favorite composer."

"Well, I'm a huge fan of Franz Liszt. I love his octave spans."

"Hmmm…. you need to hear Franz riff with some of the more contemporary players. I saw him with Charlie Parker just the other night. He's really gone off the deep end since he's died. Wouldn't you say so, Virgil?"

Evius nodded.

Pablo continued, "But tell me, Christian. Do you plan to play here in Machpelah?"

Staring to the earth's burning heart, Christian looked down at the ground. Reflected through that world's hallucinatory core, he could see the great pianists performing there on a daily basis: Chopin, Horowitz, Schubert… And those were only the names he knew. He sighed. Frowning, he said, "I don't know if I'll get a chance."

"You have to," James interjected, "Our part of the household has the three arts covered now. We could start our own movement."

"There are more arts and there's more to a movement than that," Evius snorted.

But realistically, in a friendly manner, Mike nudged Christian's shoulder. "You're here forever, man. I'm sure you'll get a chance."

Evius laughed. "Not if he dies. That's why I say – *carpe diem*."

With a quickly reversed frown, Pablo clapped his hands as if to magically imply: *take your mind away from all that*. Out loud, he said, "So it's agreed, then. Tonight, we'll see the quintet. For now, let me dazzle you all with what I've been working on most recently. A few glasses of absinthe should make it that much more extraordinary. Anybody for another?" All four of them rushed to fill their cups.

As each individual performed the sacred ritual of dissolving the sugar cube as if its grains were the sand flowing through Death's hourglass, Pablo disappeared like a shadow at midday into his apartment. When he returned a triumphant shaman from out his cave, he was lugging with him a good-size canvas he promptly laid down on the dirty, white plastic table.

With one simple look, Christian realized it was well beyond him. The layering of paints gave it an almost three-dimensional appearance, and the contrasting yellows glaring at one another hinted a fourth.

Sure enough, it was recognizably a nude, but a nude like nothing Christian had ever envisioned. The legs turned into hands; the arms, into feet. The face had more than even four dimensions. The very experience of the canvas itself was akin to that joint Christian had smoked with Evius back at what he'd thought was his old apartment. The shapes themselves broke apart not on the canvas itself but inside your mind. In fact, the entire composition visibly occurred not outside but inside the process of your very own thoughts. It bridged the gap between the external sensations of art and the internal experience of a dream. It was something like a mythical reality: not something you would ever see in actuality, but a psychological entity more vivid than any moment ever perceived by memory.

Like a serpent granting knowledge, it slithered through the brain and where its tail's rattle struck – something like an over-amplified snare (a rhythm popping on the upbeats) – it left a slight pain. The work was so good, it caused your mind to physically ache as if the knowledge were granted by fangs, and the venom was pumping, thumping, swelling through your arteries and veins. Your mind grew from the poison. It reached the point of bursting, but the membranes held you to a mere migraine. An aura appeared around the canvas. Christian was amazed. There was as much intellectual space between the art he had experienced every day of his life prior to that moment and this piece as there was between the mechanical intricacy of the computer Mike was writing his novel on and the stone flakes humanity's ancestors once upon a time used to chop through to the marrow of the bones they scavenged.

Evius kissed the tips of his fingers as if to say: *Mama Mia!* "Another extraordinary piece, Mr. Picasso," he exclaimed – a smile plying at the corners of his lips, his funk from Theo finally lifting at the sight of pleasurable brilliance. "I've got six of his works back at my own place," he completed in a whisper to Mike who raised his eyebrows at the words, but who, in a glance, couldn't tell if this man he called Virgil were lying or telling the truth.

"If you like that, Virgil, I can't wait to show you my new piece," James added.

Pablo patted the neophyte's shoulder. "Just wait until you hear the band tonight. Some things can be neither taught nor understood," he said, and as he picked the painting back up to return it to the safety of his darkened alcove, at Christian, he winked mischievously.

16.
A Night in Tunisia

The Bohemian Sepulcher wasn't the biggest club Christian had ever been to. In fact, it was more of a bar than anything else: a cozy, intimate setting with a small raised stage in the alcove behind the glass front window. James mentioned offhandedly, but with the definite intention Christian and Evius should both know, a friend of his had built the tiny stage by hand, all on his own. In his state, Christian found himself sizing up the work and determining whether or not he could have done the same, and just as he realized, why, yes, he most certainly could have, Mike whispered it was more an acquaintance than a friend.

The roommates and Evius crowded around a table too small for their party of five. A candle burned at the table's center. Smoke congealed in the air around them. Some of it came from the cigarettes all five of them smoked. The rest of it swirled off the cigarettes nearly every other patron burned.

Still consumed with the synaptic processes of their seemingly intensely important conversation, Gilles and Jean-Francois sat together in the corner. A waitress tattooed from nearly head to toe brought the five new and old friends a round of drinks: gin and tonics for Theo's three existing masters and whiskeys neat for Evius and Christian.

Evius told Christian the woman who glowed from the ink decorating her skin was one of the prostitutes killed in a London alleyway by Jack the Ripper. Even with her sideshow history, Christian found her exceedingly attractive. Her eyebrows were perfectly spaced apart, and her nose had an interesting lilt to it.

Evius went on: every tattoo carved into her (whether known or imbedded in the unconscious recesses of her soul) had been placed in a place where the psychopath had inserted a blade to dismember her – a videotaped confession had once upon a time been found in the woods on Machpelah's outskirts.

It was a phenomenon the small city-state's psychologists were extremely interested in, but she refused to reveal the depths of her knowledge. She was an enigma. However, with the colors emanating from her epidermis, to Christian, she appeared a bird.

Like a hawk on a telephone wire, Christian scanned the room repeatedly. His eyes lingered on every body walking in through the door. Every movement, every motion arrested his attention. A girl in a halter top stood up to go to the bathroom. Another patron twisted her wrist to unlock a couple of tangled bracelets. Christian stared at them all. He was looking for something. He was looking for someone. He was looking for Sophia.

She wasn't her. Neither was she. She had to be there… somewhere. She'd never been a fan of jazz in her previous life (electronica had been more her style), but in the afterlife who knew what pleasures she might have discovered. For the devil's sake, she'd been in his dream. When he'd asphyxiated himself, before he'd come back to life, she'd called out to him. She'd asked him whether or not he still believed in them. He did. Goddamnit, he had to admit: he did. He always had. He'd just never made the admission until it was too late, until he cried into a bottle of cheap wine with his eyes opened wide from the effects of the crack melted through the stem placed securely back in his pocket, that he'd promised himself that morning he'd throw away but that he just didn't want to let go of until tomorrow, and thank the Lord, he hadn't.

He'd told her before. She'd asked him, and he'd said it – "I believe in us." Tears had trickled down from behind her black sunglasses. They'd dripped beside her nose. She'd wiped them away with her pinky. "When you see the stars, you will know that I see them too because we are both alive, and as long as we are both alive, I will still believe in us," she'd told him, her Germanic accent thicker even with pain. She wrapped her arms around his neck. She stood up on her tiptoes. She kissed him. Her breath tasted of sadness. He breathed it into himself. Then, he was on a train, and it was too late. Too late.

His memory clogged his throat. Even on top of all the absinthe, he choked on the intangible intermingling of thought and emotion. He couldn't wait for his whiskey neat to show up. When he got it, he downed it in two gulps. Luckily everybody else was engrossed in a conversation that to Christian had to be meaningless. He quickly ordered another whiskey from Jack's victim. She noted it on their tab, and brought out to him what the barkeep poured – a few fingers of Machpelah's homebrewed equivalent of The Glenlivet.

Christian's head swam as it had every night previous for as long as he couldn't remember. He knew tomorrow he'd have the shakes again, but he didn't care. Tonight, he had that soothing sweetness burning his throat. It washed the memory back down into his gut. The painful sensations lingered at the base of his tongue. In the air of every breath he exhaled, warmth withered the atmosphere. As if the memory now smoked in his bowels (his mind a magnifying glass on it, the ant), it consumed him further from the inside out. The fire flared up from his stomach. Empowered by the alcohol's effects, he was a dragon. Let me show you my drunken style.

The liquor's sensation spun right between his eyes, in that spot where, if he had taken the meditation class, the Buddha would have told him his third eye looked out at the spirit realm. There, he was going as blind as an old bluesman. In his whirling darkness, a sudden thought asked him: *What if Sophia already died here, and you don't get to see her even in death.* He clenched his fist. His nails dug into his palm, but not deep enough to draw blood. "Then, I want to die again," he said out loud, and he downed his second whiskey.

"What?" Evius asked him. A little late, he reached for Christian's tumbler. "Whoa, whoa... Hold on there, killer. Leave some for the rest of the patrons..." he shook his head. "I'll get you another one, but sip this one, man. Alcohol is insanity."

But insanity meant nothing to Christian anymore. He needed out. He needed away. His insides were aflame. There had to be some hero to squelch the pain, some Christ-like figure willing to sacrifice his life in order to ease his brethren's suffering. Little did Christian know, or at least he didn't remember, the Holy Spirit descends in a tongue of fire. Perhaps that was what was alight in Christian's soul. Nobody ever said the experience of God was a pleasant one. Perhaps salvation had been conferred upon him through glass after glass of alcohol. Moses struck a stone to give birth to water, and Christ turned that water into wine. If I didn't know any better, I'd say that was a job only for Zeus's son by a mortal woman, Dionysus – the one who men never believed was a God... women did, though. Like a male frog, Zeus sowed him into his thigh.

And, of course, Dionysus (according to Heraclitus) was one with Hades – because both of their gifts are insanity – who is the ruler of the underworld, and thus the devil, sometimes known as Satan who is Iblis, Samael, Lucifer, the one angel who would never bow to humanity: the Judeo-Christian version of the Native American creator, Coyote, the trickster, Loki, the blood brother of the gods, the shapeshifter from Norse mythology: Mercury, the messenger of the gods whose symbol is the serpent-entwined caduceus. Kundalini is coiled like a serpent. It unravels up the spine and brings with it enlightenment. Lilith (some say the whole universe is fucked up because Yahweh fell in love with her) is the shapeshifter, with her consort Samael (the serpent with a lion's head (something like a Chinese pageant dance (*He* shall return as a lion)) – could it be?) the mother of Nosferatu, the vampire, the eternal, the damned. And that means Jesus was...

But the Gnostics already told us that was the case because all things are Buddha things and both Shiva and Vishnu are only attributes of Brahman, He who told Agni He makes the fire burn. And the preserver Vishnu manifested as Krishna who made love to the Gopis as Lucifer made love to Eve. And Krishna is the same Indo-European root as Christ meaning the anointed of God. Dionysus traveled with a band of loyal Gopis. But the intercessor is the son of Shiva, the simultaneous generator and destroyer: the elephant-headed Ganesha, Saint Michael, the archangel. El is now synonymous with Hel.

God is an alien like Enki, the father. The alien is a hermaphrodite, the concept of the circle enclosing the yin and the yang. So it's safe for us to return to the lord of the living and the dead – Osiris (defeater of the dog-headed Anubis (Iblis turned into a dog)) who was overcome by his brother Seth who was then overcome by his nephew Horus in the same manner Michael cast Lucifer into the pit only to build his own kingdom and rise again (but what if Michael (I've heard it said that *Michael* is Christ's name in heaven (Michael is the Jewish Messiah after all)) cast Lucifer out of heaven only because Saint Michael was the archangel Lucifer (the angel of the revelation has one name across his forehead, another on his thigh) who left never to return to his throne at the head of God's army (given the world I see, I'd say that's the most logical case)). And Marduk slew the dragon just like Hercules (who immortality was conferred upon in the form of a constellation like Draco) eventually defeated the Hydra as St. George did in England, but Tiamat is dead not dreaming, chewing her own tail, coiled in a double-helix like DNA, like Kundalini around the spine, as if she were Loki's third child, the World Serpent who will uncoil on the day of the Ragnarok, which, like Shiva, is both destruction and creation.

We've already uncoiled DNA. Amon-Ra was the first attempt at a monotheistic God, a merging of the deities ruling Upper and Lower Egypt. But Lucifer means Venus, the morning star, the love goddess, Ishtar, worshipped by prostitutes such as Mary Magdalene named for Jesus's mother, the virgin, Mary. *Everything's the devil,* Charlie Manson said. How Freudian... Samael is the ruler of the seventh heaven, and Zeus had to kill *Cronos*: Time, who killed his own father just like Oedipus had to do right before they all broke the incest taboo. Kill the Buddha inside of you. Was that Jesus's fate? So what does all this mean? "It means the world is insane, my dear friend," Gilles said in the corner with a flippant wave of his hand

and a lightning glint to his eye. Christian couldn't take it anymore. But luckily he didn't have to. Mike interrupted his manic-depressive thoughts. "So now he's disappeared for a second, what's Virgil's real name? I'm tired of playing this game."

"Evius," Christian responded.

"What?" Mike asked the dumbstruck newcomer to speak up overtop the din.

"Evius," he said again.

"Oh…" Mike thought for a moment. Trying to remember something from once upon a time, he glanced inward. Then, he said, "But Evius is another name for…"

Before Mike had a chance to complete his insight, the self-proclaimed Virgil returned and set a glass of whiskey in front of his Dante. "Now, hold on to this one for a little while," he said with a minor shake of his head as he plopped back into his chair to continue nursing his own drink.

An announcer in a tan suit stepped up to the microphone placed at the stage's front. "Good evening, ladies and gentlemen," he said. "We've got a wonderful show for you tonight here at *The Bohemian Sepulcher*, a truly stellar ensemble who've gathered together to delight your ears with the sounds of a jazz colder even than the cool. Like dry ice it'll burn you quicker than the red hot. Welcome one and all, old friends and new, to music Machpelah style. This is been-bop."

In a flash, the lights went out. Darkness engulfed the bar. The deep, resounding tempo of a floor tom echoed across the blackened room. Strobe lights flickered over the audience, capturing them in various attitudes of drink and expression. Along with the snap of a snare, the crash of cymbals splashed through the black, exterior space to rattle like the collective unconscious from one patron's mind to another. The ping of wood striking metal created an interior sensation akin to the white strikes of cocaine's blur. With a heavy thump, the standup bass joined in.

On what moments before had been an empty stage, a five-piece band stood. Seated on a stool, a goateed Charlie Mingus slumped over his bass. The attitude of a demon consumed him. His fingers found the notes on his fretless instrument with insane precision. Thelonious Monk, hat and beard in place, rattled his leg and gyrated atop his stool to the rhythm Art Blakey's six piece drum set pounded out. John Coltrane and Miles Davis, their instruments at their sides, stood in front of them all like twin angels (Lucifer and Michael) nodding their heads in time to the beat.

A warmth like the love he'd once felt for Sophia welled inside Christian's breast. It mingled with the whiskey in his stomach. He lit a cigarette. The flame danced to the pounding wind pulsing off the stage. Monk's huge, ringed fingers caressed the piano's keys with a grace that a hand of his size should never have possessed. The keys hammered against the strings, and a wave of sound washed out the percussive instrument. It ebbed and flowed from front to back, off one wall then the other. With a golden light, it glimmered through the atmosphere. The sax came in.

As if he were simply warming up, Trane blew a slew of chorded notes. He finished one run and started up in another key another one. The sheet music itself visibly manifested out his sax's bell. Miles's horn picked up to complete the melody. He weaved in and out of the rhythm section's cues to fill out the head riff with stately importance. The trumpeter stood still. His head nodded forward, his instrument a proboscis protruding from his face. Light years ago, this tune had been penned by Dizzy Gillespie, but death had morphed it into the psychedelic sensation of Sufi cities spinning out the heavenly spheres as whirling dervishes, of desert sunsets and African skylines, a call to prayer of the wildest kind. With a short remark from Trane's sax, like a car crash, the madness careened off into a brand new direction.

Still, though, it maintained the structural integrity it had already displayed. The foundation had been laid. The walls had been raised. The rest of the piece was all decorative baroque: colors for the interiors, landscaping for the garden.

The music shifted as if on an ocean of quicksand. The world appeared solid beneath the boats of notes, but as soon as the listener set foot upon the water's semblance, the hidden depths sucked him down to drown him in its complexity. Clawing for air, the mud filled the listener's throat, eyes, and ears. In death, the listener was finally able to hear.

For Christian's been-bop virgin ears, the harmonies were enough to make them nearly bleed. The rhythm contained more soul than all those imprisoned in hell. Following a last multitudinous gasp, Miles ushered in Trane's first solo proper.

This is what it means to swing, Trane's saxophone told the audience, and Christian felt it rocket from his feet into his heart. In a moment, he envisioned the three steps it takes to swing on a parquet dance floor. The next moment, his heart thumped to that tap-tap-tapped rhythm. He felt the whole history of jazz from its days in the parlor rooms of New Orleans brothels, through the clubs of the black Broadway in Washington, DC, all the way up to the sophistication of Lincoln Center in the self-proclaimed Capital of the World. History exploded in sound behind his eyes as he watched those dead men spontaneously compose such honorific music.

Monk, Mingus, and Blakey kept the rhythm tight and

punchy behind the saxophonist's wall of notes. A precise
flourish on the keyboard, and the saxophone ascended to
heaven and descended to hell. It traversed the world of
music from Europe to America to Asia and ended right
there in Machpelah. It told tales of sorrow and joy and lust
and abstinence in time to the rhythm section's cues.

After a number of measures, Miles showed the
audience what he'd learned about scales and modes in
death. He held one note out until it hurt the listeners'
hearts. It battered and bruised their aortas. It ripped their
superior vena cava in half and left the audience nearly
vomiting blood, but right when the pressure became too
much on that most precious of organs, Miles let go of his
key and changed the note. He took the listeners on a trip
backwards through time to when he played with Bird. He
hit the horn's keys with a speed he'd never been
comfortable accomplishing in life. He used the circle of
fifths to propel himself masterfully through a meaningless
symbol of Christ's crucifixion, a symbol once used by Bach
in a vocal piece, which was lost on most of the slack-jawed
audience members. He quoted tunes many people listening
at that moment had never even heard: a piece from Chinese
folk music, a piece from the pop standards of his youth, a
piece from a Wu-Tang album in the nineties. Shaking his
head and smiling, Trane, a full head taller than the
trumpeter, stood still behind him. For some strange reason
he didn't even know, Christian wanted to cry.

The world is amorphous. It affects our unconscious.
Music is the semen building in our minds' testicles. It
ejaculates spiritually to impregnate our brains' eggs with
unknown emotions and thoughts. Before we know it, we're
Zeus giving birth to Athena. Just like with Mike as he
swung his head loosely on his neck. If Christian had had
the wherewithal to ask him, his new roommate would have

told him in the darkness he was discovering the next step in his absurdist comedy. It was something like the *Rite of Spring*, which he didn't know consciously.

In a different key, Miles was quoting the pagan ballet's notes right then. Improvising his own drunken harmonies for the sacrifice, evoking physically what Mike was only thinking, Christian found his classically trained fingers tapping non-existent keys across the tabletop. He went on a run of scales. Closing his eyes, he shed his skin, crossed his middle finger overtop his thumb, went as far as his reach could take him, and started back down. Breaking into his silent reverie, Pablo tapped him on the shoulder. "Bet you'd rather be up there than back here just watching Monk," he smiled warmly at him. Misunderstanding his new friend's intention, Christian scathed him with a look of anger and disappointment. Pablo opened his eyes wide and quickly went back to watching the show.

His dream intruded upon, Christian placed his numbed hands back in his lap. If he'd been paying attention, he would have noticed Evius glancing at him from out the corner of his eye, a subdued smile plying his lips.

Onstage, however, Monk inverted Christian's earlier self-conscious action while acting in consort with his embarrassment as the pianist took his ringed fingers off the ebonies and ivories. Miles's horn drained out and the rhythm section hammered manically on. Monk pulled his sunglasses up on his forehead and stared blankly at his keyboard. In place of a solo, his eyes darted from spot to spot across the piano. At every presumed strike of a heavy finger, his eyes bulged from their sockets to indicate there, right there, was the note he would play if he felt like making any noise.

But he didn't feel like making any noise. It was as if he were communicating psychically with the audience, a skill that, had Christian listened when Evius and he had begun their walk through Machpelah, he would have known many of the town's inhabitants were in the habit of attempting to cultivate. But unlike so many would-be deadbeats, Monk had succeeded.

The strike of a chord, then a single note, then a piece of a scale exploded out the spontaneous composer's brain into everybody else's... or so Christian assumed. Maybe only he heard it. Maybe he was linked with Monk spiritually. Maybe he was making it all up. He was probably drunk.

Monk's eyes ran from one end of the keyboard to the other. The tinkle of 52 notes resonated inside Christian's mind. The shattering sounds were a whole year's worth of wasted weeks, something Christian, with a frown, realized he was quite familiar with.

The pianist pushed himself away from the piano, stood up, and started dancing ludicrous circles around his stool. He flailed his arms like a caged bird finally set free, like the sparrow from Christian's floor reborn. Blakey banged on. Mingus powered away, occasionally shouting something like, "Go, man!" Miles and Trane stared with shared smiles at the great artist performing his unconventional solo.

Monk sat back down. Twisting his head atop his neck, he set his fingers on the keys and reinstated harmony. The whole crowd burst into applause. Evius leaned back to Christian. "So... what do you think?" he asked.

At the words of the one who had gotten him into that whole mess, Christian drained his tumbler. He licked the remnants of burning whiskey from off his lips. He felt infinitely cooler than he did a few moments earlier when Pablo had upset his serenity. In fact, to anybody who had been paying attention he even *looked* cooler.

His eyes lit up. He rubbed his hand down his face. With the liquor floating freely in his mind, the memory of other substances set his teeth chattering. With his unconscious thoughts racing out to where the right alleyway in Machpelah might lie to find what he really wanted, he spoke mechanically, "Fucking amazing, man. If I remember this, I'll remember I've been waiting for it my whole life." But inside, all he could think was: *where in the hell in paradise can you find cocaine?*

Evius smiled like he could read his mind. "I was just thinking the same thing," he said. "Another drink?"

By the time the show was over, Christian didn't realize it, but he could barely walk. Arms draped over one another's shoulders, humming melodies they didn't understand, the five of them stumbled out the bar: Pablo and Mike, neither of whom had drunk as much as the other three, supporting James who babbled on and on about the promise of his next day's rendezvous with Zoe, and Evius, who had easily drunk as much as his baggage, supporting Christian like he was the cross Christ had to bear. Like with Socrates at Plato's famous symposium, the alcohol appeared to have had no effect on Christian's savior.

"Now why the fuck are you carrying me?" Christian, his eyes rolling wildly in every direction, suddenly slurred as they stepped into the cool, springtime air outside the door. He didn't know why, but he knew he needed to get away from his new "friends". Something deeper than his soul was begging to be fed. Like an empty stomach, it rumbled beneath his nerves. He needed an excuse. He needed to think about that. He hiccupped. He forgot. He shoved himself away from Evius. He tripped over his nice new shoes. He landed on the ground, and he started laughing maniacally.

His housemates looked at him askance. Evius, however, laughed along with Christian. He stuck out his hand. Christian slapped it away. "Well, get up on your own, then," Evius said. "I won't stop you. But to give you some incentive…" he added while pulling – with no regard for who might be passing them in exit – a joint from out his hip pocket. "It's Christmastime, baby."

Like a dog offered a treat, Christian cocked his head to the side and stayed zoned in on the joint as he lifted himself from where he'd fallen. *Christmastime? What does that mean?* his mind knowingly salivated.

(*Once upon a time, there was a little boy who still believed in Santa Claus. He stared out his window at the snow fallen on evergreen trees. It was so pretty, white sprinkled atop green, life continuing in the midst of death. In his little boy way, he reflected upon the great philosophical debate raging through his elementary school classrooms at that point in time: Is there such a thing as Santa Claus? Is there really a man with a long, white beard who flies through the sky on Christmas Eve, who sticks his finger beside his nose, and who shimmies his way down chimneys to deliver presents to all the good little boys and girls? He knew there was because he'd seen him sitting in a chair at the mall just the week before.*

But a nagging thought had begun to plague his mind: that might not be Santa Claus. That might just be an old man in a red suit dressed to look like Santa Claus. The issue had been raised at recess the other day. He stared out at the evergreen trees coated with white snow, and he sighed. He needed an answer. He needed to know the truth. He stood up, and he went into his parents' bedroom.

"Mom," he said. She was lying on top of her bed, reading a book.

"Yes, honey?"

"Is Santa Claus real?"

His mom set her book aside. "Oh, baby," she said, and she patted the space next to herself on the bed.

The little boy jumped at the opportunity. It was getting rarer and rarer that his mom invited him up into her sanctuary. He still remembered the many times he'd slept there just a year before when he'd been tormented by nightmares. His mother eventually told him to stop watching HBO, and he'd listened. He was still at an age when he'd do that. Sometimes, though, he wished he hadn't. Because the nightmares had stopped, and without an excuse, he'd had to stay in his own bed, reading with the lights on so the monsters underneath wouldn't grab his feet. When you're only eight and a half, a year is an eternity. He climbed up beside her. She put her arm around him and pulled him close.

He smelled the subtle scent of her perfume wafting off her neck and wrists. Years later, he'd learn it was Opium.

"Do you really want to know the truth?" she asked him.

The little boy nodded.

She sighed. "Well," she began. "Real can mean different things. Like that table over there, it's real. But also, the love I feel for you is real. Does that make sense?"

The little boy nodded.

"Even though you can't see my love?"

The little boy nodded again.

"Well, Santa Claus is real like my love, not like that table."

The little boy scrunched up his face to indicate he didn't understand.

"What I mean is that Santa Claus is real in here." She patted the little boy's breast, right above his heart. "He's real in here," she said, patting her own chest. "But not out here," she added, opening her arms to encompass the world surrounding them. "Santa Claus is the spirit of Christmas, the spirit I give gifts to you with. He's real because we make him real with what we feel. When we love someone, and we give them something, then we're all Santa Claus. But there's no Santa Claus at the North Pole."

"Okay," the little boy said, "I thought so. I'm gonna go back to my room now."

He went back to his room, and he stared at the snow covering the evergreen trees outside his window, and a tear trickled down beside his nose (right where he used to think Santa Claus placed his finger to magically go back up the chimney) as he realized if Santa Claus wasn't real, Rudolph wasn't real either. And that was just too much to take. He'd never before realized the implications of what he'd been discussing with his schoolmates. He started to cry. White snow on evergreen trees never meant the same thing again.)

Evius stuck the joint between his lips and lit it. The light from the club door tinted his profile. With the veins in his neck tightening, his Adam's apple stuck out more prominently than ever before.

Smoke trickled off the paper tip. The lascivious crew awaiting the night's next event got a few strange glances from exiting patrons. But Christian was back up and swaying on his feet in record time – a seemingly impossible circumstance given how quickly he'd gone down.

Evius handed the joint off to James who was staring as incredulously as his comrades. Christian licked his lips. Nearing a growl, he whispered, "Don't take it all."

Nobody seemed to hear him, but Evius shook his head. James's eyes opened wide with his hit. He coughed and handed the joint off to Pablo. Pablo took his turn.

With his irises registering his mind's tremors, the great artist looked uncomprehendingly at the tiny marijuana cigarette for a moment, and the joint made the rounds to Mike who took it gingerly between thumb and forefinger and partook with a great deal more care than his housemates.

By the time the Christmas tree finally reached Christian, the newly dead man puffed like a fish re-submerged in murky seas, a lungfish returned from his muddy cocoon, the missing link between land and ocean alive in his natural environment.

Through the widening of his synapses, he felt – perhaps it was only psychosomatic – the implied cocaine in the concoction. It was a rush through his veins and into his heart's straining cells. (Are the dead still composed of cells?) It thumped there with a beat more rapid than that which had left. He felt himself the drums Art Blakey had spent the last hour and a half banging upon. His body's time signature changed. As if he had just received a first-rate massage, all the tension left his body. His shoulders dropped down from around his neck. Unafraid of the effects on his heart, Christian killed the burn with a series of quick tokes and handed what was only a roach back to Evius who stomped on it – with no regard for what the trace amounts of cocaine might have cost or what they could have done to one's body – and smiled eerily at his charge.

For a brief second, he had fangs and a forked tongue. Blood pooled at the corners of his mouth. Christian remembered hanging through that hole in his ceiling. He blinked and reminded himself, like for a cared for plant in a garden, the weed was just fucking with him, sucking out his sanity and replacing it with madness. Gilles would be proud. That thought was gone.

Back at the house, Christian's insides had twisted into a Gordian knot. He could still see, but his memory was blind. He didn't recall a single inch of the walk home. The world came in disjointed segments – no sensory impressions were being formed. He was here. He was there. Life was like the strobe light preceding the quintet's show.

He thought he was still sitting on the ground in front of the club, but he found himself seated on the couch he'd been introduced to James in. It was so confusing, so maddening. Alcohol had blocked nearly all of his malleable circuits. They criss-crossed wires and burnt out beneath the liquid concoction overpowering them. Smoke clouded the visions behind his eyes. His pupils swam alone… no brain behind them to receive. Only his locomotion remained intact. All he knew was another drug could cut the rope his organs had tied themselves into, and he knew which drug that needed to be.

Not even certain what he was doing anymore, he whispered to Evius, "You got any more coke, man?" His companion's response: "Show some restraint. They're civilized here in Machpelah." He didn't remember it, but Evius ended matter-of-factly with, "Maybe this just isn't where you belong."

Christian leaned in deep for a tête-à-tête with James. The latter had a very serious look on his face. Christian wanted to talk about art. He swung his hands wildly, and he narrowed his eyes to slits. James suddenly shied away as if he were afraid of being hit.

"*Am I really going to die again?!*"

Typing away on his computer, Mike was in the back of the living room. Sitting on the couch, Christian wanted to know what he was writing. He was wondering if he was writing about him. He was certain he was. His head lolled loosely on his neck. He screamed something, and somebody put his arm around him.

Tears: "I know I'll never see my mom again..." "...None of us will..."

He was outside in the dark next to the house. Vomit was spilling all over his new leather shoes. Was all that slush really coming from out his own mouth?

Trying to walk up the stairs, he couldn't get his legs to move forward. He had to strain them backwards. That made him smile. Then, he fell down the two steps he'd managed to clamber up. He was bleeding.

"*Where's Sophia?*"

A scuffle broke out in the hallway. Christian found himself on the back of his head on the hardwood floor. It felt like something had cracked (his mind, his brain, his skull?). Above him, Mike's face puffed red. "*Who the fuck do you think you are?"*

15.
This Ain't Your Dream

*D*aylight *ignited swaths of warm light across Christian's cheeks* and lips. As he rolled his head from side to side, he felt the wood his skull rested upon, a mere quarter inch of fluid protecting his brain from the floor he had conceivably fallen upon. The dull sensation of a bruise proved that to be the case. Beneath the bones of his elbows and buttocks, the same wood dug through his thin skin. He didn't want to – but he had to – open his eyes.

Through the dusty bay window taking up one wall of this unknown room, the sun filtered into the house he must have passed out in. *Where in the hell am I?* Above his queasy stomach, a slight panic twanged his breast. It rose into his throat. In the moment between sleep and full wakefulness, the day before disappeared, and all that remained was the too common occurrence of reliving the fluidity of liquid dreams.

He glanced to his right: floor. To his left: the floor led into a couch. In front of the couch sat a pair of boots attached to legs covered in tight jeans, a tight tee shirt, and, ah yes, Evius smoking a cigarette, his black hair hanging down over his ears and shadowing his eyes. His long nails gingerly flicked the ash from the butt. Christian closed his eyes.

Everything from the sparrow on his floor to dangling the rope through the hole in his ceiling to meeting Pablo and leaving for the concert flashed in front of his mind's eye. He remembered just about everything up to smoking a joint in front of the bar (...*It was Christmastime, and a little boy still believed in Santa Claus*). He thought: *There's no way around it. I really am dead.*

He smacked his terrible tasting tongue against his mouth's dry roof. He needed water. His parched Adam's apple bobbed to the tick of a swallow. He stifled a vomit encrusted burp. In the pit of his stomach, a silent rage built.

"Well, I'm glad to see you're still with us," Evius said. The sound of a smile tinged his words.

"What the fuck are you so happy about?" Christian moaned.

"It's morning, man. We made it through another day."

"I didn't want to make it through yesterday."

"Well, you could have fooled me. But either way, you don't have a choice. We don't have control over these things. Unfortunately, death just keeps going. Man, you gotta find some faith."

Faith... he didn't care what that meant. His life wasn't a theological study he'd chosen to embark upon. In fact, the idea of theology was the furthest thing from his soggy mind. Mere practical philosophy was too much for him to comprehend. Forget about metaphysics. At that moment, all he wanted was for the light to go away. He shielded his eyes with his hand. *Why do we ever have to be awake? Why can't we just forget about the day?* "What time is it?" he slurred, his tongue still drunk from his night in Tunisia.

"Time for you to get out of here," Evius said, and he stood up.

Evius' boots clicked across the wood until they were even with Christian's head. With a grunt, the tour guide leaned down and pulled Christian to his feet by his shoulders. As if he'd seen himself as a ghost again for the very first time, the dead man's knees felt weak. He drooped amid Evius' chest-high embrace. His feet barely touched the floor.

"I'm not gonna carry you," Evius said. A note of disgust colored his tone, and he let go.

For a brief moment, Christian thought he might fall. Left to its own devices, his head swam lightly. Then, he was standing all on his own, the soles of his new boots (the square toes of which were peppered with crusted chunks of last night's puking) firm against the floor. His favorite shirt had a hole in the elbow and dried blood caked to the sleeve. "Is that mine?" Christian asked.

Evius nodded.

A slight relief resonated through Christian's pained features, but he failed to make any verbal mention of it. His legs felt shaky beneath him like a child's who has just done battle with the ocean's waves. They roll in and out beneath, follow you onto the shore, and leave you standing on fluid ground until you drift off to sleep that night rocked in the sea's arms. Christian squinted. "Where are we going?"

"I thought we'd go get a cup of coffee. We sure as hell can't stay here. After the shit you pulled last night, I'm not so sure if we're welcome anymore…"

Years of awakening guilt deadened Christian's breast. He didn't even want to ask what had happened. He felt the same as he had so many years ago in college when he'd still had the wherewithal to spend his time with others, and then, he remembered why he had fled the company of his fellows. With a growl – so unlike anything Evius had ever heard him mutter before – he said, "Well, if they have a problem with me, they can throw me the fuck out."

A light, not of amazement or recognition but rather of panic, lit behind Evius' eyes, "You don't understand this place yet, man. If we don't get out of here, they very well might call the cops."

Not sure what that entailed in paradise, but certain it couldn't be good, Christian took his guide up on his advice and deigned to use his seafaring legs to carry him across the living room, out the door, and down the threshold back into the yard where so much promise had appeared to him the day before.

Had he killed somebody? He didn't know, but he sure as hell hoped not. As far as he knew, nothing like that had ever happened yet. But the truth is, after most nights of his adult life, he could have been told he'd shot the pope, and all he would have been able to say was, *You're kidding me, right?*

Evius, seemingly as ashamed of his own actions as those of Christian, followed close behind.

"Wake and bake?" Evius asked as he removed a joint from his hip pocket. Christian nodded, and the lighter was sparked yet again.

Soothing chemicals flowed into Christian's mind while he tried desperately to remember how to put one foot in front of the other as they stepped off the grass of his newly vacated brand new residence and onto the sidewalk glittering beneath the morning sun. Christian caught himself wondering if he'd left any clothes behind since he may not ever get back to his new home (which he didn't). Then, he realized he hadn't been there long enough to move in while a subtle thought asked him if maybe he'd had the chance to check out his bedroom if he might not have found a wardrobe as fitting as those shoes that seemed to have come directly from the cobblers of the gods. No matter. As he'd read once in a short story back in the days when he used to read, he was throwing everything away to follow Jesus. Yes, this was most certainly paradise.

Evius led them back to the same café as the day before. As if in replay – although slightly slower from the marijuana and hangover, and a little more rugged in appearance and tone from the remnants of the previous night's debauch – Christian sat down in a chair on the patio as Evius asked him, "Coffee?" Slightly lost even to himself, Christian nodded, and his companion disappeared.

As he settled himself in to take in the day's rays and forget about as much of what had happened the night before as humanly possible (*never pay attention to what happens to you when you're drunk,* a female friend of his had once told Christian (of course, for Christian that meant he could never pay attention to much of anything)), a grizzled old man supporting his aged weight with a cane shuffled up to where Christian was sitting. A few days' gray growth shaded his cheeks. His white hair wisped away from his baldness. He was wearing a white dress shirt, unbuttoned at the neck and slacks. His shoes were that same comfortable kind you can buy on the cheap at any K-Mart. And as he puffed away on a wicked looking, hand-rolled cigarette, he seemed like he might have been one of the gentlemen who Evius had waved to on the porch the day before as the two of them had begun their walk through Machpelah (*you never know who God is. So you better be nice to everybody. That's what I always say …*).

"You're sitting at my table," the old man grunted as he rapidly blinked his eyes three times in succession, each blink punctuated with a backwards nod. Like a stripper's jiggling thighs, his jowls quivered with the motion. It seemed quite a strange habit to have acquired. When he was done with his routine, the old man stared at Christian in an uncomprehending way as if he'd expected the younger man to have disappeared from the effects of his odd ritual.

Not in the mood for a crazy dude, Christian thought. He mumbled, "Sorry, I'll just…"

"No. Stay where you are. Guess I'll join you." With a grimace, the old man struggled his awkward bulk into a chair. He rested his cane between his legs and rested his hands upon his cane.

Christian didn't bother to move more or less because the torment of lifting his legs seemed like more trouble than entertaining the old man's inane conversation. Motion required energy. Listening, that required absolutely nothing… or so Christian had always conceived, which was why he knew so little about Machpelah despite all Evius' lost admonitions. Learning to listen is as much a skill as learning to read, and unfortunately, most of us know how to do neither.

"What's your name?" the old man asked, his nearly toothless mouth gumming his cheeks, his bottom lip hanging loose and collecting spittle.

"Christian, and you are?"

"Christian, you can call me Joshua."

"All right, Joshua. If that's what you want to be called…"

"Yes, goddamnit, it is. For Christ's sake, I just told you…" With his words, the old man's eyes grew wild. His body struck rigid. In disbelief, he shook his head. It started strong but ended with a mere tick in his neck as his gaze drooped towards the ground and his shoulders slumped over. That big head of his simply seemed too heavy to keep on holding up. And he looked tired.

Which Christian felt. He leaned back in his chair and let out a sigh.

Joshua said, "You ever look at the number of that

building over there." He pointed straight ahead of himself. Christian turned and looked over his shoulder. The building was a toy shop with the number *999* inscribed across the red, white, and black striped awning. He shook his head, *No.*

"Upside down, it says *6-6-6.* Makes you wonder if this is really heaven we're in, doesn't it?"

Christian shrugged. He didn't care where he was. So far, all he could tell was nothing had been much different from earth. He pursed his lips.

Joshua kept going, "And that makes you wonder: where are we, and what is?"

Christian didn't understand a word of what the mad old man was saying. Even though he was obviously speaking English, the meaning made it seem as if the breeze had never blown in that spot the day before and shaken the foundations of Babel. Christian leaned deeper into his chair and prayed for Evius to return to chase the old man away like a fly who had buzzed onto the table's metal grates and that Christian was just too damn lazy to chastise (the name *Beelzebub,* the Lord of the Flies, I've heard, was a deliberate Hebrew mispronunciation of a neighboring Semitic tribe's God, *Baalzebul,* the Lord of All). "Whatever," he mumbled. Vomit crept back into his throat. If there'd been food for him to eat, the casual internal observer may have believed Christian himself was the fly.

Joshua grunted. "The question that always concerns me," he began a bit more intellectually than before, "Is what happens when we die."

"We come here," Christian flippantly answered.

"But after we die here," Joshua continued, a panicked look enkindling his heavily lidded eyes. "Because I'm not always sure this may not just be my dream, and if I die, you may disappear."

"Trust me," Christian said, "I won't disappear."

"But how can you be so sure? I don't want to be responsible for your disappearance. I'm so confused." He shook his head.

"Look. Did the earth disappear when you left there?"

"I don't know," Joshua appeared honestly perplexed. "I may not have left yet. I might still be asleep down there somewhere."

"You're not, and I was there just yesterday. It was, too."

"Maybe that was just your dream."

"Christ, maybe this is my dream."

"No. Because I'm here. And if you think this is your dream, and I think it's my dream, then maybe we're both still asleep somewhere else, and we haven't even seen the real world yet. Did you know it's a fact two people can have the same dream? I read an article about it once... or maybe it was a short story. In which case... Nevermind."

"I'm pretty sure this shit's real."

"What makes you so sure?"

"Jesus, I don't know, maybe because I hung myself yesterday, and I've still got the fucking bruise to prove it."

Joshua squinted to better perceive Christian's neck. Then, he snorted a short laugh, a disgusting little sound coming from such a repugnant countenance. "And you think this is your dream? The only thing I'm certain of now is you're definitely dead, my friend. Me, I'm not sure of. You, you're dead. This ain't your dream," expressing his satisfaction with a nod, Joshua leaned back into his chair.

"Thanks for the insight, my man. I really needed it this morning."

Joshua leaned forward, and he very coolly countered, "Don't call me, your man, buddy. One thing we can definitely agree on is I am not your servant. If I was, I would have heeded your wishes and disappeared right off the bat." His eyelids fluttered as his pupils rolled to the sky in order to imitate the direction into which he seemed to perceive Christian wanted him to take flight.

"Sorry. I'll try to remember to show you the respect deserving of my elders," Christian said, shaking his head and looking away.

"Don't be so presumptuous, Chris, I may not be your elder. I could have been born looking like this. In fact, I think I was..."

"Doubtful," Christian snorted. Joshua scowled at him, but Christian simply determined he was going to look even more interested in the nothing he was looking at. He'd had enough of insanity. The years previous had been as full of it as Joshua was.

"You know, I killed a man once," Joshua suddenly admitted.

Christian wasn't paying attention. Maybe he should have been. The story might have made a little more sense out of everything. But Christian didn't care about sense. He'd never discovered any.

"Yes, I did, I didn't want to, but he had it coming. He challenged me, and I couldn't allow myself to back down. It was like somebody slapped me in the face. So I hit him, and I hit him again, and then again, and then again, and then... I started banging his head against a wooden floor. You get the picture. I didn't even know my own strength. Before I knew it, he was dead. I swore I'd never do that again, but you know what... I may have. I can't remember if it happened *here* or *there*, but it could have happened to anybody..."

Christian continued staring off into space; Joshua continued staring off into... "Ahhh, she is beautiful," the old man said – all the peevishness gone from his voice – as if he were agreeing somehow with Christian's vacant gaze.

The acknowledgement of beauty brought Christian back to himself. It placed him firmly in his groin. Even amid the thought, *Sophia?* he was grounded only to the earth... or Machpelah, as the case may be. Such higher notions of the transcendent power of the body were lost on his minimalist spiritual understanding. Perhaps, he needed the same lesson James was convinced he would receive from his Zoe – whatever that lesson may be. But as Christian let his eyes focus on the terrain ahead of him – a sidewalk with buildings lining the borders – he found himself entranced not by Sophia's dream, but instead by the same wistful green-eyed siren who had barely sat down at the table next to him the day before.

Bewitching. Their eyes had interlocked then, and Christian thought he perceived their eyes interlocking again now. But then again, what man when confronted with an object of such feminine designs wouldn't imagine such happenings?

Her rose colored lips lit against her pale skin. Her shock of red hair stood up in a very hip posture. Her tee shirt and jeans were tight. Her long legs flowed along with the breeze. Suddenly oblivious of himself, Christian smiled. He was squinting to see, but she might have smiled back.

Joshua mumbled, "I think she's looking at me." Brought back from divinity to paradise's perceived madness, Christian, still in need of that meditation class, glared sidelong at his newest absurd companion. The old man was smoothing down his few hairs and grinning from ear to ear.

"She's not looking at you," Christian scoffed.

"You think she's looking at you?" Joshua snorted. "Fat chance. That woman's got taste. I can tell. She's looking at me."

Ready to vomit at the thought (for real this time, not

just from last night's revelry), Christian growled, "She's not looking at you." *Why in the hell am I arguing about this with an eighty year old man?* he caught himself wondering. *If Joshua's not insane, he's at least senile.*

"Well, if you're so sure, then, go over and talk to her, killer, and when she disrespects you, tell her to come back and talk to me. I've been waiting for her for an eternity." Joshua shifted in his seat. He reached his hand into his crotch, and he mumbled, "I'm sure the old boy could get it up for her, at least." He shot a pained glance Christian's way. "Do you have any idea what it's like to feel desires you simply can't satisfy?"

"None," Christian said without a single thought to the day before – tearing through his ramshackle bedroom unable to find a misplaced little baggy of green as he cried to a faded photograph of a then dead girl. It's truly maddening how we choose from something not to relate to those who wish with all their beings to relate to us. Makes one think of God, doesn't it?

"Oh shit, I think I wet myself," Joshua mumbled. That was Christian's cue to finally stand up. As he did so, without even wanting to, he glanced at Joshua's lap. Sure enough, a dark wetness was spreading across the old man's crotch and dribbling down his left leg. A look of disgust passed over Christian's features. Again, if only he could have remembered yesterday.

He looked away and towards his supposed prey. The girl was coiling up like a snake that in a split second would strike and was sliding herself into a chair. The mouse was Christian, and as unsuspecting as any rodent could be, he trembled at the thought not of what awaited him but from the thuds of his very own heartbeat. Like that very same mouse picked up from a pet store and dropped alone in what could only be an empty cage (or so his meager understanding of life would assume) and therefore completely safe, if his roots had been just a bit more Southern rather than Midwestern, he may have whistled a sweet melody through his teeth. Instead, he swallowed slowly and began a million mile walk to where his newest dream was now sitting, unfolding a newspaper left behind by the last patron.

She didn't seem engrossed, but at the same time, she didn't seem to notice Christian's approach. His palms sweat. He wiped them on his jeans. He ran a hand through his hair. He walked straight up to her (something that under any normal circumstances he wouldn't have had the audacity to do, but nothing about the current circumstances were normal. So... what did he have to lose?), and he said, "Hi."

The woman to whom he spoke looked up from her paper, drew her head back on her neck, nearly hissed a forked tongue through her teeth to scent the air, tipped her head to the side imitating a dog this time (her nostrils even flared), and sat silently, taking in the awkwardness of the moment, before she answered – a coy smile approaching her lips, "Hi back at you."

With no bait for him to hook himself with, Christian stood still for what to his stoned mind seemed eternity yet again before he asked, "Do you mind if I sit down?"

"Suit yourself," the awakened beauty replied, "I don't bite. At least, not yet."

With a shaky hand, he pulled out a chair. He told himself it was the DTs causing him to tremble, but as anybody watching would have assumed, the girl he was attempting to flirt with figured it was because of her. That's what caused her to nimbly cover her mouth as giggles escaped. Only an omnipotent observer would have known the truth. Christian sighed, and aware of her laughter, mistaking it for a judgment on him proper, for a brief second, he bowed his head as he realized the shape he must have cut that morning: dried blood on his holey sleeves, vomit spattered across the tips of his new shoes, eyes glazed from the morning marijuana, and the taste of stale alcohol covered with regurgitated tobacco coating his tongue... What the hell was he thinking walking over there?

"So what did you want?" she asked.

Christian shook his head. He had to think about that for a moment. He chuckled dejectedly, "Actually, I just wanted to get the hell away from that crazy old man I was sitting with."

"What crazy old man?"

"The one right over there," Christian said. He pointed over his shoulder. He looked. He blinked. Joshua was gone. To disappear so fast, he must have huffed it on that cane of his. "But he was..."

"I know," a sly tremor resonated through her syllables. As Christian turned back around, she was leaning towards him. From between her jet black lashes, against her pale skin tinged pink, her green eyes sparkled brighter than Hades' treasures. "You just wanted an excuse to talk to little old me. Thank you. That's very flattering."

With her words and her smile, warmth oozed through Christian's guts. It relaxed him in the same way a hit of weed would have coaxed him into a falsified sense of security. He rearranged himself in his seat, crossed his legs, and tried to think of what to say next. Maybe he should have asked her name, but instead, before anything registered in Christian's brain, the siren spoke again. Her voice was lilting and sweet – hints of a magnolia accent with a slight rhythmic blemish, "It's starting out to be a beautiful day." She folded up her newspaper as if there were something on the page she didn't want to read.

Christian chuckled. "You could say that now."

"I just did," she countered, jutting out her chin defiantly.

Embarrassed at his own optimism, Christian looked down. The ground came up towards him, but he wasn't falling. It only felt that way. The individual stones in the pavement broke apart into sublime points: gray, silver, white, and black. It was a whole universe contained within each individual speck of concrete. A point is infinite. Infinity is merely a point. Where does that mean we are? We don't exist, but we are everything. Christian had to close his eyes. Evius packed some heavy shit. That's for damn sure. Maybe, though, it was the strange energy from that enigmatic woman producing the sensation. Either way, Christian wiped his face.

"Are you okay," she asked.

Christian nodded. Whatever that means.

She didn't seem to know either. A far away look drifted into her eyes: listening... to what? Her head tipped back on her neck. She turned her perfect profile to Christian. Fluid flowed through his veins at the subtle purse of her lips, the distant dimension of her irises. When she spoke again, her thoughts were calculated. "When did you get here?" she asked.

"Yesterday."

"Well, then, you need someone to show you around."

"Somebody said something like that to me once before," Christian said, and he lapsed into rumination. His features contorted. His face blanched. Against the backdrop of his mind, the entrance to an Austrian train station unfolded: brick and concrete. A man was in front of the tunnel, leaning his head to the side to light a cigarette. Christian had just hung up a phone call back to the States. He needed a smoke, but he didn't have any money. He went after the man. However, as if the man were psychic, he picked up his pace and disappeared into the station. Christian turned around. He dropped his head into his hands. "I hope this turns out better than that did," he mumbled.

"I didn't mean to…" but she thought better of it. "I'll tell you what, meet me here tomorrow, and I'll show you sights you'll never believe. There's a place… well, you'll see tomorrow."

"Why not today?" Christian asked supernally, a longing awakening in his gut, a longing he hadn't experienced in years. The hormones sent his blood racing. He wanted to leap across the table and embrace her right at that very moment, but then she said –

"Because I think your friend's coming back."

Christian glanced over his shoulder. He expected to see Joshua shuffling closer on his cane, gumming his lips and pulling at his crotch with urine dripping across his comfortable shoes. But instead Evius held two steaming cups of coffee in his hands. With long strides, he was approaching Christian and his desire. His brows were knit. His lips were pursed. Over the course of his conversations, as if in a trance, Christian had forgotten all about his savior.

How the hell was he going to get away from Evius tomorrow to meet up with this woman? The man was practically codependent.

No, there was absolutely no gratitude in Christian's mind for the drugs and information he'd been supplied with, only a need to escape and fulfill his wishes. The need centered in his stomach. It twisted into rage when he saw Evius' attractive face. It morphed into jealousy as he glanced back at her and saw her repositioning herself nervously in her seat as if she were a groupie in the presence of 1969 Mick Jagger. Christian half expected her to say, *And bring your friend.* But she didn't. So... never matter. He'd figure it out. The devil knows he'd figured out trickier situations when he was alive.

And then, as if to relieve all the tension building in Christian's neck and shoulders, as if she could sense his thoughts and wanted to reassure his masculinity, she whispered, "Try to make it... alone." And she reached across and squeezed his hand before she stood up and, with a quick smile and a quicker pirouette, disappeared as quickly as she had the day before.

When he got to Christian, Evius asked, "Who's your friend?"

Christian realized he'd forgotten to ask the siren her name. "I don't know actually," he said as he leaned reflectively back into his seat.

While across from them, with a hesitant nod in their direction and a sidelong glance at one another, Gilles and Jean-Francois slid into chairs across from each other.

"As I was saying last night..." Jean-Francois began. Christian thought he noticed the man's hands trembling ever so slightly. He wondered what they'd thought of the quintet, and at the edge of his hearing, he believed he heard a wolf howl... or maybe it was a coyote. What the hell was that doing in Machpelah? What the hell was it doing out in the daylight? Gilles shivered. Maybe at the sound. As if reading his thoughts, Evius smiled not quite reassuringly.

14.
The Labyrinth's Mysteries

From the café, Evius and Christian strolled down Machpelah's brick plaza. Shops lined either side of the walkway. Doors were opened and curtains drawn back. Art dealers hung paintings in their windows. Shop owners primped mannequins. Morning travelers going about their business flitted in and out of coffee houses and breakfast nooks. Hot cups steamed in peoples' hands. Conversations continued amid bites of food. Peddlers were setting up their wares on tables: necklaces and bracelets, scarves and woven shirts, rings and paintings. The homeless sat down on corners to spare change or rant about whatever question was tormenting them there in paradise. A group of people formed a circle around what appeared to be a labyrinth set in the stones. But nobody placed a single foot in the maze.

Christian remembered seeing such things in cathedrals during his collegiate European travels. They never made much sense to him. Supposedly something about the contemplation of existence and the spiritual path. If life were a labyrinth, there was no end, no point to be reached, only an endless series of twists and turns eventually spitting you right back out where you started, and foolish you, you set your foot back into the maze to be consumed. Still, for some strange reason, for the first time ever, Christian wanted to try it. Evius stopped and gazed along with the gawkers at the air contained between all of them. He narrowed his eyes. "Do you see it?" he asked.

"What?" Christian wondered.

"The funnel cloud. It's rising from the center of the labyrinth. Those who can say it's God. I don't know. I think it's a freak of nature. Far as I can tell, God doesn't exist. At least, not here."

"I don't see shit."

Behind them, a trolley car rolled across an intersection. According to Evius, riding the trolley along its loop was free... one of Machpelah's few real perks, an influx from Pandemonium's sentiments, perhaps. Perhaps not. Evius was actually quite unclear about it, which made Christian even less clear.

Nevertheless, regardless of whether or not he could see the funnel cloud and regardless of whether or not he could understand the labyrinth's mysteries, the newcomer kept following his guide, his seeming companion, his veritable savior.

They reached the end of the plaza where a good sized amphitheater had been built. The stage was set up outdoors with a metal pavilion covering it. The seats were a grassy knoll along a hill's downward slope – perfect for a second sniper if Machpelah had had a president. But alas, the great community didn't. Its leaders were but trusted servants.

A concrete slab implied the possibility of a dance floor. Amid a blink, Christian saw ghosts partaking of their amusements. Then, they were gone. Too much weed, man. According to Evius, the community held concerts and gatherings there... none of which were really any fun. Too many kids. Christian had no choice but to believe him.

There was a tunnel leading away from the stage. "Normally we'd go that way," Evius said, "But today the path appears to be occupied."

Sure enough, sitting at a picnic table at the tunnel's mouth – a scenic wall of red and white graffiti sprawling behind them – swallowed by the expanse, two lovers hid amid an embrace. In his state, Christian pictured them as a sperm and an egg being discharged during a menstrual cycle. The guy's short hair was a mess, and the girl's hair was long and curly with the guy's fingers firmly tangled in it. Her hands ran up and down his broad back. Their heads pivoted around their mouths' fulcrum, which seemingly fit together as smoothly as a key in a lock. It left an empty aching in Christian's breast for Sophia... for that girl from the café... for... *what the hell is her name?*

Instead of walking through the tunnel, then, they headed straight up the grassy knoll and through a gate in a chain link fence, which to Christian's surprise was adorned with neither razor wire nor barbed wire.

They made their way down a street, Evius pointing out various office buildings he'd worked at over his stay in eternity.

"You could probably get a job in the mail room there," he said. Christian scowled at him.

"I'm sure they need somebody to do some filing," he went on, pointing at another building. Christian narrowed his eyes and looked at the ground.

"They might even be hiring for their call center." To that, Christian didn't even deign to respond. Work was something always better left behind. It got in the way of more important things like overcoming the morning's hangover, sitting through the first hit of marijuana's mind-blowing effects, and lacerating oneself with the guilt of yet again smoking crack the night before. No, there were better things to do with the day than work. Besides, if you didn't have a home, why did you need a job? And right then, it appeared, Christian didn't have a home. There had to be shelters in Machpelah, and maybe there people wouldn't be so picky about little rules like no pints in the bunks. It was paradise, wasn't it?

A corner store appeared along the landscape to the left. "I need to run in there," Christian told his companion.

"They won't have what you're looking for," Evius responded, nearly shouting at Christian's back he took off so fast.

Christian didn't care. He was licking his lips. He had to see for himself.

He stumbled through the aisles while running his hands through his shaggy hair, and went straight to the coolers in the back.

Sure enough, there it was. Like a beacon in darkness, like Sophia's voice when Christian had floated through the ether, the sight was still more comforting than her disembodied presence. A reddish tint glowed through the bottle like it always did on earth: Wild Irish Rose – lifeblood.

Vampirically, Christian grabbed the bottle from its place. The chilliness froze him to the bone and sent him quivering like a lover getting ready to spread his beloved's thighs. He looked over his shoulder. Nobody was at the counter. Nobody was in the store's main lobby at all. Christian stuck the bottle down his pants.

When he exited the store, after they'd walked a little ways, Christian glanced back in the direction they'd come from, and when he saw nobody was following them, he removed his prize.

Evius stared at him in disbelief. But not to give Christian the wrong idea, all he could say was, "Damn, I wouldn't have expected that. The gods sure are looking out for you, buddy. But if you'd asked, I could have bought it for you."

Christian didn't care what other ways he might have gotten the mystical liquid. All that mattered was he had it. He unscrewed the metal cap. With the shape of the bottle nestled in his hand, his last true sexual escapade rose to the forefront of his mind. Must have been a few years ago...

She had blonde hair, short and spiked, hip clothes, a ring through her nose, and a tattoo of a star around her bellybutton. They'd met at a bar, and they'd made plans to go see *The Passion of the Christ* that evening. They even got a newspaper to see where it was playing. Sometime over the course of their conversation, they realized there wouldn't be any alcohol at the theater. "Besides, I don't know if I could handle watching what happens to Jesus," she said. "I think I might cry." So instead, they stopped by a store and picked up a bottle of Wild Irish Rose.

It was her idea, and Christian realized she was the woman for him: his soul mate... more so perhaps even than Sophia. They went back to her place. She danced in her Chuck Taylor's, and she showed him nude pictures of herself that a professional photographer had taken. They didn't make love that night. They were both too drunk. But the next morning... some things are too painful to remember. She never answered the phone when he called, and she never called him back whenever he left a message. He'd thought he was in love. He'd thought he'd been good in bed. He'd thought. No matter... some things are too painful to remember.

He turned the bottle upside down into his mouth and took a gracious swig. The bitter nectar was both sweet and sour... nothing like Chinese flavor to offset a rotten afterlife. It's the dichotomies that need to be moved beyond, though. It's the sauce, thick as semen, encompassing both palatal sensations we need to taste. And right then, Christian tasted it.

One sip and the flower budded in his brain. Like Kundalini, its stalk thread up his spine. Its thorns pricked his mind. Its aroma overwhelmed his senses.

"Mind if I get a sip?" Evius asked.

Oblivious to the insights he'd made, with a sidelong glance, eventually, Christian shook his head, *No*, and handed the bottle off to his compatriot. Evius treated the treat with the same aplomb as his charge. "Thank the gods for Dionysus," he grunted as he removed the bottle from his lips. "Not that this is quite what he had in mind when he first distilled grapes, but still, it does the trick." He handed the bottle back to Christian, and after a pause, he added, "Now, if only we had some Maenads to accompany us on this long and arduous journey, my dear Arjuna." He laughed.

Christian, however, didn't find his joke quite so funny. In fact, he didn't even understand it. He shook his head and drained still more of the bottle into his gullet, proving Dostoevsky wrong for saying the sensualist always saves half his wealth. For, all of Christian's wealth consisted in that bottle, and he didn't seem to have any intentions of saving even a mere finger. But, of course, in Machpelah, a finger is not really a finger... or so Evius was trying to explain to Christian's loaded brain. What did it matter? Another sip made all philosophical quandaries disappear.

The road continued on. The alcohol swirled through their minds. Cigarettes were sparked, consumed, and discarded. The day dragged on. The sun grew hot. An itch grew below Christian's clothes, across his skin. He pulled at the neck and chest of his damaged shirt. Evius appeared unaffected. Christian's unwashed, uncombed, uncut hair grew sticky and stuck to his forehead, ears, and neck. Evius never stopped smiling and pointing out the sights.

There were statues to various artists and philosophers, plaques to people Christian had heard of on earth and some to those who'd made a name for themselves in the afterlife. A huge monument of Saint Michael rose out of a roundabout at an intersection. It wasn't like the statues on earth. There was no serpent being trampled underfoot, just a winged, androgynous creature. It actually appeared to shimmer between male and female both in visage and in body while standing stoically, staring at the sun with an impressive golden spear glimmering light. But still, even in paradise, the marble appeared dingy and the stains of some graffiti that had been cleaned off besmirched the archangel's exterior.

Evius snarled at the statue in the same responsive manner he'd snarled at Theo the night before, but not too far beyond, he spoke, "Right now, we're in a neighborhood called 'Paradise of Fools'. It's a new name, used to be called Heaven's Gate or something like that, but mentalities have changed in the past century. You could say they've inverted. I think it's a sign of… oh well, nevermind."

Christian glanced around. The houses were smaller than the abode where he'd been offered a chance to reside. They looked more like duplexes and triplexes, a little more urban flair, not quite as suburban. Christian could picture himself living there.

With a sly grin, his tour guide whispered, "It's where all the hipsters want to be nowadays. I wouldn't be surprised if your siren from the café lived out here somewhere. She looks the type." A butterfly fluttered in Christian's chest. He *could* picture himself living there. "Really, it's just a poor man's excuse for Pandemonium… a place for people who want to seem like they're down, but nobody here really is.

Except maybe for you... The verdict's still out on that one." As Evius' smile grew, Christian noticed his teeth seemed to have yellowed a bit. Maybe it was just a discoloration from the liquor swimming behind Christian's eyes.

Without warning, the road came to an end not at a stone or brick wall or even a cul-de-sac but instead at a dense clump of seemingly useless trees. "Let's go," Evius said as he lit a joint and plunged into the forest. Branches snapped shut behind him, but the marijuana's pungent odor lingered.

Entranced by the scent but with a foreboding premonition offsetting his buzzed bliss, Christian swallowed and followed.

The dirt path they tread upon ascended through the overgrown undergrowth. "Glad you could make it," Evius said, and he handed the joint back to Christian who took a deep hit. After a moment, Evius wondered, "You gonna give that back?" Christian complied, and Evius, flicking the cherry off the joint and sliding the roach back into his pocket, was off.

A green peak poking above the treetops in the distance intimated this path perhaps led in that general direction. Christian thought about asking, but he was too busy swatting twigs from in front of his face. One scraped his right cheek, right underneath his eye. A fear of possible blindness caused him to proceed with more caution. Of course, the fear of alcohol-induced blindness never led him to that same conclusion. However, like with so much of his life, he felt no blood but only the scar.

His caution was merely momentary though because the deeper they went, the more he realized how much he needed to rely on Evius to lead him back out. The path forked here. It turned there. Besides, he was a little high again, and Evius showed no intentions of slowing his pace. So, overcoming his internal distress, Christian thrust onwards. How much more of a metaphor could one ask for?

Metaphors come to be out of thin air. They materialize in the deepest recesses of space and find existence here on this plane. An abyss opens in the back of the mind, and then, there's something tangible where before there was nothing. When looked at in the right light – the stars' night lights, for example, all of existence is a metaphor.

To the left, a shadow seemed to be keeping pace with them. It might have been a trick of the light. It might have been a trick of the crossed wires in his mind, but by that point in time, Christian believed anything possible.

The shadow appeared a man but with horns like a goat, something like cleft hooves for feet, deeply bent legs, and a flaccid phallus hanging down at least a foot or more and swinging along with every step. Christian paused. The shadow paused along with him. It threw its head back in mimicry of a howl – a billy-goat beard adorned its chin. But instead of sound, only wind rustled the trees' leaves. Still, it was as if the wind manifested from the shadow's open mouth. Christian wanted to grab Evius by the shoulder and ask him what the hell was happening at the edge of his vision.

Because every time Christian looked directly at the shadow, it disappeared. He swallowed hesitantly, picked up his feet, and saw the shadow move along with him.

Laughter echoed across the trees, and Christian forced himself to believe the noise must have come from Evius even though there was no evidence to support that conclusion. The shadow lifted a jug to its lips and took a sip. Fire looked to shoot out its mouth, and Christian could feel the heat radiating off the branches. He felt the flames

might consume him. His breath stopped. His steps paused
– one foot still bent halfway off the ground as if in a
Renaissance allegory. He touched his hands to his arms and
chest. He was still in one piece: no burns, no smoke.
"Fuckin' weed, man," he whispered, and he shook his head.
But the vision remained stumbling along in time with the
travelers.

Marijuana's never really an excuse, though. Eventually,
we have to confront what we believe.

They hiked along in quiet. The shadow just at vision's
edge. Evius at least a full three steps ahead of his
companion. The light transformed. A spectrum shot
through the leaves. The shadow morphed into an almost
full-color silhouette – deep brown hair matted its chest.
The sun was setting. Christian looked up. Between the
trees, the sky turned into a purple bruise on heaven. "Evius,
are we going back to Machpelah?" Christian asked.

"Not tonight," his guide answered. "I figure it's a good
evening for camping. Full moon should make for an all
right night hike, and the weather should be good. There's a
clearing not too far ahead where I figure we can set up
camp. Why? You got somewhere you gotta be?" Christian
shook his head sadly, *No*. Without even looking back, Evius
said, "Didn't think so."

But Christian did have somewhere he was meant to be.
He didn't have to be there immediately, but tomorrow…
And he was already nervous to miss his appointment. One
should never put too much faith in tomorrow, though. It
may never come. But still, he found himself wondering:
*Does Evius know about her? Is he jealous? Is he keeping me from
her? When is he planning on taking me back to Machpelah?*

Then, panic attacked Christian's breast: *Who the fuck is
Evius?* It might have had something to do with the weed.
As William Burroughs would say, Christian perhaps had

"the fear". But it might have had more to do with the madness of the past two days, not the madness of the alcohol and drugs (that was habitual), but the panic of waking up dead. That's the type of trauma one really needs to go see a shrink about. But we all have trauma we should be seeing shrinks about. Most of us simply can't afford it, or we haven't thought of it, or we figure if everybody's going through the same shit, how bad could our shit be?

Christian was at one of those points, but he wasn't sure which. He hadn't considered psychological help since his senior year of college, and even then it had only been a fleeting thought dealing with his father's walking out on him. The impetus had been a girl he was dating who'd wondered why he couldn't open up to her emotionally. Instead of telling her the story of Sophia, the only answer he'd been able to come up with was his personally, parentally tormented childhood. But how self-indulgent is that – even if both might have been lies? The truth was more likely of a much simpler gender. Since then, he'd never really entertained the possibility. And there'd been lots of trauma: illegal drugs and illicit sex and nightly blackouts and drawn guns and nights in the drunk tank and mornings in court and street beatings and more things than those who don't travel the paths Christian had traveled could even imagine.

As night came on, the moonlight streamed through the trees in front of them onto what appeared an open field. The sky turned indigo. Stars poked pinpricks through the leaves' canopy. Briefly, Christian wondered if Machpelah had the same constellations as earth. He thought about asking Evius, but before he had a chance to speak, his guide, nodding ahead, said, "That's where I was thinking about staying tonight. But," he added as he stopped walking and his tone grew paused and pensive, "It looks like somebody might have beaten us here."

Half expecting to see the shadow that had kept pace with them throughout the whole hike lit brilliantly by the moonlight, Christian peered through the foliage. The shadow should have been howling and beating his chest and pulling on that jug he carried in his hand, his phallus exposed to a harem of every species of female as his horns pointed to the night and his hoofs beat the ground to a bloody pulp. But instead, a couple, nothing more than silhouettes, nowhere near as vivid as the earlier couple from the tunnel, appeared to be occupying the field. What had happened to the shadow? Before Christian could finally broach his concerns, Evius wondered, "Is that who I think it is?" He paused as a sly smile crept into his voice, "I'll be damned if it is."

What the hell was Evius? A fucking owl, a cat? Christian squinted into the night. *Sophia?* No. Christian had to keep his head straight. How would Evius have known her anyways?

But what he did see surprised him perhaps even more. If the moon hadn't been full, he never would have been able to make out their features. He and Evius might have simply left, but they didn't. In the field, James, Christian's apparently ex-roommate held in an embrace none other than… yes, Christian's siren from that café.

So that was his Zoe, then, the same girl who'd promised to show Christian Machpelah tomorrow. Tonight, she'd determined to create an artist. Tomorrow, she'd determined to create… Christian had no idea, but he felt a bit queasy. If Evius had been watching him, he would have noticed him blanch. Christian tugged on Evius' sleeve. "Let's go, man," he almost whined.

"Are you kidding me," Evius responded, spinning around, reminiscent of Krishna revealing to Arjuna his entrancing many-armed form. "This looks like it's just about to get good. Besides, they're friends of yours. Don't you want to see how your friends spend their free time?" There was something hypnotic about Evius' presence. Christian couldn't say no. He followed his guide over to a fallen tree they crouched down behind.

The leaves rustled as they settled into their seats. Christian thought he saw Zoe look out over James's shoulder in their general direction. If she did, she didn't notice them. Or if she did that even, she at least pretended she didn't. Perhaps she enjoyed being on stage. She went back to ecstatically swooning in her apparently new lover's arms.

Christian was certain her excitement was feigned. James leaned over to kiss or nibble at her neck. From his vantage, Christian couldn't tell which, but he wished it was him who held the beauty tight to his chest, feeling her breasts press firm against him from beneath two sets of clothes. In his state, he thought he knew how to make her feel like a woman. How absurd... she always felt like a woman.

Like partaking of a mere appetizer for a main course that would never appear, longing as if for a drug never experienced excited the juices in Christian's gut. He couldn't tell if he was sick or excited... maybe a little of both. Sick at the thought of what he'd hoped to experience tomorrow being experienced by another tonight, or excited at the chance to take a sneak peek at what he might be able to indulge himself in on the following day... if he could get over his revulsion at one of the men who seemed to be responsible for him now being homeless (what did happen last night anyway?) enjoying the flavor of a fruit he'd wanted to hide away all for his own greedy taste buds. That was it – he was sick. If only he knew in how many ways...

In the clearing, the two lovers delighted in the ecstasy

of experiencing another's desired body for the very first time. Although who desired who – if minds could be read – wasn't quite clear. As to whether or not both were desired by the other no one could be certain of as anyone who has ever watched a man embrace a woman is sure to know. Very little in this life is mutual. Any pleasure can be falsified. Any revulsion can be masked. All things form a circle with the two poles converging to one. And at that moment it seemed the masculine and the feminine were on the verge of completing their circuit.

A fallen tree, burgeoning with a fruit Christian didn't recognize, rested on the ground near where the two lovers stood. Christian didn't even think about how the dead could give life. With branches extending up to James's shoulder, its shadowy form was magnificent. It seemed to contain all of life within the veins its sap had ceased to run through.

James shifted his weight on his feet in order to better position his Zoe to lay her across a flattened spot along the tree's trunk where no branches grew. But like a master of kung fu dance, the woman, by sliding her hands along James's ribs, resisted his maneuverings.

"It really is quite symbolic," Evius quietly laughed. Christian scowled at him. Evius must have sensed his scorn because he added in a whisper, "Oh, come on. Think about it." But there was nothing to think about. The vision was too captivating. Oozing drama from its every pore, it read like a play from another world, one we've never seen on this plane.

The actors were familiar – we met them at the opening, but their actions were incongruent with their characters. It must have been a trick of the weed. Even love Machpelah style was like the concert the night before, like Pablo's newest painting. As stage-lights would, the moon illuminated the sky above. As the perfectly constructed set, the grass grew up to their knees. The tree provided a proscenium. The dance looked to be getting violent as James tried again to lay Zoe across the tree, but she resisted. Christian imagined them biting one another's lips. Zoe took a step forward, and with a shift of her right foot, James collapsed upon the tree's flat surface.

He appeared stunned. He appeared shocked. But before he could make any move, Zoe ripped a few leaves of grass from the ground and bound his wrists to two protruding branches. She stepped back.

James smiled at her. As nonchalantly as any man in the presence of a woman assumed weaker, he went to break free of his seemingly effete bonds, but as he flexed his arms, stretched like Jesus's as he cried with his wrists nailed to the cross, his shackles only tightened and brought out the veins in his fleshy forearms.

He tugged again. His smile inverted. He looked to his left and his right, and he tugged a little bit harder. A slit of blood dribbled down his wrist – again, a reference to Jesus?

With his speech slurred, apparently oblivious to the pain he should have been feeling, he spoke, "So this is what you're teaching me?" Attempting seduction while simultaneously feigning comfort, a crooked smile slid onto his lips.

"Oh, it will be," Zoe said. Unlike James, she sounded completely sober. From her back pocket, into her hand appeared a serpentine dagger. It must have materialized miraculously, for it was far too long to have fit into her jeans. Bewilderment tinted James's face. "Now, if you're who I hope you are, in the morning, this won't have hurt a bit." And then, amid a masculine scream that shook the forest's very dirt and roots, she plunged the dagger through James's shirt and into his chest.

Her sparkling eyes enkindled in the darkness, she wriggled it around, carved a squared circle. She reached into the cavity she created, and with a cry as triumphant as when a lion has finally slaughtered a lamb, she pulled out – beating, bloody, full – his beating, breaking heart.

Like a cat toying with a still living mouse, she scraped her long fingernails, which were perfect for clawing through a bed sheet, across its soft flesh. James was still breathing, but as he grew weaker, as the pooling blood soaked deep into his shirt's tattered remnants, he stopped screaming. A grimace like nothing Christian had ever seen before distorted his facial features. His head tipped back on his neck. With their final ounces of pressure, the veins in his neck pulsed, but having nothing to thrust the blood up through them any longer, they went slack. One more brain appeared to go offline in Machpelah's darkness. And unlike with Joshua's empty threat, unfortunately, Christian was still there.

Behind Zoe, the shadow that had kept pace with Christian materialized.

It was more horrifying than even his nightmares could have imagined. It did have horns, and hair, and hooves, and a penis dangling down to its knees. With brightly lit fangs, it ate the massy pulp of James's heart from out Zoe's small hand.

Blood matted its beard. And then, as Zoe began to remove her blood-spattered clothes, as the phallus dangling down grew almost to the ground and began to rise, Christian couldn't take it anymore. Not caring how much noise he might make, not caring whether or not the beast and the beauty might hear him and pursue, he leaped up from his place and began running.

He ran into the night, branches swatting at his face, coming still closer to blinding him. He pumped his arms.

As if in a dream, thinking he'd been through all this once before, he breathed heavily, and he panted over and over again, "Holy shit. Holy shit. Holy…" If only he'd known how right he was. In the woods, in the night, with a vision torn from the marriage of heaven and hell etched into his mind, the only sounds other than his plodding feet and his heaved words were the simultaneous cackles of a monster and a woman.

Σ.
Ponerology

13.
Mandelbrot Sets

Running, swatting... leaves... branches... A tree! To the left, to the right. *Am I running in a circle? I don't want to wind up back there. I don't want to wind up staring that fucking thing in its bearded face as it chomps down on the heart of a man I knew, as it spreads the legs of a woman I thought was beautiful, as that huge piece of flesh between its legs starts to...*

Dear God, I knew him. I drank with him. I may have even fought with him. I watched what she did to him. She cut his fucking heart out of his chest. He was alive. It was still beating. He was still breathing. He was alive! We die even in Machpelah. What the fuck is wrong with this place? What kind of afterlife is this? I'd rather take what the preachers told us about with all its singing, all its righteousness – floating bodiless through eternity. She wants to do the same thing to me tomorrow. She wants to do the same thing to me. It'll hurt. God, it'll hurt. Oh my God, that looked like it hurt. Tomorrow... I won't be here. I can't be here. I want out. I have to get out. Jesus, let me out! (Who taught you to pray to Jesus, Christian?)

Suddenly, without warning, as if he were Jason from *Friday the 13th* walking in his black boots as his prey runs, Evius materialized in front of Christian, and the latter ran smack into him. He'd appeared from out of nowhere. He couldn't even be dodged.

As Christian picked himself up off the ground – sticky leaves matted to each palm – his panic reached a critical threshold with the realization that perhaps he'd run in circles. That's what forests do to you, isn't it? They spin you around a single point like shit flushed down a toilet. Perhaps, he was right back where he'd started, with a demon and a murderess somewhere within eyesight. He glanced to his left, his right. There was nothing but trees, fallen leaves, and the night – darkest, darkest night. But one never knew, did he? "Evius, man, we gotta get the fuck out of here," Christian panicked and turned every which way like the victim of a bomb attack digging through the rubble of what had once been her house. His eyes grew wild and mad. They bulged – a zombie's from out their sockets. The cops would have locked him up just for that gaze – ***chk, chk, crackle*** *we've got a real live one here; I need to get him to a mental ward.* But like after being told he was dead for the very first time, before Christian could move, Evius' magnetic embrace graced his trembling shoulder, and, of all things, his guide through the labyrinth laughed.

Yes, Evius' lips lifted up to his eyes, his tight cheeks trembled, and laughter burst out his thin chest. Christian was dumbfounded. How the fuck could that psychopath be laughing at a time like this? For God's sake, there were killers afoot. Somewhere not too far from there, a man who'd seemed decent enough was beginning his decomposition. In front of his ravished body, a monster was having sex with a human woman. Human? Well, who knew? What she did sure as hell didn't seem too human. But then again, what humans have been doing to one another since the dawn of time doesn't seem too human.

After his chuckle, Evius caught his breath and said,

"Calm down, man. Clam down. Remember, I told you: some sketchy shit goes down here in Machpelah. I'll tell you what, though. If you really want out of here," immediately, Evius became deadly serious, "I know a place where we can go."

Evius' black eyes deepened, and Christian felt his soul falling into their depths. He remembered an acid trip when he was quite young where he'd envisioned his body descending onto the surface of a deep red, comic book-type eye. When he'd told his grandmother about it (omitting the part about the acid), she'd said it was him coming in touch with his "third eye". Christian shook his head in a vain attempt to come back to himself. With a shaky voice, he said to who was hopefully his friend, who was his only possible chance of never seeing that kind of physical suffering ever again, of not having the same thing happen to him, "Anywhere, man. Anywhere. Just get me the fuck out of here."

"Cool, then. It's time for you to check out Pandemonium."

Pandemonium. The name didn't sound too enticing. In fact, it sounded like the very same insanity Gilles had been discussing with Jean-Francois the day before. But, truthfully, what were his other options? To stay in that forest? To return to Machpelah and maybe bump into that Zoe who had done the unthinkable? He'd lose his mind, if it wasn't already lost that was, if he ever saw her again. He was certain of that. He was certain there was no life left for him in that purported paradise. Wherever Evius wanted to go, he was willing to follow. He wasn't in control. He knew that now.

Had he ever been? Drugs had held him in their grip from the first moment he'd realized that with a little bit of money he could buy a plastic bag whose substances would take him away from wherever he was. Alcohol had only preceded the drugs. Marijuana wasn't the gateway, alcohol was, but everybody did that. What the hell had gone wrong with him? That was a question for another time.

Sophia... she herself had called their meeting *kismet*. That implied some foreign presence guiding their motions like the invisible hand toying with world markets. Suicide... his last choice was the only choice he'd ever made. Now, he was too scared to try it again, too scared to find out what might possibly come next, if anything. When he'd believed in nothing, it had been an option. But existence still, that was too much. Yes, he was under Evius' power. And who the fuck was Evius?

Christian stared at the lines creasing the man's face: around his lips, his eyes. He might have been older even than Christian had first imagined him, or had he simply aged over the past days? It didn't matter. Things were really quite hopeless. Insanity surrounded him, and the unknown one leading to the unknown place was his only option. Tell me, was that so different from anybody's regular life?

But nothing is regular about life other than its irregularity, and for that reason, systems dynamics is the most complete worldview humanity has yet to encounter. Euclidean geometry, with all its perfection, all its postulations including non-intersecting parallel lines, describes our vision of how we *want* to see the world. But as anybody who's ever tried to create a piece of art will tell you, as anybody who's ever performed a scientific experiment will tell you, what we want is not in our power to get. Newtonian mechanics, with all its force ratios, all its Biblically deduced laws, makes about as much sense to the modern mind as a baroque performance. The world is freestyled over a microphone. It's spontaneous composition without even a head melody, unless one counts the past. But the history books have taught us even the past is relative. Life is a skater going up a ramp. He either wipes out, bails, or lands the trick. Existence is akin to a Mandelbrot Set. Only digitized art can capture it in brilliant, pixilated reds and blues.

Art is anything. It's everything. Define it for me.

Evius turned his head to glance over his right shoulder. His nose seemed to have lengthened in the snout. His face had shrunk in the cheeks. His sideburns even appeared coiled and curled, somewhat Hassidic. He was chosen. His profile glimmered beneath the moonlight. God, it was still night.

"Pandemonium is that way," Evius said, a longing quality to his voice as his Adam's apple bobbed, like a metronome, up and down to the rhythm of his words. He turned back around and stared overtop where Christian had, as if he'd been in Gethsemane, kneeled penitently. With a backwards nod of his head, indicating the direction with his chin, Evius said, "Machpelah is back that way."

Like with Theo before, he narrowed his eyes in mimicry of some forgotten hatred. Again, he glanced over his shoulder. Evius sighed. "I've had enough of paradise's tricks for this trip. I'm going this way. If you want, follow me." Behind his wistful glance, proving he wasn't possessed, Evius turned his long body all the way around, and his long legs carried him off in the direction of what he claimed led to Pandemonium.

And although Pandemonium frightened him, although Evius confused him, Christian brushed off his hands and knees, and stumbled through the woods a mere two or three paces behind his apparently eternal guide. For, truth be told, Christian had had enough of paradise for that trip as well, for any trip for that matter. He'd stake his chances on a potential abyss.

Like they usually did in the mornings but never in the evenings after a few bottles of cheap wine, his hands were trembling. Like they usually did when he closed his eyes to sleep but never when he was still awake, visions of horror and madness flitted behind his eyes, in his mind. He never even paused to wonder whether or not his lovely Sophia would have ever made this trek as well, and if she had, had she stayed in Pandemonium or had she returned to Machpelah to wait? She probably hadn't because deep down inside, beneath her atheistic veneer, she was actually quite religious. Whether or not Christian knew that was anybody's guess.

This time, there was no path. Evius and his follower cut through the forest's thick trees along a route only Evius could have known. He never even paused to get his bearings. There was no looking for chalk marks on that tree. There was no searching the branches for a broken one in this direction here or there. There was no panic while staring at the ground for a trail of breadcrumbs that never materialized because, like the rest of life, they'd already been eaten by the birds – the sparrow's insight.

This time, Hansel knew precisely how to get out of the witch's candied forest, and for the first time since he'd cut her down from that hole in her ceiling, Gretel was grateful that was the case. All she wanted was for the labyrinth to end. Little did she realize (although after his suicide attempt, Christian definitely should have known) once you step into that labyrinth, you can't get out until it's done with you. The mysteries are endless. They repeat at ever more minute levels until eventually they become too small to see – a wavicle vibrating at an unknown frequency. What does that say about the macrocosm? If you really want it to end, you're better off not escaping back to your father and step-mother (they'll just send you back into the woods anyways since they sure as hell don't want you) but rather finding your way to the witch's house because she'll make sure it ends for you, and she'll make it quite pleasant in your cage as you're waiting to be cooked and eaten. I guess that's what we're scientifically attempting anyways. As you sleep pleasantly – nothing else to do – on a bed of straw, she'll fatten you up on roasted meats and baked goods... so much of what those not addicted to drugs or sex find heavenly about this plane. But remember, you'd rather be her meal than her slave. You'd rather be Hansel than Gretel, regardless of what fourth wave feminists and white-male apologists might wish to say. Hence, the reason humanity is superior to angels.

Intruding upon his avian thoughts with an amphibian reality (a sort of inverse evolution that bypassed the reptilian), Christian realized they'd been walking along the side of a slight stream for quite some time. It seemed to have suddenly materialized because Christian had never been aware of anything possibly leading them. Although, if he thought back to it, it might have been there from the get-go. It's hard to keep straight the mind. Perhaps, it was the urine flowing out that huge phallus issuing off the monster that had been ready to make love to Zoe. Created by the banks confining it, it wound through rocks and gulleys. It carved a path for itself even though the path itself created it. However, like with a metaphor, Christian didn't know whether or not the stream actually was something they were following or just a simple stream with no symbolic referent. Either way, like John the Baptist, he was stuck behind a maniac on a manic trek through the unending woods swallowing him in their eternity until eventually... Evius stopped.

Christian asked, "What's going on?"

Evius looked back, smiled, then turned his head and

nodded to what was in front of them.

What was in front of them was the toilet bowl the stream they'd been following eventually issued into. Carved into a massive rock wall, as if it were the Buddha soon to be blown to bits by the Taliban, the stream entered a cave – its enclosing stone miraculously rolled away – stretching deep, dark and endless as the womb a Tibetan Buddhist spirit improperly freed from the Bardo realms might have been getting ready to enter. Maybe somebody should have recited *The Book of the Dead* into poor Christian's ear while he'd hung limp at the end of that rope. But who in the hell was going to do that, his stoned roommates? Certainly none of them had ever spent any time at a guru's feet. To either side of the cave, as if they were the centurions guarding Jesus's tomb waiting only to meet the newly arrived Mary Magdalene, a set of sardonic, winged, stone gargoyles sat enthroned upon the seats they were chiseled out of.

However, these gargoyles were not quite like the ones adorning a medieval church spire. Oh, they looked the same in theory – monstrous and imposing, but the mouth of one of these gargoyles was moving as if it were a cow chewing cud. In fact, it had an apple in its hand from which it suddenly took another bite. The one on stage-right scratched its revealed scrotum. The one on stage-left cocked her head to the side. There was something vaguely orangutanian about them. The bite of the apple was finished, and just like when witnessing a primate in a zoo, Christian wondered whether or not it might not be thrown at him. It wasn't. Instead, like an inappropriate subject, it was merely dropped. In the long run, the former might have been better. But before too much pondering could be done, the one on the left exclaimed: "None shall pass!" To which the other replied: "One shall pass!" And they both burst into a fit of cheeky laughter that was actually quite frightening in its inappropriateness given the present conditions and the fact they were both made of stone.

Heaving for breath amid his chuckles, the one on the left asked the one on the right, "What good does that do them? There's two of them."

"How do you know that?" the one on the right responded as she wiped a tear of laughter from off her cheek.

"Because I see them with my own two eyes," her partner responded.

"But if your two eyes make only one sight, how do you not know there might not be only one of them?"

The other stopped laughing as abruptly as he'd started. "I'd never thought of that," he said. Then, he drew himself up to his full height, fluttered his stone wings with a rocky shudder, and in a stately manner shouted out, "One shall pass!"

To which his compatriot retorted, "None shall pass!" And all semblances of respectability disappeared as they dissolved into fits of laughter yet again.

"Gargoyles..." Evius muttered. "Such contradictory creatures." With a shake of his head and continuing to follow the flowing stream, he stepped ahead to enter the cave.

"Go on, then, follow your friend. Don't be afraid. The cave doesn't bite," the female gargoyle said. Christian looked from one gargoyle to the other and back to the cave's mouth.

The male gargoyle, sensing his trepidation said, "Let me tell you a parable, then. There was this guy, right, and his mother didn't want him to ever have sex. So... she told him all women's vaginas have teeth that would bite off his little pecker if he ever stuck it into them..."

"You're so vulgar," his companion herself, illuminating

the difference between male and female, inserted at that point. "Nobody would ever tell this parable at such a moment."

But the gargoyle simply said to his female companion, "Nobody tells any of the good parables. I'm speaking a language everyone can understand." And he went on, "Anyways… So eventually, this guy gets married, and on his wedding night, his wife gets herself all sexied up. She puts on lingerie. You know, a garter belt and all, and she crawls into bed with her new husband who she's never consummated her love with. And she asks him if he's ready to have sex. Her husband sighs, leans back against his pillow, and says, 'Look. My mom told me the truth. She told me you have teeth around your vagina, and you'll bite my penis off if I put it inside you.' His wife looks at him with a compassionate gaze, and she says, 'That's not true at all. Look. I'll show you.' And she spreads her pussy lips wide. The guy leans down, takes a look, and says, 'No wonder! Just look at the condition of those gums!'" The gargoyle cracked himself up – not literally, just figuratively – while his companion merely shook her head. "Now, that's what I call a parable!" the male gargoyle congratulated himself.

Christian didn't know what to make of any of it, but he thought of the demon and the murderess waiting for him either in the woods or back in Machpelah… if he could ever even figure out how to get out of those woods Evius had brought him so deep into. He swallowed slowly.

"Okay, okay," the laughing gargoyle said, wiping a liquid tear from his stone cheek as his compatriot continued shaking her head. "If that parable didn't make any sense to you, let me try this one: A guy's looking though the newspaper. He sees an ad that says: *Pay $5,000 cash for this car and get the fuck of your life.* He can't believe his good luck. He folds up the paper and immediately gets on the bus to head off to the address of the ad's used car lot.

"Intensely excited, he approaches the lot. He sees the salesman, and he says, 'I came about the ad.' The salesman directs him over to a beat-up, old, Chevy Nova. The guy looks the car over – it's a piece of shit not even worth $1,000, but he says, 'I'll take it as long as I get the second half of the ad, too,' he adds with a: *wink, wink, nudge, nudge*.

"The salesman whistles, and out the door of the lot's office steps a beautiful blonde: short skirt, high heels, huge tits. She sashays over to the car and gets in on the passenger side. She waves with one finger to indicate that the customer should get in on the driver's side. By now excited beyond belief, the customer hands over his $5,000, and *he* gets in. He waves goodbye to the salesman, and amid belches and coughs from the tailpipe, he putters off.

"After a little while, as he's driving, he turns to the blonde and says (he actually has to raise his voice the car's knocking so loudly), 'Can I put my hand on your knee?' She nods, *Sure*. He drives a little farther, and when they're stopped at a light he asks her if she'll kiss him on the cheek. She leans over and does so. At the next light, he finally swallows slowly. He leans over and whispers something in the blonde's ear. As he pulls away from her, she bursts into a fit of cheeky laughter. 'What's so funny?' the guy asks. 'Oh,' the blonde says, 'Nothing except that you got that when you bought the car.'"

A guffaw exploded from out the female gargoyle. The male gargoyle glanced sidelong at her. As he winked one rocky eye in her direction, she doubled over in a fit of absurdity.

With his apparently female companion lost in a humorous rage, the seemingly male gargoyle went on: "See, that's why I always say we need to be more careful about how we *use* language. To get 'fucked' should be a good thing, right? I mean, it feels nice to get fucked. If we used 'fuck' the way it felt, as something good, perhaps even as a compliment... For example, if instead of saying 'Thank you,' we were to say, 'Fuck you, fuck you very much', and the person to whom we were speaking were to good-naturedly respond, 'Well, fuck you, too. In fact, go fuck yourself', then the main character of that parable never would have gotten into that mess in the first place. See," the gargoyle went on, explaining the intricacies of the humor Christian believed he already understood, "What he thought was going to be a *good* thing turned out to be a *bad* thing, right? Humans really need to listen to us gargoyles a little more. One should *feel* language when one speaks it."

Shaking his head, still unsure of himself, of the gargoyles, of everything, Christian stepped forward. Following the stream as if he were an excess element included in the forest's urine, as the sun finally began its purple rising over his shoulder, he embarked upon the next phase of his journey.

Behind him, the gargoyle shouted: "One more parable! A nun and a priest are playing golf. The priest takes a swing at the ball, misses, and says, 'Goddamnit, I missed!' The nun says, 'You say that two more times, and God will strike you down with lightning.' The priest shrugs, swings again, misses, and says, 'Goddamnit, I missed!' The nun says, 'You say that once more, and God will strike you down with lightning.' The priest frowns at her, swings again, misses, and screams, 'Goddamnit, I missed!' Suddenly, a bolt of lightning comes crackling out of the sky, strikes the nun, and burns her to cinders. A booming voice comes out of the clouds, saying, 'Goddamnit, I missed!'"

12.
The Porcelain God

Trickle, trickle, dribble, dribble, water tinkled through the rocks.
Behind him, Christian heard the muffled laughter of the
gargoyles from their newest parable as yet another one
formed from that direction ("Speaking of God: what's the
difference between a golf ball and a clitoris?" (pause) "A
man will spend twenty minutes looking for a golf ball!" *Ha!
Ha! Ha! Ha!*). While to his right, a whispered, "Hey,"
greeted him.

Light emanated from somewhere, and Christian saw
Evius – leaning forward, a grin touching his lips – in
profile. "Sorry about those gargoyles," he whispered a bit
louder. "I've never cared much for them myself, but who
would ever imagine I was in charge of this world?" As if
he'd just stepped out of the bed of some mellow-thighed
chick, his hair seemed even more mussed up than usual.
From his hunch, his spine was a bit out of place.

"Follow me," Evius whispered still louder, and his
leather boots splashed through the banks of the ever-
widening stream. He disappeared into a darkness that
somehow lightened as soon as Christian, his own vomit-
spattered boots soaking up the mucky water, stepped into

it. He dragged his hand along the cold, craggy, gray walls echoing of what sounded like splashes of the world's piss. His hand dampened. His fingers crinkled. And when he stuck his whole appendage up to his nose, it had a mildewed odor to it. This was so different from the vision he'd seen when he'd been hanging through the hole in his ceiling. He liked that death better. Why in the hell did Evius have to cut him down?

"You didn't wanna die," Evius said.

"What?" Christian asked – some vague premonition that perhaps his guide was reading his mind.

"I was singing a song from my youth: '*To-diddly-widdly-lie*.' You know it?"

"No. I thought you said something else."

"What was that?"

"Nothing."

"Oh, then, *To-diddly-widdly-lie, do-middly-liddly-die*... You ever notice how music is really just noise, and words are only sounds? How in hell's name does it ever come to mean anything? It has something to do with silence, but I don't know."

Christian shook his head. Evius couldn't have seen that, and Christian muttered, "Filling up those silences is what jazz is all about..."

"No. It doesn't fill the silences. It just creates smaller ones. Crazy. Didn't you pay any attention last night? Silence must be infinite. But then again would there be silence between the notes if there were no notes? I mean, isn't it the notes themselves defining the silence? So... the infinite must be created by the finite, no?"

"I don't know what in the hell you're talking about, man..."

"You will. Just wait till you get a load of Pandemonium. It's so full of notes it takes a real effort to notice the silence.

Like John Coltrane's *Ascension*, you know? And that's meditation, my friend. That's meditation."

"I don't know what's going on with *Ascension*," Christian said.

"Neither do I, but it sure as hell is good, wouldn't you say?"

Christian shrugged. Evius had been dead for so long, he couldn't have known anything about Coltrane's masterpiece. Evius sure seemed to know an awful lot though. It was as if he traveled not only between Machpelah and Pandemonium but also had some sort of secret entrance into the world Christian had just left. He needed to ask him about that. Maybe if there was a secret entrance, he could go back. He could make that peace with his mom he'd promised himself he'd make in the shower. He could live again. He could get sober and clean and…

He was getting ready to ask about all that when, drowning out the echoing piss, a cried scream resounded through the tunnel. Where it actually came from, who knew. Christian froze, though, because he knew it hadn't come from him. And Evius was too close to have allowed such a rising pitch to emanate from his screeches. The scream was a buzz saw slicing through Christian's ears, ripping into his brain. It was so lazy that, like an Alaskan wind, it didn't bother going around the body, instead it cut right through and froze the heart in mid-beat.

Like for a zombie newly arisen in its tomb, Christian's heart started beating again. Immediately, a cold wind blew strong into his face. The same scream given physical presence, it whipped his hair back in place. Christian shivered as if he were standing at a urinal and needed to shake. If he'd had a coat, he would have pulled it tight around his neck. He glanced over at Evius. He'd heard the sound as well. Like a penis with an instant reaction to a pornographic woman's moan, he was perked at attention. He didn't seem chilled by the wind, though. Rather, he appeared quite comfortable... keyed into the scream's presence.

"What was that?" Christian muttered, a slight edge to his voice as if adrenaline's metallic taste had been sparked by the breeze's cold fusion.

"I don't know," Evius said with a grin sliding up his cheeks, "Let's find out."

"I don't know if I want to find out."

"You want to go back to the woods?"

Christian didn't respond.

Coldly, Evius answered anyways, "I didn't think so."

Splish, splash, drip, drop... they followed the stream as it flowed deeper into the cave. The ethereally emanating light turned the water a blood-like, reddish tint. Was it; was it not? It thickened into plasma, into bloodily discharged semen as if the ejaculator had a testicular ulcer as if he/she were hermaphroditically menstruating and cumming at one and the same time. Regardless of what the actual case may have been, Christian didn't want even his shoes to touch the mess.

Closing in tight on the dank smelling wall (but not touching it since it seemed coated in the same substance flowing down river), he scooted along the path. Evius, on the other hand, boldly splashed through the mess. Darkening his legs, it splattered off his boots and landed on his jeans. The thought of that shit touching him made Christian want to vomit, and watching it actually stick to Evius brought the vomit to the back of his throat.

"You okay?" Evius asked.

Christian nodded.

"Good. Because we've got a ways to go yet. Don't let this part freak you out. You ain't even seen freaky yet. But if I know you as well as I think I do, that shouldn't bother you one bit. For Christ's sake, you're American. And Christ had a lot to do with that country. For better, for worse, in sickness, in health, all that mess…"

Christian mumbled, "What do you mean *had?* America's still there." He didn't add he wanted to know whether or not Evius had ever been there, and if he had, how could Christian get back.

Like a tornado, Evius spun around. He exclaimed, "Don't you ever listen to anything I say? Nothing's still there, man. I told you all about that on the way to the mountain-top. Look. If you want to say things are, that's fine. If you want to say they aren't, that's fine, too. But just remember the truth is they neither are nor are not. They both are and are not. Jesus, man, think for a freaking change. You're here, but you're not. You don't exist, but you do. Hasn't the reality of that gotten through to you yet?"

Again, Christian didn't think for one moment about what Evius had to say because they actually did seem to be there, and as far as Christian could tell, there most definitely existed. Here might not have, but there did. Evius shook his head and turned back around. In front of him, as if they'd passed into the vagina, broken through the rectovaginal septum, entered the rectum, and now stared at an anal exit, one of the cave's deeper orifices opened beyond Evius' silhouette.

Christian stared at the brightness emanating from the possible exit… Was that outside? Was that where the scream had come from? Christian's mind fluttered between joy and trepidation: joy at leaving the cave, trepidation at finding what had provoked the scream. Perhaps, the monster was there again. Perhaps, Zoe was there with another maddening encounter. Either way, though,

Christian didn't have a choice because he knew, at the very least, they were both quite possibly outside. Don't choices drive you crazy? Which one's better: the known or the unknown?

"Let me give you a koan, then," Evius said. "The gargoyles posed this one to me years ago, and I've been meditating on it ever since: If you were one of three people walking through a haunted house, would you want to be in the front, the middle, or the back?"

Christian shook his head. "I don't know. The middle."

"Why?"

"I don't know. Maybe because I don't want to bump into anything first, and I also don't want anything to grab me from behind."

"But if you're in the middle, you might see what takes the person in front, and then you'd *know* death was on its way for you, too. So you might just want to be in the front and simply go right off the bat. The other problem with the middle is: what if you look behind you and suddenly the last person is gone? Now, you're last, and you know something might very well grab you, too. Besides, you're going to be first or last sooner or later, and then the whole question doesn't matter. Once one person goes, you're probably not making it out alive. Did you ever think maybe that deal was your whole problem?" Evius shook his head. "You really need to be more certain of your answers before you say them. Otherwise, you'll never get the dharma-transmission. But, I guess, since there are only two of us in this haunted house, the question doesn't really apply."

"Haunted?" Christian asked.

"Jesus, man, you never think, do you? We're ghosts. This place is definitely haunted. We're doing it." Evius shook his head in seeming disbelief, and he started walking toward the exit, the entrance, whatever it was lit up and opening wide in front of them. Not knowing what else to do, Christian followed.

The stream expanded ever wider, turned into a narrow river. Christian moved closer to the wall. He scowled at his proximity to the bloody, semenic mess. As they approached the end of the darkness, a breeze picked up again. Hidden in it, as strange as this may sound, were words.

They weren't spoken. They were felt in the coolness brushing across Christian's skin, lifting the nervous sweat from his pores. If he'd been schizophrenic, he might have recognized the voice. It said: *My name is Lucifer. How do you do? I believe I have a question for you. There's not one answer, but two. Would you like to reign in hell or would you rather serve like I do?*

For a moment, unlike he ever did with anything Evius ever said, Christian found himself physically pondering the psychic sensation. Images came with the words. Images of... *Fool! Only Loki reigns in Hel!* Christian put his hands over his ears, but it didn't stop the sound. *My name is Lucifer. Now, tell me, does this make sense: Would you choose hell or non-existence?* Christian didn't know whether or not he'd answered the question. Something told him he had and he'd answered wrong.

To a tune from his childhood, a screechy voice sang, very low-key and quite off-pitch: *Lucifer, Lucifer... Never before did an angel want more.* Children's voices joined the first. They were maddening. A Jamaican accent chimed in, cooing: *I Bliss, baby.* And, then, a purr: *Luciferrrrrr... (Lucifer doesn't exist; there is only Iblis).* Laughter! – audible this time – broke up everything inside Christian's mind. "Stop it!" he screamed, his hands blocking his ears, though the sounds came from inside.

From in front, Evius asked, "Where else do you want me to go?" Without a hitch in his step, seemingly oblivious to the madness Christian was encountering, he stepped into the light beyond. It shimmered on his hair of midnight. Had he heard those voices before? Was he immune to them? Christian didn't know what to think anymore. Stopping mid-stride, he glanced askance at his guide. Evius turned around. As if he were being invisibly crucified, he extended one arm to either side. But unlike Christ's howling as the pain split his wrists, Evius grinned instead. "You coming or not?" he asked. Christian had no choice but to go forward.

He reached the light. Feeling as heavenly as cocaine, it shined through the layers of his skin straight into his soul. It felt strange to once again envision his reflected flesh. Like a baby in the presence of its mother, Christian closed his eyes, tipped his head back on his neck, and let the light caress his cheeks and lips. As far as he was concerned, he'd made it. There was no Zoe, no monster waiting for him. Even through his eyelids, the source of the light was as blinding as the sun. Although, Christian was certain he was still inside the cave. And still, the light manically disintegrated all the earlier voices' pains.

As if it were a charismatic leader, the light washed them clean from Christian's mind and shoved them straight into the dustbin of history. Unfortunately, as any inhabitant of the postmodern world knows, that dustbin is already overflowing. Where will we put our ghosts of Christmases future? They'll suffer along with our ghosts of Christmases past.

The river of filth widened ever more. It flowed straight up to a cliff and spilled over the edge. In the light, as if they'd earlier suffered in the eerie presence of a living black light poster, its color was hardly as red. Instead, it appeared even more semen-like. With it came a salty scent, like the ocean, like… From this side of the cliff, across an invisible chasm, a rickety wooden bridge stretched. The rope railings appeared ready to split, and Christian gulped as he pondered the thought of crossing it as it swayed in a mild breeze emanating magically from the stone walls. He asked, "Evius, where's the light coming from?" because, even with the changes in tone, they were most definitely still inside their haunted house, and Christian still wished he were in the warm middle of two others.

"I don't know, man, but it sure is nice, isn't it?" Then, more seriously, "Let me tell you something, though, and listen to me on this one: When we cross that bridge, whatever you do, don't look down."

But Christian knew all about that. When you look down, you might feel dizzy. You might feel the urge to jump. You might lose your balance. You might... whatever. He shook his head and nodded anyways. He wanted to know about the light, but like with so much of the afterlife, there didn't seem to be an explanation for that one either.

But the truth was that after everything he'd been through over the past few days – How many days had he been dead already – two, three... how long had it taken them to walk through that cave? With the way the bridge looked, the least he was concerned with was actually looking down. Instead, he was more concerned with the process of crossing. The wooden slats composing the floor appeared a bit spacious for his tastes, and the stability seemed still murkier... especially if he wasn't supposed to look down. But because of the cave he would have had to return through – this really did keep getting worse and worse – he managed to say, "Okay."

"Well, then, let's take some medicine and head across," Evius intoned. Christian wasn't a hundred percent certain what type of medicine they were going to take. He'd yet to experience a diagnosed psychosis, but when still another joint appeared miraculously from Evius' pocket, he began salivating. The guide sparked a match. The guided took a few hits, and with at least one of them blown out of his mind, they strolled on up to the teetering, tottering bridge.

Right before Evius dropped the sole of his boot onto the bridge's first slat, though, Christian – his mind, once again, in a lifted state – finally got up the nerve to ask him, "Is that shit laced?"

Evius laughed. "Tighter than a corset. Now, remember, don't look down." And they stepped onto the bridge.

But even though Christian had heard his guide this time, he still didn't heed Evius' advice.

What else was he supposed to do? How was he supposed to walk across that bridge without looking down? The whole thing was one huge hole. He tried keeping his vision trained straight ahead, but before he even completed his first step, with one hand out to either side grabbing tight the worn, wobbly rope rubbing raw his palm, he looked right down at where he was placing his vomit-spattered shoe on the loosely spaced slats. A peephole appeared. Through it, he should have seen a river, a ravine, anything other than what he actually did see. Between the slats, he witnessed a sight that sent his jaw crashing to the ground and caused him to pause mid-step.

It wasn't fear necessitating his hesitation. It was another emotion entirely, an emotion twisting like a hatchling breaking open its egg in his gut and slithering straight up his chest, coiling and crushing his heart like a constrictor, to his throat. There it paused, tickling his esophagus with its tail before it shot into his eyes to blind him.

With Christian unseeing of anything other than what existed beneath – peripheral vision was gone, the constrictor flexed amid his brain. At first, he wasn't quite sure if he were really witnessing what he thought he might be. At first, it just didn't seem possible that, amid all his trepidation, *God bless Pandemonium* was his primal thought.

Because there was a river beneath... only it wasn't composed of water. It wasn't even composed of the bloody, semen-like mess running through the cave. What it was was a river of humans, a river of flesh, most specifically of living, naked women.

They writhed over top and beneath one another, buxom breasts to bubbled butts, tiny feet to voluptuous lips, glistening vaginas to thick legs. They were nude and smooth, bodies as hairless as a newborn, though as developed as any full-grown woman's. Their long hair, short hair, trimmed hair shimmered in the light from above: red, black, brown, blonde. Their skin-tones were as many and varied as all the earth's: white, black, brown, red, yellow, and everything in between. The shapes of their eyes were round and almondy. Their irises were blue and green and black and brown. Christian's own eyes nearly burst from out his skull. The women stretched endlessly in either direction. The semen-like substance gushed a waterfall over the plateau's wall. It thickened into gooey, white spots as it struck the wriggling bodies, and the women, with red, wet tongues, licked it off one another's flesh. Like a billion *Venus de Milos*, they reached up above the mass – breasts of perky nipples fully exposed – drinking it with endlessly open mouths as it fell.

Directly beneath, a black haired siren pulled herself up to straddle a red headed body beneath her. She locked eyes with Christian, opened her arms, and with long nails ushered him to come down. She licked her lips. *Come on,* she mouthed in slow motion, *Come on*. A blonde noticed him as well and did the same. Before Christian knew it, he had a whole fan club of African, European, Asian, and American women rubbing their crotches, lips, and chests silently begging him to join them.

It was like nothing he'd ever experienced in life – not even in his younger days of frequenting strip clubs. He'd never been a bad looking guy (although, the last years had taken their toll). He'd also never been a rich man... And he'd never had a bevy of naked women begging him to join them in bliss. Their mannerisms ricocheted through Christian's groin. Without – as one of the gargoyles' koans had once pointed out to Evius – enough blood to work two heads, he couldn't even think. Before Evius had a chance to realize what his companion had seen, with no thought for what it might mean for one body to topple onto a horde of others, as the gargoyle's first parables flitted through his mind, Christian flung himself over the rope railing and leaped feet first to the sea of women.

Through the pulsating, glowing air, he fell. Wind whirred past his ears. With each micro-inch, the flesh-filled feast came closer.

Evius' cry, "Chriiiiiistian!" echoed from above.

But Christian was Superman descending not to save somebody else, but for the first time, to save himself. He couldn't have gone on... not with the possibility of eternal salvation beckoning him to join them. For the first time since he'd first seen the house he'd thought he was going to live in, he was happy to be dead, more than happy even – elated. This was how he'd always presumed heaven to be.

It took only a moment to fall, but a mere millisecond of bliss's anticipation is eternity... just ask any crackhead waiting on a rock to melt. The drug is dropped into the stem as gases condense in what will become space. The lighter licks the crack at the moment of combustible expansion. The flame finally burns your thumb as oxygen molecules begin to bond with other elements. Smoke seeps down the stem when life crawls out of the primordial ooze.

The chemical taste doesn't touch your tongue until this very moment, and as the sun finally explodes, your eyes pop out of your skull.

Like any addict waiting for a lift, Christian closed his eyes. As he shivered in his soul from his groin to his brain, flesh caressed the soles of his shoes. Hair wrapped around his jeans. Dragging him down into heaven's sea, frail fingers ending in wicked nails reached up to rub through his thighs. A random palm cupped his crotch. Its fingertips lifted up his shirt and tickled the hair of his happy trail. Unable to contain himself any longer, he stiffened like cooked and cooled cocaine. The pressure of bodies against his stomach shoved him down beneath the musky scent of naked sex. This was the very ocean every man dreamed of... a thousand virgins for every martyr wasn't enough. Why not ten thousand, a million, a billion? As he opened his eyes in that warm sea, immersed in what should have been a bevy of writhing beauties waiting only for him to unsheathe himself, everything changed.

What he had expected to see was an unending landscape of unclothed, female flesh... What he had expected was to have long hair wrap around every extremity of his body...

But there was no hair. Instead, there was flesh most definitely, but it didn't feel human. It was warm and muscled, and it writhed through his mouth and around his crotch and arms and legs, and in certain directions it caught rough and tumble against his skin. In other directions, shielding muscles beneath, scales lapped overtop one another. His eyes open, Christian saw markings of colors no human should have had: blue and blood red, jade green and jet-black, gray and yellow. Diamond-shaped heads caught in his hand. Baby's rattles ricocheted around him. A forked tongue followed by fangs darted straight for his eye.

Christian screamed. A green snake shot into his open mouth. Blocking his vocal chords' noise, its head caught against the back of his throat where it sat still writhing, trying to find its way into his stomach. Instead of bathing in an ocean of beauties, Christian was drowning in a sea of reptiles.

He pulled the snake out of his mouth. With a hint of the desired sexuality, it bit his tongue, his lip. Salty blood flowed through his mouth. Pushing against long bodies wrapping around his legs, trying to pull him further down, he fought his way – much like he had when reaching for the knot of that rope he'd looped over the beam through the hole in his ceiling – to the surface.

Teeth sunk through his jeans into his thigh. They were glass piercing his flesh. More glass seemed to slice into his leather boots to bury themselves in his Achilles heel. As if amid vampires, long needles poked through his neck. Venom pumped thickly into his veins. He felt his whole body swelling. Constrictors writhed around his forehead and neck. He reached the surface. Like a leech, a black snake stayed stuck to his chest via its fangs.

More so than from the mere earlier scrape on his elbow, he was dripping blood through his clothes. Hands other than his own ripped the venomous teeth off his heart. Standing astride the bodies of worms, Evius stared at him concernedly. He ran his worried hands through his hair. "Grab hold and follow me," he said.

Barely above the reptilian surface, Christian grabbed his eternal savior's leg. Like a truck pulling a car out of the mud, like a branch pulling a man out of quicksand, Evius surged forward.

Weaving above the surface of its brothers or sisters, a cobra in front of Christian's face spread its hood. To no piped beat, its tongue flickered back and forth. As if in sneak attack, from either side, venom was spat into Christian's eyes. He went blind. Human hands grabbed hold of him underneath his shoulders, pulled him upright, draped one of his arms over an invisible neck, and carried him forward. The world writhed beneath his feet.

"Put your hand here," Evius said, placing Christian's palm against what felt like a stone wall. "Put one foot here," Evius said, kicking Christian's sole into a nook. "Now, go here," Evius said. "Now, here…" In such a manner it seemed they scaled a wall to take them away from the snakes. Woozy, Christian heard the rattles and hisses descending ever deeper.

On solid ground again, Evius ordered Christian to kneel. Penitently, the wounded man did as he was told. The sensation somehow reminded him of being in a youthful church with his mother at his side, her hand on his back as he prayed through tears for his grandfather's dead soul.

Something cool, chunky, and liquid was rubbed into Christian's eyes. Within a minute, as a sheen of tears, just like in that church so long ago, welled up and dripped down his cheeks, amid a burst of brightness, he could see again. Like the Arizona landscapes he'd never been witness to, the world appeared sandy and deserted. A stream of some sort of red chunky mess ran beside him. It was the same stream that had appeared to be semen when it splashed on what had seemed to be women. Christian realized they were back where they'd started from on the other side of the bridge. Evius' hands were smeared and stained with the same menstrual substance flowing through the river whose banks they rested upon. It dripped off the sides of his lips, and Christian realized that was what had been rubbed into his eyes. If only he were still blind. He wanted to vomit. Aware his charge could finally see, Evius pointed to the soupy mess. "Drink it," he said.

Pained from fang gashes and bloating from venom, Christian begged, "What?"

"Drink it," Evius said again. "It's the only thing that can save you."

Christian didn't want to drink the bloody discharge, but he wanted even less to experience whatever may come beyond Pandemonium and Machpelah. Things were too much of a mess as they were.

Still feeling he might vomit, now feeling he might split apart at the seams, Christian crawled over to the river that could be likened to a flow through the feminine world's thighs. He leaned his face down to the mess. The sickly, sweet scent of innards greeted his nose. Having seen discarded tampons in some of the dumpsters he'd dug through, he was certain of what this was. He cupped his hands in the mess he once didn't want to have touch even his shoes. Like John the Baptist bringing holy water over Jesus's head, Christian brought his palm to his lips, and he drank. He lapped up everything in hand. It tasted salty and vaginal. Then, at Evius' insistence, he dipped his palm and drank the discharge again and again and again.

"That should be good," Evius finally said – his own mouth caked with the same bloody mess.

The pain began subsiding. The immanent swelling drained from out his wounds. Christian was soaking wet from his own blood, from his sweat, and from the ounces of venom unclogging his system. His shivering limbs ceased their frenzied wracking. He lay prostrate, gulping, and parched on the dusty ground. He stared at Evius haloed by the light emanating from nothing. With a heavy sigh, his savior put a cigarette between his lips and lit it. "Why... why did you save me?" Christian asked him.

With red goo dripping from his fingers and mouth, Evius shrugged. He said, "You could call me your guardian angel, but truth be told, you're the best friend I've made in centuries."

11.
A Desert Corposant

They were back on the rickety, old bridge again. This time, though, there was no admonishment to Christian not to look down. Evius must have realized the danger was passed. Reality has a way of draining fantasy's fangs, and those fangs had been drained all through Christian's still pained body. Grimacing, he carefully watched where he placed every footfall. Now, his only fear was he might make a false step and fall back into that ocean of whatever lay beneath.

Visible between the cracks in the boards, the sea churned through amorphous shapes: a woman whose torso turned into a snake's tail rolled overtop the thighs of a true, human woman who sat astride a huge serpent. A beautiful blonde with reptilian eyes motioned Christian to join her. Her body excited his – stimulus, reaction – but her forked tongue sent a chill shivering through the healed holes in his neck – stimulus, reaction. Dizzy, he realized he had to focus more succinctly on exactly where each foot landed. He was extremely aware he'd almost gone on to whatever life came on after the afterlife, and having experienced that space, he had no desire to comprehend what lay beyond. If possible,

Pandemonium would hopefully make for a fine eternity, and Pandemonium was exactly what they were headed for.

The bridge crossed, the descent into madness lay behind. Ahead – a wasteland yet again. In this cave whose ceiling was still visible though light burned from it as if it were the surface of the moon's sunny reflection, desert plains rose into dunes on every side. It was the shores of Kitty Hawk with no ocean beyond. Just looking at the Saharan monstrosity parched Christian's throat. "I sure could use a drink," he croaked.

Evius grinned. "Patience," he said. Then, he coolly asked Christian, "Cigarette?"

Christian nodded. A butt was lit and made the rounds between them as they strolled through the sands. Christian's god-given, leather shoes were getting duskier and duskier. Chunks of vomit coated in the river's menstrual blood now magnetically attracted grain after grain of non-metallic dirt to them. Where a crown of thorns possibly could have rested, sweat broke out across Christian's brow. A trickle of it dribbled down his cheek. With his already bloodied, now even holier sleeve, he wiped it away. His armpits were swimming. His crotch grew sticky – and not in the way he'd hoped it would when he'd plunged into what he'd thought was an ocean of a trillion virgins for every martyr. On the other hand, Evius, though panting a bit from heat, looked as fresh as a man with a five-o'clock shadow ever could. They walked on and on and on and on... feet burning through soles, up dunes, down hills, until something sparkled in the distance.

A mirage, maybe, and the mirage would disappear as soon as they approached. Christian was yet dreary enough to hope. He refused to question Evius with his parched throat. The sparkle grew brighter and more glittering as the two dead travelers drew closer.

Coming on from nowhere and disappearing into forever, like a serpent's never-ending scales, it shimmered in a thousand places. It didn't seem to attain the ephemeral, liquid quality Christian always assumed a mirage would gain. Instead, it appeared more substantial as they got nearer. After a few moments, it disappeared off to the left. A few moments later, it reappeared from the right. Christian feared perhaps for that moment where it wasn't there he might have actually gone blind. But no, he could see. Without the sparkle, there was simply nothing there. Regardless, it didn't look anything like liquor... or water for that matter.

Like a baby child who's learned just because the glass door was there once doesn't mean it's there any longer (he leans forward to press his hand against the solid substance that always catches him, and as his mother – screaming his name, *Chriiiiiistian!* – reaches forward, he falls into the backyard to bruise his forehead), Christian was quickly learning in the afterlife things were never quite what they seemed. Usually, they were much more frightening. What a strangely moving mirage.

The mirage was gone yet again when they'd walked for what seemed like eternal miles, and Evius said, "All right," before he stopped walking.

"All right, what?" Christian asked – parched so much that forming the words was quite difficult. With nothing to wet it, the inside of his throat stuck to his windpipe.

"This is where we wait."

"For what?" Sand surrounded them, nothing but white in every direction. Evius must have become delirious.

But Christian's guide shook his head and said, "For the train, silly. Don't tell me you didn't see it."

Christian had seen something – a sparkle, a movement, a train... maybe. But how did Evius know where to wait?

There were no stop markers. There was no bench. It didn't even look like there were any tracks. The fool himself had fallen for the mirage. Evius must have been in worse shape than he appeared. His addled mind had invented and invested some sort of meaning for the illusion.

But there's nothing ever before us other than illusion. If Christian had stayed in Machpelah, somebody might have been able to teach him that, somebody Indian and dead, somebody like the guru Vasishtha, like Rama after he'd talked with Vasishtha. But that would mean he was talking to the great God Vishnu Himself, and Christian had already said, "Fuck you," to Krishna. Who was… well, so much for the Dharma (*I'd* never say, "Fuck you," to Krishna. I've seen His many-armed form. It exists inside my mind). Machpelah itself was an illusion. The desert was real, or so it seemed at that very moment.

The sweat sure felt real. It stunk. It was sticky. The sun seemed real. The heat… No, here he was – sweating, running from something he wasn't even sure what: death, fear… He was already dead. He was already afraid. As far as he was concerned, he was the last person in the haunted house. That was the answer to the gargoyles' koan. Evius had already succumbed to the monster – delusion. So why didn't Christian stop?

That's exactly what he did. He waited in the middle of a desert with Evius on what he assumed was a non-existent train. One more non-existent among myriad such things. He didn't even pause to think a mere hit of weed (like it had back on the couch when he'd still thought he was alive) might have made him realize he himself was non-existent.

And if what exists needs what exists to reify it, the same must hold true for what does not exist. The problem with marijuana: Nobody takes seriously what they experience while it clouds his or her brain. Again, a finger to the so-called Hindu trinity. We don't need Shiva or His realizations. Let Him sit in meditation alone. That's exactly what He does. Hence, the reason Gilles's theory at Machpelah's café would never work. This is reality. That isn't. What is? The desert.

From stage left, a silver train entered glistening in the sun as if it were a dolphin throwing sparkles of water from its nose. Before its feet, like for a fall blower taking care of some leaves, the dust scattered in front of its low-lying mouth like fish fleeing a whale. Directly in front of it, the tracks it ran upon miraculously appeared from beneath the rapidly diffusing sand. Its slick roar sounded of wind rushing off aerodynamic jowls. Dumbfounded, Christian felt his eyes grow wide. Where had such a metallic beast appeared from? He and his sole guide were supposed to be in a cave. Of course, though, the world over, such monstrosities roar through caves beneath every major city. Why should this cave away from Machpelah and Zoe and her frightening beast be any different? All it was missing were the mole people. And if Christian had imagined such a prospect, panic would have taken hold. Needing more than ever to be the middle person walking through the haunted house, he might have even jumped into Evius' arms to flee the white skin, track-marked forearms, and long fingers reaching out to take something, anything…

With a screech and a whoosh, the train came to a stop directly in front of the two dead travelers. Pressurized doors slid open to welcome the newest coming occupants. Evius stepped into the train. Since Christian didn't immediately follow him, he turned with a smile, waved his arm towards himself, and whispered, "Come on."

Seemingly reluctant to leave the desert heat for whatever lay beyond, Christian followed. But as he stepped into the train, he caught, out of the corner of his eye, a glimpse of the conductor at the front leaning out a window to watch the two passengers step on board. Christian might have been mistaken, but he could have sworn when the man smiled, he had dripping fangs hanging over his bottom lip while poking through his flat cap were two red horns. But again, what choice did Christian have other than to follow his guide. With his heart in his throat, he was on board, and then, he was sitting down in a window-facing, subway style seat, and then, with a recorded voice saying over the loud speaker, *"Hold on for your life,"* the train started chugging along again.

Before Christian knew what was happening, outside the window across from him, the dunes and desert flew past at speeds akin to a Chunnel bullet train. Only, it wasn't a tunnel beneath a channel they flew through. It was the barren landscape of the same terrain that had dried Christian's throat to the point where he could barely even swallow.

Bringing his parchedness more to the forefront of his own mind, desert dust flew up on all sides. Like staring through a storm of gnats, it blurred the blinding, sunny scene beyond the window. "Is there anything to drink in here?" Christian asked Evius who leaned forward, shook his head, and laughed. Christian's lips went askew. He leaned back into his seat. *It's not like I was asking for liquor for Christ's sake... I just want a freaking water fountain.* To be immersed, like the initiate with a downward thrust to the head, choking as he makes the sign of a cross from fingers dipped in the baptismal font... John the Baptist *did* eat honey and locusts, sweet and crunchy vegetable blood and parasitic bugs. Baptism: symbolically cleansing original sin. A fountain – gushing upwards in a spurt of creativity – sexually Freudian. Like with Rumi, the two spiritually coincide on a physical plane due to the natural inversion of all innate drives.

But that wasn't Christian's desire. His was more base, based upon life. "Someday you'll have to give that up," Evius said.

Christian croaked, "I just wanted a glass of water."

"Acceptance, man, that's the key. Just be where you are, and it's a hell of a lot easier to deal with."

But we haven't gotten to that point yet. Instead we're on a train that instead of flying through a tunnel is locomotivating its way, full-speed ahead, straight through the desert inside a cave that seems to have, nonetheless, disappeared (much like the walls of a padded room might fade away into nothing if the cracks of a psychosis could have their way)... just like the desert seems to disappear into, well, nothing as well. But wait. Here it comes. A screech slid through the gears, the wheels on the sand-obscured tracks. The train slowed. It stopped. As if some sort of medication were kicking in, the obscured world outside the windows came back into focus. Christian had seen through a glass darkly. Now, things appear as they truly are: infinite. "What in the hell's going on?" Christian asked – his face turned towards Evius.

"Added a stop," Evius noticed. Unlike everybody else, unimpressed by the prospect of a stranger, he returned his hidden glance to the sky. But the unexpected stop broke even its trance. It peered down through the blistering sun shining through the cave to cast a spotlight on a paunchy figure.

With cheeks covered in white whiskers, wearing a dark suit, sweat-through the chest and armpits, and a bowler hat over wispy, white hair, the man waited beyond the sliding, glass doors. He rapped his cane against the glass and curmudgeonly mumbled something. The doors opened and the man, in some type of comfortable, support shoe – so in contrast to the rest of his outfit – stepped into the air conditioning.

He pulled a handkerchief from his pocket and wiped his forehead. Recognizing the hunched, decrepit stranger, Christian tipped his own head to the side. But recognizing the hunched, decrepit stranger, Christian didn't say a word. He didn't even have a logical thought. As if re-witnessing some traumatic event – perhaps unconsciously – his breath caught in his throat, his eyes widened, and he straightened in his seat. The old man kept gumming his nearly toothless mouth and moving his cracked lips as if he were speaking to somebody who obviously wasn't there externally but might have existed inside his head. Continuing to wipe the sweat from his forehead, cheeks, and neck, he sat down on the bench across from the two travelers and nodded unknowingly at them.

"Reminds me of my father," Evius whispered into Christian's ear.

Christian merely produced a choked gag reflex of disgust at the memory of Joshua's earlier wetting of himself on the patio of Machpelah's café. As if he were giving the universal symbol of, *Off with his head*, though he was merely externally rubbing away the disgust blocking his throat, Christian rubbed his fingers across his bruised neck.

That very well might have been the exact wrong thing to do. Because Joshua looked right at him. A period of recognition passed across the old man's features. He made the same symbol back to Christian, and he mumbled: "I remember that neck." He laughed. "You'd think I was a vampire saying something like that: *I remember that neck*. I can assure you I'm not, but you might want to see for yourself."

Joshua opened his mouth wide to reveal not only did he not have fangs but he had hardly any teeth whatsoever, and those he did have hardly looked to be in any sort of shape to pierce skin, much less drain blood. "But now you probably think I'm a faggot who wants to nibble on your neck. No worries. Even if I am, faggots burn witches. And really, in this hellhole, which are you more scared of, a little buggery or some real trickery." As if intentionally trying to make the travelers still more unsure, Joshua rubbed his crotch and smiled a decayed grin.

Christian was reminded of Evius' earlier koan, and he reminded himself he wanted to be the middle person walking through the haunted house regardless of how Evius might have deconstructed the analysis. But where he was to stand with respect to a haunting was not the issue at that point in time. His very vision was haunted by a living ghost – both in objective reality and in subjective thought – from Machpelah, which thought, if he were to have considered it, might have made him giggle, rather than gag, a little at its reality. But in reality, he didn't think that thought. Instead, he recalled the siren from the café who Joshua had claimed was looking at *him*. And Christian remembered the absurdity he had considered that statement and his own mistaken move of trying to pick up the enchantress, the murderess, the sorceress, the... whatever she was, which, of course, led him to consider the murder he had witnessed (another stifled gag at the horror and disgust of that thought (a still-beating heart consumed by a beast – *Jesus, I knew that man*)) and all that had transpired since. And now, on a train coming from and bound to nowhere, Joshua again. *Dear God*/dear devil, *when is this going to end?* (*Never* – as far as *I* can tell.)

"So I see that you, too, made it out of that purported heaven they call... What do they call it? Make-a-playa? I can't recall," Joshua continued. "But I don't believe I had the pleasure of meeting your friend," he added with a nod towards Evius.

"Eosphorus," Evius – since Christian sure as hell wasn't going to say it for him – said as he extended his hand.

For his part, Christian hardly noticed Evius' gesture of friendship towards the old man. He was too caught up in the awareness that his guide had chosen yet another name with which to introduce himself to yet another person. For a brief moment, Christian found himself wishing he were the writer his former roommate Mike had claimed to be and he were writing the novel of his afterlife simply so he could go back through the pages (and skip ahead to future pages) in order to keep track of who Evius claimed to be.

However, cutting Christian's thoughts short, Joshua grunted as he slyly shook Evius' hand, "Now, don't go greeting me in recently concocted languages, youngster. You might simply be concocting a bunch of cockamamie, if you know what I mean."

"I do know what you mean, and I assure you, man, there's no made up languages here, just a true name you can call me by."

Joshua winked. "Well, I thank you for referring to me with the proper respect due an elder. But I should hope you don't mind if I simply call you Eos. All that 'porous' crap is too much for a man my age to take. And if that's the case, you can call me Josh."

"That is the case – although it's technically 'for-us' not 'poor-us' – and I will call you Josh, then," Evius/Eosphorus/Virgil responded. The name didn't really make a difference, though, because, for the most part, the man appeared to look more or less the same at all times – of course, that "more or less" was quite preponderant in Christian's pondering of the names his purported "friend" chose to go by.

But before he completed his thoughts on the nature of Evius, Joshua started up again, "Funny enough... I was just wandering through that damnable desert myself – all alone, mind you – wondering if anybody else had let themselves get caught up in this mess... And I'm glad to see you have."

Christian shrugged, but Evius answered, "We didn't have much of a choice, Josh. It's the only way out of Machpelah I know of."

"Well, then. You," Joshua's voice became gruff, and he nodded at Christian, "Should have followed me and your siren out of that café. She knew another way, and judging from the looks of you and your friend," he said with a grimace, "You could have used a short cut."

"Really?" Evius perked up, "you've found a short cut?" Under his breath, he added, "I've never cared much for the stability of that bridge."

Mildly ill, Christian nudged Evius and muttered, "If you remember, that 'siren' was James's murderer."

Evius shrugged.

But Joshua growled, "Murderer? I'll never let you accuse my Zoe of such a heinous crime... especially in the masculine declension."

Joshua jumped up as quickly as his aged body could – which wasn't really all that quickly once you got down to it. He had to struggle and push himself up a little bit before he could actually lift his bulk out of the seat. It took about three tries, and with a switch from anger to wistfulness happening verbally and mentally (and, therefore, in a sense, spiritually) much quicker than he'd been able to move physically, he added, "How could such a thing like that piece of sweet ass Zoe gave to me ever, and I mean EVER!" Joshua bellowed (switching as quickly from wistfulness back to anger), "Be responsible for the murder of anything other than a pigeon, a rat, a FLY... if that even? I challenge you, young man. I will defend my love against your jealousy. I will be Lancelot to your Arthur, Arthur to your Mordred, Mordred to your... your...," for a moment, it appeared Joshua's mythologies had confused even their author. Then, he continued his diatribe, "I told you she was looking at me. *En garde,*" he finished as he raised his twisted, awkward cane as if it were a rapier with which he was ready to fence to the death.

Christian slunk back in his chair. He'd never been much of a fighter (he usually got beaten up when he tried, but then again, he was usually drunk at those moments) – not that he was a lover either (he was actually a thoroughly practicing alcoholic), and Joshua's rage, even in such a laughable frame, scared him a little. The cane twitched between the old man's trembling fingers. Christian's breath stopped. Evius made no response while Christian wished only that his savior would stand up in his stead, but the newly dubbed Eosphorus merely stared out the window beyond the absurdly angry old man.

In that same window out of which Evius was staring, silhouetting the crazy, old, decrepit warrior's stance, the desert disappeared to be replaced by a hard stone wall. Christian was impressed by what, even with the speed they were moving at, he could tell was masterful stone work. However, with no respect for the men who had laid those stones, somebody – or somebodies – had spray-painted shades of what could only have been graffiti. As the walls zoomed past, the art work appeared to be some sort of mural of reds and whites. A demon's horns appeared to grace one of the designs, and Christian was reminded of the train's conductor – art always is nothing more than a mimicry of reality... or is it the other way around. Either way, we can only produce what we see. The train jerked to a stop.

Joshua stumbled. Kicking one leg against the other, in his slacks and comfortable looking shoes, he tripped to his side and fell into the aisle.

Without a pause to help the ancient, would-be combatant up, without the merest recognition of the old man's unveiled threats, Evius, much quicker than Joshua had been able to, jumped to his feet. "Sorry, my man... But this is our stop," he said, and as the subway doors swooshed open once more, he stepped onto what, with its columns supporting the roof of some new cave the travelers had entered, could have only been a commuter platform without any commuters.

"Empty... must have missed rush hour," Evius observed, and he quietly added, "I wonder what time it is anyways... Or what time rush hour is for that matter."

Dumbfounded, mildly trembling still from his fear, Christian followed, but behind him, he heard Joshua muttering, his voice darkened and veiled by the floor he was speaking into, "I'll get you... I will have my revenge."

And as Christian set foot on a damp, cold, stone walkway, he heard Joshua scream, the echo resounding from the sticky floor to the graffiti-covered walls to the flying-buttressed ceiling to the dirty columns to the quickly closing, fingerprint-smeared doors, "I WILL AVENGE MY SWEET ZOE!" But before Christian could even look back over his shoulder to see if the old man with the cane were rushing after him like an American, Civil War-era, Southern diplomat tearing into an anti-slavery Yankee, the subway car had taken flight.

10.
Death-De(i)fying

"*Jesus, man, weren't you paying any attention to what the hell* was happening on that train?" Christian suddenly exploded on his guide. "I mean, that crazy old man was ready to kill me!"

But Evius simply shrugged and responded, "What difference would that have made? You're already dead."

Nearly apoplectic, Christian continued, "But – but you told me we can die here again."

"And would that really be so bad?" Evius quite coolly countered.

Which left Christian at a loss. Yes. It was that bad. First off – still reeling from the trauma of choking himself to death by means of a frayed rope – Christian was quite aware of the pain being beaten to death would bring with it. For Christ's sake, his throat still hurt. He'd been hit enough times on the streets to know what it felt like to receive a blow to your cheek, a kick to your ribs, and with a cane... It could only be that much worse.

Secondly, there was the fear of what may exist on any plane that may come next. Things had been strange enough. They'd been painful and scary enough. If there was one thing Christian was now certain of: things could definitely get worse (and they would).

Thirdly, there was still the possibility of ultimate nothingness, a sensation Christian's selfishness refused to accept as the eventual, timely end of his thus far seemingly meaningless existence. Pain was one thing, but nothing? That brought a mental suffering to the mind that seemed to split his brain right down the middle of its two hemispheres to leave each division dangling by nerves as frayed as the rope with which Christian had hung himself to the other half. It was that unfathomable. And if it hurt that badly to consider the great nothingness, imagine what it would feel like to actually experience it in all its non-existent grandeur. Yes, it would really be so bad. But Christian didn't say that. Instead, through angrily clenched teeth, as anybody still emotionally stuck in high school would, he responded, "If you hate it here so much, why not just kill yourself?"

Evius spun on him as quickly as a vampire revealing his fangs to a previously supposed lover as he spat, "Don't you think I've tried that? Unfortunately, for some of us, it simply doesn't work."

Now, that revelation left Christian reeling. He'd yet to contemplate the idea there might actually be people on that plane who'd been unable to escape. That sounded like an afterlife, the type of afterlife always promised to him. And it made him wonder, were there people on earth who'd been unable to escape? Tangible ghosts? Physical phantoms? Why couldn't Christian have been one of those? It took leaving to realize it, but he'd loved the plane he still referred to as earth.

Sure, it had its problems, but he'd grown quite used to it over 27 years: its laws and rules, its seemingly existential flux. But away from such sentimental pondering, back to the question at hand. Why couldn't Evius die again when it seemed apparent to Christian, at the very least, James had, and he had it on decent authority James had witnessed others die? The thought sent Christian into a panic – what if things got still worse, which they apparently could… and after they got worse, what if he was stuck in that worst of all possible existences forever – a sort of anti-panglossian inversion of a utopian worldview? Maybe he shouldn't be going to a place named Pandemonium, but on deeper inspection, Machpelah hadn't seemed too cool either.

Suppressing all such thoughts as he had suppressed so many others over his short life span, aloud, he merely wondered, "How many times have you tried to kill yourself?"

It wasn't the most prominent thought in his mind, but many times, the most prominent of our thought's layers are too personal to express. Instead, we relieve a pressure valve on our minds and say something not too painful, not too personal, in order to hear ourselves speak, to reify our own terrified existences.

Evius responded, "Enough," as he slowly turned around, apparently not too happy at being reminded of his failed attempts to escape from life after death.

Probing perhaps too much, Christian went on, "But, I mean, did somebody save you, or could you just not, you know, die?"

"Does it make a difference? I've been stuck here for what feels like an eternity. Other people come and go. Me, I seem to be stuck here." He shook his head. "But couldn't we just walk? There are still things I want you to see."

They escaped the platform by walking up a spiral staircase of metal steps. The stairs – nothing more than grates, really – twirled and twirled in an almost unfathomable fashion making them appear, to Christian's mind (unconsciously trained by his years of building stone chimneys and walls), as if there were no earthly means by which they could support themselves, which there weren't. The spiral spun so tightly Christian was afraid he might get too dizzy to continue. Gulping down the fear he may fall again, hoping if he did he might just die of a cracked skull this time – and not wind up in a bed of human-sized serpents, Christian kept his hand safely planted on the guardrail.

The guardrail was as cold as a lizard's body in the dead of night before it had a chance to cook on a rock like a naked yogi in the daylight sun. Given Christian's nervous palm sweat, it was as slimy as a fish's skeleton just removed out the anus of its scaly body. But Christian held on for dear life until he reached the top, which wasn't an exit as he had hoped, but had all the appearances (this time, rather than with the earlier cave, for real – complete with concrete and graffiti) of being an unused sewer. To perhaps brighten Christian's afterlife, at least there was no mess, no sludge running around his feet... only the echo of his and Evius' footfalls as their respective boots tap-tapped along the stained concrete.

They hadn't gone too far when, ahead, an alcove appeared to open off to the right. Again, Christian recalled Evius' koan, and again, he wished there was a third person with them (provided that third wasn't Joshua (or Zoe)) so he *could* be the middle person walking through the haunted house.

But then, Evius' response to his response popped back into his mind as he realized his guide had been right. There would be nothing scarier than having something appear in the midst of that alcove, grab the first person, and carry his screaming body away right before Christian's uncomprehending gaze. And the only thing that might be just as scary would be to pass by that alcove and realize, amid an attempted conversation, the person behind him had disappeared. Briefly, Christian thought about asking Evius if he could go first, but then, his bravery vanished, and trembling ever so slightly at the memory of his trauma in the woods, he began trailing along a few steps still further behind.

They reached the alcove. Evius stopped, turned, and stared straight into it. He clapped his hands, and amid a chuckle, the seemingly eternally dead hipster said, "Damn me if he's still there." He turned to Christian who had stopped dead in his tracks. "Hurry up, man," he said, "You gotta see this shit. I mean, literally, shit."

Christian was loathe to continue, but, truthfully, he had no choice. Coming up on Evius, he turned towards the alcove as well. If what had happened thus far hadn't been enough for him to want to turn around and climb right back down through that hole in his ceiling and into his earthly body, this certainly was. After this vision, how could he possibly go any deeper into what the afterlife held in store for him? He couldn't, but he didn't have a choice. More often than not, as long as breath still fills our lungs and sight still entrances our eyes, we have to do what we can't. Hence: depression.

Behind what could only be a plexi-glass window – smeared, stained with a deep brown that must have been feces caked in chunks, spread and streaked by remnants of frozen breath and fingerprints – sat a fat, bald man on a lone stool.

Balancing his stool in an unequal equilibrium, he wore a black cape he appeared nude beneath. At least, his thick chest and legs were exposed. His genitals were covered by the cape's drapery. Finger-painted above the window, in messy red lettering mocking the sneering vision behind the glass, were the words: *The wickedest man alive.* And beneath the window, welded-on old English metal letters – rusted and corroded – contained the phrase: *The Great Beast: 666*.

"Magick, brother, magick," Evius said.

Sending the equilibrium of his stool completely off balance, the man jumped to his feet. In a second, with a scowl across his face, the "Great Beast" was up. His cape billowed back to reveal, sure enough, he was completely nude beneath. Christian jumped in place, but before he could run, the now thoroughly naked man – his minuscule penis with its tiny testicles flapping up and down – charged straight ahead, growling audibly even beyond the glass, to slam his forehead into the cage's window at the precise angle of Evius and Christian. Running straight into one of the smeared stains, he sent chunks of it splattering in all directions. A dull thud ricocheted across the cavern's walls. The Great Beast stepped back.

On the window now, mixed in with the brown muck was a thin, dripping trail of blood. Blinking, seemingly dazed, it appeared the Great Beast had wanted his charge to ram straight into one, if not both, of the travelers and bowl them over. For a brief second (before it registered with him the goal had been to hurt his target), Christian was afraid the man had broken his neck.

Like a sparrow fleeing a hawk, unaware clarity can't always be traversed, confused as to why he couldn't get past the glass, the nakedly caped creature – with a brown stain where he'd hit the glass and blood drying into a slight cut across his forehead – tipped his chin to the side, turned around, and, heaving breath, slowly retreated back to his stool. If he were still capable of it, he appeared to be thinking. Splatters of the seeming feces dotted his face, shoulders, and chest. Maybe he'd only wanted to frighten the one he'd never seen before.

Enthroned again, balancing in an unstable equilibrium,

the Great Beast stared straight at Christian's face, straight into Christian's eyes. To Christian, it seemed the Great Beast stared straight into his mind, and Christian, in that respect, was blind. The sensation made him quite uncomfortable. As if he'd achieved anything approximating comfort since... well, since the devil knows when.

For his own part, the Great Beast – in distinction to his recent outburst – appeared as comfortable as a sage king facing south in order to survey his domain. He brought his feet up, and as the stool crashed again onto its equilibrium, he crossed his legs in the lotus position – one foot atop each thigh. Given the form of contact the two of them had made, it appeared apparent to Christian the "man" was focusing his eyes' attention at a point in space just beyond his face, perhaps, given the way his eyes seemed crossed, even on the very tip of his nose. He straightened his spine in such a way that, from behind, must have forced his butt to jut out a little bit. His hands formed a sort of circle in his lap, and his breathing – obvious through the ins and outs of his diaphragm – deepened for a moment. He rocked back and forth (seven times to be precise), and his breath steadied into a shallow pattern. Forgetting his smile, Evius nodded.

"What's he doing?" Christian, recalling Evius' last short phrase, hesitantly asked his companion.

Evius merely shrugged: as if he knew, as if he didn't... The truth was unapparent.

Without too much of a shift out of his contemplative position, the Great Beast scraped some of the brown muck off the side of his stool. Like an orangutan imprisoned in a zoo, he held it in his hand, contemplated it, and then – much like Christian thought the gargoyle might have done with the masticated mess that had been in his hand – he lobbed it in an outfield ball player's arc towards the two travelers.

Forgetting for a moment there was an inflexible pane of plexi-glass between them, Christian ducked. But the brown muck, subject to the simple laws of physical bodies, didn't make it out of the cage. It smacked against the plexi-glass and slid down a little bit. Then came another lob, and another lob, and another lob until a good portion of the window – directly in front of Christian's face – was covered in the sticky, brown mess.

It sure looked like shit, and that made Christian stifle yet another tremor at the thought of the smell in the cage and the crap that must now be caked to the Great Beast's fingers and hands. The mess would have cemented itself underneath his fingernails. Thank God, Christian still hadn't had anything to eat. Like with a man just bearing witness to his oldest friend dead on a chair in front of a still turned on TV set, it wouldn't have remained in his stomach much longer. Anything there would pour out across the hardwood floor, lap at his friend's cold, bare feet.

The Great Beast stepped off his stool again – his hands a brown mess. Christian flinched, but the Great Beast walked slowly, stately, this time… no manic charge to his gait. He nonchalantly strolled up to the window and touched his dirty finger to his forehead to daub a bit of the blood left over from his head-butt. Then, he stuck his finger against the glass, into the shit.

On the pane of glass, through the brown mess, drawn in blood, the Great Beast made a five-pointed star, a pentagram to appear. He started drawing a shape inside the pentagram. It started with a curve following the lines of the top-most point. For some odd reason, Evius snorted a quick laugh. And after a glance in his death defying guide's direction, Christian looked back at the Great Beast to see, inside the pentagram, the would-be yogi had imprisoned the image of the figure of a man. Hastily drawn, it retained all of Michelangelo's imperfections. One arm reached to either of the points pointing off to the infinity of the number line's infinite sides. One leg reached to each point holding the star aloft. Genitalia were succinctly in place where all lines come together – much like in the living figure of the image of a man.

"Figures," Evius chuckled, "We've got another da Vinci on our hands. A wizard... of the highest order, I suppose," and with a circular flourish of his right hand Christian's guide mockingly tipped forward at the waist to drop his neck and hang his hair in front of his seemingly sculpted face. "Re-naissance always deserves a bow," Evius explained.

For his part, Christian didn't quite understand what his companion might be referring to, and he certainly couldn't discern the true purpose behind the bow (even whether or not it might not be in earnest), but he found himself entranced, mesmerized by the Great Beast's manipulations of the blood and shit.

There was a hint of the multi-dimensionality of Pablo's earlier painting-in-progress from the basement of Christian's old home in Machpelah. There was a remnant from all the madness thus far experienced throughout Christian's journey amid the afterlife. As if the Great Beast were somehow characterizing that entire journey by means of one artistic product. In fact, not only did the representation seem to characterize the last day or two days or... it seemed to characterize the entirety of the young man's unfortunately conscious existence up to that moment in time – from birth till wherever he was in between the journey from Machpelah to Pandemonium. And for that reason, for some strange reason, it made Christian miss his home in that far away, once upon a time town – not where he had killed himself, but rather where he prayed his mother still resided in seeming obliviousness to the fate that had befallen her once so-loved only begotten son.

For his part, the Great Beast appeared in rapt concentration. His forefinger trembled ever so slightly as he painstakingly completed his diagram. His lips pursed as he reveled in the quite authentic detail of a tiny, little scrotum hanging above the point of two points like a pit atop a pendulum above a treetop bed rocking him off to sleep. His masterpiece done, the Great Beast, apparently in order to admire the work, stepped back from his portrait. He cocked his head to the side, put one stained finger to the side of his nose, and again, from behind the blood and shit smeared art gazed purposefully into Christian's mind.

From out his eyes attached to that very same mind, Christian finally noticed how kind the Great Beast's own eyes actually were. Envisioning them, he'd pictured them set on fire by rage and hate, but they weren't. They sparkled with tears that hadn't yet cried themselves away. *Do you love me?* they seemed to ask. *Do you love my painting?* Christian shook his head. He couldn't answer that question. "*Speak to me,*" he found himself whispering.

From his side, a short laugh turned into the question, "What?" and Christian realized only his guide had heard him.

"No-nothing," Christian mumbled.

"Oh," Evius chuckled, "I thought you asked me to freak with you, and I was all like: *I know we're friends and all, but I don't fly that way, if you know what I mean.* I thought you might have misrepresented my birds-of-a-feather statement from eons ago, and I was thinking... well, nevermind what I'm thinking. You didn't say anything."

But as Christian turned to hear Evius' last words, for a brief moment, he saw his guide's eyes *were* set on fire by rage and hate. However, as soon as Evius noticed his companion gazing at him, those very same eyes appeared to soften into the same question the Great Beast's eyes asked. It must have been a trick of the light... or lack thereof. Christian imagined himself gazing into a mirror. He must have looked too long and too hard at that mirror because, somehow, he gave life to something like its thoughts, and it shouted words that had no air to breathe: *"Look at me! If you want to know what's true, if you want to know what's real, then look at me!"*

"I don't think I really want to know."

"Yes, you do. If you didn't, you never would have stayed."

"I didn't want to. I tried to leave, but you trapped me."

"You trapped you."

"I want to go to sleep."

"How do you expect to sleep when you'll never look at me?"

"I'll close my eyes and let my thoughts fade into nothing."

"How can you escape what you'll never face?"

Was he coming up with those thoughts? Did he put those words into his mind? Or was it the Great Beast, was it Evius, who implanted such thoughts into his head. Stranger things had happened. Why, just the night before (or was it two nights before?), Thelonious Monk seemed to have performed such a feat of mysticism upon Christian by means of his silently stared at piano solo. Dear God, whose thoughts were in his head? Where did any of those thoughts come from? Was he an autonomous being, or was he subservient to another's mind? God... who thought for him? *Jesus, who am I?* Christian didn't know. He looked away from Evius' steady stare. He didn't greet the Great Beast's gaze.

Instead, he glanced down at his own vomit-spattered shoes, his seeming household gift from the gods. For a second, he wondered what kind of painting he could make if he were to scrape the vomit off those once-so-nice leather half boots. Then, those same half-boots looked like nothing more than a pair of beat-up, old, black sneakers, and for some strange reason unknown to him, Christian wanted to cry.

Unaware of what he was doing, Christian bent over. He reached to his shoes, and he picked a fleck of vomit off them. With his middle finger, he pressed the tiny chunk of vomit against the glass, against the forehead – as if it were Shiva's third spiritual eye – of the man in the great beast's painting. As if the painting were done in Hebrew, Christian suddenly saw it staring backwards out of a mirror of the world into the Great Beast's cage. It was emblazoned in gold. He met the Great Beast's saddened gaze. And again, for some strange reason still unknown to him, Christian wanted to cry. He couldn't handle looking at the man in the cage any longer. He couldn't endure what he was seeing any longer.

Almost silently – so quietly even Evius right next to him couldn't hear the words, Christian mumbled (as if it were an incantation), "I wish I could ask you your name. I wish I could at least ask you your name because now, I can't cry it out. Now, I can't catch your attention and let you see what you're doing."

Charlie... Christian thought. Then, the Great Beast broke eye contact with the traveler. He started moving his hands in a manic manner.

"Let's get out of here," Evius said, tugging at Christian's ripped sleeve.

But Christian didn't want to go. He wanted to stay. The motions of the Great Beast's arms and fingers appeared some sort of simian sign language, and for a brief second, Christian thought if he stayed still for long enough, the madman's digital ramblings might make some semblance of sense to him. He wanted the man to make sense. He wanted to know what was happening, what this was all about. For some reason, the naked man in the cage drawing in his own blood in his own excrement seemed like the one who might be able to provide Christian with the answers.

"Christ, man," Evius, still tugging at Christian's shirt sleeve, increased the mania in his own tone, "Let's get the *fuck* out of here... if for no other reason than to get *you* to stop acting like an idiot, child."

It was then Christian realized his middle finger was held against the glass, a piece of vomit cemented to its tip tight against the backside of a bloody, shitty piece of art. "What the fuck?" he mumbled. There was something in his mind about gold and Hebrews. As if he were now aware a snake hid under the rock he was trying to escape from the world beneath, Christian got control of himself and snatched his finger from the glass. He set the rock back on top of the baby copperhead, and the poor child never even had to contemplate a bite.

Immediately, the Great Beast's mania dissipated. Rejection took its place. If Christian had been paying attention, he would have noticed all the light in the man's eyes went out as he returned to his stool, climbed back up into his unstable equilibrium, and criss-crossed his legs again in mimicry (mockery?) of the foundation supporting the world. But Christian wasn't paying attention. With another short laugh from Evius, and the off-handed comment from his guide of, "Now, *that* was fucking weird... and I don't mean in the sense of Norse gods and all that. I don't think so at least..."

Christian, now shaking his head, began following Evius' footsteps down the sewer trail again.

Alone inside his cage, the Great Beast narrowed his eyes. He focused on a point in the air just in front of the tip of his nose, and after a few deep breaths while rocking steadily from side to side, his body grew erect, and his breathing settled into a shallow pattern. Walking away from the assumed serenity of the man's cage, Christian was completely unaware of the fact he still had a dried chunk of vomit stuck to the very tip of his middle finger. Without realizing it, he wiped that finger across his face and left it sitting in the very middle of his forehead – as if it were Shiva's third spiritual eye. That same dried chunk of vomit.

"You got something on your face, man," Evius said.

"Oh," Christian off-handedly muttered, and with a quick wipe, he wisped the chunk of vomit onto the sewer's floor to be lost amid the dust and debris of nothingness.

"You're good," was all Evius had to say about that.

9.
So There Are Three Doors...

For all intents and purposes, it appeared the tunnel the two travelers had been traveling through on this most recent leg of their respective journeys came to an abrupt end. Unfortunately for Christian (or perhaps fortunately for him considering the terrors he would have had to return through in order to re-traverse the path he had already traversed), the dried up sewer didn't end with a wall. There was no point at which Christian could say, *Well, my friend, it appears we've gone far enough. Let's just end it here.* And the two of them could have sat still, seated in cross-legged positions, for all of eternity. No. Instead, Evius and Christian were greeted by the closed fronts of three red doors – each studded with black metal dots as if they were the entrance points to some sort of tribunal of heavy metal prisons.

"Damn," Evius said, "I can never remember which one we're supposed to go through." And he stood still, shocked into torpor by the triumvirate.

Nervous at the suggestion and trembling at his very own words, but not sure what other insights he could offer, Christian countered with, "Why don't you just open one and look?"

Quite out of character, Evius appeared, this time, shocked. He stuttered, "But-but you have no idea what's on the other side of the wrong one."

"Haven't you chosen the wrong one before?"

Evius shook his head. "I don't think so," he said. "But still, if I can't remember, you've definitely got an idea." He reached towards the one on the far left. But before pulling the knob, he said, "Wait a second. It's your first time here, and besides, it's your idea. You choose. I'm petrified of my mistakes."

"Petrified of *your* mistakes? I have *no* idea which one is right."

"Neither do I."

"But you've been here before."

"What does that matter?"

"You must have *some* idea."

"Come on, Christian, you saw what we had to go through to get here. Do you really believe I can ever remember *anything* about this place?"

Standing still for a moment, realizing Evius wasn't going to act, and contemplating what he would have to return through if he didn't want to either sit for all eternity at or bash his brains out against (still with no guarantee he might die) a concrete wall, Christian swallowed. He pointed at one of the three identical red doors studded with black metal dots.

And Evius opened it.

9.(x)
Behind Door #2:
Who Turned out the Lights?

Staring into an apparent abyss. "I think I'm going to head on in."

Christian couldn't believe what Evius was saying. What had happened to the man's previous trepidation? As far as Christian was concerned, via Evius' recollection of the gargoyles' koan, they'd already discussed the "haunted house" prospect, and although he hadn't said so explicitly, Christian was fairly certain at the very least he'd *implied* he didn't have the fortitude to enter one no matter what the situation. That was all Christian was able to think, though, before Evius disappeared across the threshold and into oblivion.

For Christian, a moment to consider: monsters, bridges, Joshua, the Great Beast, and all that waited for him if he could even find his way back out of that maze his guide had led him through. Or else, nothing. Truthfully, there was no choice to make (if he'd had a little more courage, he could have tried a different door, but...). Christian steeled himself and followed the one man who claimed he was his best friend. Which was actually quite funny because Christian hadn't had a best friend – or a friend of any sort for that matter – for at least as long as Evius had made it sound as if he'd been without one as well. With his eyes closed, Christian prepared himself to fall headfirst into a leap.

But he didn't fall. In fact, he didn't even stumble. Rather, his foot landed on packed dirt, and once through the door, light appeared. Not a great deal of light, but still... light.

What the light shone upon was another cage, but this one differed considerably from that of the Great Beast. Rather than a postmodern, plexi-glass prison cell designed to discipline and punish, this one appeared to have been lifted from a medieval dungeon whose purpose was not to confine the soul of its inhabitant but rather his or, as the case may be, *her* body. Thick, rusted, metal bars stretched from floor to ceiling. They descended into the dirt floor and ascended into the apparently earthen, dripping (Christian wondered if maybe they were now *under* the disgusting river of discharge they'd had to drink from) ceiling. And behind the bars, this time, was a woman, but a quite unordinary woman.

She wasn't one of the inhabitants of the stream Christian had almost lost himself to. At least, she wasn't one of the inhabitants who had initially beckoned him to join her, but she might have been one of the inhabitants after they'd revealed their true selves. Seated on a falling-apart wooden stool a mere few inches from the thickly corroded bars, with her head downcast, the woman's body was easily as enticing as the café siren's, known to others as Zoe. But completely nude, she appeared an ocean, an entire expanse revealed of blue flesh.

Her breasts, her thighs, her legs, her neck were as deep a shade of aqua as if she were a drowned mermaid became one with her watery home. In contrast to her flesh, spinning Kandinsky's color wheel (a feat Pablo might have been quite excited about), her hair was bright red – as if her brain had ignited the top portion of her head and set her mane afire. She turned her face towards the two travelers.

The shape of her jaw was majestic. The purple cut of her diamond eyes was magnificent. As if she had just arisen from the river Styx itself, had just dragged herself out of that artistic canal, her hair plaid back like an angry horse's ears – beauty of the truest, most horrific kind, a model for Hollywood's darker visions, the type of beauty imprinted upon Christian's mind since long before he had ever been aware of such a concept. If her skin tone hadn't possessed the shadow of death itself, Christian might have found himself twittering again in her presence, as he had done in the wake of every female's stage-entrance since arriving at Gilles and Jean-Francois's café in Machpelah.

Unfolding at least six feet, the woman stood up to her full height. As his eyes opened wide, flowers budded on the TV screen of Christian's mind. The woman opened her mouth for what appeared a scream, but no sound escaped her cavernous lips. Instead, her mouth revealed a tongue split and forked down the middle like a snake's complete with non-retractable fangs that, like the bars she was trapped behind, reached from the top of her palate to the bottom. As the silent scream entered her lips, they began trembling ever so slightly. The unescaping air traversed her throat, which sent it into a shiver. It entered her lungs, and her torso convulsed violently. The trembling spread through her flat stomach to send her hips into a gyration sending each leg twirling as if a hula hoop were spinning down her body to end in tiny ripples spreading from her toes into the dirt floor. Christian was petrified.

But Evius mumbled, "Now, that's what I call hot," and he took a step towards the cage.

Christian reached out to grab the man's arm, but in a movement as fluid as if he were a master of kung fu dance in the midst of a subtle attack, Evius shrugged him off. "What are you doing?" Christian whispered. The man appeared in a trance comparable to the one Christian had entered by means of the visions creating his river beneath that bridge. *So this is how it ends…* Christian caught himself thinking.

Right then, though, the strangest thing appeared to be happening to the woman in the cage. Where her feet met the floor, where the gyrations seemed to culminate, the blue color of her skin began transforming. It began below her toenails and spread through each appendage into her feet.

At first, Christian thought it was a trick of the light. His hand outstretched, Evius was still walking forwards. His hands pinned to his sides, Christian was still standing in place – his own mouth mimicking the woman's. And for her part, the woman's mouth was still open in that silent scream, but around her soles and through her shins to drape her calves, her skin's drowned shade seemed to be transforming into a much livelier variation on an almost human pink.

Then, came the noise. It started in the stratosphere beyond the registers of human hearing. Although, if a dog had been there, that dog's howling might have alerted the potential sapiens listener to the coming aural intrusion. Like the big bang's background radiation leaking through a set of Bose speakers, its initial audibility was mild… at the edge of perception much in the same manner as the big bang still exists at the edge of our known universe. Then, the ringing dropped down in pitch and built in intensity. It contained the rush of a police siren's wail. It was a mild mourning. Then, the world's cry grew louder. As it eventually settled into Christian's brain, he realized it was actually the siren's call of the wailing blue woman who wasn't quite as blue as she'd appeared a mere moment before.

As the gyrations spread up her body, her color began to wobble more and more through the realm of human dimensions. Much like the river Christian had passed over before, it shifted subtly among the spectrum of the world's skin tones – Asian, European, African, American. Eventually, as her flaming hair devolved into a singular blonde, her skin, too, settled into a flavor approximating the healthy flesh of your average, suburban, North American princess enjoying her summer vacation of swimming and sun bathing. With her still in her nudity, Christian, enamored by her body's remaining perfection, was too impressed to notice Evius' hand falling on her bars. Much less did he notice the man brushing his fingers across her lock. In fact, (like any good American on a European vacation) he didn't notice anything other than her breasts until the cage door was open.

"What the fuck are you doing?" Christian shouted, and unbeknown to his own timidity, he lunged towards Evius and the now open cage door.

But when he realized where he was heading, with the memory of his earlier swim still fresh in his queasy stomach and mind, he stopped short.

The woman ran one hand up the length of the doorjamb, and her molten shape solidified against it. She cocked her head against her raised arm. The metal frame liquefied and filled in the gaps around her heat. She curled her tongue and cheeks and slid them around her words. "Come in," she breathed.

Evius shook his head. "I don't accept your invitation," he said, "But I'm coming in anyways."

"Are you..." but before Christian could finish his thought (is a thought ever truly finished?), Evius had crossed the threshold, while Christian, still reaching a strained arm towards him in order to save his jailer savior, stumbled in, through no fault of his own, behind him.

As Christian tumbled onto the hard earth at the feet of the woman's strange morphology, Evius mumbled, perhaps to himself, perhaps to her, "My companion, on the other hand, appears not to have entered quite of his own volition... I hope you won't hold that, at least, against him."

In replay of his awakening an eternity ago earlier that day, Christian found himself glancing across the cold ground to a set of feet. Only these feet weren't in masculine boots leading into a pair of jeans. Those were on Christian's other side, his blind side – as dark and unknown as one half of the full moon – behind his head. Rather, this set of feet were a pair of bare female feet, not as dainty as Confucius may have hoped for from his own lover's anciently broken toes, but still quite as enticing given the rapturous size of heel and arch. Each toe was long and thin, the nails as healthy and pink as the recently metamorphosed skin. With a flex, as if settling deeper into the earth itself, as if settling deeper into the body she had either chosen to exist within or she had been forced to inhabit, the transubstantiated woman stretched each toe one apart from the other and brought them back together.

Christian blinked. Like a child on the eve of a burgeoning Freudian foot fetish, he traced his gaze along the flatness of her arch up her ankle to her calf. Perhaps for the betterment of Christian's own mental health (perhaps not), there was no skirt leaving exposed the mere inkling of Victorian ankles. Rather, the calf ran straight up her thigh to precisely what Christian had hoped to find a million of waiting for him in a terrifying serpentine ocean. Whether or not that would cause a complex, only Freud could have told him (but that overly astute psychologist of the self, munching on his own penile fascination, had been left behind on the outskirts of Machpelah in an attic apartment where he was working through the intrigues of his newest set of thoughts (a quaint little volume with the working title of *Driven Beyond Death* – a volume Pablo couldn't wait to get a hold of)).

Either Freud would have told us Christian was on the verge of his newest complex, or he was ready to overcome us all – which very well may have been the same thing. Only time could tell, and as it does, it told quite quickly. With a nervous jerk, feeling the blood rush to his face, Christian brought himself back onto his own two feet...

For his own part, in the previous moment, Evius himself desired Christian's gaze. In fact, he would have embraced the situation.

Arisen yet again, Christian found himself out of breath – too many cigarettes, too many joints… hopefully. His heart was beating from falling, the exertion, the sight, quite literally – life. And in keeping with such a state, he didn't know quite what to do. He licked his lips, glanced over his shoulder, thought to escape from yet another terrifying predicament, but realized he had nowhere to go.

Truly. For, somehow, unbeknown to him, as he lay for what could only have been a moment on the ground, touring the magical woman's mystery, the metal gate he had entered through had closed seemingly of its own accord, which very well may have been for the best. There was nothing but blackest pitch on the other side. Appearing not quite as panicked as he actually felt, Christian reached for its latch only to find himself locked in with the entrancingly odd woman and Evius who merely said, "I figured we didn't have anywhere specific to be tonight."

His fingers slipping off the latch the same as they'd slipped off his own front doorknob so long ago, Christian glanced at Evius on his right. Shocked into his own torpor, Christian desired only to visit some act of unforgettable rage upon his guide… an act that would never materialize, an act that had been building ever since Evius had first asked Christian to pause, reconsider, and smoke that joint with him on the couch. Because Christian was certain it was his own trusted guide who had locked him into that nightmare.

Although, even that guide couldn't have been responsible for the nothing beyond the nightmare itself. Apparently in tune with that very impotence, perhaps via an imaginary omnipotence, Evius greeted Christian's disgruntled scowl with an immediate smile, one quickly turning into a wide-eyed statement, "Don't worry, I think she invited me in before... but as for you – have no fear, I *always* refuse."

Christian, however, didn't care about Evius' state of being. He had his own enkindled panic to contend with. But then – to the onlookers' surprise – the morphological woman herself opened her scrumptious lips. With honey dripping through the saliva creating a glistening sheen across her teeth, she asked, "What can I do for you?"

As the other half of a potential sandwich, Evius' own words sounded like peanut butter. Christian recalled the gargoyle's parables, "Well, I can think of a million things, but none of them are worthy of mention. Christian?"

Who was naturally dumbfounded the Amazonian beast could speak.

The tan, blonde (though previously blue, fire-maned) bombshell continued, "Then, why did you come here?"

Evius again asked, "Christian?" but when our hero, his jaw practically at his feet, still couldn't speak, Evius continued, "My friend appears a tad bit tongue-tied. So... let me just put forward the proposition that the two of us are a wee bit lost. You see, we were looking for Pandemonium when we stumbled upon you in your cage."

"Seek and ye shall find," the strange woman, still completely nude, said with all sincerity. But amid such sincerity, her voice retained a tonal quality making her sound – if Christian had been sitting in a darkened movie theater rather than experiencing death in all its Technicolor vivacity – like some sort of horror movie spoof. Given the immediate circumstances, however, the moment itself was more horror than spoof.

But our newest entrant from stage-nowhere was still saying, "But as you do follow me." And she turned on her bare heel to head deeper into what had previously been a washed out field of black but now appeared a room that was (complete with skirts for the tables' legs), on the one hand, exceedingly well-equipped for a Victorian era salon... bright, flame lamps even burned atop metal stands. On the other hand, the mutant's outfit (or lack thereof) was entirely inappropriate for such a supposedly repressive occasion. But dichotomy is always what makes life – or death – so fascinating. It's the antinomies themselves that keep us so intrigued with philosophy.

The woman herself was settling stiffly onto a couch. Unconsciously covering the lower half of her nudity, she politely crossed her legs at the knees. Her back she kept straight.

Across from her, upon a wooden table – with legs carved quite immaculately and a top inlaid with designs reminiscent of Pablo's own postmortem work, sat what Christian had needed so desperately in his journey, so desperately on the train: a clear pitcher of water. Smacking his dry tongue against the roof of his mouth as deserted as the desert they had wandered through, Christian gazed longingly at the life-giving liquid and at the three crystal wine glasses beckoning beside the pitcher.

The terror of the cage suddenly felt quite inviting.

In its patience, in its subtlety, water remains the most destructive of our five, natural elements. Fire burns, but of course, where there's smoke there's fire. Heat gives us warning. Water waits. It drips. It softens. And Christian wanted its Shaivic properties inside himself, filling his mouth, coating his esophagus, quenching his need... for life. For the first time in a long time, Christian hoped the clear liquid in the vessel *was* water and not the source of life's more sinister Russian cousin.

Oblivious to what Christian so desperately needed,

Evius, much as he had done in Christian's own ramshackle earthen dwelling, took a seat across from the water, across the table from the strange woman. He appeared intent on something in the woman's features – not, as Christian found himself intrigued when he glanced away from the pitcher, her body but, rather, her face. The would-be Virgil, who still had yet to recite a true poem, tilted his head to the side as he studied...

Christian, still staring longingly at the water and the glasses to be filled, took his own nervous place beside Evius' seeming stability.

The woman glanced at Christian, and as if reading his mind, pointed to the pitcher and the glass to drink. Christian didn't hesitate at the offer. The only one, he snatched a glass from its place. As his hand slipped from the mouth, a sonorous ring sang through the hall, and he poured into the crystal glass a full amount of crystal liquid. He began to drink. The water filled his cheeks. It dripped out of his mouth, across his shirt, and into his lap. He filled the glass once more and drained it yet again. Cooling his insides, washing his soul, the Lethean floods relaxed the thoughts that had tortured him when he was imprisoned in the train.

Evius turned to look down on his right. He shook his head, and he continued to speak, "Too bad there's yet to be a way for you to share your artistic predilections, my dear Christian."

But now, there was. For, at that very moment, as Christian set the twice drained glass back on the table (did the drink cause it to materialize?), as he looked up, he saw shimmering beyond the strange woman's head what appeared to be a magnificently long, ebony grand piano.

As the musical monstrosity glowed in the soft lighting like a beast in a forest clearing, the water was forgotten.

Like the introduction to a tale, it stated nothing but implication. Like a minimalist piece of composition, it contained all its magic hidden in its own simplicity. Like a metaphor, it made sense of mystery.

Evius didn't seem to have noticed the instrument. He was reaching into his pocket, staring at the previously blue woman, and carrying on in his manic way, "Hey, you guys wanna smoke some pot?"

But for the first time since his adventure began – maybe it was the water allowing him to do so – Christian *was* paying attention. He shook his head, *No*. Evius appeared a tad confused at Christian's unprecedented reaction, but something else had finally captured the addict's mind. It had been so long since the tips of his fingers had graced the majesty of those keys that he had to… It had been so long since he'd created anything other than another brick in a wall that he just had to.

His burning throat satiated, Christian stood up.

Evius stared – dumbfounded.

The woman, seemingly intrigued, curled a corner of her lip up in a smile. She turned the perfection of her neck to look over her shoulder, and she whispered, "Be very wary of fairies bearing gifts."

"That's right," Evius said, "Never accept a gift from a fairy… but it may be a little late for that, Christian. Christian?" Evius shook his head as Christian walked around the white couch the woman was seated upon. Apparently not caring at this point in our story, Evius shrugged, "He never pays attention anyways." And he whispered to the woman, "I never caught your name."

Shrugging as well, the strange woman said, "Call me Belle. Because every time I chime another fairy gets her wings," the newly-denominated "Belle" added with a lively wink.

"Did you hear that?" Evius said to nobody since, now, Christian definitely wasn't listening again. But still, Evius asked, with a somewhat defeatist quality to his voice, "Christian?" But when his charge still didn't respond, Christian's afterlife tour guide simply stated, "Well then, I'll be sure not to ring your knocker, my dear, because I certainly hate fairies. If there's one thing we don't need on this plane, it's any more of those pesky buggers. I swear, in some places, they're as thick as flies." Evius said. With a swipe of his hand in front of his nose, he closed by adding, "Wish I could say the same for my friend. But he's so unpredictable... or... maybe he's predictable, it's just the world he's enmeshed within one can't predict. I don't know. Really, it all beats the hell out of me."

With a slight smile, Belle said, "That's the best way to be beaten."

Simply sighing, given his apparently repressed desire, Evius shifted his weight and said, "You sure drive a hard bargain, little dearie."

"Maybe I just like to tinker," Belle added with a wicked wink.

Evius shook his head in something like exasperation.

Christian remained oblivious to the entire exchange – though it might have cast some light on the darkness of his future situation. But since he hadn't reached his future yet, he basked in his present's glow.

For the first time since his journey in those now vomit spattered leather shoes that fit so tight and snug around his ankles had begun, for the first time since he had fixated (and asphyxiated) himself on that hole in his ceiling, for the first time since he had wrapped and re-wrapped that rope around his hand, he was focused on one thing only, settling onto the leather bench and touching his fingers to the coast of ivory keys. He believed he could open worlds with those keys – even if the worlds were only in himself, even if nobody else experienced what he felt, even if his emotion itself was incommunicable... as the commentators on the recital he had given for his rejected entrance into graduate school had told him.

He still remembered that day. Even death couldn't erase *that* disappointment. A screw twisted in Christian's gut. He would play...

Pulling the piano bench back from where it sat underneath the keyboard, with a fluff of his non-existent tux tails, he sat down, bent his arms, placed his foot over top the damper pedal, arched his wrists, and set his fingers on the keys.

But right before he began to play, as he scanned the length of what would soon be his musical canvas, he noticed, out of the corner of his eye, a tiny plastic baggy of beautifully enticing white powder placed next to the highest of highest keys. It looked so forlorn there, white against the black piano. All the way up there, it appeared lost and looking for an owner. Packed into the plastic, it seemed thicker than it actually was. Heaped atop itself, it appeared an almost single substance rather than individual grains, and the burgeoning tickle in the back of Christian's throat told him it certainly wasn't flour, by God. There wouldn't be any cooking done with this shit... unless it was to merge the chemical's combination to baking soda's. Christian licked his lips. He knew he had to be the lost, little powder's possessor (or was it, rather, he had to be possessed by the lost, little powder?).

Either way, he glanced quickly in the direction of Evius and Belle. They appeared engrossed in a conversation all their own. Without making a sound, Christian slid his hand up the keyboard's length, grabbed hold of the little baggy with his fingertips, and nestled it tightly into where it belonged – his own jeans' tight pocket – while wondering if Belle had a bathroom where he could go snort the shit.

Christian glanced in every direction: nothing but unending, unadorned white walls. His heart pitter-pattered in his chest as if the cocaine were already up his nose, but since it wasn't, he knew that emotion was panic... or excitement... or desire... but not bliss. How strange that the same physical sensation in one instance is so desirable, in another, so not. Maybe, then, there's more to this body than just simple, physical stimulus-response mechanisms. Maybe there's such a thing as... we don't even have a name for it (but how could we name a completely intangible "_____" – language needs a referent). Regardless, Christian took a deep breath and set his fingers on the keys to play.

From the ebonies and ivories, the tones should have sung a tune to the mind. They should have painted the walls with their unmistakable sound of hammers striking strings. Frederic Chopin should have tinkled through the room. His unmistakable, nocturnal solitude should have disturbed the two interlocutors engrossed in their oddly flirtatious conversation. The two talkers should have been looking up to see where the beautiful melody emanated from.

But, instead, where there should have been song there was silence. Where there should have been music, there was the muffled madness of Christian's own empty brain, the blindness of his own uncomprehending eyes. To him, the keyboard appeared something he'd never seen before. This instrument that for so long had been a desired piece of his life (that through so many a snowblind night he'd wished to sit at the feet of and play once again), he suddenly had no idea how to make work. What was the white? What was the black? Where was the tool to create the sound? What are you doing with that beast in here?

It must have been because of the water. It must have been something in that drink... What was in it? What *was* it?

Unbeknown to even his own consciousness, Christian's fingers began tapping, as if it were the solidly cooked embodiment of the powder in his pocket, on the white. Over and over and over again, one single note at a time, he tapped a simple melody. He couldn't remember the notation for the sound. He had no idea what it said, no idea what it meant. He unconsciously cried from the depths of his soul as Evius' apparently perfectly pitched ears deciphered the tune's notation: A-B-B-A, A-B-B-A, A-B-B...

Evius, exiting his own engrossing conversation for a mere moment, said, "Nice progression, my friend, but I have to tell you, if you want to unseat Monk, you're going to have to do better than that. Honestly, I don't think music's really your calling. What else did you say you did?"

Christian mumbled something, but at the moment, he appeared as apparently unable to form words as he was to create music. In fact, in all actuality, he didn't even hear Evius' voice quite right. At least, he couldn't remember there being any meaning behind the seemingly vocal sounds that had just echoed across the room. And this time it had nothing to do with his own broken attention span. Instead, it had more to do with the empty hollow of his mind. He couldn't have heard Evius even if he'd cared to.

It was like Christian was in an alcohol-free blackout *(Hallelujah,* he might have thought had he still had the power of thought): the moments happened, but he had no recollection of them. If he still were in the midst of a physically reductionist plane, the scientist would have told him, at the moment, his synapses weren't properly recording his memories. In fact, all they were recording was the moment necessary to make his heart beat, his lungs breathe. But Evius didn't care. Lost in his own momentary absorption, his lessons for Christian were forgotten as soon as he appeared to have more pressing business in dissecting the internal workings of the once-upon-a-time foul, but now quite fair creature the two of them had so recently encountered but that only one of them had the desire to put up on the table to tinker with in an actual vivisection – in order to get to the root of the labyrinth's mysteries.

Lost entirely in the moment, Christian looked over his shoulder. And there, right there, there appeared a door. A door to what? *The bathroom*, Christian's mind calculated. *Remember what's in your pocket, Christian*, the unobservable observer told him. *Get up and move towards that door. Use your hands to push yourself up and pry your ass off this boring seat. Use your hips. Move your fucking legs. Step. There you go. Move one leg, now the other. Step. Step. Left. Right. Left. Right. That's right, boy, just keep walking. Keep moving. Follow me. Follow me deeper, eventually arriving to here.*

The doorknob was in Christian's hand. He twisted it ever so slightly. The lock clicked, the teeth loosened, and the portal opened: darkness on the other side, but every bathroom has a light. So once again, Christian stepped into pitch black. And once again, as Faith led the way, he didn't fall. Yes, once again, he didn't even stumble. Onward, Christian soldier. Instead, he stepped onto…

At which point, with a disappointed shake of his head, Evius politely excused himself from their most inviting host with the polite statement, "I would love to stay and continue tinkering with your knocker, Belle, but duty calls, and I must retrieve my charge from the devil knows what. Christian? Christian. Damn it all to hell. Christian."

And soon, with a grin lifting the side of her lip, which

was rapidly transforming from the liveliest pink to the deadliest blue, as Evius disappeared through the door that had just appeared in her otherwise unending, unadorned white wall, Belle unfolded her rainbow-hued nudity from the couch, snapped her fingers, and plunged into darkness herself.

Who turned out the lights?

9.(y)
Behind Door #1:
No. Really. Who Turned out the Lights?

No. Really. Who turned out the lights? Evius suddenly caught himself wondering as he stepped through the door and could no longer find his way back to ring Belle's lovely knocker, which, unbeknown to the two travelers was actually the exact same thing Christian was thinking – not about Belle, but rather about the lights. Did one of them speak the separate words out loud in order to put the other's unitary thought into the one's mind? Or was there only the one mind controlling the other's two? Which was it? Was that mind controlling me? Was it controlling you?

Then, somebody flipped the switch. The world flashes red. A perspective painting appeared –

Soft lighting at the gilt edges… On a plush couch with feet of silver unicorn hooves, and the crescent head of a horned moon… two women reclined. One woman's legs – clad in black leather tight beneath her white, frilled shirt – stretched across the red satin upholstery to end in feet imprisoned by hard stiletto heels. The other woman, from her choked neck to her tight-fitted ankles in leather as well, rested her head in her mistress's lap. With a wrist of silver jewelry, the raven-maned mistress stroked the seemingly younger woman's shock of short, magenta hair. Both women wore what was presumably eyeliner stretching their occidental eyes into oriental shapes. Both: their hair cropped short, red and black (*In the beginning, there were two*...), blown into twisted halos atop their heads.

Then, as the magenta one blinked and revealed the green irises hidden beneath her lids, Christian started in place. He had seen her milky flesh before. In Machpelah... in the woods beyond Machpelah. A cold panic seeped through his limbs as he realized he had nowhere left to run. He was stuck, confronted by the woman who had possibly made love to the real beast who had trundled along beside him up the mountain bellowing smoke, the woman who (apparently, once upon a time) had introduced herself to Christian's former roommate James as "Zoe".

Gulping, Christian reached into his pocket to feel what had become of his sole source of comfort: the little baggy of what appeared to be cocaine. Shocked, he found it wasn't there. He reached deep as if he were a miner seeking a mineral far more precious than gold. But only nothing was there... not even an empty pack of cigarettes, only imprisoned air. His heart sped up faster. His mind raced harder. He felt short of breath. He broke out in a cold, cold sweat. He... (might as well have already snorted a mound of the purest of cocaines).

Intruding upon Christian's solipsistic panic, Evius stepped up beside the sober addict already overdosing on a yet-to-be-ingested substance and addressed the couch's pair of carefully writhing vixens, "Well, at least one of you appears familiar, but I don't think any of us have yet had the opportunity of being properly introduced. I apologize for the rudeness of my friend's apparent loss of speech – I'm sure it's simply from a lack of heavy substances. You can call me Samuel," Evius ended, which sounded familiar to Christian, but the poor lost soul, in the very midst of his death, couldn't quite place his deja-vu.

To which the mistress of the game responded, "I don't know if I want to know your name," and without a pause in stroking her long, black nails through her partner's hair, she added, "In fact, I don't even remember asking."

Which stopped Evius short, but a smile slid across his lips and toyed with his five o'clock shadow as he cocked his head to the side, "I don't know if you know quite what you asked or when you asked it," he said, and, in his turn, he added while pointing to his own partner, "This is Christian. It's not his religion, just his name. Confusing, I know."

The one Christian recognized as Zoe reached her arm up to cup her psychic's palm behind her mistress's head. She pulled the mane of black hair down towards her shock of red, and with a stretch of her neck, she whispered into the woman's ear...

Smiling and widening her delectably blue eyes, the mistress said, "For your part, you can call me Vesper. And my dear friend here says you already know her as Zoe."

"Actually, I don't think I do, but now that you mention it..." Evius tipped his head to the side as he spoke, "Maybe I do. Only the devil knows. Regardless. We're sorry to intrude upon your little world, Zoe, Vesper, but, you see, we're trying to make our way to Pandemonium, and my friend here stumbled through your door while looking for what I can only assume was the bathroom while we were being entertained by a lovely lady who goes by... what the hell did she call herself again? Oh well. Nevermind."

Vesper smiled quite devilishly. "Well, that's easy enough," she said. "The door to Pandemonium is right over there." She pointed straight ahead of herself, to Christian's and Evius' left.

As they turned to follow where her finger pointed, to not be confused by the sign for the thing-in-itself, Evius and Christian were greeted by the closed fronts of three red doors – each studded with black metal dots as if they were the entrance points to some sort of tribunal of heavy metal prisons. "But which one is the right one, I can't quite recall," Vesper finished amid Zoe's stifled giggles. And Christian's heart sunk still further into the ocean of his drowning emotions than it had already immersed itself when he had realized – amid the terrible panic of recognizing the murderess of Joshua's aged desires – somehow his gram of blow had disappeared.

"I've an idea," Zoe suddenly piped up while sitting up from her mistress's lap. She scooted forward on the divan and crossed her leather-clad legs at the knees before continuing, "One of the two of us might be able to tell you which one is the one you want… if only you can ask that one of us the right question."

"And what sort of question might that be?" Evius quickly queried.

To which, with a shake of her head, Zoe immediately responded, "Nope. That's not it."

As Vesper added to the stakes of her friend's wager, "Well, there's one down. Careful, now. You only get so many tries before we decide to send you through the wrong one entirely."

"And you know what's waiting on the other side of *that* one," Zoe concluded. And Christian may have been wrong, but amid his panic, he could have sworn – he would have staked his soul upon it – she winked at him.

Go ahead, you supply the mythological symbolism's compass for a change. There are only so many answers left in Zoe and Vesper's game, and like the bunch of trapped animals we are, we've got to get out of this place.

At which point, right on time, Evius wondered out loud, "What do you think it feels like to die?"

Intuiting his question was perhaps meant for her, Vesper retorted, "It feels better than being alive. But still, wrong."

Her response brought a nod from Evius but due to his own selfishness, it only turned Christian's stomach yet again as he mumbled out loud, "This is crazy."

To which Zoe responded, "That's not it either," and she smiled, "Careful, my dears, you're both running out of time."

"Wrong," Evius laughed, "That's only if time runs forwards, and we both know, existentially, time *actually* runs in the direction we might call backwards."

Zoe scrunched up her eyes, "That's merely a result of either analysis or paralysis, but on the other hand... who's the both? You and him or you and me or you and her?"

Like the Buddha making a point, like a cross-legged Christ on an Orthodox church ceiling, Evius pointed one finger towards the heavens, and he said, "Now, you know you'll never find out from us which door is the right one if you keep asking silly questions like that."

Vesper frowned and shook her head, "Even infinity has an end, my friend. As for you, wrong again."

Apparently being careful not to speak the words that might be misconstrued as the end of time, Zoe looked at Christian confused. *Aren't you?*

While Evius pointed out, "The ladies seem to have forgotten infinity can be construed as nesting in sets. In which case..." As he had done so often when Christian had first met him, Evius finished by rhetorically lifting one shoulder to drive his point home – as if he'd spoken one of the good-natured gargoyle's favored koans.

A thought that caused Vesper to shake her black mane.

She said, "You'll never get to where you're trying to go with statements like that. Because if there are smaller infinities inside larger infinities, then this infinity itself must have an end."

"The point at which parallel lines meet."

"Infinitely wrong again!" Zoe shouted.

Suddenly, Christian, insanely shaking his head, broke his nearly catatonic silence. He covered his eyes with his hands, and he shouted from between the megaphone created by his forearms, "Stop it! Will you all stop it?!"

Silence settled over the hotly debated infinity of the room... Carefully standing up, Zoe slowly walked over to Christian. One foot in front of the other, she put a soft hand on his vexed shoulder. As Christian manically ran a hand through his unwashed hair, she smiled sweetly at his contorting face, and she said to him, "Sorry. But that isn't the right question either." And she dropped her hand back to her side, doubled over in a fit of laughter, slapped her knee, and returned to her seat at the simultaneously smiling Vesper's feet.

Christian didn't know how to make heads or tails out of any of it... as if he were playing with a kitten that had been cut in two and the pieces simply wouldn't hold together being already hacked into such a bloody mess. But then again what sort of heads or tails had he made of anything since first being introduced to Machpelah? For that matter, what sort of heads or tails had he ever made out of his life on earth? The cat he played with was, of course, neither alive nor dead inside Schrodinger's famous box. Instead, it was severed into two horribly separate pieces – one that fit into each separate hand, two halves writhing in painful spasms as death croaked a purr out the severed lungs of its aching throat.

"I think what my friend was getting at," Evius casually

explained to the two laughing ladies, "Is the rules of your game seem awfully – how should I say... malleable? I know, wrong again... And, no doubt, to your histrionic benefit."

"Quite right, was it – Samuel? But not right enough because it's not *our* game, it's yours," Vesper, quite soberly, responded as she, with the long nail of her little finger, wiped a humorous tear from her heavily made-up eye.

"Well, that's certainly one way of looking at it," Evius mumbled, in a muted tone so soft – given the lack of commentary from the women – only Christian could hear. In which case, the cat was most definitely alive. "But it's certainly not the only way." In which case, the cat was decidedly dead, but either way, at least (far beyond Christian's meager grasp), intact.

In fact, the whole situation was not unlike the afterlife thus far in its entirety – neither dead nor alive, simply "unknown". "From what source, then, do I derive my existence?" Evius asked.

"Why... the source is the origin, of course, but, of course as well, at the very least, 'origin' has two senses, in the sense of both the chicken and the egg. In other words, with respect to the source, does it precede or is it retrospective. Which came first, the cause or the effect? But the real question isn't about the source. Rather, it's about the origin: Is it this or that? Either way, you're still wrong."

"I could say the same for you – to both of your questions," Evius, appearing somewhat perturbed, responded. "But we're not getting anywhere in our little game. I've been flying blind. Christian, we need a new strategy for overcoming their defenses. From now on, I'll play the wingman. Try a new line of attack. Your responses are so much more invigorating than mine."

But Christian had absolutely no idea what to say. In

fact, he was at a complete loss. His eyes shot from Evius to the two women waiting for him on the couch, then back to Evius. He licked his lips, but no sound tripped off the curled tip of his tongue. He was so confused. Instead of sense, his mind experienced the same emptiness that had confounded him when confronted by Belle's magnificently grand piano. As Chopin was unable to speak then, the night remained silent now. All Christian could see behind his still open eyes was a scene from beyond the Paradise of Fools: a tree fallen across the hard ground, a smile drunk across a man's lips, a serpentine dagger flashing in a woman's hand, a heart beating through a monster's palm, a phallus pulsing from out the earth's womb…

Christian blinked. For a moment, the visions disappeared. He opened his eyes. Nothing had changed… except he'd found the words he wanted to say. He mumbled as if lost to himself: "Will I ever see Sophia again?"

On the couch, Zoe and Vesper glanced at one another. After a silent second, Vesper nodded. Apparently disappointed, Zoe shrugged, then spoke for the two, "That seems right to us." She sat up still straighter, "But there's one catch. We can't let you off that easily… not after so much foolishness…"

And Vesper picked up on Zoe's train of thought, "You see, we'll tell you which door is the right one, but we won't tell you which is the wrong one, which may wind up leading you in through the out door, as they say. Now, tell us – and this question is only for Christian, Samuel, the game's victor – which is more important: knowing what you want or knowing what you don't want?"

"Careful with this one, Christian," Evius whispered, "These women strike me as being more serpentine than the actual serpents we encountered earlier. Maybe it was all just a misogynist's metaphor to begin with…"

"Zip it, Samuel," Zoe cut in. Much more kindly, with wide eyes open at Christian, she continued, "It's his moment to shine, not yours."

Evius snarled as if he had encountered Theo the dog all over again, but still he bowed, with all the flourishes of politeness, to the enchantress.

There was no indigo glow emanating from Christian's moment, though. With a dejected sigh, he shook his head, and he said, "I don't really care," as if he were a man in the midst of the lull of a war, "I just want to know, truthfully, will I ever see Sophia again?"

"Sounds like you're a man who knows what he wants," Vesper smiled. "That's important for a man, I've heard. Too bad you didn't know what you didn't want. But listen closely, Christian, here's the trick. The door out is the only one in. Go on, then, thread the needle for a change. This one's all yours. What you're looking for lies behind door #4."

At those words, Christian glanced to his left. His lips moved silently. He said, "But there are only three doors."

"Exactly," Zoe responded, moving into a more excited and (to some observers) more exciting pose, "All you have to do is figure out which one is the fourth."

"But how can there be a fourth if there are only three?" Christian begged.

"Look," Zoe coldly responded, "We don't have the space or the time for the trinity's mystery right now. Instead, why don't you try, for a change, to find your own way out of the labyrinth?"

"Just watch out for the minotaur," Vesper giggled.

Which, Christian knew, meant he had to be quite careful. For, if Vesper were at all serious, he was certain he couldn't take another monster. Not at such a late point in this absurd, schizophrenic comedy of a lunatic laughing at insanity's own lunar surfaces. She rides side-saddle. Her toes point towards the earth she has escaped; her peaked hat a compass straight to the moon, her mistress, Luna.

With respect to that most precious of internal resources, his own sophistic sanity already stood barefoot, its head bent forward at the neck, its black eyes staring emptily into darkness, contemplating the descent at the edge of the precipice, gazing into something "other" than an existential abyss. He feared his mind alone was now the sole wanderer through the haunted house's madness. Those in front and behind (Gilles and Jean-Francois?) had already been picked off – at the toll of a bell – by some great beast of a ghastly sniper. Now, Christian's worse fear appeared to be coming true: whether he was with an*other* or not, his misdirected thoughts seemed entirely alone, alien even to themselves, petrified of whatever lurked around the next corner... at the top of the next page. If only he could understand the gargoyles' parables...

"Now, don't lose any sleep over it – not that you need to," Vesper continued. "As a man who knows what he wants... just leap – like I'm sure you've done a thousand times over again."

"Come on, Christian," Evius encouraged him, "Remember that story you told me..."

"What story?" Christian wondered.

"Exactly," Evius continued, "Well, this is just like that."

Christian shook his head, "I don't know what you're talking about."

"I do," Evius finished with a knowing nod as he retreated, like a vampire fleeing the sun, out of the foreground.

"I really don't understand," Christian, left alone in the spotlight, whispered as he touched his forehead as if he were suffering from a dehydrated headache, "And I just want to go home."

"Look, Christian… if that really is your name. For my part, I'm not convinced it is any longer, although there doesn't seem to be a more fitting moniker for a man of your description – it's simple," Zoe smiled quite kindly at him. Then, smiling still more broadly, she went on, "If you're scared of the minotaur (and why wouldn't you be?), just think of it like this: *Buffalo buffalo, Buffalo buffalo buffalo, buffalo Buffalo buffalo.*"

"What?" Christian, still shaking his head in disbelief, wondered.

Explaining precisely what her friend had in mind, Vesper continued, "The answer to your question: *Buffalo buffalo, Buffalo buffalo buffalo, buffalo Buffalo buffalo.* The trick is to catch the appositive."

"Sounds like a mathematical solution to me," Evius coolly piped up, like the demon sitting there, from over Christian's shoulder.

"Exactly," Vesper responded, making sense out of even Zoe's confusion to Evius' unprovoked insight.

"Think of it like this, Christian…" Evius began whispering in his friend's ear.

But before he could finish, Vesper shrieked, "No cheating, Samuel! It's his decision, let him make it! If you don't, I may turn you into a pup, a golden retriever, and I don't think you wanna be our dog. That requires too much devotion, I'm sure. Besides, you know what *they* say they'd do to a defenseless, little, dog – or was it god – in Pandemonium."

As Vesper turned her cold blue eyes into a freezing glance at Evius, the over-dead man, as if in the midst of a childhood game of hide and seek (if I can't see you, you can't see me), quickly crouched down behind the one he had led so far.

But Christian, visibly shaken, nervously wondered, "What do they say they do to dogs in Pandemonium?"

"Well, it depends," Zoe giggled, "But for the most part, it's an easy answer. *They* say they pop them right into a warm bun..."

"And slide them down their throats," Vesper finished, "But you know what 'they' say about what they say..." she finished with a knowing shrug reminiscent of Evius' trademark trick – for that mere second, she could have been his twin, developed inside the same egg... perhaps even with the same name. But we both know that couldn't possibly be the case. For, logically speaking, a man and a woman could never be the same, but if we invert one half of that simple statement (equation), such that, for example, $V = \Lambda$ and $L = \Gamma$, then, symbolically speaking of course, not only are we *speaking* Greek, but we also derive something entirely absent from both our original and our transitional metalanguages, something backwards, something inverted, something that could only be described (poetically) as $\aleph, \{\emptyset\}$. Wouldn't that be nice?

Christian, however, didn't have any such sophistical intricacies in mind. Instead, he was anxiously wondering whether or not he still wanted to go to Pandemonium, whether or not he'd made the right decision in those woods that night beyond where the woman he was now looking at had cut out the riddle called "James's" heart and fed it to her well-endowed behemoth – he should have been wondering whether or not he'd made the right decision in his broken-down bedroom while staring at the hole in his ceiling.

He replayed the incident in his mind. As if searching through underlined words in a novel open on a desk in front of him, he replayed everything that had happened from the moment his absurdist comedy began: Belle... the Great Beast... the bridge... Zoe... Sophia... the sparrow... What did it all mean?

The thoughts brought him to a point of such indecision that – as he shifted, with a frown upon his face, from one foot to the other – it appeared to those watching as if he had to go to the bathroom immediately, as if it were the case that if somebody didn't direct him to the alcoholic's well-worshiped porcelain god soon, a stain may spread down his leg much as it had down Joshua's all those eons ago on a café patio in Machpelah.

But would that really have been so bad? Most people consider age dignified.

Contemplating his seemingly immensely uncomfortable state, Zoe had to stifle yet another untimely laugh. Not feeling quite as humorous as her frivolous friend, Vesper coldly slapped Zoe's shoulder while shooting her a look that said: *cut it out – you're scaring him.*

And indeed she was. As if an immediate, unpredicted winter storm had hardened a summer stream of urine into ice, Christian's pee-dance-esque shifting of weight from one foot to the other instantly transformed into a rigid stiffness. He knew he had to make a decision, but he didn't know which one. He knew he had to get out of there, but he didn't know how.

"Maybe I can help you make up your mind," Zoe said.

Christian turned an unwanted glance in the women's direction. As Zoe smiled yet again, Christian noticed in front of her canines, where a set of incisors should have been, gracing her palate was, instead, a set of fangs. Had those always been there? Whether they had been or not, Zoe smiled still broader, proudly revealing her fangs in all their glorious horror. She slid her hand along the couch, closer to her waist, and as she started to push herself off the plush seat and towards the two travelers, Christian couldn't take it anymore.

Taking off at a sprint, he didn't even bother checking which door he pushed open. He simply knew he had to get out of there. It might even have been door #4. Anything, nothing, was better than Zoe and the terror she seemed to bring everywhere she went.

Like with the gargoyles, laughter once again greeted his exit. Christian leaped across another black threshold into darkness. This time, however, there *was* nothing there. He did fall. He spilled through the air much like he had when he had leaped off that bridge. He merely prayed, as he tumbled head over heels – screaming, he hadn't tripped and fallen in there yet again.

8.
Behind Door #4:
Lost in (Neither Time nor) Space

Christian must have passed out. Whether it was from the fear, from his own exhaustion, or from the forgotten comfort of floating through nameless space he could never know, but one thing was certain, Christian woke up with his cheek firmly planted on rough concrete. The possibility of abrasion hearkened to the depths of his every pore. There was nothing newly sore about him, however, which caused him to wonder whether he had actually fallen or not. Perhaps the whole sensation had merely been akin to that of one drifting off into the world of dreams: the sinking feeling in your stomach as you clutch at your sheets and your chest while wondering how close you are to the bed's edge. How one could sleep while tumbling through seemingly infinite space, Christian certainly had no clue, but the reality of his situation forced itself upon him. He was there, somehow unhurt, lying upon cold concrete.

For a moment, he caught himself thinking whether or not he was perhaps back in his economically-depressed Rust Belt city where he might have passed out behind the corner store after drinking his regular bottle of Wild Irish

Rose without the usual crack chaser. Maybe Zoe, Vesper, Belle, the Great Beast, Joshua, and the entire host of the afterlife's maddening encounters and characters had been nothing more than a twisted alcohol-fueled nocturnal emission. If that had been the case, then everything that was about to happen wouldn't have, and fewer questions would have remained. Instead, the glad tidings of, "Nice of you to rejoin us," spoken with the intonations of Evius' characteristic frivolousness lay all thoughts of that once-upon-a-time dream to rest.

Christian was numb. "Did we fall?" he asked.

"You could call it that," Evius responded with his usual cavalier verve. "But what difference does it make? Welcome to Pandemonium, Christian. You chose the right door. We finally made it." And, indicating he should look in the indicated direction, Evius tipped his head forward and added, "Well, maybe we didn't quite make it there, but at least we made it here."

A statement which, at first, Christian didn't quite understand, but as he raised his head and the rest of his body from off the concrete and as he rubbed specks of dirt and pebbles from his palms, forearms, and cheek while looking in the direction Evius nodded, he could understand what his guide meant.

Across a wide, black river over which a silhouetted suspension bridge arched, a gray field hung across pitch: clouds polluted by city lights. The fullest of full moons weaved in and out of the shifting cloudscape. Spires cut the nighttime sky out of which no stars shone. Something like New York or Tokyo or Hong Kong, but the shapes of these penetrating monstrosities were akin to nothing those skylines had to offer. Punching holes in the sky, towers coiled around one another like a thousand octopi writhing in a sea of weeds. Shining in lights of myriad horrific colors

– blood red, evening purple, and stolen silver, they toppled over top one another like row upon row of a shark's serrated teeth. From between the decaying masterpieces of stone and rock and steel, a glow, white as the deathly lights of a hospital's intensive care unit, shot upwards into what one would normally assume to be the heavens. Even from across the river, the screeches of cars and trains, the grinding saws of construction, the screams, shouts, and curses of human beings sliced through the air. A feeling of oppression and madness emanated from the city across the pithy river. Pandemonium – what it was called, and what it appeared.

"I can feel the city seducing me," Evius whispered. Christian turned a stunned glance at him. His guide's eyes glowed eerily, maniacally to Christian's fretful gaze. Then, as Evius stood up, he appeared, to Christian's amazement and fright, to have grown. He'd always been a little taller than his charge, but now he seemed to tower a whole head above him at least. Like a survivor of Auschwitz, Evius' cheeks had sunken still more than they had back on that path to the first bridge. His black hair had grown longer. It curled down to nearly his shoulders, which somehow now seemed a little hunched over. His whole gait shifted into an almost limp as he stepped forward and put one hand on Christian's shoulder. At which point, with a downwards glance, Christian noticed his guide's nails had grown longer, and they appeared a bit murky as if he'd clawed his way out of his own tomb.

But before Christian could check his most recent recognitions, Evius heaved a sigh and continued, "Can you feel it? I can't believe we finally made it out of that hillbilly, stick town... Machpelah," he spat out the syllables like they were so much bitter fruit, "I thought it would be the death of me. Not that that would be so bad... guess that's why I keep going back. Whatever. Took some wrong turns along the route, but what the hell? Like they always say, just turn left and don't go straight. The Earthly Paradise they call it? Hah! Pandemonium's so much more my style. Let's go."

With strides even longer than before, Evius set off. As always, Christian had no choice but to follow.

They were on the bridge, heading into a city Christian was no longer sure he wanted to visit, much less settle into for what could wind up being the entirety of his short eternity... which, in the end, is where we always settle. Perhaps if we looked at the world from that Epicurean vantage more often, we might not wind up in so many of the predicaments we often find ourselves in. Perhaps we wouldn't subject ourselves to whatever objective masters the world might muster: drugs, alcohol, pornography, ideologies, marketing – a slave's value system. Perhaps, then, we'd be authentically free, exercising that myth we've heard of since the moment of our first taste of forbidden fruits. Free will – which may or may not, in actuality, exist. But perhaps, then, we'd realize we need to live, not later, not tomorrow, but rather today, right now – our own masters.

Such a realization our dearest of dear friends, Satan (that Promethean figure), might have had in Heaven – floating amid peaceful eternity: tomorrow may never come. Perhaps, he left paradise to share his secret realization, like man's sacred passage of fire, with his one true love – humanity... if myths could only speak true. The future...

Suddenly, to Christian's eternally fried mind, Machpelah didn't appear quite so bad. A realization (like Adam's after tasting from the knowledge of good and evil) arrived at, yet again, too little, too late. He shook his head. Maybe, someday, he could apologize to those potential roommates... at least, to the ones left dead alive. He gulped.

For now, the miraculously retraumatizing bridge. It was quite different from the one crossed before, but the mere necessity of passing over a ravine that couldn't be traversed by foot sent Christian's mind reeling and his legs quivering. He'd been through too much both in his short life and in his much shorter death. It all weighed heavily on his supposedly threefold existence of mind, body, and soul. He thought of that photograph of the pensive girl once upon a time on his desk, now crumpled up on a dead man's floor. Sophia contemplating her descent. He thought of the rickety slates he'd had to cross once before (so different from the wide expanse he now set his feet firmly upon), of the rough rope rubbing against his sweaty, grasping palm, and of his own descent into… madness: the fall.

As foreboding as the other side – with its ominous towers and audible hints of terrors – may have appeared, the bridge itself, to Christian's surprise (such is the way of trauma) did not appear to cross over anything other than mere rushing water. To add to the oceanic illusion, however, the world – although overwhelmed by the odors of powerfully polluting chemicals – even smelled a bit briny after a few steps left the land behind. Evius inhaled deep the sooty scent, and with his exhale, he said, almost to himself, "Brine and smog. Styx… Smells of paradise to me. What do you think, Christian?"

"Sounds like L.A.," was all Christian could think to say.

"Yes, the City of Angels. Like I said, Paradise…" Evius responded, "Or Pandemonium. Same thing." He smiled and threw his arm over Christian's shoulder in the conspiratorial manner that had begun their journey, "Though our dear Styx flows a little stronger than their dry, concrete riverbed, I must say. So tell me, who wins?"

Shrugging Evius' arm off his shoulder, Christian

narrowed his eyes. He slowly turned his neck, and with an accusatory quality in his voice, he asked his companion, "When have *you* ever been to L.A.?"

"Well, that's a very interesting question," Evius coolly countered. "I don't know that I have. I think, maybe, I just heard about it..."

"Because I'm telling you. If you know a way out of this crazy place and back to the one I left, you'd better tell me about it..."

In the bridge's warm darkness, amid the oceanic urban scent, Evius spun on his friend like a cornered serpent. A viper, he spat, "Or what, Christian? What are you going to do if I don't... if there is one?"

Christian didn't say anything. He didn't move. For a moment, his world was completely still. Something like heroin, something like nirvana.

Opposite him, Evius' tense posture relaxed. "That's what I thought," he said. He smiled as kindly as his disturbed features would allow, and he added, "I don't know why in the hell you'd *want* to go back there, man. Don't you remember? You killed yourself to get *out*. And not just killed, man, but hung... I mean, you fucking *strangled* yourself to death. Why would you *ever* want to go back? Jesus sure as hell doesn't. Come on, let's go enjoy Pandemonium for a change. We both deserve it," he ended with a diabolical grin.

All of which Christian knew was quite true, but still there was something unsettling about his guide's answer, something unsettling about the entire situation. Christian couldn't quite put his finger on it, but there it was, squirming around beneath his very own index finger like a worm chopped in two, like an orgasming woman who Mick Jagger might have, many eons ago, falsely claimed was already under his thumb.

Something didn't add up, but before Christian's warped mind could even begin doing the math (there was so much division to do that, without some sort of technology, it was hard keeping all the numbers straight), Evius – not quite so unhappy in heaven – swerved upon him and said, "Holy Christ, man – or is it holy shit, brother, oh well, whatever – I almost forgot," he reached into his pocket and brought out yet another joint, "Smoke?" and he smiled a comic book Cheshire grin, "Always enter Pandemonium lifted. That's what I always try to remember to Nobody who's with me," as his smile grew wider and toothier yet.

Christian gazed beyond to the bridge's end. It ended in nothing – a mist, a brackish fog breathing off from atop the River Styx. The fog was beginning to engulf them now. The world's harsh edges were slowly eroding, rotting away... maybe it had something to do with the weed Evius had already sparked. The spires of Pandemonium – daunting and impressive, vividly painted by horror – diminished in their grandeur and vivacity. What an odd optical illusion as one got closer. You would expect the opposite. London Bridge took the place of the one they crossed as Christian rubbed Styx's sticky film off his slick skin hoping this one, unlike the nursery rhyme, wouldn't fall down with a bubonic ring around the rosy and a pocket full of posy to keep away the plague.

"Jesus Christ," Christian mumbled.

To which Evius, under his breath, muttered, "Not here, brother, not here."

Christian, however, in his own mind, was more stuck on the tangled web of what he was actually doing rather than the mental state he should be in when entering that apparently terrifyingly odd place. But if he isn't careful, his mental state might be the only thing he should be concerned about as his entire mind is consumed by the web's widow, a match made in hell for the male (heaven for the female). For, it was there, in his mental space, where he could no longer fathom the decision he was making... not in any sort of sane manner (as he should have done eons ago, wondering what he was thinking getting that rope out of the bucket, wrapping it around his hand, looping it over the exposed rafters beyond the hole in his ceiling)... only in the question of fear.

In an act of psychic foreshadowing, he was terrified of what Pandemonium had to offer, but there he was, a few feet away from the end of the suspension bridge leading right into its tainted heart. Truly (like any of us), he had no choice.

"Not such a bad walk," Evius said. "We used to have a gondolier here, but he disappeared as soon as they built the bridge. It was a nice trip... Charon, I think, was what he called himself – although he didn't speak, actually. I heard he works for the PMS now – that's the Pandemonium Metropolitan Services – drives a subway... maybe even the one we took so long ago just to get to almost here." Stoned, Christian envisioned a man smiling with dripping fangs hanging over his bottom lip and two red horns poking through his flat cap. "I don't know for sure, but I always feel good about the possibility of somebody moving up in the world... makes you feel like the system's working. Can't stop progress. That's what I always say."

Christian nodded knowingly. Although, truthfully, he didn't hear a word Evius ever said.

At the other end of the bridge, out of the mist, a scent of something other, something deeper and more profound, than life reached Christian. It contained the sickly sweet odor of the inside of a workman's socks majestically coupled with the labored sweat from a prostitute's inner thigh. Christian couldn't quite place it, but he knew he'd smelled something approximating its hermaphroditic, inner stench sometime before, perhaps sometime during his early teen years. At the tip of his tongue, had he known the reference, was the long-forgotten taste of Proust's madeleine. But, like the reference, the thought was unknown and, hence, immediately forgotten. Always searching out one in the bush, Christian's scrambled brain simply couldn't keep a bird in hand.

Setting both feet squarely on the asphalt of the other side, inhaling deeply the fog and nearly reveling in the sickly stench, Evius, his eyes darkening to their depths, growled, "Now, we're here, Christian. For real, this time – Pandemonium."

Christian shuddered.

"All we need is a place to sleep," the afterlife's tour guide finished with a subtle laugh as his long legs carried him away from the bridge, deeper into the fog and deeper into the darkening city. Christian struggled, for more reasons than just Evius' lanky speed, to keep up.

The mist dissolved black skies.

Silently, Evius and Christian walked past the skyscrapers towering along the city's outskirts, its downtown. The buildings stretched up… up, and unlike in any earthly dwelling place, they coiled around one another, intersecting like a brood of snakes, at the tip tops of their heights. Sometimes, amid their Siamese relationships, they appeared snarled, dripping fangs in the distance. Sometimes they appeared strands of entangled, braided hair ready to be pulled, weeds uprooted from out their solidity, by a gardener, a playground bully. How could such living monstrosities have ever been conceived or designed? To Christian's earthly, constrained brain, especially given his own background of sweating away his day through various construction sites, he couldn't fathom how they could have possibly been built.

The streets, however, for all intents and purposes, were a financial district as abandoned as the stock exchange after the bulls had crashed headlong into a bear and all the brokers had leaped from the angels' own unknown heights. Only, like with all the other angels, the bodies were missing. Vesper's statement about buffaloes rang emptily through Christian's mind otherwise as vacant as the streets he and Evius carefully meandered along.

"It's all for show," Evius suddenly broke their silent trance with a misty breath exhumed from off his lips. "Nobody bothers working here in Pandemonium…"

They twisted and twined through overtowered streets. Not a soul in sight, Christian remained locked inside the building unquiet of his own mind with thoughts as odd as the world discovered, the subjective passively imprinted on the objective (or vice versa) – while Evius, forcefully imprinting the objective on the subjective (or vice versa), turned his head from left to right until… unexpectedly, he spoke, "This way."

Before Christian could protest, Evius' long steps click, click, clicked on the cobblestones down the descent of an unknown, seemingly abandoned alleyway. With his unquiet mind quickly shutting quietly down – as if the Buddha had finally taught him something through action at a distance, Christian, still not wanting to be the last person in the haunted house, gulped.

For, as he had already learned – in the afterlife – not everything is as it seems. However, (as has been mentioned before) what choice did Christian ever have: the interminable calculus of existence rolls on and on…

At the very end of the alleyway, underneath darkness, beside a large dumpster's murky outline, appeared the slight shuffling of shadow upon shadow. It could have been a trick of the night, but still… Christian stuttered mid-step amid the thought: *Rats?* If he'd had a pistol, he would have shot that rat between the eyes. However, to his chagrin, he was almost certain that along with the play of shadows shuffling along the ground, he could make out, attached to the shadows, the thick form of heavy legs, which meant the shadows must be feet. And attached to those legs appeared something like the oversized torso and the hunched shoulders of what could only be (or, at least, would hopefully be) a man.

Christian gulped yet again, but before he could grab Evius by the shoulder and tell his guide he thought maybe they'd made a wrong turn somewhere along the line (how far back, only the devil knew), that the stall they were heading towards appeared to be occupied, a gruff voice barked, "Halt! Who goes there?"

Like a middle school girl suddenly made aware of her burgeoning body, Christian wanted to dissolve into the ground… dust to dust. One would think, elementally, that would be quite simple: fluids flow into one another. But solids are different – especially when one body of earth is still animated by the breath of life (or death in the instant case).

From that same occupied alleyway's end, the rough sound of a match spark sounded. Christian started in place. From between the illuminated tips of shaky fingers, the small glow of a flame raised up in the night, traced out what was certainly the buttons of a white shirt stretching over a man's puffy chest. As the flame approached the face, Christian wasn't sure what he would see.

What he did see wasn't quite as frightening as what he had feared, but it was just as frightening as what he had hoped against hope wouldn't be the case. The face was human – not monster, but against Christian's every wish, he

actually recognized the visage. It wore the same sloppy
jowls, the same haggard appearance of that aged madman
from the café, that verbose maniac from the train, the
inane, insane, old man – Joshua. Christian lowered his eyes
and shook his head.

As Christian glanced up again, Joshua's dead-fish eyes
bulged from out their sockets. Like a blind witch, he
growled, "Come closer, I can't quite make you out."

Evius followed Joshua's mad advice and took a step
towards the alley's end. Like at the entrance to Belle's cage,
Christian wanted to stop his guide, but as they both lived
their separate experiences of respective fear and curiosity
each, the seemingly unflappable dead man laughed, "That's
because there's a flame not even two inches in front of your
eyes, friend. It's simple optics. Put the match out, and you
might be able to actually see us," which was precisely what
Christian didn't want.

But against Christian's wishes, a wisp of Joshua's
wicked breath extinguished the match.

For a micro-second, blackness engulfed the world.
Then, by what light the devil must have provided, sight
returned. It must have done so for Joshua as well because
the old man let out a sigh as he seemed to hang his head
and say, "Ah, I remember you two." At which point, he
released a belabored breath.

Evius quite uncharacteristically wondered
compassionately, "What's wrong, friend?"

Christian thought he heard a sob from Joshua's end of
the alley. There was a pause. Then, Joshua cried, "I thought
you might be my beloved Zoe come to save me."

To which, Evius said, "Save you? From what?"

"From this!" the old man shouted. Evius shushed him,
and Joshua, swaying, stood up. Not sure what to expect
next, Christian jumped. His adrenaline rushed. But Joshua,

leaning heavily against the dumpster, meekly croaked, "From Pandemonium."

Which sent a shiver through Christian's frazzled nerves as Evius snorted a short chuckle. Joshua shot a wicked gaze in Evius' direction. Evius shrugged, "Don't hold it against me, friend, but we just had a run in with your 'beloved' Zoe…"

Joshua growled, "Don't fill me with the same lies you pandered last time we met." His broken fingers curled into fists, and he hunched his large shoulders over his thick arms while Christian recalled the story Joshua had told him on the patio of the café in Machpelah, the story about how, once upon a time, a man had challenged him, and how Joshua had hit him and hit him again and again and again until he just wasn't sure whether or not the man was dead… And Joshua whispered, "Blasphemers…" Again, Christian shivered – if only he could have remembered so well the many stories Evius had told him throughout their journey.

Fearlessly, though, Evius continued the challenge, "No lie, no blasphemy, friend – although, for the record, the statement my erstwhile companion mumbled the last time we met was no lie either, but we'll let sleeping dogs lie – or should we let them lay? *No*, better not. The fact is, your 'beloved' Zoe is yucking it up right now, at this very moment, as she reclines across the lap of some temptress in their siren's lair on the wayward path to this very place you find so terrifyingly horrid. In fact, by means of some ingenious – or was it ingenuous, I was always get that vowel confused – detective work, my dear compatriot here was able to trick the deceptress into revealing the door to the path to this very realm where we have – both for your sake and for ours – luckily stumbled upon you… which – Q.E.F. – proves, should she want to, your 'beloved' Zoe could certainly find you, too. No, my good man, you're as alone as God here in this place."

Joshua snorted, "I know that feeling." He shook his head. "Figures... Women... Can't live with them; can't die without their help... Why else do you think Eve was imagined? What choice does a man ever have, then, but to live alone... as Adam, naming things in whatever absurd way he pleases..." Joshua started pointing at objects and mumbling, to himself, in some sort of guttural gibberish as he slumped back down into his former posture.

Interrupting Joshua's unintelligible ramblings, Evius answered, "That's too Heraclitean for me. Adam could have always tried a mirror image. Things might have turned out better for a certain species that way."

Joshua shrugged, "Whatever your pleasure: Heraclitus... Parmenides... But I'll tell you for certain (I've heard it on good authority) serpents prefer not to have their legs. It would be best if you weren't to judge a species you knew nothing about. What was Hui Tzu's story about fish? Besides, Narcissus wound up in a comparable predicament – probably because he couldn't see the fish." Joshua snorted again. "Whatever... Men... Can't live alone, too vain to die without somebody's help..."

"I've heard tell there was once a gifted troubadour who versified that sentiment, but you know, on a preliminary evaluation, that seems to be your problem, friend," Evius inserted. Joshua looked him in the face questioningly. Evius responded, "Think of fish – this duality necessary to your thinking. In electrical terms, hormones aren't so different to anything other than the senses of vision and smell, which, if you ask a hawk or a dog – take Horus or Anubis, for examples – in humans is pretty fucking weak... possibly too weak to notice the subtle similarities."

Joshua gave a slight smile. Christian noticed the molars

missing in the back of the aged maniac's mouth as the old man gave a Valhallan cheer, "Ra! Now, you speak the fluctuating truth." His mood completely changed, Joshua happily continued, "Come, sirs. Sit. Join me for a nice evening meal beneath the stars," and with a flourish towards the heavens (if one could still call the sky such when entombed within the wide-open bowels of Mother Earth) he produced a can of something from out each of his hip pockets while from out his back pocket appeared a single silver spoon.

Christian swallowed slowly. He remembered something. He remembered that...

He was hungry. He remembered that...

He hadn't eaten anything since long before he had died. He remembered that...

Food was a necessity.

If he still was alive even though he was dead, he still had to eat. Like a confused canine, Christian licked his lips, and finally, hesitantly, he took a single step towards Joshua and the cans of whatever were proffered from his hands. He took another step, and he took another. Until almost magically, Christian was nearly begging (if he'd been Mike's Theo, and Joshua had been Master Mike, Master Joshua certainly would have slapped Christian on the nose and hissed: *No*), standing directly in front of Joshua and Joshua's magnificent hands full of canned food.

Like a heavenly angel running an errand in Pandemonium's hell, like a priest offering a penitent the Eucharist, Joshua slowly set one of the cans into the outstretched hands of the suddenly starving Christian.

Christian couldn't believe it... here was the food he hadn't been waiting for for so long! Here was the potion that could ease the starving belly he hadn't even known he had... Here was the body of Christ for his everlasting, never-known (or was it neverlasting, ever-known) soul... Here was the answer to this very momentary problem encountered in the afterlife... Here was – food!

By means of a ring, Christian ripped off the can's metal top. Amid the peeling sound of metal from metal, the jagged edge peeled back, and Christian stared deeply down into the soothing depths of his never-sought-for meal. He gazed at the life-giving nectar he had seen somewhere before. He inhaled the pungent odor and realized he knew that effervescent scent, he had smelled it many times over the course of his life. Yes, he knew that deep, olfactory sensation of meaty innards. During his childhood, he'd slopped the dark, grisly producer of that same smell from many a can, and he had spooned it into the bowl of his mother's dog. Christian opened his eyes wide and looked again. Yes, it was true. The cans Joshua held were full of nothing but wet dog food.

Amid such a revelation, Joshua still smiled.

While Christian licked his lips – whether in hunger or confusion neither Joshua nor Evius was certain (though each had his own respective idea). Christian shook his head – whether in preparation or in wonder neither Evius nor Joshua was certain (though, as always, each had his own respective idea). Christian blinked – whether in awe or in amazement none, not even Christian himself, knew.

Regardless, the food was to be consumed. It waited, wet and sloppy in its can, for a spoon to a mouth to scoop it out with the sucking noise of vacuous pressure released. It waited, dark and mushy with a sheen of water across the top, for some starving entity to devour its moist, life-giving properties – however meager and tasteless those properties might be. Of course, though, life itself is always quite tasteless, and in that respect, the food in the can had more to do with the food Christian had always loved than he could even imagine at that point in time.

What was happening to his starving guts was not the reaction food should produce in a body internally wasting away for only the devil knows how many days. His gorge rose in his throat. He thought he might vomit when Joshua said in a kind voice, "Go ahead... eat," as the aged lunatic proffered his spoon.

Now, Christian had a choice, and choices had never been that easy to make... not for one of Christian's caliber, at least. There'd been the choice years ago, after he'd finished studying at college, after he'd been rejected from graduate schools: should he keep practicing music and apply again? Should he keep playing and see what happens? Should he alter his desired career trajectory and try to teach high school? Or should he give it all up and just drink? If you've read this far into the story, you know which choice Christian made, and, of course, his "choice" had actually been more of a simple cop out, like copping a plea for a crime he didn't commit (although, the crime was committed by virtue of his psychology, at the very least) – *I won't kill myself, I'll stay on this plane of existence, but I won't partake of it. I'll nullify my reality as much as I possibly can.* Truly, what else can a man ever do? Nothing... which is exactly what Christian did.

In the meantime, the choice regarding the food was still to be made, and with regard to that choice, Christian felt as if he were confronting that dynamic duo, Vesper and Zoe, all over again.

Then, his temper changing as quickly as a prostitute's fabricated desires, Joshua held forth his trembling hand and growled, "Well, if you don't want it, give it back. Christ, man, show some gratitude, some of us were looking forward to a nice, home-cooked meal..."

A notion to which Evius spoke as well, "He's got a

point there, Christian. If you're not going to eat, then pass that morsel on over to me. I'd be happy to devour whatever it is you're holding in your hand. I'm freaking starving…"

"No…" Christian, feeling the emptiness inside him in a way he never had before, mumbled, "I need to eat." With a thlwop, he stuck his utensil into the muck. With a fwlup, he pulled it out. Catching the light of distant street lights, dog food glistened on the silver spoon, which, like a newborn, Christian, while holding his breath, quickly put into his mouth.

It wasn't half bad, that dog food. It tasted something like liver against the tongue (rotten liver, but liver none the less), which Christian had never had anything against. In fact, he kind of liked it. It reminded him of the Eastern European neighborhood he'd lived in in that abandoned Rust Belt city where his journey had begun. Christian plunged the spoon into the muck again. He jerked it out. For Christ's sake, if he'd known the dog food would taste like that, he never would have questioned his own desires (but one should always question his desires, shouldn't he?).

With the brown mess dripping down his cheeks and chin, with his molars still mawing the remnants of slop, before Christian knew it, before he had passed the meal along to either of his compatriots to share, the can was empty. The heaviness of a post-Thanksgiving bodily blood-letting coursed through Christian's body. He needed a couch to lie on and a football game to pass out in front of. Instead, Christian stumbled where he stood. Before he knew what was happening, he was on his knees. Before he could ask, *what the hell's going on*, his face hit the abrasive ground. Before he even caught himself snoring, the world was as dark as his fall yet again, and Christian was asleep with his scruffy cheek on the cold concrete. Thus, as if none of this had ever happened, we end where we began.

Ω.
Phlogiston

7.
Let Your Lord Make an End of Us

There was a dream, but Christian didn't remember it. He never remembered his dreams anymore – even when he *was* alive. Every night, he slept the sleep of the dead: beyond that welcome embrace of the Reaper's less formidable cousin – if we cease to dream, we very well may die. Christian opened wide his eyes. He blinked only – yet again – to gaze upon the brick and concrete landscape made rich by Death Himself. His throat sunk into his stomach, which sunk into his feet.

The sun shone brightly. As if he were the vampire so often feared as he lay in bed as a child praying to the God that he had, once upon a time, believed in that he had never inadvertently invited Dracula into his home, Christian shaded his vision from the distant star's burning warmth. He smacked his terrible tasting tongue against the roof of his mouth and lolled his head from side to side. Still in the alleyway where he had passed out after eating the can of dog food, to his surprise, he found himself, for the first time since his journey began, alone. Evius... Joshua... neither were anywhere in sight. Meeting his vision, the abandoned point between two buildings intertwined at their highest height while housing nothing but an overfilled dumpster, an empty can of dog food, and, apparently, Christian himself. Panic gripped Christian's breast. Where his allies had gone, only the devil knew.

Thrusting his trusting hands against hard concrete, Christian bolted upright. Thinking maybe he had merely overlooked one of his two earlier companions, he spun a circle as wide as one of salt: to keep the demons out. But there was no salt, no sword, no candle, and no wand. There was certainly no grimoire Christian was aware of. His companions couldn't be missed (one was too tall, the other too large), and they weren't there. Maybe they'd always been figments of his imagination. Maybe this entire journey was a figment of his imagination: a trip taken on some bad acid many years before, before he'd ever even breathed that name – *Sophia*. None of this ever happened. He should have read *The Bible* instead. It might have helped to explain the significance of his own name. A few others he'd come across in his time as well. The Upanishads would have done him some good, too.

Christian had never felt so alone in the wide world, and perhaps that was because he wasn't in the wide world, hadn't been for quite some time. The buildings' external walls shrunk in on him to entomb him out of doors. He was in the realm of death. One might even say: *beyond the realms of death*. He was, after all, a suicide. And no religion ever treated them quite as kind as they did themselves.

Stumbling, he figured maybe if he could get out of the alleyway, he might happen upon either one or both of his lost (or found) newfound (or lost) friends. Though the mere night before he never would have used that term to describe madmen such as those. Maybe they had simply wandered away to forage for something more to eat. Now that his stomach had been awakened, Christian, like his mind, couldn't put it back to sleep. He needed either Evius or Joshua to explain something to him – what that was he still wasn't quite sure ($\{E \lor J = J \lor E\}$)... and maybe they could have explained that question to him as well: What *did* he want to ask them?

Nevermind, he should have asked the Buddha instead. *He* would have told him it was all a process of codependent origination. There was no answer without the question. There was no question without the answer. Thus, Christian had already reached the point for which to strive. Nothing. If only such a reality were so simple to accept.

Sunlight and dust mites loomed at the alley's end. Like the light at the end of the tunnel, like the dream he'd had when he'd hung through that hole in his ceiling, Christian approached it. Only, this time, there weren't wings attached to his back. There were only his feet sliding along concrete. He stuck his hands in his pockets. He noticed, for the first time in ages, the hole in his shirt's elbow. He hunched his shoulders over still more. He stared at where his now scuffed and battered shoes met the pavement. He reached the alley's end and glanced to his right.

From behind – "Hey!" The voice startled him. It wasn't spoken in recognition as if coming from a friend. It was spoken in admonition as if coming from an assailant. Christian started where he stood. He turned his head, squinted his eyes, and as if he could see through to another time and place, to the lens of time and space, he peered to the left, deeper in the voice's direction.

Emerging, like reason, from out the blinding sunlight, a strolling figure appeared. It didn't seem a monster, but Christian didn't recognize the gait. It was human all right, but not one Christian might have recognized. Although, back on earth, he'd been quite accustomed to such sights. His heart slowed a frenzied beat.

The policeman appeared to be walking his own beat. His uniform was a little more disheveled than what Christian's city's finest would usually have let themselves be caught dead in, but given the fact this officer was quite literally caught dead in the uniform he had chosen to don at some point in the past, he managed to cut quite a sharp figure. Giving him a rakish aspect, his hat tilted a little to the side. Paunching around his middle and hanging over the butt of the gun and the handcuffs on his waist, his shirt was untucked a bit. His pants didn't appear freshly pressed. But it struck Christian as so odd to bear witness to a denizen of law and order in a world that had been, up until then, nothing but chaos. Christian smiled at the incongruity.

That smile, however, was cut short as the officer, barreling forward, increased his pace. The disorderly policeman pointed his finger directly at Christian as he exclaimed, "You've got a lot of explaining to do, mister."

Taking a step back, Christian immediately realized he had nowhere left to run. There was a walled alley behind him and the devil knew what in front of him. He gulped down his fear and, to his shocked dismay, stood his ground. As a teenager, that never would have happened. But the world changes as we age, especially after we've stared madness directly in its grotesquely absurd face.

What possibly could have happened? What possibly could he be responsible for? (Nothing, so far as he was concerned.) Destruction of property? Drunk and disorderly conduct? Murder? (How right he was on all counts – if he'd known that, he definitely would have run, and he never would have stopped, not until they shot him dead... again.) He wished he had a cigarette. The nicotine might have taken off some of his fearful edge as if he were merely looking over rather than stumbling off the ledge.

But he didn't have a cigarette, and the cop was quickly

approaching. As the officer walked – it must have been the light alternating between dark and light – beneath the cop's reflecting sunglasses, the officer's nose appeared to morph between a human nozzle, a pig's fleshy snout, and a wolf's furry muzzle. For Christian, it was all quite disconcerting. He had to blink a number of times to keep his mind right. But when the cop stopped less than a foot away from him (so close Christian could smell his garlic encrusted breath), even in his uniform, he was nothing but a human being. Albeit, a human being in a very imposing outfit.

The cop whipped his shades from his eyes as he poked one finger hard against Christian's bony breast. "Where are you coming from, son?" Officer Ygg (for, Christian could now read his nametag) snapped.

Christian didn't answer.

"I thought so," Officer Ygg nodded. Quickly shoving his glasses into his breast pocket, he dropped one hand to the butt of his gun. With his other hand, like he was Zoe's beast devouring himself rather than the brother of Christ – a zombie, cannibal corpse eaten back to life, he pointed the walkie-talkie, which was attached to his chest, as if it were his heart, to his mouth: ***chk, chk, crackle*** "*We've got a real live one here; I need to get him to a mental ward.*"

In a flash, Officer Ygg pulled his gun from its holster. He stepped back, assumed a strong stance, and pointed his weapon directly into Christian's petrified face. With the barrel of the cop's gun less than an inch from Christian's nose, Officer Ygg told him, "All right, buddy, your days of immortal mayhem are over. You're coming with me."

To which all Christian could say (although, as if he were channeling Franz Kafka himself: *pour une littérature mineure*, it was more of a mumble than anything else) was, "But what did I do?"

Before those words even finished tripping off the tips

of his lips, Christian was face down on the concrete, screaming nothing to nobody, with a knee in the small of his back, right where Kundalini could have been uncoiling from, as his arms felt they were being ripped out of their sockets, and Officer Ygg's handcuffs, like a shark's serrated teeth, were biting into the veins of his wrists. *"You make another goddamn sound, and I'll crack your skull!"* the officer screamed.

Really, it was suicide all over again.

Christian was in the back of a white van. He knew that from when he had been shuffled inside with Officer Ygg's grip firm on the back of his head. The inside of the van was dark and hot and moist. There weren't any windows. The inhabitants' sweat clung to the sticky atmosphere. The sun must have reached – that is, if the sun could reach underground – something like midday. Again, Christian was parched, but this time, even over his thirst, he was terrified. He had been shoved into the van to share it with, at least, fifteen other prisoners. As if they were in Auschwitz's converted cattle stalls, there wasn't enough room on the wooden benches lining the walls for all of them to sit.

Being one of the last to arrive, Christian remained cross-legged on the floor – his hands still cuffed behind his back, his butt bruising to the bumps in the road. He wanted to ask his companions where the "officers" were taking *him*. But like everybody else in the van, Christian's mouth was taped shut. All he could do was stare – out of his own wide-eyed gaze – at the other eyes enkindled into bovine appearances by their respective panics. The collective nervous energy corroded the van's overbearing interior.

Knowing something was about to end (though he wasn't quite certain what that "something" was), Christian reflected back across both his life and his afterlife. Neither had been particularly "good" – but what is good when measured against an equally relative "bad". There had been joy in each (the pleasures of the highs, the anticipations of greater conquests). There had been comfort in each (the stillness of a drink, the rest of stoned thoughts)... And there had been pain and fear and suffering throughout (much more of the last three than the previous two). Really, the latter had merely been a surrealistic interpretation of the former. Writhing in discomfort on the van's floor, unable to speak his mind, Christian reflected on such things.

Then, the van stopped... as did Christian's thoughts. The symbolic tale rolled on and on.

Squealing, the van's double backdoors flung open. A horde of uniformed officers piled in. They grabbed and shoved and kicked the terrified occupants out into the light. Nobody seemed to *want* to go. They *wanted* to exercise their free will as they preferred not to. But by means of nightsticks and batons, the officers didn't give the would-be Bartlebies much of a choice. The prisoners – male and female, all, Christian included – stumbled out the van, so often tripping to fall their last steps as sweat broke through their foreheads and armpits while the sun dazzled them blind by means of its white light.

But, to the outside world, Christian wasn't blind enough. Amid his horror, he could still see an officer, smiling a Joker's psychotic smile with a rusty pair of scissors in hand, approaching. Whatever the officer would cut with those shears, Christian didn't want to know. He wanted to run, but he was held in place by a minion who he couldn't see but who must have been, at the very least, twice his size... or so the overpowering grasp implied.

Christian writhed. His torso contorted and his legs twisted out of place as the blade of the rusty scissors snipped through the hem of his jeans. A whimper sounded in back of Christian's throat as he tried to shy away from the blade.

"Now, if you don't hold still," the officer holding the shears methodically whispered, "I might wind up cutting you... And we certainly don't want to damage any merchandise."

At which words, Christian writhed harder still. A whine slipped from behind the tape across his lips, which brought a smile to the cutter's face and a brief machine gun burst of laughter from the captor. But like when he had tried to get to the top of his rope to untie himself from where he hung, Christian's struggles were in vain. Much like in the real world, like a rat battering its head against the wall of an unending maze, his strength was spent upon an object that simply wouldn't budge: his overbearing captor.

Cold metal slid up Christian's leg as if it were the inversion of a woman's sensually warm touch, and Christian watched himself slowly be stripped bare of what, once upon a time, had been his favorite outfit. The French-cuffed shirt with the hole in its elbow was cut off his chest and ripped from his back. His undershirt was cut off his body. In a final act of destruction, even his shoes, those gifts from the gods to the hero beginning his quest (now sprayed with crusts of vomit and stained by the bloody, semenic mess) were sliced off his feet. The leather gave so much easier than Christian imagined it should have. Truly, those were heavenly hellish shears. In full nudity, Christian closed his eyes as, leaving even his socks behind, he was shoved forward from behind.

Like a young heart with an emotion, he nearly tumbled head over heels, but like an aged heart with an emotion, out of necessity, he held his balance to keep from falling on his face. He set his jaw and walked forward in the nude – the sun burning cancer into every inch of his bare body.

The concrete was hot upon his feet, but he stepped with the attention demanded by the horror of his situation. Where he was going, only the devil knew.

___

As if his soul were the salty water leaking out of him, the sun sucked life out of the sweat from Christian's pores. Replacing Officer Ygg's now quite comfortable handcuffs, heavy shackles stretched from Christian's ankles to his wrists. With every subtle motion, a metallic clank.

Naked in line with other naked bodies – both male and female (though, at the moment, neither caused Christian any sensual excitement) – Christian waited his turn to step his bare feet up on what appeared to be a concrete auction block, which was a better alternative than his initial thoughts: prison, a human sacrifice... At least the block contained life (but was that something to even want?).

The shouts of the elated crowd, bartering for the body atop the block, echoed through the agora. Horrified (even after everything he'd already seen), Christian closed his eyes – reality's burden is harder to bear than fantasy's has ever been. If he had to hear, at the very least, he didn't want to see. A deal appeared to have been reached, and with a metronomic clank in time to the rest of the line, Christian was shoved one step closer to his turn.

When Christian opened his eyes, from his position in the middle of the line-up, he couldn't really see the crowd shouting empty figures at the auctioneer succinctly dressed in a shapeless black robe from head to toe and speaking into a microphone. Whether the auctioneer was male or female, Christian couldn't know. The voice coming through the loudspeaker was being run through some sort of distortion pedal filtering it into the high-pitched screech of Norwegian black metal vocals. Christian couldn't understand what was being said. How the elated crowd could, he had no idea.

The nudity of Christian's fellows suddenly formed a disturbing juxtaposition with the master's full-frontal covering, which meant something. Even in the sun's heat, Christian began shivering. The glass of water with Belle was long lost, and Christian's shivering didn't stop, especially not when it was finally his turn to step up onto the block. That meant something, too. What that something was, Christian could never know.

Atop the cement block, Christian stared down into a pit – Times Square, the crossroads of the world – overflowing with abundant consumers. As far as he could tell, they were relatively humanoid. Although, they appeared something out of a novel fantasy: in reality. Next to Christian, the auctioneer fired up his/her rant. His/her black metal vocals sliced through the microphone out through indistinguishable speakers. He/she pointed at the hair atop Christian's head. He/she waved his/her flowing robe of an appendage down Christian's naked body – pointing out every intricacy in our hero's physical design – to his toes. The intellectual sensation of overt objectification (something Christian had never truly experienced before) did nothing to ease Christian's physical tremors. Where in the hell had Evius disappeared to? He scanned the crowd for his lost afterlife tour guide. He turned to scan the line he had stepped up from, but an unknown jailer behind him, by means of oversized hands, whipped his head back into place, staring straight ahead.

At that moment, Christian certainly could have used a tidbit of Evius' seemingly worthless advice. Although, if Christian had paid more attention (he was finally realizing) he might not have found himself in the midst of his currently terrifying predicament, which, Christian was certain – though his thoughts were too petrified at the moment to even begin to imagine the fact – could only get worse.

From inside Christian's sternum, emptiness opened out to the world. It was the codependent arising of the world outside himself within himself, and Christian was nauseated by the sensation. Outer space suddenly turned into his physical inner world, but the physics were too frightening (what *is* at the center of an atom?). It was as if all the filth Christian had subjected himself to over his 27 years of dying had finally found fruition within that one, very moment – absolute emptiness. As he swallowed, his throat clicked like the hammer on a revolver, his existential body ready to pull the trigger on his non-existent soul and send him to Nirvana once and for all. The Buddha would have been proud. All it took was less than one full day in Pandemonium. Now, that's what *I* call enlightenment.

The auctioneer, by means of the chain running from Christian's wrists to his ankles, spun his/her human product around as if our hero were nothing more than an object – a playful dreidel for a child's Hanukkah. In Christian's own mind, of course, he was so much more than that mere object, that naked slab of meat for sale. Although, when he jumped off that bridge not so very long ago, that's precisely what he'd hoped to become. But how do our own minds' perceptions have anything to do with the reality of what others perceive of us? Just ask any middle school girl wearing the short shorts her society simultaneously both sold to her and sold her on around a group of grown men. As far as Christian was concerned, he was a breathing human being, no longer living, but certainly still breathing, which to his mind, made him a subject… which he was: the phenomenologically perspectival subject of an auction.

The consumers in the pit below began throwing out

their bids on whatever purposes they had in mind for what they could see of Christian's naked body, which was everything – but we're so much more than our bodies, aren't we? So, in fact, the consumers, much like the consumers (both native and foreign) of Christian's own home country, saw nothing – blinded by what they see.

One voice rose above the unending din and snarl of the auctioneer's shredding vocals. However, the chaos was too complete for Christian to understand which body the voice emanated from. As the guttural counterpoint of the auctioneer's higher squeal, the voice from the pit reacted to every demand the auctioneer appeared to make. Then, a gavel appeared in the auctioneer's robed hand. For a brief second, Christian thought it might have been meant to bash in his own brains with, but instead, the auctioneer, bending into the posture of a penitent kneeling his/her nose to the grindstone, struck the hard earth beside Christian's right foot. A ring sang from the tip of the gavel's mallet. The shock traveled up Christian's leg into his groin. It swirled around in his testicles like that first puff of smoke off the first of Evius' joints back in that home Christian had, then, thought was still attached to the rest of the earth. The first recognizable word Christian had had the displeasure of hearing since stepping atop the block came from behind the auctioneer's ventilated mask. He/she shrieked – a banshee's wail – overtop the crowd's elated heads: "SOLD!"

At the word, what could only have been a hood cut through the sunlight and darkened Christian's sight.

Christian could barely breathe. The bag over his head was getting hotter. He felt himself suffocating. Panicking, he gasped deeper into the quickly warming atmosphere for something like cooler air, but there wasn't any. He'd been shuffled off the block, shoved into what could only have been the trunk of a car, and now felt himself being pulled out of that trunk he had spent the past – the devil knows how long – kicking and screaming in as it wound through what must have been the labyrinthine streets of Pandemonium. His voice was hoarse. His wrists and ankles burned from straining against the shackles. A door creaked, and Christian was pulled into a cooler atmosphere.

The truth (or so Christian now knew) was that Christian would never find his way back. He would never find Evius. He would never find Sophia. He had to have faith they could find him, and faith was one thing Christian sorely lacked. In more ways than one, both he and all were lost. In more ways than one, he had finally found hell. But the thing about hell (what the demons might truthfully tell you) is it's bottomless – there are levels even the Devil has yet to explore. He'll never admit that, though. It keeps going deeper, deeper, eventually arriving to here.

Where the bag was removed from Christian's head and thrown into the corner of a long, narrow disheveled apartment, the floor of which – like some sort of Coney Island funhouse room – sloped down to the right. As muted bulb light blurred Christian's sight, the walls were adorned with the most decrepit, disturbing canvases (monsters and tortures) Christian had ever seen... nothing like the promise of Pablo's and James's paintings from his home in Machpelah. No windows anywhere to be seen. Flies buzzed over trash everywhere.

In front of him, breathing unwashed breath heavily into Christian's petrified face was a balding man, twice Christian's height, hunched over at the shoulders so his head didn't brush the ceiling, with a round face and narrow eyes. Jesus, those eyes were intense. A long scar ran down his left cheek. His uncovered belly, matted with thick hair, bulged over his pants' line. Even as he stood, in his acid-washed jeans, his spindly legs appeared a little bowed. He thumped his hairy chest, and he bellowed from between broken teeth, like a literate silver-back gorilla, at Christian, "I AM MALIK! I RULE THIS WORLD, AND YOU ARE MY SLAVE, SLAVE."

Obediently, he accepted his title; Christian nodded. He had surely met the devil responsible for this charade: Beelzebub, the (current) Lord of All.

Malik grabbed the chain running between Christian's wrists and ankles. As the demon turned around, Christian noticed patches of black hair running up his Lord's back as well, connecting through his armpits with the hair on his chest. Kicking aside bags of rotting trash, the stench of which was noxious, creating a swarm of buzzing flies obscuring Christian's sight, Malik dragged his slave through the apartment to a door in the back, which opened onto a pitch black room.

There was no threshold to cross over, no cliff to another world to spill off into. Only reality, only hard wood beneath Christian's bare, shuffling feet as he was pulled to the wall and chained, amid clanks, in place to the cold bricks against his back and ass – his arms above his head, his legs spread-eagle. Closing the door on darkness, Malik left.

Something invisible shuffled in the corner. It sounded alive.

6.
Darkness Burns

There was definitely something in that corner, and Christian didn't like that thought. He didn't like it one bit. He strained against the chains binding him, but he only succeeded in rattling his shackles and possibly attracting the attention of whatever lived in the darkness. *What* lived in the darkness? Would it consume him, destroy him, or just terrify him? The truth was much worse than all three.

There was a room in the home Christian and his mother had moved into after his dad had left, the home Christian had left as soon as he was old enough to... one room Christian never went into unless he was ordered. For the family before them, that room had probably been a den. There was no window, and Christian's mother had left boxes of objects from her previous marriage starving for life alone in the pitch black. Even by the time he was in high school, a young man in outward features at least, whenever his mom asked him to get something out of one of those boxes nobody had ever taken the time to unpack (which was quite rarely... even she didn't seem to want anything to do with the memories in that room), Christian would run into the room with fear cramping his chest.

He would hurriedly fumble through whatever box he'd been asked to as if scorpions and serpents might be upon him at any moment. When he found the desired object, he would run to return to the hallway's light. Later that night, as Christian would fall asleep (even as a teenager) with the fear of unearthly monsters writhing through the room's darkness, he determined the room itself had been haunted before they'd even moved in. He never realized we haunt our own rooms. We haunt ourselves. That room was so much of the reason, after high school, Christian left his mother… alone. That room was so much of the reason, eventually, Christian had never gone home.

And now he was chained, alone (or not quite alone) in a place carrying the same terrifying sensation as that unpacked room. If we will never willingly confront on our own what terrifies us, time will, eventually – unwillingly – force us to do so… again, on our own.

As Christian quieted the rattling from his own straining, from out the dark corner, rattling continued. Christian's heart beat profusely. The tinkle of metal link on metal link and wooden floor increased intensity. Something was waking up. Something was coming after him. *What* lived in the darkness?

Darkness: the nothing out of which we are born, the something making us sleep… which wouldn't come to Christian. Instead, tears plied the corners of his eyes. He whispered (softly – so very softly – so that the entity in the corner wouldn't further awake), "God, if You are Anything, if You are Something, please help me…" *Help me* – the prayer of life's selfish desire, uttered by convicts and alcoholics alike, both of which, at that point, Christian was.

But such prayers remained, as they had for so long, unanswered. Was it because Nothing like God was there? Or rather, was it because Christian had gone deaf from the din of his own sins? They'd been screaming above even the Adversary's good news. Either way, in the heat of the cold darkness, a screeching silence reigned.

Until a lone voice peaked out from amid the shadowy corner where the motion had begun. To that voice, Christian could listen. Because it wasn't as frightening as he'd expected it to be. However, as both he and we have learned, in Pandemonium, amid the jangling chords of notes with no audible silences – as Evius had promised – to distinguish them, things are not always as they seem. Perhaps, it wasn't the din of Christian's own sins that might have made him deaf to God's voice. Perhaps, it was the din of the world's sins that had dampened his ears (along with the rest of ours) to a single harmony sounding amid the discord. Listen: can you hear the harmony in this work? In *this* world?

That voice spoke quietly. It spoke carefully... something soft, something sweet. With the safety of a young girl's resonance and the hint of a Southern accent, it asked, "Is somebody there?"

At the sound of her polite tones, relief welled in Christian's breast. He'd expected to hear a demon's growl, the guttural contusions of Zoe's monster, but that wasn't it. The tears plying the corners of his eyes now dribbled down his cheeks as he almost happily responded, "Yes. Yes, I'm here."

"Oh," the girl from the darkness responded, "I thought you might be Him come back for me."

Christian wasn't. He was certain of that. "What's your name?" Christian asked.

"Anne," the girl responded, "But He called me Saint Annie."

At which words, light – as blinding as the Glory of God radiant through the clouds – burst in upon them in the room. For the first time, Christian saw Saint Annie. She *was* a girl, no older than 15, chained by her neck to the wall. She had blonde curls spilling over her bare shoulders. At the sight of the light, she curled back into the corner, deeper into a ball.

And there, looming in the doorframe, was the shadow of the great bulk of their combined Lord, Malik. Saint Annie averted her eyes, but Christian, in his terror, did nothing but stare at the magnificent loping shape stepping into their shared room.

Holding nothing in his hands, Malik wore the same acid-washed jeans below his bare, hairy chest he'd had on when Christian first encountered him in the antechambers of his "palace". Like Jesus walking across the desert, burning his feet on the scorching sand, Malik was barefoot... but his own wooden floor was cool. It was cold enough to comfortably walk across with all the weight of one's foot, which Malik did. He must have stood close to seven feet tall.

Saint Annie and Christian, nakedly chained to opposite walls – Malik between them. The moment couldn't have been more symbolic. It reminds me of this moment, right now, right here, sometime, somewhere: a stranger in a strange land lost somewhere in time, locked up in the iron maiden.

A fate Christian would have relished given what came next – to have the infinity of life pushed out from you by a finite number of tormenting spikes entering every square inch of your visible body, blood pulsing out your pores with every beat of your speared heart. A new realization of terror plummeted from Christian's breast through his stomach to his guts.

Into this newfound depth of his terror, Malik plunged a growling declaration as if it were a chainsaw kicking back into the soft flesh of your neck – a horrid, many-toothed vampire bite like that from a metallic shark ripping through the flesh in your leg because, to the shark, you're nothing but a fish struggling in the water, "SLAVE, you will bear witness to everything I inflict in here. *That* is your purpose – to be nothing but eyes gazing upon the suffering Skye."

The suffering sky? But there were no windows in that room. How could Christian bear witness to the sky in such a world of walls decaying with dead plaster, wooden floorboards spattered by various hardened fluids, and chains running around the necks, arms, and legs of Saint Annie and himself? How could anybody understand the sky's pain amid the world of, Dear God, Malik?

Although, Christian would have traded seeing the suffering of anything else, anything he could possibly understand, for what he did bear witness to. It made no sense... even in Pandemonium's serpentine depths. He couldn't comprehend why Malik would do such things to someone who was little more than a child as far as Christian could tell. He couldn't comprehend Saint Annie's vacant stares even after and amid her screams. Christian couldn't understand, but still, he watched as Malik smiled eerily at him and asked if he, too, enjoyed it.

"I know you do," Malik cooed, to whom, Christian wasn't quite sure.

But still, Christian watched. He didn't want to. He was compelled to. Whether that compulsion was internal or external, even he wasn't sure. Whether he was subject or object – in either sense of either word – even he wasn't sure. But he couldn't turn away from what he was witnessing. Like the world itself, it held him captive.

An entire lifetime of emotions welled from his feet through his legs, his stomach, his chest, his face, and into his mind. Even less than what he was seeing could he comprehend what he was feeling – something born by and returning back to the unconscious, something to be forgotten that never would be: images burned deep inside the blackness of his self, sensations tattooed onto the underbelly of God's own eyelids, never to be forgotten, never to be removed. The darkness harnessed by all the world's ages sedimented itself in Christian's mind. In a sense, Christian went blind. For, what is the glory of God other than the forever sublated phenomenology of human spirit: driven unconsciously by the darkened corners of our desires?

And Christian knew why he had run from that room in his mother's home, but then, he forgot.

What he saw was too much, much too much. Unlike the Christ, Christian could never return to earth now. Even if Evius had been able to find some hidden Rainbow Bridge between worlds that he might, someday, be willing to share. Precisely like the Christ, Christian *would* never return to earth now – but (H/)he didn't know the future. He was wholly human. Instead, as if it had been a premonition, he'd been swallowed by the sensations of that abandoned room in his mother's home. The unholy secrets of the damned dead must never be brought back to life: the transmigrated zombies of this plane of existence – Osiris. Truly, it's madness. Thus, how different from life: the truth we all know but we all too often refuse to reveal even to ourselves. What the terrors of the insane frighteningly, unwittingly teach to us. There is no essential self... an-*Atman*.

What do we know – (*Nothing*...) Exactly?

Amid the cries, the screams, the grunts, the groans, sense was disintegrating. The world was melting. Veins pulsed and turned inside out. And still, Christian watched. Still, the horror continued.

As if toothpicks pried them open, Christian's eyes wouldn't close. The nightmare might never end either for Saint Annie or for Christian... or even for their current Lord, Malik. None of them could get what they truly needed (what do any of us truly need?) because the Master had lost his mind, which was apparent as Malik strained Saint Annie like she was a piece of fruit in a juicer.

Her skin sloughed off to become mere pulp. Malik would never be satisfied: not with this scream, with this torment, with this pleasure. As if he were Dr. Mengele experimenting on an undying corpse, he redressed her bones, her nerves, and he began his tasks all over again. His living possessions cried (both internally and externally). His living possessions shook (both internally and externally). His living possessions, as if they were his own bifurcated soul, died (both internally and externally), and then, like seeds planted in January outside somebody's window, they mystically came back to life.

He should say something, Christian thought, which, unbeknown to his own subjective experience, was precisely what Saint Annie subjectively thought as well... only, who *He* was differed, as it always does. But the thought, in itself, that was the same.

Externally, nothing changed as the madness in Christian and Saint Annie's cell went on and on. Malik would grunt and groan. Saint Annie would scream. And still, Christian would stare. If it didn't stop soon, he might lose his mind. To see such suffering and to be unable to do anything about it, to be unable to stop it, to be chained in place, to be naked... Christian strained against his bonds while Malik simply smiled a wretched grin. Internally, a whole new world was opening up.

From beneath Malik's hairy back, Saint Annie's childlike shrieks burrowed into Christian's soul. They found a home there, and they twisted around like worms inside your intestinal track. Feeding on everything you've ever fed upon, the inch worms grew into tapeworms. They became serpents, and they chewed through Christian's insides just as the unending river of beauties below the bridge had chewed through his outsides. The same. Only there was nothing to heal his suffering in this predicament. Evius was gone. Everything was gone. Emptiness, like that of his long ago ache for Sophia, remained deep down inside.

And Christian, whose external gaze was fixated on Saint Annie's body, found himself gazing inwardly at an entirely different scene. He remembered that a forlorn tree grew through the pavement outside the window of his earthen home. That tree's lifeless, winter branches rattling, like a chorus of cicadas, in the wind consumed him. He remembered contemplating that tree through his nights of unbearable internal agony. And he wondered what that tree outside his window had meant. What had it *symbolized*?

What is a tree? It is life: a mass of cells and vegetal organs. It reaches to the sky seeking light and sun. It speaks in its massive silence. What is a dead tree? It is knowledge: a swirling mass of atoms and electricity. It grounds the earth by ripping through surrounding vegetation. It remains silent as its world speaks. Suddenly, Christian understood: all, but then, as always, he forgot.

He remembered the way the moonlight cascaded down the tree's branches when the only drug in his system was marijuana. He remembered the tree's twiggy fingers scratching at his window as he writhed in the horrors of his drunkenness, when a blackout simply wouldn't come. He remembered the summertime and the emerald leaves blinding him to the sun, stealing its jeweled light for themselves. He remembered icicles dangling like crystal fangs from those same branches in the winter, refracting that sun into rainbow intricate patterns upon Christian's wooden floor... the same wooden floor, that now, and for all of time (as far as Christian was concerned), remained the final resting place of a little, lost sparrow.

Christian didn't close his eyes, but all he saw was that tree outside his window. He fulfilled Malik's desired contract. He watched, but he didn't *see* anything any longer. That tree outside the window inside his mind kept him safe from everything he perceived. His external vision had turned to white. His internal vision was green. Saint Annie was in too much pain for a helpless man to contemplate. He understood the suffering sky: from its nuclear heart, it bled light for life... only now, it was far too late. A lavender bruise spread across the sky. Malik's tormenting voice receded into nothing, and when Christian opened his mouth, only a dry sound clicked in the back of his throat.

As suddenly as he had begun, Malik removed himself from Saint Annie. He glared at Christian and Christian thought, for a moment, the same horrors were about to be visited upon him. But Malik didn't move to consume him. Instead, casting Saint Annie further aside, the demon said to Christian directly, "Now, Slave. Tell me what you call yourself."

Christian stuttered out his name.

"Are you telling me the truth?" Malik authoritatively wondered, "I asked your name!"

"That is my name," Christian answered, and then, he whispered, again, "Christian..."

"How fitting..." Malik shook his head, "From now on you can forget that moniker. From now on, this is your name: Slave. And I want you, Slave, to gaze upon the suffering Skye, and tell me what you feel. NOW!"

Christian didn't know what Malik meant. His head dangled loosely atop his neck, but the desired final blow still didn't materialize. "I feel... I feel... empty," he finally answered.

Malik laughed with his lips while he raged with his eyes: "So do I, Slave. So do I. And now, I will leave you alone with the suffering Skye. Contemplate that."

5.
Hummed, So Pretty...

When Malik left the room, plunging his two slaves back into darkness, Christian didn't know what to say or do. Chained to the wall, he was completely impotent. In awe at what had just occurred, he remained totally silent.

Eventually, uncharacteristically concerned for somebody other than himself, he stuttered, "Are – are you okay?"

Saint Annie didn't respond with words. However, even amid the darkness, Christian could hear her biting her lip to muffle quiet tears.

To which Christian said the only thing he knew to say, "Please don't cry," which sounded absurd given what she'd endured.

"I'm not crying because I'm sad," Saint Annie said. "That's been happening to me for what feels like forever. It's no big deal. It hurts, but it's no big deal. I'm crying because there's never been anybody here to ask me that question. There's never been anybody here... I've felt like I was dead for so long, and your question just made me feel so... so... human." Even with the blackness engulfing them, Christian could hear, solely from the inflection of her words, Saint Annie was smiling... for what, she didn't have to tell him, had been the first time in "what feels like forever", which caused Christian to smile, albeit sadly (if anybody had seen the tormented eyes above his smile – but as Saint Annie had learned so long ago, there was nobody paying any attention), as well. And then Saint Annie finished her statement with a question, "Are you human?"

Christian smiled still more mirthlessly than before. "I suppose so," he answered.

"I'm happy to hear that," Saint Annie said, "Because when He found me, He told me I may not be human anymore – after He started calling me Saint Annie, that is, before I wound up here. And Mr. Malik, if he's human at all, then I was totally wrong about what humans were like before I ever came to this place. Even after... well... even after 'all that' I still didn't think humans could be as horrible to one another as Mr. Malik is to me. Sometimes I wish I'd never come here."

"Me, too," Christian said, "Both me and you." Then, he wondered (Saint Annie seemed so different from him), "How'd you wind up here?"

"That's a long story," Saint Annie responded amid sniffles.

"You can tell me if you want," Christian whispered, in what felt like forever, kindly.

Saint Annie paused for a minute as if gathering her thoughts. Then, with a sense of determination Christian couldn't see but he could most definitely hear, she said, "Okay, I'll tell you..."

...Three Bright Nights
(The Story of Saint Annie –
As Told by the Suffering Skye)

My parents live a long way away from here... I don't really know where any more, it's been so long. But I grew up there, not here. Maybe that's why I don't really understand Mr. Malik. Not what he says, just the way he is.

I was a bad girl. I really was. I wish I hadn't been, but I was. I come from good people. I don't know why I was so bad. I've spent so much time here thinking about how good my people are, and I can't understand why I'm so bad, why I wouldn't let them just be good to me, but I wouldn't.

I was always trying to run away, ever since I can really remember. I don't have any brothers or sisters. So my parents always took me back. They shouldn't have, but they did. They always took me back.

My best friend was a boy named James. Me and James were going to run away to Los Angeles together. He was going to be a rock star, and I was going to be a stripper. I know now that that's a pretty stupid dream, but it's what James and me wanted to do. Maybe he got to do it. Maybe he got to become a rock star. I don't know. I haven't seen James since the day before that day.

My parents and I were fighting a lot. We were always fighting a lot, but around that day, when all *this* started, we were fighting a lot. It was because of this boy, not James, but another boy, a boy I'd started dating – Ike.

Ike was older than me. He had a driver's license, and he had a car. I thought I was in love with Ike, but now I know I couldn't have loved him. I couldn't have loved somebody like that.

My daddy told me I couldn't see Ike anymore. I couldn't see somebody who drove a car because I was only in middle school. I told my daddy I'd run away... only this time, I wouldn't come back. I'd run away with Ike to Los

Angeles (he promised he'd take me there)… and I'd never come back. I should have gone with James. I should have waited for James.

But when I called Ike and told him my daddy said I couldn't see him, Ike asked me if *I* still wanted to see him. I told him of course I did, I loved him. He told me he loved me, too, and he said that if I ran away he'd take me to Los Angeles. I believed him, but I should have waited for James.

I didn't go to school the next day. I met Ike at the corner around the corner from my bus stop. Ike had a friend with him: Donnie Church. Donnie Church was dating a girl at my school, too – Kat. Kat didn't like me. She didn't like me at all. When I started dating Ike, she and Evie (Evie had really liked Ike for a long time) had tried flushing my underpants down the toilet in the girl's locker room, and they told me they'd kill me if I didn't leave Ike alone. I didn't because I knew Ike would tell *them* to leave *me* alone. He did, but I wish he hadn't. They all lived in the same neighborhood: Kat, Evie, Ike, Donnie Church, and my friend Gabby who introduced me to Ike at the mall that one time.

I asked Ike if Donnie Church was going to come with us to Los Angeles. He said he was.

Ike and Donnie Church were drinking beers. I didn't like beer, but they had a bottle of Wild Irish Rose. I drank that instead. I didn't like it, but it was better than beer. I liked Boone's Strawberry Farm, and Wild Irish Rose sounded like it was kind of the same thing. It wasn't, but it was better than beer.

I don't really know why we stopped, and I don't know why we went into the woods, but there we were, in the middle of this clearing with this old, abandoned washing machine in it. There we were: me, Ike, and Donnie Church, the two of them drinking beer, and me trying not to get sick off that bottle of Wild Irish Rose.

I remember I asked them when we were going to get going to Los Angeles, and Donnie Church asked me what I was planning on doing there. I should have asked him the same question, but Ike just said, "Go ahead, tell him."

Ike knew about what me and James were planning on being in Los Angeles. So I told him: I was going to be a stripper.

"You'd make a pretty nice stripper," Donnie Church said.

I didn't think that was very nice for him to say to me in front of my boyfriend and all, but he and Ike just laughed.

"Go ahead, show him how you plan to be a stripper, Anne," Ike said.

I told him I didn't think he'd want his friend to see me like that, and Ike said if I was going to be a stripper, he'd just have to get used to it. I thought that was sweet. "Go ahead, Anne, dance for us," Ike said.

"But there's no music," I said.

"Doesn't make a difference whether or not there's music, Anne," Ike said, "Just dance for us."

I'd never had sex with Ike. I'd let him feel me up, but I'd never had sex with anybody. That's the truth. Ike had never even seen me totally naked... no boy had ever seen me totally naked. But I danced anyways.

"Take your shirt off, Anne," Ike said.

"Shouldn't we get going?" I said.

But Donnie Church said, "You need to practice if you want to be a stripper in Los Angeles, Anne."

So I took my shirt off. I don't know why I did it, but I took my shirt off.

"And your bra, too, Anne," Donnie Church said.

I looked at Ike, but he just nodded. So I did it.

I didn't think either one of them would touch me. I thought I was safe since my boyfriend was there. Because I certainly didn't think Ike would let Donnie Church touch me, but I was wrong.

When they were all done with me, I didn't want to go to Los Angeles anymore. Especially not with Ike and Donnie Church. It hurt too bad. Not just on the outside, but on the inside, too. That's why it hurt worse than what Mr. Malik does to me. Because it hurt on the inside, too.

But that didn't make much of a difference. I don't think they were ever planning on taking me to Los Angeles anyways. I think they just wanted to get me into the woods. And that's what they did. Sometimes, I'm so stupid.

I'd thought Ike had loved me. I sure enough loved him, but you can't love somebody who you let your friend do those sorts of things to. So I guess I was wrong. I've been wrong about so many things. Sometimes I think that's what Mr. Malik is punishing me for... for being so wrong. I don't know. I don't know why Mr. Malik does what he does.

But after Ike and Donnie Church left, I just stayed in that clearing in the woods next to that old, abandoned washing machine. I didn't cry. I didn't do anything. I just stared at all the dead leaves and where they were all torn apart from where they'd thrown me down. You ever feel that way? Like you're just too sad to even cry. So I put my clothes back on, and I walked home.

When I got home, though, I was in real big trouble. You see, a teacher had called my parents and told them I'd never shown up to school that day. What with the argument we'd had the night before, they were real mad at me. But I didn't fight back this time. They kept asking me where I was all day...

I never said anything. I think I just looked down at the

ground and tried not to cry. That made them both real mad. I didn't mean to make them mad, but I did. I kept promising myself I wouldn't cry because I didn't want to tell my parents how stupid I'd been. Not both my parents, but my daddy. I didn't want to tell my daddy how stupid his little girl had been. So eventually, when they were done yelling at me and telling me they didn't know *what* they were going to do with me, after they'd told me I was grounded for as long as I could think of, I just went to my room, and that was when I finally started to cry.

The next day, when I woke up, I promised myself I would be good from then on out. I promised myself I would never make my daddy angry again, that I was *happy* they'd grounded me. That way I could prove to them, both my mom and my daddy, that I could be good.

But I still wasn't good, and that's why I think I wound up here with Mr. Malik. He would have saved me, but I'd been too bad already, and that's why He couldn't.

I know He *wanted* to… He just couldn't. I guess that's how the whole thing works.

But that next day in school… I really wish she hadn't done it, but Gabby (that same girl who introduced me to Ike that time at the mall), she asked me if I wanted to go ride a horse with her after school that day. She had a horse, and she wanted me to ride it with her. I should have told her I couldn't. I should have told her I was grounded. That's what a good girl would have done. But I wasn't a good girl… Maybe when I was really little I was, but that was a long time ago… A long time ago then, and an even longer ago time now. I don't know how long I've been here with Mr. Malik. But I'm sure my parents are really scared about me. Because Ike might not have loved me, but now, after meeting Mr. Malik, I know *they* loved me. And He *wanted* to love me. He just couldn't. Not with the type of little girl I've been.

So here I am with Mr. Malik...

But that day, the day all this *really* started. Gabby asked me if I wanted to go horseback riding with her on her horse. I didn't really want to say yes. I had this funny feeling in my stomach the whole time I was thinking about it and then when I said it... like I knew something was going to go wrong, but still, I said it. I knew I was grounded, but I told Gabby – yes, I'd go horseback riding with her.

She seemed really excited when I told her I would, and that's what made me feel like it would be okay. Even though that meant I wouldn't go straight home from school just like my parents had told me to... And even though it meant I was going to be in even more trouble since I wasn't going to do what they said again. And even though it meant, and I knew it meant this, that my daddy was going to be disappointed in me again, and he'd give me that look he'd give me that made my stomach feel like I was going to flip inside out. Even with all that, I still told Gabby I'd go horseback riding with her after school that day. Because I wanted to ride a horse. It just sounded so nice. And I wanted her to be my friend. I wanted Gabby and Gabby's horse to be my friend... You can be friends with an animal, you know. It's not very hard...

When we got to the farm where they kept Gabby's horse, I was still real scared... But just because I thought I was going to be in trouble. Not because I thought anything else was going to happen. But maybe I knew bad things were going to happen, real bad things, and maybe that's *really* why I was so scared. I don't know. But I was so scared I felt kind of sick.

Until I saw the horse, at least...

I hadn't seen many horses... Not in real life. I'd seen

them a lot in movies. But to see one in real life… I couldn't believe how big it was walking around that circle they kept it penned up in. There was this white fence the horse was walking next to. And the horse, it was light gray with darker gray spots on it. And it had the prettiest mane stretching down its back. Its mane was so beautiful. Such beautiful hair it had… I wanted my hair to look that pretty. And there was a barn right behind that circle with the white fence. But I didn't really look there. Why should I have looked there? Now I know I should have paid more attention to the barn. But I should have paid more attention to everything. And I didn't. I just decided then that I made the right decision not to do what my parents told me to do. And that it was okay if I was going to be in more trouble. Because that horse was so pretty, it was worth it.

"Do you want to pet him, Anne?" Gabby asked. And I nodded I would.

Gabby took me in behind the white fence. She introduced me to the horse. Israfel was his name. I thought it was some made up word. But then Gabby said it was the name of an *angel*. She said she learned it because it was the name of a poem her grandfather had read to her mom once. I don't remember who Gabby said wrote it. But her grandfather had liked the poem when *he'd* been a little boy, and her mom had always thought it was such a pretty name. So when Gabby got a horse, her mom asked her if she wanted to name him Israfel.

"It *is* a pretty name," I told Gabby.

Gabby tied Israfel up to a post, and she said I could stay there and pet him while she went into the barn to use the bathroom. She said she was going to get Israfel an apple, too. I remember I hoped she'd let me feed Israfel that apple. Because I wanted to be his friend. I already felt like *he* was my friend. But I wanted me to be *his* friend.

I didn't have to wait for him to be my friend though. As soon as Gabby left, I went up to Israfel. "You're so pretty," I told him. He neighed. And it was like he nodded his head at me.

"Can you understand what I say?" I asked him.

He neighed and nodded his head again. And you might not believe me, but I *knew* that meant he could understand everything I said to him. So I told him about what had happened to me the day before. I pet his face, and I told him what had happened to me the day before. He listened to me, but his eyes looked real sad while I said the things Ike and Donnie Church had done to me. And I know it was hard for him to hear. Because his ears kept twitching like he didn't want to hear anymore. But he knew like I knew that I had to tell somebody. And I needed to tell somebody who understood me but wouldn't tell anybody else. I didn't know anybody like that. Not even James. I could have told James. But he would have wanted to do something about it. He would have wanted to fight Donnie Church and Ike. And I loved James, and I know James loved me. But I knew they would beat him up. I knew they'd beat him up real bad if they knew he knew what they'd done to me. And I loved James. So I didn't want to let them hurt him like they'd hurt me. And *that's* why I didn't know anybody like that except for Israfel.

It was because I was petting Israfel and telling him that story that I didn't really pay any attention to who was walking up behind me. I heard the footsteps. I just didn't pay any attention. You should always pay attention to what's going on behind you because you never know what it might be.

But I wasn't paying any attention. I wasn't paying any attention until I heard a girl say, "Why don't you turn around and look at me, bitch."

And I did. I did because I knew it wasn't Gabby's voice I heard… even though the voice sounded real familiar. And as soon as I turned around, sure enough, it was familiar. It was familiar because it was Kat, Donnie Church's girlfriend, and for a second, I knew why it sounded familiar. It sounded familiar because it was the same thing she'd said to me with the same tone of voice that time her and Evie, that same girl who liked Ike, flushed my underpants down the toilet in the girl's locker room.

I got real scared right then. Some of it was because I thought maybe Donnie Church and Ike were there, too, and I didn't know what they were going to do to me again. But a lot of it was because Evie was standing right behind Kat, and I remembered what they'd said to me when they flushed my underpants down the toilet in the girl's locker room that time when they said they'd kill me if I didn't leave Ike alone. Even though I should have. I should have left him alone not because they told me to but because my daddy told me to. And I didn't. So now I'm here with Mr. Malik.

"Did you fuck my boyfriend?" Kat said.

I didn't. But I didn't know what to say because in a way, I did. In a way, I did fuck her boyfriend even though I didn't want to.

"I said, did you fuck my boyfriend, bitch!" Kat screamed at me.

I started to cry. Because where was Gabby? She wasn't anywhere. And she'd brought me there. And that was when I knew she'd brought me there just so they could be there. And that was when I knew she wasn't my friend at all. Just like with Ike, she wasn't my friend at all. I didn't have any friends. I didn't have any friends except for James, and he wasn't there right then.

So I looked at Israfel. I looked Israfel right in the eyes. And he nodded again, and it was like *he* told me what to say. Israfel told me to tell Kat I didn't have sex with Donnie Church. And once Israfel told me to say that, right then, I made up my mind I didn't. I didn't have sex with Donnie Church, and I didn't have sex with Ike.

But Evie stepped up beside Kat, and she said, "I think you did, bitch. I think you fucked him and Ike in the woods down on Paradise Lane just yesterday."

I started shaking my head, and I told them again, "I didn't do that."

"You know," Evie said, "That was your one chance, bitch, because if you'd told us the truth, we would've let you go. But now we know. Now we know... You're not just a slut. You're a liar, too."

I was crying so hard by then I couldn't believe I was still standing. I probably should've run, but I was crying too hard. Why would they have called me those things? I didn't lie to them. And I wasn't a slut. I'd never even had sex before, not before the day before, and I didn't even want to have sex then. Evie and Kat had had sex. Everybody knew that. Kat had sex with Donnie Church all the time, and Evie had had sex with Ike before. Everybody knew that. I was a virgin until the day before, and I still wanted to be a virgin then, but I couldn't be a virgin anymore. So, I guess, in a sense, I thought maybe they were right. Even though Israfel was saying I wasn't, maybe I was a slut and a liar. Israfel shook his head right then, and I knew that meant he didn't think I was. But still, I should've run. I should've run, but I just didn't think they'd do to me what they did to me. Like the day before with Ike and Donnie Church, I didn't think they'd do to me what they did to me.

Kat was the first one who touched me. She shoved me real hard, and I fell down.

It all happened so fast. It was like the day before with Ike and Donnie Church. It all happened so fast. I guess that's how life is. It all happens so fast. They were kicking me and punching me, and it didn't really hurt. It didn't really hurt like the day before with Ike and Donnie Church. I could feel this coldness all over my face, and I knew it was blood. I knew my nose was bleeding, and it was splashing all over me. I could feel my eyes puffing and swelling. And Evie was screaming, "You ain't so pretty, now, huh? You ain't so pretty now, are you, bitch? You ain't so pretty now."

And I remember thinking I never thought I was pretty.

But then Evie got a hold of my hair. I know it was Evie because I saw her face right in front of me. I saw her face outlined by the sun when she banged my head against the ground, and I felt a real sharp pain in the back of my head, and that was when I knew she'd slammed my head into a rock. And then, everything went black.

I had a dream. I had a dream, right then. I dreamed I was flying. I dreamed I was flying down a long, dark tunnel with a light at the very end of it. It was like I was flying into the sun. And in the light, I could see all these angels. There were all these angels flapping around me. All these angels with golden wings. And I knew they were angels because they looked just like I'd always known they looked.

But I got real scared then. I got real scared because I was afraid I was dead. I was afraid I was dead and I'd never see my mom and my daddy again. And the last thing I'd known was that they were angry with me, and I hadn't even told them I loved them. I hadn't told them I loved them in a real long time. And I did love them. I knew right then – I loved my mom and my daddy. I knew that right then. And I felt like I was going to cry. Even though I was flying through all those angels, I felt like I was going to cry.

But then I heard a voice. I heard a voice say, "Annie? Are you there my little, orphan Saint Annie?"

And the first thing I thought was that it was Israfel talking to me. Because nobody spoke that nice to me anymore... nobody except James, that is. But it didn't sound like James. It sounded like Israfel. So I opened my eyes, and all the angels disappeared.

I was lying on the ground in Israfel's pen, but Israfel had disappeared. It was still light out. It was starting to get dark, but it was still light out. And Israfel, Evie, Kat, and Gabby... they'd all disappeared, but there was a man. There was a man crouched down beside me. He had blond hair, and it was real long and wavy. And he was dressed like he should have been in a music video. And he had the prettiest eyes I'd ever seen. Blue eyes, and they were the prettiest eyes I'd ever seen. He looked like somebody from somewhere I'd been before. But he also looked like somebody who lived some place far away, some place like Los Angeles.

"Who are you?" I asked him.

"I'm Israfel," he said. "I'm the angel, Israfel."

I asked him if I was dead. And he said he didn't think I'd ever die. Then, I asked if he was real. And he said he was as real as I was. And he told me to stand up.

I didn't think I'd be able to... not after everything Kat and Evie had done to me. But I did. I stood up, and the angel Israfel stood up right along with me. He was a lot taller than me, and above him, the moon was poking through the blue sky. You know how it does that? Right before it gets dark, how the moon looks like somebody just pressed it out of the daytime sky like it was some sort of button? Well, it looked just like that. Just like that above the angel, Israfel. And I started to cry.

"Why are you crying, Saint Annie?" Israfel asked me.

"Because of what I look like," I told him.

"And what do you look like?" he wondered.

"I don't know," I said. "I don't know what they did to me, but I know I'm not pretty. I know I'm not pretty enough to meet an angel."

"They didn't do anything to you," he told me. "You're pretty enough for an angel."

"What do you mean?" I asked him.

"Do you know what sign you are, Saint Annie?" Israfel asked.

"What?" I asked him.

"Your zodiac sign, Saint Annie…" Israfel said.

"I'm a Virgo," I told him

"And do you know what it means to be a Virgo?" he asked.

I shook my head, *No*.

He said, "Virgos stay pure. No matter what happens to them, they always stay pure. In fact, you're so pure, you may not even be a human anymore…" And that was when he told me people could do all sorts of things to me but that I would always heal. Because I was a Virgo, it didn't matter what happened to me. I'd always come back to being his little, orphan Saint Annie. And that's why I was *Saint* Annie. Because nobody could hurt me forever.

But that's also why Mr. Malik eventually wanted me. Because I'm a Virgo, and he can do whatever he wants to to me, and I'll always heal. So he can do it all over again. And that's what he likes to do. He likes to do all those things to me you saw him do to me. And then, he likes to do them again.

But I didn't know about Mr. Malik back then. I just listened to the angel Israfel tell me how I wasn't anything like anything I'd ever thought a human being was before. I was a Virgo, and that meant I may never die. And that meant I was special, that I was *Saint* Annie.

"Can I go back to see my mom and my daddy soon?" I asked the angel Israfel.

"You'll see them soon enough," he said, "But first, there's one place left for you to go."

"Where's that?" I asked him.

"Los Angeles," he told me.

So the angel Israfel brought me here to Los Angeles. But Los Angeles wasn't quite like I always imagined it. I'd never been here before, but this isn't how I imagined it. I thought there'd be beaches and movie stars, but I haven't seen anything like that from the day I got here.

Instead, when we got off the bus, the first person we met was this gray-haired old man. He didn't really walk quite right, he kind of hobbled like he'd just been alive too long to stand on his own two feet anymore. He carried a cane, and he was sort of bald, and it looked like he hadn't shaved for a while. He was wearing black pants and a white dress shirt that was unbuttoned at the neck. His shoes were that same comfortable kind that you can buy at any K-Mart. And he smoked these wicked looking, hand-rolled cigarettes.

He walked right up to us when we stepped off that bus, and he told us he could find us whatever we needed.

The angel Israfel whispered to me, "You never know who God is. So you better be nice to everybody. That's what I always say…"

I agreed. Maybe I shouldn't have, but I did. Maybe if I hadn't agreed, the angel Israfel would have been able to stay with me in Los Angeles. And maybe if the angel Israfel had been able to stay with me, I never would have wound up here with Mr. Malik. But he couldn't stay. The angel Israfel couldn't stay in Los Angeles with me. God had to take him away. Maybe it was because there was somebody else he had to help to get here. I don't know. God took him away, and I never got a chance to ask him.

The old man gave us some food. I was really hungry because I suddenly realized I hadn't eaten in days, and as soon as I ate, I fell asleep.

When I woke up the next day, the angel Israfel and the old man were both gone. I went looking for them, but there was this policeman. He wore his uniform all out of place, not like the policemen in my hometown who kept their shirttails perfectly tucked in. And his hat, it tilted to the side like he thought he looked cool or something. He scared me.

I didn't want to ask him where the angel Israfel and the old man might have gone, and I didn't. When I saw him walking down the street towards me, I turned around in the other direction like I'd never seen him at all.

But he shouted at me, "You! You, young lady, where do you think you're going?"

I turned back around real slow because I didn't want him to talk to me, and I wished he'd just disappear. But you can't tell a policeman to leave you alone, and people don't just disappear, do they?

So he ran right up to me. He pointed his finger in my face like he was my gym teacher, and he said to me, "Your motley crew is poison, young lady. No more fun and games."

Next thing I knew, I was in the back of this white van, and there were all these people chained up all around me. I was chained up, too, and the van was so uncomfortable. The chains cut into my wrists and my ankles and my neck. We kept bouncing around because it felt like we were racing through all of Los Angeles, turning really sharp turns, and knocking us all around like the driver didn't even care there were people in the back.

Mr. Malik paid for me. He paid for me as soon as they

took me out of the van. I didn't think you could do that to a person anymore, but I guess Los Angeles is different from where I grew up. I saw Mr. Malik give money to this person wearing a really long robe that covered everything from their hair to their feet, even their face, and the person in the robe gave Mr. Malik my chain. He paid for me. I didn't think you could do that to a person anymore, but it's like he was waiting for me. It's like Mr. Malik was waiting just for me. He brought me here.

I don't know how long ago that was, but it's been a really long time. Mr. Malik nailed my chain into the wall, and he started doing to me all those things you saw him do to me. He told me my name was Skye. I tried telling him my name was Anne, but he wouldn't listen. He got so mean, even meaner than usual, when I tried to tell him my *real* name. He said I was Skye, that I was the suffering Skye. So I never tried to tell him my real name again.

I just want to see my mom and my daddy again. I want to tell them I wish I hadn't always been such a bad girl. I just want to see my mom and my daddy again.

4.
The Death of Sophia

Christian didn't know what to say to what Saint Annie had told him. The world was so dark… Both inside and out, everything was black. The pitch crept in through Christian's open ears. It spun his mind through his head. It trickled out his eyes with every tear only to reenter his mouth with every heaved breath as if the darkness were a conscious blackout. But the whole purpose of a blackout is to not experience consciousness. Instead, to experience… the sublime: nothing.

"Are you still there?" Saint Annie asked him.

He responded, "Yes. I'm still here."

"Oh, good. I was worried maybe you'd disappeared like He did…"

"No. No, I didn't disappear," Christian, unfortunately, had to respond yet again – as if the iron maiden were forcing the breath out his chest, spearing his heart, and tearing his spleen for its own torturous ideal – an experience sublime, yet again, in its magnitude.

"And then I'd be here all alone again. I don't want to be alone again. I'm sorry you're here. I really am. I'm so sorry you have to be here, to see all this, but I don't want to be alone again."

"You're not alone, Annie."

"Thank you. Thank you for being here even though I can't see you. At least I know you can hear me."

"I can hear you…"

So the days of endless nights wore on. And Saint Annie's screams ossified Christian's soul. In other words, they made it *real*, a core, a being around which a body could form: Christian.

There were always lulls between Malik's visits. In the darkness, Christian and Annie would speak to one another, cry with one another, and through the intervals Christian lost his sense of time.

One day, after a particularly brutal visitation, the little orphan, Saint Annie asked Christian, "My friend, have you ever been in love?"

Christian strained against his metal bonds, but eventually, he had to say, "Yes. Yes, I've been in love."

"What was it like?"

"I don't know anymore."

"Could you tell me the story?"

"I don't know if I can remember it in here…"

To which Saint Annie mumbled, "You don't know anything, and neither do I. Just tell me a story to keep my mind off my own."

And Christian began…

Through Days of Endless Nights
*(Christian's Love of Sophia –
A Slave's Story in e minor)*

Allegro:
I Was Scared, Then, but Not So Much Now…

I don't know how long ago this was, but it was right after my junior year of college, which, before I showed up here made it six years ago, I think…

Why I bought the ticket to Europe is another story entirely – one I'd like to tell you sometime, but not right now. Suffice it to say, I went to Europe alone, to get away from things in the States. I guess I wanted to have an adventure. I still believed in adventures back then, but not anymore.

I'd met this guy from Rome, Giovanni, the summer before, and he was my pretense for the trip. He'd offered to let me stay in a guesthouse there with his family, but I figured I should do some backpacking across the continent first.

I flew into London, took the ferry to France, crashed in hostels in Paris and Amsterdam, and then made my way through Berlin to Poland and down to the Czech Republic. That's where I met Melinda, at a hostel in Prague.

I opened my eyes one morning from this crazy dream about these people called "the dwellers in the fourth dimension". They were manipulating all these machines that somehow affected my life, and right before I opened my eyes, I heard one of them say: *He's ready.*

That's when I saw Melinda.

She isn't who this story's about, but she's an intricate part of how it all happened. So I have to tell you about her, too.

The sun was shining in through the windows of this big warehouse room we were all sleeping in. She wasn't wearing a shirt. She wasn't even wearing a bra. "Laundry day," she said to me while popping some gum, and I smiled.

"I noticed," I told her, probably grinning because I was young. She had brown hair and dark skin, and she reminded me of a girl I'd thought I was in love with as a kid. But that's another story, too. One that probably explains a lot about me...

On that morning, though, those days of being the new kid on a middle school bus were the furthest thing from my mind. That morning, my body was on fire with optimism and youth. I was a caged bird set free feeling, for the first time, my wings. It's a shame they melted so fast. I hardly even had a chance to fly.

You see, what I haven't said so far is, back then, I had a girlfriend in the States. She wasn't the reason I'd bought the ticket, but she *was* the reason I'd wished I *hadn't* bought the ticket. Because I'd bought the ticket before I'd started dating her... since another girl had broken my heart, and when I bought that ticket to Europe, anywhere on the same continent as Eve (the girl who broke my heart) was just too close. But like I said, Eve's a whole other story. Someday, I might tell you about it...

Michelle (the girl who I was dating at the time) and I were supposed to meet up in Germany somewhere near the end of my trip. We hadn't decided on an exact date or place yet, but she was going there to visit her brother who was in the army, and we were planning on touring the castles along the Rhine. It sounded wonderful and beautiful. I called her once a week, Wednesday afternoons on the dot... since she was taking summer classes then and had those evenings free. I believed whole-heartedly back then that I was in love with Michelle. She'd saved me from Eve. But, this time, Michelle isn't who the story is about either.

I'd been in Europe about a month and a half at that point, and I had about a month and a half to go. I guess, you could say I was midway through my journey when this story starts. And like I said, that whole time, I called Michelle every Wednesday evening on the dot. In fact, I'd called her just the day before Melinda strolled into our communal warehouse room at that hostel with her shirt off. But that phone call the day before was the last time I spoke to Michelle that whole time I was in Europe.

Oh, don't get me wrong, I told Michelle I was going to call her the next Wednesday so we could nail down our plans for touring the Rhine. And we told each other we loved each other and we'd talk in a week. But that was the first time I ever lied to a girl who wasn't my mother. Even though I didn't mean to.

I really didn't mean to.

Melinda and I had breakfast together that afternoon. I remember that old hip hop track *Ghetto Supastar* was playing in the kitchen. Melinda and I hit it off quite nicely. She was from New York, and she wanted to be a dancer. I fancied myself an artist of sorts, too, because I wanted to be a jazz musician back then. She'd studied tap when she was younger and loved jazz... especially rag time. So she asked if I could play Scott Joplin. I told her, of course I could. And she said we should do a duet together someday. I laughed, but to be completely honest, I was scared, then. Because I really liked her. Which threw me into a total panic with regard to Michelle because if I was so in love with Michelle, how could I want to be with Melinda so badly? But I kept my feelings to myself and spent the day touring around Prague with Melinda.

In fact, I spent that day and the next touring around Prague with Melinda. I remember we went to see a puppet production of *Don Giovanni* that night, and the next day, I bought this picture from some crazy artist on the Charles Bridge who drew these really wild portraits of the devil. We saw Mozart's *Requiem* performed in an old church, and we went to this modern dance performance that intertwined all these sheets and ropes and wrapped them around the performers like they were strangling them. Both nights, we were eating three course meals for the equivalent of what was, like, ten bucks (there was no such thing as the Euro back then). We went out clubbing until the sun came up, and one night, this old, drunk guy who could barely speak English (but that was okay, I mean, we weren't in America) asked me if I wanted to buy some Viagra so I could spend all night with my girlfriend. Melinda and I just laughed. But we developed such a connection that when she said she was leaving for Budapest on Saturday, I told her I'd go with her. And I did.

I hadn't even thought about Michelle when I'd said yes, and every time she popped into my head, I felt so guilty. Melinda and I hadn't really done anything, but I wanted to. I really wanted to. And on the train ride down to Budapest, when Melinda curled up in the seat beside me and went to sleep with her head in my lap, I ran my fingers through her black hair. I was afraid I was going to cheat on Michelle, and I was afraid there was nothing I could do about it.

It was just like my drinking. I didn't always want to drink, and back in those days, sometimes I didn't. But whenever I did drink, even all the way back then, there was nothing I could do about it.

We found this really amazing hostel in Budapest. The living room was covered in travelers sitting on brightly colored pillows, and there was a gazebo in the backyard. It was a wooden structure, about ten feet tall in the center, with a ceiling that arched down and expanded into posts that dropped into guardrails that folded into seats. And it seemed like in the nighttime, lovers retreated to the shadowy alcove. Old or young, it didn't matter because lovers are the same for all eternity. The boy would write or carve their names into the gazebo's soft wood so that coming generations would always know that somebody had been in love, once. Then, he would sit down and the girl would curl her head into his shoulder or lean against one of the posts of one of the benches. They would whisper about how lonely they'd been before they'd met, and they'd shield one another from the wind. At least, that's what I thought.

That first night in Budapest, Melinda and I went to a jazz club on the Pest side of the river. I remember walking there through this bombed out building that looked like it had probably never been rebuilt after the war. The skylights were all shattered, and the concrete walls had what looked like bullet holes puncturing them. I haven't thought about any of this in years... so many years... not consciously, at least.

The next day, we met some of the other travelers. There were three of them in particular – Kristen from Australia who was on walkabout, which she could do since Australia had socialized healthcare. She wore her hair really short, and she dressed super punk, but she was really into drum and bass. There was Bill from the Bay Area who had quit his job as a programmer after making millions when his company sold. And then, this Canadian guy named Gary. The three of them invited me and Melinda to go to a brewery with them. Melinda wanted to go, but I didn't. I mean I wanted to go, and it wasn't because I didn't want to drink. I just didn't know what would happen if I drank one more time with Melinda. You see, I felt like that train ride down there, when she'd fallen asleep on my lap and when I'd played with her hair, I felt like that had pushed us closer to the edge, that, pretty soon, we'd have to leap. And I didn't want to cheat on Michelle. I really didn't. So I didn't go.

But Melinda did, and all day, while she was gone, I just

sat around the hostel reading *War and Peace* – I'd started it in London, at the beginning of my trip (I figured it would last me the whole summer), and I remember reading the section on the Battle of Austerlitz when I was in Paris and realizing the arch in front of the Louvre was built out of the cannon captured in that battle – and feeling sorry for myself. I was eating chunks of thick Hungarian bread, and waiting for her and our new friends to get back.

I was running out of money, and I knew it. There was no more cash in my bank account (I'd overspent myself in Amsterdam), and I was living off cash advances on my credit card. The card had a $1000 limit because my mom had co-signed on it for me when I'd started college. But I could only get out $500 in cash advances. And like I said, I was only halfway through my trip. So I just sat around the hostel reading *War and Peace*.

By the time Melinda and the rest of them got back, I wasn't in the best of moods. I've never been in the best of moods when I want to drink and I'm trying not to. And the fact that all four of them came back trashed out of their minds didn't help with my mood at all. Melinda went back to our room and passed out. Kristen told me what a great time they'd all had and how I should have gone with them, but the fact they'd wanted me there didn't cheer me up... especially since Bill and Gary were thrilled they'd had an opportunity to see Melinda naked.

I guess somewhere during the drinking process, Melinda had taken off all her clothes and gone running around the barrels. I was jealous. I'd wanted to see her totally naked from the moment I'd met her, and I still couldn't admit that to myself. So I stayed up late into the night playing cards with the three of them, drinking their wine, and trying not to let anybody know how hurt I was that I hadn't been able to go with them and that while I was separated from her, for some reason, Melinda had chosen to share a piece of herself with them she'd yet to share with me. It never even crossed my mind to excuse her because she'd been drunk. I certainly would have asked for that kind of forgiveness from her if the roles had been reversed.

Needless to say, when I woke up the next morning, mildly hungover and probably still a little drunk from all their red wine the night before, I wasn't particularly thrilled with Melinda. She tried talking to me during breakfast, and I was pretty cold as she told me about her experience at the brewery and how much fun she'd had. She followed me when I went outside to smoke a cigarette, and we sat down in that gazebo I told you about earlier.

"I'm so glad I was there instead of church yesterday," she said since the day before had been Sunday.

"Church serves a purpose," I said roughly.

"Really?" she asked, "And what purpose is that?"

I was a little dismissive, but I shrugged and said, "It forces you to wonder about God."

"I don't want to wonder about God," she said.

I looked her straight in the face, and I said, "But you have to. Once Jesus showed up here and said what he said, every human being has to make a choice – Do you want to believe in God or not?"

"I don't think I have to make that choice."

"But, don't you see, you do," I told her. "Once Jesus said what he said, you have to make the choice whether you want to go to heaven or hell."

"I don't think those are the only options."

"They may not be, but in Christianity, they are. So once you learn about Christ, you have to choose – Do you want to believe and go to heaven, or forget about the whole thing and take a chance on hell?"

"Really?" she asked me, visibly perturbed, "And have

you made that choice, Christian?"

"Yeah," I said. "I don't believe."

"Well, that's fucking great," she told me, and she went back inside. She didn't speak to me the whole rest of that day, and she left without telling me the following morning. I told myself I was comfortable with that.

But the whole reason I told you about Melinda was to get to this point. Because, like I said, I was running out of money, and I didn't know how I was going to afford the rest of my trip. So when Kristen asked me the following morning, "Where'd Melinda go?"

And I said, "I don't know."

And she said, "I thought you two were, you know…"

I told her, "No. We were just friends. I have a girlfriend back in the States." But it really hurt to say that.

So she said to me, "Well, if you're looking for some new traveling partners, me, Gary, and Bill are heading out to Salzburg tomorrow. You should come with us."

I told her I'd love to do that, and even though I was still angry at Melinda since I didn't get to do what I'd wanted to do with her, I was also relieved I wasn't going to cheat on Michelle. Or so I thought.

We left super early the next morning, and when we got to Salzburg, we all went out for lunch. I remember we were sitting on this patio with these sheer rock faces surrounding us and stretching up like they were the buildings of downtown New York. The three of them were so impressed with me. Because I could explain all the intricacies of the music in Bach's *St. Matthew Passion*, and I could tell them what made it such an incredible composition, but I could also recite the entire Wu-Tang *Enter the 36 Chambers* album. And their accolades about how I was the smartest hipster they'd ever met made me forget all about losing Melinda. But I wouldn't have been in

Salzburg in the first place if it hadn't been for her.

When it came time to pay, the restaurant didn't take cards, but they said there was an ATM around the corner. I strolled on over to where the waiter had said to go, and that was when I discovered I couldn't get any more cash advances on my credit card.

Alla tedesca:
My Bank Account Had Finally Gone Dry

Maybe everything happens for a reason. I don't know. I don't really believe that, but I don't know.

You see, I was scared. Like I said before, I was only halfway through my trip, which meant I still had a month and a half left in Europe, and as far as I could tell, I was practically broke. Especially since it had been my experience there weren't many places that took credit cards on the Continent back in those days. So, needless to say, I was scared.

The guys I was traveling with were happy enough to pay my lunch bill, which, looking back on it, was awfully nice of them, and we wandered off to the hostel they'd picked out for us. Me, silently hoping I could use my credit card there and panicking about what I'd do if I couldn't.

It was while we were walking that Kristen came up with a solution for my dilemma. "You know," she said, her Australian accent drawing out each vowel and dropping the end of every word, "You could probably call your credit card company and get an extension on your cash advances…"

"You can do that?" I asked her, somewhat shocked I'm sure.

"I don't see why not."

Our other two friends, who were a bit more worldly than either me or Kristen at that point in time, agreed.

The first payphone we got to, I pulled my credit card out of the wrap-around, waist wallet I'd bought back in the States, checked for a phone number on the back and placed the call. The line rang and rang, and then, a woman's voice answered.

"Hi," I said. My palms were sweating. The receiver almost slipped from my grip. I didn't know what I'd do if they said, *No.* I swallowed hard, and then, the words just spilled out, "I'm traveling through Europe right now, and I found out I maxed out the cash advances on my credit card. I still have money left on the card... I just can't get any more cash advances. Is there any way I could get an extension on those?" I bit my lip while I waited for the woman's response.

"Sure. That's no problem, sir. Just let me transfer you."

Suddenly, my stomach felt like somebody had turned a key in its lock. I was saved. The line started ringing another extension. It rang and rang, and then, the line suddenly went dead.

I scrunched up my eyebrows. Quickly, I dialed the number again. Again, a woman's voice answered. I spoke a little more emphatically this time, "Hi. I was just talking with someone about getting an extension on my cash advances, but when she transferred me, the line went dead. Is there any way you could transfer me to that department again?"

"Sure. No problem, sir."

Again, my stomach came to terms with itself. But again, as soon as the next extension started ringing, the line went dead.

I stepped out of the phone booth. On the door, a sign was posted in English – *No international calls over 3 minutes.*

I scratched my head and bit my lip, but still, I thought, *No big deal. I'll make the call at the hostel…*

On the way to the hostel, though, I checked two more phone booths. Neither allowed international calls beyond three minutes, and suddenly, my palms started sweating again.

The phone at the hostel wasn't any different. My traveling partners paid for a couple rounds of drinks at the bar. It was about midway through the second beer when I turned to Kristen and said, "You know, if there's any payphone in this town that allows international calls, it'll probably be the one at the train station."

She wiped some suds from her lips. "Go for it," she told me.

Slightly buzzed, I nodded and left my half-drank beer (which was a rare occurrence for me even back then) so I could make my way back to where we'd come from in the first place.

Outside the train station, at the mouth of a tunnel leading into where the trains departed from, there most definitely was a phone booth. I didn't see the sticker on the door saying I'd only be able to make the call I needed to make for a mere three minutes. I glanced around like I was being pursued, stepped into the booth, shrugged my shoulders, breathed in deeply, pulled my card from out my money belt, and dialed the number.

A woman answered yet again. I explained my situation yet again, and I hoped I didn't get cut off yet again. She transferred me. The line rang and rang and rang. Another woman answered. And finally… I was able to get an extension on my cash advances.

All the tension released from my shoulders. Without the panic, I suddenly remembered – I needed to call Michelle. I'd had so much on my mind, she'd completely slipped my mind, and today was the day I was supposed to call.

I figured I'd step out and see if I could scrounge up a cigarette since I hadn't bought a pack all day and had simply been bumming from my travel companions. Then, I could call Michelle and tell her about my last week's adventures (leaving out, of course, everything about Melinda). But there was nobody in my vicinity.

A man appeared outside the train station. He pulled a pack of Marlboros out of his pocket, shook a cigarette out of it, stuck the cigarette between his lips, tilted his head to the side, and lit it. I raised my hand and shouted out, "Sir!"

But it was as if he read my mind. Because as soon as he saw me and heard my remark, he flipped his Zippo closed, shook his head, and disappeared (with a clickety-clack of his dress shoes' heels on concrete) into the station's depths.

I didn't know quite what to do. I bit my bottom lip because I knew I needed to call Michelle, but I wanted to smoke a cigarette first in order to celebrate my trifling victory. Then, I could tell her peacefully of my earlier panic. And I didn't have to mention anything about Melinda. And we could laugh about everything because we'd see each other soon.

Then, I turned around. Approaching me from down the sidewalk, there was a girl. She had short, black hair parted boyishly to one side and cut to the nape of her neck. Sunglasses shaded her eyes, and she was stylishly dressed all in black. So European, she was perfectly puffing on a delicious-looking cigarette.

Although, I certainly wanted to, when I approached her, I definitely wasn't hitting on her. Not just because of Michelle. She also looked so distinctly out of my league… I simply couldn't imagine she would possibly be interested in me.

I was wearing a pair of oversized blue jeans as was the American style back then. My skinny torso was covered in a tattered white undershirt, and my hair was all out of place. My tennis shoes had holes in the toes and the soles. I hadn't even shaved in a couple of days. No. A woman like her would never be interested in me.

Sheepishly, I approached. "Excuse me," I asked. "Cigarette?" And I put my fingers to my lips to mimic the act of smoking since you could never be sure who actually spoke English in Europe back then.

"Yes," she said, her Austrian accent thick with her Germanic tongue. "I have a cigarette."

"You speak English," I said in near disbelief. I'm sure I sounded a little relieved as well. Having just come from the more Eastern parts of Europe, it had been a while since somebody on the street had spoken to me in my native language.

But she simply said, "Yes," and she set the tiny bag she was carrying with her on the ground. She crouched down, and she began picking through the bag's contents, apparently looking for a pack of smokes.

As she bent over, though, I noticed her back. Not only were her muscles perfectly proportioned and writhing with every subtle motion of her arms, but her back was beautifully highlighted and simultaneously shaded by a Renaissance crucifixion scene tattooed across her pale skin. Beneath the tattoo, the words – *Eli Eli lama sabachthani.*

"Nice tattoo," I off-handedly mentioned, not remembering my last conversation with Melinda and certainly not expecting any response from the gorgeous European meticulously digging through her belongings to provide what I'd asked for. As I said, I couldn't imagine somebody who looked like her would possibly be interested in me.

But quite matter-of-factly, she stated, "Yes. It was finished today."

"It's really great work," I said, no hint or evidence of the lie that didn't exist in my voice.

"Yes?" she asked. "Thank you," she said. And she stood up and handed me that cigarette I wanted so badly.

I assumed, although she'd been so polite, she was probably done with me. But she asked, "Do you need a lighter?"

I laughed a bit at my own oversight. "Yeah," I said, "I guess I do."

And she lit my cigarette for me. "You are at the train station," she said. "You are leaving Salzburg?"

My head filling with the much-needed nicotine, I shrugged and answered, "No. I just got here. What about you? You going somewhere?"

"I have three days off from work," she said, "I was thinking I would go to Italy."

"That would be nice," I said.

She nodded. "But you," she went on. "You just arrived here?"

I nodded back at her.

"You are American?"

And I nodded again.

"Come, then," she said. "I will show you Salzburg."

And for a second, I remembered I needed to call Michelle. But I figured I'd follow the beautiful woman to wherever she wanted to take me for just a minute. Because she certainly wasn't interested in me. And then, I could go back to the train station later, and I could call Michelle.

"Nice to meet you," she politely said to me as we slowly strolled away, cigarettes in our hands, from the entrance's open mouth waiting to swallow me and spit me up into another foreign land. "I'm Sophia."

"Christian," I politely responded. "And it's nice to meet you, too, Sophia."

We shook hands, and I noticed she had the bluest eyes – like see-through sapphires.

Sophia asked, "What were you doing here at the train station, Christian? You don't have your bag with you. And if you just now arrived here…"

I chuckled. "Actually, I didn't *just* get here. In fact, it's kind of a funny story if you want to hear it."

"Of course," she said. "We have the time as we walk…"

And I recounted the day's adventures' tale with regard to my credit card situation. Even though, somehow, I entirely left out that I needed to get back to that international payphone and call my girlfriend back in the States…

Sophia nodded intently along with my story. As I spoke, she gazed up at my profile. Her blue eyes turned on me were like a sun-warmed sky caressing my cheek. They lit a burgeoning fire beneath the hardened ice of my too-often drunken gut, and she serenely led me to a fountain in the middle of some pavement park.

I'd spent a lot of time in a lot of parks in Europe that summer. I'd left The Netherlands after bumping into an American student named Gabriel in Vandal Park, Amsterdam who'd been strolling that city's canals for over a year believing he was an archangel simply because he'd seen Christopher Walken in *The Prophecy*. He'd been enamored by my name and believed he'd been sent there just for me. And I'd realized I needed to leave right then or maybe I never would. In a marijuana induced panic, I hopped a train to Berlin that very night.

But in that park in Salzburg, as the city's residents went about the ends of their days, Sophia seated me on the fountain's edge with my back to the pulsing water. She handed me a native coin, "Make a wish and throw it over your shoulder," she said, "But don't turn to see where it lands. The wish won't come true if you do."

I did as I was told, and Sophia did the same. The sun was as bright as a dream, and I remember a drop of water landed on my neck, but I still didn't turn around to see where my coin landed – because I really wanted that wish to come true.

"Did you make your wish?" Sophia asked me

I told her I did.

And she said with a certain nod of her head, "Don't ever tell anyone what your wish is because, then, it will *never* come true."

And you know what? You want to know a secret? I'll whisper: *I've never told anyone what that wish is, and I'm sorry, Saint Annie, but I'm not going to tell you either. Because that wish still hasn't come true. And I still really want it to.*

Our wishes made, Sophia decided we should continue our stroll. She sat me down on a wooden bench on a slight rise overlooking the park, and she pulled out a can of Red Bull. "Do you want some?" she asked.

Back then, they didn't have Red Bull in the States yet. So I longingly asked her, "Does it have alcohol in it?"

"No," she responded, "I don't really drink alcohol."

"Oh," I mumbled a little ashamed, "I wish I didn't really drink alcohol."

"Yes," she told me, "When I was younger I had a drug problem."

I glanced at her with my head cocked to the side – not judging, just curious.

"Yes," Sophia went on, "I lived in London for some years, in what you would call a 'squat'. Do they have those in the United States?"

I nodded my head – *Sure.*

And Sophia continued, "I did a lot of drugs there. So I try not to drink, and I never do drugs anymore. Do you do any drugs?" she asked.

I told her, with complete honesty back then, "Just soft stuff like marijuana."

And she smiled. "That's okay. Marijuana is not bad."

I smiled and nodded. "So you learned English in London?"

"No. I learned English here, but I learned how to speak it in London."

I was impressed. I'd never really known anybody who'd lived in a squat. I'd heard about that stuff, gutter punks and all that, and it seemed so cool to me. But I was a college student. I didn't know anything about that sort of life… not yet, at least. And to think this immaculate woman on the bench beside me had been a drug addict, homeless in a foreign land just a few years before, well…

"How old are you?" I suddenly wondered.

"21," she responded. "And you are?"

"Same," I said. "21."

"Come," she said, "I want to show you my favorite place in Salzburg."

And she took me by the hand and dragged me from the wooden bench back down into the park. The sensation of her palm sent childhood butterflies fluttering through my stomach. Just like with Michelle. But Sophia's fingers slipped from mine as quickly as they'd intertwined. Side by side, making our way through children, tourists, and townsfolk, brushing shoulders every once in a while, we strolled the city of Salzburg. And I don't know quite where anymore, but somewhere, we made our way up a stone path along a grassy hill.

Atop that hill, a regal bust of Mozart tilted his gaze on

us. "Do you like it?" Sophia asked me.

I couldn't even see the city in the distance I was so enthralled by the composer's dark appearance. I smiled, and I wanted to put my arm around Sophia's shoulder, but I didn't think that was appropriate. So all I said was, "He *is* genius."

"Yes," Sophia responded, "I think so, too."

And she pulled a blanket from out her bag to spread overtop the grass in Mozart's shadow. The sun was still warm on my face as I sat down, squinting beneath the light. Sophia handed me a cigarette. We smoked, and then, she asked, "Would you rub the medicine across my tattoo?"

Of course, I wanted to – to put my fingers to her flesh, however tender that touch may be. By then, I knew I'd gone too far. I knew I should say, *No.* But I didn't. Against rational judgment, I said, "Sure…" And Sophia handed me a tube of ointment to moisten her new tattoo with.

When my oily fingertips caressed her back, electricity pulsed from *her* skin into *my* arteries. I don't know if she felt it, too, but her blue eyes glanced at me over her shoulder. I looked down, burying my vision in the fresh ink across her back. To me, the sensation was akin to the shock of winter's electric charge. Her tattoo's flesh was still raised from the incision's scars. Running my hands overtop her crucifixion, I experienced the passion of the Christ.

As the meat of my hands more fully experienced her back, like a spider crawling the water spout, my palms crept up her shoulder blades. And when my fingers curled overtop her shoulders, she slowly turned to me. Our eyes interlocked, and I saw her gaze longing for something I felt in mine. We hesitated. For a moment, I was lost in her pupils' reflection. Then, our necks tilted forward through sunbeams. And our lips interlocked.

Adagio:
Before You Can Learn to Sing the Blues

It's like coming up from the bottom of the ocean when a kiss ends. Sophia and I stared at one another in bewilderment. She broke the silence, not me – "That was amazing," she said.

"Yeah," I agreed. "It was."

Then, my fears must have overcome my gaze. Because Sophia scrunched up her eyebrows, and she asked me, "What is wrong?"

I looked down at the grass and rubbed a lone blade between my fingertips. "I have a girlfriend," I finally admitted. And I told Sophia all about my relationship with Michelle.

When I was done, Sophia asked. "Do you love her?"

I tipped my head to the side. "I thought so," I said, "But now, after all this, I don't know."

"It is okay," Sophia said, "She is there. And you are here. Be here. With me."

For the first time since my story started, I looked into her eyes again, and I couldn't help myself. Her lips were like a fucking drug, and I've always been an addict. That's the truth. *I've always been an addict.*

Sophia wanted to take me out to dinner. So she took me to the one place she said she knew Americans ate. She kept our destination a secret as we strolled the streets of Salzburg talking art and music. She thought I'd be so excited when we got to the restaurant she *knew* I would love.

But I burst out in laughter when we arrived. I told her, "Americans don't *really* eat at McDonald's. That's such a stereotype." She frowned and asked if I wanted to go somewhere else. I shrugged. "No. This is fine."

I was so fucking hungry. It was like when... nevermind. When we got up to the counter, I knew exactly what I wanted. I ordered a Big Mac. But when I asked Sophia what she was going to eat, she simply responded, "I don't know. I have never eaten here before."

"Ever?" I asked her.

She shook her head, *No.*

And that was when I realized, regardless of what I might have wanted to believe, I was an American through and through. I told Sophia she might like Chicken McNuggets.

"So really you don't eat here ever?" she asked me while biting the head off one of her nuggets (she didn't eat many of them, by the way). "I thought all Americans eat at McDonald's."

"I grew up eating this shit," I said. "But I don't eat here much anymore. I mean, I get cravings. For Christ's sake, I've eaten this food my whole life. It's like something you just can't get away from in the States. It's almost... addictive. You've seriously never eaten here before?"

She shook her head again, *No.*

"What *do* you eat, then?" I laughingly asked her.

"Typical Austrian food," she answered. "Have you ever had *Wiener schnitzel?*"

It was my turn. I shook my head, *No.*

She said, "You must have *Wiener schnitzel* while you are in Salzburg, then. Tomorrow we will have *Wiener schnitzel.* And we will go to the lakes. Would you like to go to the lakes with me?"

I told her I would love to go to the lakes with her... not a thought of Michelle crossing my mind.

"Good," She said, "We will go to the lakes tomorrow, and my grandmother will cook us *Wiener schnitzel.*"

I told her that sounded like a great idea. Because I'd completely forgotten all about the phone call I was supposed to make to my girlfriend back in the States.

After dinner, Sophia walked me back to my hostel. I kissed her goodbye somewhere beyond the glare of the streetlight outside. "So I will meet you here tomorrow morning," she said to me, looking up from my embrace as the moon reflected in her blue eyes and turned her black hair to purple midnight.

With a smile, I responded, "Of course." Still, not a thought of Michelle clouded my mind.

When I got back to the hostel's bar, my travel companions immediately asked where I'd been. Of course, they'd been drinking beers since before I'd left, and they ordered a fresh round to include me in as I told them my evening's story. Adventure welled in my chest, making me feel quite animated as I recited my tale. Gary and Bill were enamored by my luck, but it was Kristen who finally wondered, "And what about your girlfriend back in the States?"

I took a hard swallow off my pint. Wiping the suds from my lips, I looked away, and I mumbled, "I don't know. I just don't know."

That next morning, I was up bright and early, packing my bag for my trip to the lakes with Sophia. I said goodbye to my travel companions and made tentative plans to meet them in Venice sometime after the weekend, but I never saw them again. Some things are like that. Sophia was waiting for me outside.

I don't remember if it was Gary or Bill anymore, but one of the two of them gave a big cheer for me and shouted their encouragement as I strolled away from the hostel with a pack on my back and my arm around Sophia. I felt so very triumphant. I've never felt like I triumphed in that way ever again. This story I'm telling you now probably has a lot to do with that.

Sophia smiled in the sunlight as she asked me, "Have you eaten breakfast yet?" I told her I hadn't. "Come, then," she said, "We will have a typical Austrian breakfast."

She took me to a small café where we dipped croissants in coffee thick with sugar and tan from milk. As she wiped a stray drop of coffee from off her chin, she told me *that* was the proper way to eat a croissant, and I've eaten them that way ever since. Because I believed her.

After breakfast, we went to a market to get bread and cheese. No wine since Sophia didn't want any, and for the only time ever in my life, I believed I was okay with that. A fact that wasn't lost on me. In fact, it meant so very much to me... even all the way back then. We hopped on a city bus to head out to the mountains, to where Sophia lived on Salzburg's outskirts... to get in touch with her grandmother and fully prepare for our weekend getaway.

Sophia explained to me over the course of our bus ride together that she worked at a hotel on a big hill in the middle of Salzburg, and she lived in a house with five other kids who worked there as well. However, she was the oldest and acted as a sort of "elder sister" for the entire group. She was off through Sunday, and it was only Friday. She hoped I wouldn't mind meeting her housemates, but she knew I would love them as they would love me, which they were looking forward to ever since she'd told them about me the night before.

They were so excited Sophia had finally met somebody who piqued her interest, she told me. Many boys liked her, but she never liked any of them, she said. At that point in my life, I didn't believe anybody had ever bothered taking the time to tell people about me before they met me... and certainly not under the assumption they might like me.

Needless to say, I was beyond flattered. In our shared seat where my arm rested over her shoulder, I pulled Sophia tight against my body, and with a smile, she nestled into my grooves.

Sophia's roommate, Bettina, greeted us at the door to their home. They looked so similar – Bettina and Sophia, as if Bettina were Sophia's younger sister. She offered me a smile of joy, and I accepted while she said something to Sophia in their gutturally shared German. Sophia shrugged and translated for me that she had to call her work before we could go anywhere. There was some sort of problem with their computer system, and Sophia was the only one who could tell them how to fix it.

We dropped our groceries off in the kitchen, and Sophia walked me into her bedroom where she quickly closed and locked the door. A bouquet of dried, dead flowers hung down from the middle of her ceiling. For some strange reason, a rusted machete was in the corner. Sophia kissed me, and I didn't want her lips to ever leave mine. Something had awakened in my soul. But then, she sat down at the edge of her bed, phone in hand – offered me a cigarette and started dialing her work number while I paced the room, smoking, glancing at the black and white photos of landscapes and her spaced around the walls.

Behind me, on the phone as she spoke to her work, Sophia's guttural German slowly dissolved into a softer tone. All the jagged edges of her native language were lost. Somewhat concerned, I turned to look at her. Just like with her words, her shoulders, too, had slackened. She was furiously writing on that worn pack of Marlboros she'd offered me a cigarette from the day before. As I stood there stupefied, she looked up and cleared a stray strand of black hair off her forehead. Tears lit in the depths of a newfound sadness I'd yet to notice in her... as if a constrictor would sometimes flex its muscles around her smooth heart. Because there was something in her gaze that said this pain was familiar.

"Okay," she whispered again into the receiver – the only repeated word I'd understood that far. And she hung up the phone.

The phone dead, Sophia sat still for a moment or two. The heaviness of her silence weighed upon me as well. I didn't move either. Then, she looked down and mumbled, "I can not go to the lakes with you." Her trembling lip seemed to drag her words down even further than her mood itself had caused them to descend.

As suddenly as it had been filled when we'd kissed... Just as quickly, my soul emptied. I felt myself turn pale. "Why?" I gulped.

"Because I have to work. The computer system is not working. And I have to fix it," Sophia said.

"There's nobody else who can do that?"

"No. I tried to tell them to find somebody else, but I am the only one."

"Well, I'll just wait, then. We can go to the lakes after you finish."

"No. I am supposed to have three days off, and they want me to work for today and these next three days. Then, I can have three days off... Will you come back for me after this weekend?" Sophia begged.

I have to be honest... Michelle never even entered my mind. "Of course, I'll come back for you," I said. "I'll go to Rome and visit my friend, Giovanni, and then, I'll come back for you in three days."

"Yes," Sophia said, "Come back for me." And she handed me that pack of cigarettes she'd been writing on through her whole phone conversation.

Scratched into the top of the pack, over and over again

with a black pen, were four words: *Ich habe dich lieb*. Below it was a bunch of numbers: 00 049 662 456838 (I can't believe I still remember that). And below the numbers – Sophia Freund. I asked, "What does all this mean?"

"It means '*I love you*'," she said. "In German. Below it is the telephone number here. And now you know my surname. Call me on Saturday at midnight. I will tell you when to come back for me."

Sophia stood up. She walked over to a desk in the corner where, from the top drawer, she pulled out a picture roughly 3 inches by 6 inches, and she handed that picture to me. The picture was a black and white photograph of her. In black pants and a white shirt, she climbed overtop the railing at the edge of a cliff. Her short black hair was brushed back, and her immaculate jaw line was settled in concentration. Barefoot, her perfect toes bent in the air, she perched, balanced on the arch of her foot, on the bottom rung. Both hands, long fingers wrapped to whiteness, gripped tight the top rung. Her head bent forward at the neck, and her black eyes stared emptily into darkness as she contemplated the descent.

"So you don't forget about me while you are gone," she said. "You will keep it with you always forever now. And now, I will take you back to the train station where I will see you again in three days." She tried to smile, but with her tears, she could only make a half-hearted attempt as if the pressure from her lips would cause the salty water to drip, and all semblances of our happiness together would disintegrate. We were so young back then.

I wanted to tell her I didn't have to go. I could wait for her… if she would let me. But I swallowed hard, and I nodded.

We took the bus back into the city proper. Rome was such a long way away. And the next train wasn't leaving for over an hour. Sophia didn't want to go to work while I aimlessly wandered the streets of her hometown. So we sat down in another café.

She kept her sunglasses on while we sat, and she looked up at the ceiling when she said to me, "I want to tell you my life…

Through Days of Endless Nights'
(The Objective Truth Behind
Christian's Love of Sophia –
Chorale in b minor)

I was born here in Salzburg. But my father went to prison when I was very young. He was arrested for bringing drugs into this country. He was a heroin addict, and so was my mother. I have not seen my father since I was a child. I believe he is still in prison, but I do not know. I am the only child.

My mother contracted HIV when I was in grammar school. It was from injecting heroin. She died of AIDS… nearly seven years previous now at this point. My grandmother, my mother's mother, tried raising me – out by the lakes where I wanted to take you today. But she did not like my father, and she blamed him for my mother's death. So I was forbidden to have contact with him. Not even letters. I was to go to high school there out by the lakes with my grandmother. But I was not a good child. And I ran away from Salzburg and Austria when I was 16.

I was homeless. I was alone. And I was on the streets. I slept on benches, and I slept in alleys.

But I stayed in Berlin for almost one year because I met a boy there. I thought I loved him, and I thought he loved me. But one time he hit me, and I knew – I had to leave him. Because I did not believe a person would hit another person who they say they love. That was how I knew he did not love me really. So I left him, and I left Berlin, too, with a friend. She brought me to London.

In London, my friend and I were homeless, too. But we were not alone. We had one another. And we met squatters everywhere who showed us where we could sleep, and how we could eat. But in those squats there, I became addicted to heroin just like my father and just like my mother.

The addiction was horrible. It was more painful than death, but I met another boy in London. He was a squatter like me. And he was a heroin addict, too. I loved him very deeply, and he loved me as deeply as I loved him.

He died of a heroin overdose when we were 18 years old. And I knew I had to stop doing the drug. I wrote to my grandmother, and I asked her to help me come back to Salzburg. She did. I went through the withdrawal for the last time on the trains as I traveled here, but I have not injected heroin since before I left London. And I have been here now for almost three more years. I have worked at the hotel that whole time.

I have no family except my grandmother. I have only been in love twice in my life, and the first time I was wrong. But both times, my heart was broken. And now I have met you. And I knew when I saw you in front of the train station that our meeting was *kismet:* fate.

I do not want to scare you because I know that my feelings may not be your feelings, and I know that you have a girlfriend in the United States and that you will have a hard decision to make when you go back there. But I believe we are meant to be together (*Sophia finally took off her sunglasses, and as she did, I could see the tears that had been building behind her eyes ever since she'd spoken on the phone with her work were just then beginning to drip*). And I know that wherever you are, whenever I look at the stars in the nighttime sky, I will know that you will see the same stars, too. And that is because you are alive and because you live on this planet together with me. And as long as we both are here, I will still believe in us.

Scherzo:
My Secret Yin and Yang

It was an overnight train to Rome, but Giovanni greeted me the next morning at Termini Station with a smile, a hug, and a kiss on the cheek. Perhaps sensing some of my inner turmoil, his hand still resting heavily on my shoulder, he immediately asked, "How is everything, my American friend?"

"I don't know, man," I honestly answered, "Could we go somewhere and get a drink?"

Giovanni's eyes lit up with that grin I'd become accustomed to the summer before back in the United States... now, an entire eternity previous. "Certainly, my friend," he said. "Of course. Welcome to *my* home, now – Roma!"

On the way to the café and out on its patio, staring at the schizoid traffic and listening to the cacophony of that ancient city of 30,000 citizens grown to house nearly 3 million souls, I rambled out my story of the previous days. "...So I just don't know what to do, Giovanni. Is it truly possible for someone to be in love with two different people at the exact same time?"

Giovanni looked up at the pale sky hiding so many greenhouse gases, and he responded quite thoughtfully (we were both so very young back then), "I do not know. I believe you will be in love with only one person. Ever. I must ask you – Do you believe that Michelle or Sophia is this one person?"

I shook my head. "Shit, Giovanni, I don't know…"

"Of course you do not know. You are like me. You are young. And you are traveling. You will fall in love with Sophia. For now. And when you go back to the United States, you will fall in love with Michelle. Again. That is my advice."

For Giovanni, I smiled a little bit – on the outside. I think I even chuckled some as I simply told him, "I guess you're right, Giovanni." Because on the inside, I felt a deep sense of foreboding.

"Of course I am right," he said. "I am Italian. I know these things." But he certainly didn't know me.

The next night, I met Giovanni's girlfriend, Elaina, for the first time ever. The three of us went out to this restaurant owned by some Italian horror movie director. It was the craziest place I've ever been to… well, until I got here, at least, that is.

This restaurant – I have no idea what it was called any more – had coffins for tables, with glass tops revealing skeletons below our drinks and plates. Web-encrusted candelabras hung above each and every party. A live snake crawled along the bar. There were promotional posters of dead bodies and naked women decorating the red walls and dark ceiling. And the more we drank, the stranger things became. Because it's odd what humans will hold in reverence.

At midnight that same evening was my appointed call to find out when to return for Sophia. I excused myself and stepped out of the bar to a payphone beneath a streetlight on the corner where I dialed her number. The other line rang and rang and rang and rang. No one answered. I hung up and tried again. The other line rang and rang and rang and rang. No one answered. I went back into the bar. She'd told me to call her then.

Giovanni and Elaina were curious what Sophia had had to say about my return.

"Nobody answered," I responded somewhat dejected.

"Perhaps she is drunk, and she is asleep," Giovanni said quite cheerfully amid our horrific atmosphere. "Or perhaps you are drunk, and you did not dial her number properly," he laughed as he poured us each another glass of wine beneath the red lights. Elaina smiled and nodded in drunken agreement as the bar's serpent inched closer to the bracelets on her forearm.

I chuckled along with the two of them, and I tried shrugging the whole thing off, but inwardly I was disturbed. Had Sophia lied to me? She'd seemed so sincere. But then again, I didn't know her all that well. I'd been so tortured. It had to be true.

"I'll be right back," I said. I went out and dialed Sophia again. There was still no answer. I stared in disbelief at the number on her empty cigarette pack. I called Sophia two more times that night before returning to Giovanni's around 2 AM to pass out. Sophia never answered. *Nobody* answered.

The next morning, Giovanni woke me from my stupor where I slept in the guest house off his parents' home in a neighborhood outside of Rome called *Infernetto*. He'd brought me a shot of espresso mixed with cold milk and sugar. It tasted perfect, but as soon as I opened my eyes, all I could think about was Sophia.

Giovanni and I went to the Vatican that day. I stared at the frescoes across the walls. They were so lifelike, but still so dead to me. I contemplated the Sistine Chapel, but God and man meant nothing. There was only Sophia. I called her every hour on the hour, and every hour, nobody answered. I bought a rosary as I left, but I never used it to pray. Maybe I should have…

Monday morning, Sophia's first day off, Giovanni woke me again with a shot of espresso – the same as he'd done the day before. And the same as the day before, it tasted perfect.

"I am going to meet Elaina today," he said to me. "I thought that maybe you would like to go to see the Coliseum while I am with her," he added, never mentioning Sophia, but a slight frown colored all of his words and motions as he became increasingly convinced, although he'd never say it, my love was unrequited.

I nodded, but all I could think about, still, was Sophia. From the moment I opened my eyes, she was the only thing occupying my mind. So even though I'd already given up hope, I agreed.

Just like the day before, we ate breakfast prepared in Giovanni's kitchen by his mother: eggs, fresh tomatoes from their garden, and cold slabs of mozzarella. And just like the day before, Giovanni and his mother shouted at one another, waved their hands in the air as they spoke, but embraced each other right before the two of us roared away on Giovanni's mini-scooter. His sister, he explained to me once again above the rattling engine as we drove up the hill leading away from his family's home, always got to use the big scooter. He never knew why that was.

Near the Coliseum, in Old Rome, I sat on Hadrian's Wall. I contemplated what it meant for Augustus Caesar to wander the paths I tread upon, for Marc Antony to give speeches from where I stood. But truthfully, all I could think about was Sophia. History, like God and man, meant nothing to me as well. Only the present mattered.

There was a payphone in a terminal across from the Coliseum. By quarter to 5, still waiting for Giovanni to return at 6:00, I thought maybe I should try calling Sophia one last time. And one last time, only nobody answered.

Completely dejected, feeling eternally rejected, I hung up the phone. But as I did so, I suddenly noticed (how could I have been so blind?) the list of European country codes on the phone booth opposite me. I looked back at the number on Sophia's cigarette pack, and I looked back at the numbers on the phone booth.

My eyes opened wide. Because the country code for Austria was 043. The country code Sophia had written on her cigarette pack – 049: *Germany*.

Immediately, I grabbed the payphone out of its cradle. I'm sure the other tourists and commuters thought I was possessed so quickly I reacted. Without even thinking about whether or not Sophia had written the wrong country code on purpose, I punched her number – with the correct country code – into the phone. It rang only once, and then…

"Christian," Sophia breathed across the line from too many miles away.

"Yes, Sophia," I said. "It's me."

"I knew it was you, Christian. You must come to me today. I have only two days more off…"

"I will, Sophia. I'm coming," and I pulled out the Eurorail map I'd been carrying in my bag from the moment I'd first left Giovanni's with the intention of calling Sophia two days before.

"I wrote the wrong country code down for you," she nearly cried. "I wrote Germany's because I lived there before."

"I know, Sophia. I know, but I figured it out."

"Yes. You figured it out. I was afraid I would never see you again."

"You're going to see me again. You're going to see me

very soon."

"Yes. I will see you very soon."

But as I looked at the train schedules, emptiness hollowed out my chest once again. "Sophia," I croaked. "The last train today is leaving in a little over an hour. I don't know if I can make it…"

"You must try, Christian. You must try to make it. I have only two days more off."

"All right," I said, "I'll try. But I need to get off the phone right now and call Giovanni. If you don't hear from me again tonight, it means I'll see you tomorrow morning at 5:30."

"I will see you tomorrow morning, then," she said. "I believe I will. Because I believe in us. Christian, I love you."

"I love you too, Sophia," I said – without even wondering whether or not I meant what I'd said, and I hung up the phone as quickly as I'd ripped it from its cradle, which I promptly did immediately again.

Giovanni had a cell phone, which wasn't common at all in the States back then. Everybody in Italy had one, though. My theory at the time was that was because they were only charged for outgoing calls. The caller paid for incoming ones. I don't know if that's still the case or not. I've never been back to Italy since.

I dialed Giovanni's number. And as if he'd been waiting for my call, he answered immediately. "Giovanni!" I shouted, "I talked to Sophia!"

"Yes!" he screamed triumphantly back at me, contaminated by my own excitement, "You spoke with Sophia!"

"Yeah… I finally reached her. She wrote the wrong country code down, but there's a problem."

"Is no problem," Giovanni answered quickly, "You spoke with Sophia. Is no problem."

"No, Giovanni. We have a problem. I have to leave here tonight to get down there to see her…"

"Is no problem," Giovanni repeated.

I went on, "And the next train leaves at 5:55."

This time, Giovanni answered slowly – as if the serpent from the restaurant two nights before were stuck on his palate, "Is problem."

"Yeah, Giovanni, like I said there's a problem… But I have to get there tonight. She only has two more days off."

Giovanni spoke to me very matter-of-factly this time, "Is problem, Christian. I am at Elaina's. It is 25 minutes from Elaina's to Coliseum. It is 25 minutes from Coliseum to Infernetto. Then, it is 30 minutes from Infernetto to Termini. And it is already… 4:51. We will not be there until later than 6:00."

"Yes, Giovanni. I know. It's a problem. But, Giovanni, can we try?"

There was a pause on the other end. Even from all the way across the phone line, I could almost see one of the last friends I ever had thinking carefully. Then, he said, "Yes, Christian. We will try. It is 25 minutes from Elaina's to Coliseum. I will be there in ten. "

I tried to say, *Thank you, Giovanni*, but he'd already hung up.

I set the phone back in its cradle, and I went out to the street to wait in the same spot where Giovanni had dropped me off at a mere hour and a half before. I paced back and forth, rubbed my hands together in Rome's summer heat. I appeared freezing even though I was on fire. It took exactly ten minutes before Giovanni, astride his scooter, screeched into place in front of me.

"Get on," he said. He turned over his shoulder as I complied, looked at me from behind his sunglasses, handed me the extra helmet, and said, "Put on this. Because today, in Rome, for us, all red lights are green."

And off we roared.

Giovanni wasn't kidding about what he'd said, either. We flew in and out of traffic and screamed through every light – green *or* red… it didn't make a difference. Before I knew it, we were out of the city proper, on the outskirts, and flying down the familiar country road to Infernetto. That's when Giovanni cried out, "Christian, is problem."

"Is problem? What do you mean, is problem, Giovanni? How could there be a problem now? We're almost there."

"Pedro! Pedro!" he shouted above the wind roaring at me.

"Pedro?" I said, "Who the fuck is Pedro, Giovanni?"

But Giovanni simply shouted again, "Pedro," and he tapped one of the scooter's gauges.

I looked down. The gauge hand was almost in the red. "Oh, shit," I said, "Gas."

"Yes," Giovanni said, "I told you – Pedro…"

And that's when I registered what he'd been trying to say to me: *petrol*. Holding on tight to Giovanni's waist, I cried above the roaring breeze, "Do you think we can make it?"

"We will try if we can make it home. And then, we will drive my sister's scooter, the big scooter, to Termini. It is faster than this one, too."

"Okay, Giovanni, sounds good," I shouted, panicking, however, as I pictured us stranded at the side of the road to Infernetto while my train for Salzburg departed.

Every second that passed, I stared only at the gas gauge. But somehow, we managed to putter all the way down the road and up to the hill atop Giovanni's street before the gas tank went completely dry. And, then, we coasted down that hill and into Giovanni's driveway.

There was no time for celebration, though. "You will grab your bag. I will tell mama we are taking my sister's scooter," he said to me in their garage.

I did as I was told, and as I reentered the main house again from out the back door leading to the guest home where I was staying, Giovanni was pleading with his mother in Italian. But she only took one look at me. One look was all it took. She clasped her hands beneath her chin, smiled, sighed, and nodded. Giovanni and I ran back into the garage and grabbed his sister's scooter from where it sat dormant. Thankfully, it had a full tank of gas.

Off we roared again. We were back in Rome's city center, at Termini, within a half hour of when we'd originally left the Coliseum.

Giovanni ran with me into the terminal. I scoured the departures board for my train... I turned to Giovanni. "We have a problem, Giovanni," I said.

"Is no problem," he told me. "You have made it."

"No, Giovanni. I haven't. My train isn't up there."

"Yes," he said. "Your train is up there." He grabbed my Eurorail schedule from out my hand. "Your train is..." he stared disbelievingly (just as I had) at the departures board. "No," he breathed, "Is not up there."

Immediately, Giovanni grabbed me by the arm and dragged me up to the shortest line for one of the ticket windows. The grate was pulled down halfway, and the woman behind the counter waved us away. Because she was closing, you see. But Giovanni stubbornly shook his head, *No*.

When we got to the front of the line, he refused to comply with the woman's rapidly shouted instructions, which, I can only assume, were to get out of her line. But Giovanni began pleading with her in Italian. And she only took one look at me. One look was all it took. She clasped her hands beneath her chin, smiled, sighed, and nodded. Giovanni thrust the Eurorail schedule underneath the window. After a quick glance at it, she fired back rapidly at him in Italian.

Giovanni nodded. "The train is not here," he said to me.

"What do you mean the train isn't here, Giovanni?" I cried.

"The train is not here," he repeated. "It is at Tiburtina."

"Tiburtina? Where's Tiburtina?"

"Not far from here. It is near where I play soccer," he told me, consciously using the Americanism so I would understand. "Fifteen minutes away. Come. We will make it," he told me, and he grabbed me by the arm as we ran back out of the station to his scooter.

A mere ten minutes later, we were pulling up at Tiburtina station. Giovanni left the scooter parked astride the curb. I hopped on board the train to Salzburg as it pulled away from the station while I waved goodbye to Giovanni receding in the distance.

He was smiling and waving back to me. That was the last time I ever saw my friend, Giovanni.

Rondo:
April's Coming Early This Year

*A*board the train, *I immediately scoured out one of the rattling* spaces between two of the cars. A group of European travelers were already hanging out there, speaking their guttural tongue. I plopped down in the corner and lit a cigarette of relief. Striking up a conversation with one of the girls, a German, I told her my story of Sophia and the day's adventure with Giovanni. She smiled and applauded.

When I told her I was going to go find a seat, she simply said, "I will see you again." But in response to my incredulous look, she continued, "Because you will always see everybody twice," and she winked at me.

Back then, I was still naïve enough to believe her.

I found a seat in a car with a brown-skinned man. He was very well dressed, and he didn't speak English... But he offered me a banana, and I took it. He kept smiling at me and nodding as I ate it. Then, I panicked... I thought he was a terrorist poisoning me, that he could understand every word I'd said and he was simply keeping up a charade so the American wouldn't suspect him of any malicious motive.

And then, I couldn't take it any longer, I bounded out of the car I was sharing with him. He tried stopping me, implying he was asking where I was going, but that only confirmed my paranoia. I stormed back through the space where I'd plopped down for my previous cigarette (the German girl wasn't there any longer – as far as I know, despite what she'd told me, I've never met her again), convinced I was dying, and into another seat. I realized I might have overreacted a bit, probably freaked the poor guy – who was kind enough to give me some food – out. But what I didn't realize was how unconscious fears had affected my decisions...

(*Even though she couldn't see him, in the pitch darkness, Christian suddenly gazed in the exact direction where he believed Saint Annie to be chained against the wall opposite him, from where he could hear her familiar rattle. "I can't believe I never realized that before now," he disbelievingly whispered to the nothing that had to be somebody.*)

We stopped somewhere near the Italian border, and I had a two hour layover as I waited for the Salzburg connection to come. I sat down on a bench in the midnight dark, staring at the railroad tracks extending infinitely beyond the slight light from the station's bulb above my head. Another traveler took a seat beside me. I remember he had long hair and a beard... Something like I'd always pictured Jesus Christ.

"How are you?" he asked after lighting a cigarette. He had a thick accent that, even after my half a summer in Europe, I still couldn't quite place.

I chuckled a bit and told him the story of my freak out on the train. He laughed a bit along with me, but then he said, "It is funny. But you cannot be too careful. There are people in this world who want to hurt you."

"Yeah," I laughed with all the knowledge of three years of a collegiate education behind me, "This world's an evil place."

"It is not an 'evil place'," he told me. "There is no such thing as evil. Especially in this place."

"No such thing as evil?" I asked him. "That's an interesting theory." I smiled the safe smile of the junior intellectual.

But he merely shook his head. "No. It is not a theory. It is true."

He sounded so serious, but I was still chuckling. "How can you be so sure?" I wondered, baiting him like the two of us were pounding beers together at a party.

He answered succinctly, "Me? Because I am Bosnian. And I was in Srebrenica."

That one word *"Srebrenica"* sobered my mood considerably. I blinked. You see, you may not be old enough to remember this, Saint Annie, but back then, we weren't that far removed yet from the Civil Wars that had decimated the former Yugoslavia. I remembered that word (*Srebrenica*) from news reports of the time. I remembered hearing the Serbians had entered the city of Srebrenica.

And that thousands upon thousands of Bosnians had been murdered, thousands more had been left homeless and destitute only to be rounded up, tortured, and killed later. "Jesus, man," I said to him, all my humor finally gone, "How can you say there's no such thing as evil, when you were *there* for *that?*"

"Precisely because I was '*there* for *that*' as you would say."

"I don't understand," I told him.

"Listen," he said, "I was in Srebrenica when the Serbian Army marched right past the UN peacekeepers. They did nothing to stop them. Because, you see, I was also in Bosnia *before* the UN peacekeepers. And I remembered we kept saying – *Why will nobody help us? Why will the Americans not help us like they helped the Kuwaits?* So you see, I already knew they would not help us – Because I had touched our ground, and I knew... We had no oil.

"And I escaped into the mountains. Because I watched my sisters get raped, my brothers get tortured and killed. So I joined the Bosnian Army. Because I wanted revenge. And I watched the friends I made in the Bosnian Army – who had seen their sisters get raped, their brothers get tortured and killed... I saw *them* rape the sisters of the Serbians and torture and kill the brothers of the Serbians. And that is why I say this world is *not* an evil place. Because there is no such thing as good and evil in this world. This world is all there is. And, unfortunately, this world simply 'is'."

I had no idea what to say to that. He left long before the train came, but I pondered his impenetrable words until the moment I fell asleep in my seat during that final leg of my trip back to Salzburg.

At the station, the following morning, in the muted light of Salzburg's dawn, I stepped off the train and into Sophia's arms. We laughed about my story from the previous day. She thanked the gods for Giovanni, and we immediately made our way back to her group home in the mountains. She wanted to take me out that night for "a typical Austrian meal" of *Wiener schnitzel*. Because I had missed my chance to eat her grandmother's home cooking out by the lakes, but we never made it…

At her home, I met another one of her roommates, a blond, German boy a year or two younger than me named Jan.

"You are Christian?" he asked as I shook his hand.

"Not really, but that's my name," I laughingly told him, playing on the joke people had played with me for years.

Jan smiled. "Sophia has told us a great deal about you," he said, "And I am very happy you are here."

"Really?" I affably asked, not really confused, just confused he would say such a thing.

"Yes," he told me, "Sophia always brings us the travelers she meets at the train station."

My eyes screwed up in my face. "Excuse me?" I wondered.

And Sophia started laughing slightly, "Jan, stop," she said. "Christian, you know that is not true."

"No, but it is true," Jan went on. "Yes. Sophia always brings us the travelers she meets and we kill them and cook them and eat them."

"Wh-what?" I wondered, all my paranoia from the brown-skinned man the night before immediately flooding my being all over again.

(*And I wonder what <u>that</u> says about me, Saint Annie…*)

"Jan, stop," Sophia said a bit more forcefully. "You're not being funny, and I think you're scaring him."

Seeing Jan smiling, I tried laughing as well. "It's okay, Sophia," I said, "I know he's just kidding."

"But I am not kidding," Jan said. "Yes. Sophia brings us

the boys from the train station, and we kill them and keep them in here," he said, opening a freezer full of meat.

My face must have blanched because Sophia suddenly cut him off, "Jan! You're scaring him. Stop. Come, Christian. Let us go to my room."

"No. Let him look, Sophia. It will be his fate."

But Sophia turned on him, shouting in German. Jan looked like he'd been struck in the jaw. "I am sorry," he suddenly said. "I was simply making a joke with you, Christian."

"It's okay," I said even though it really wasn't. Not knowing, in some symbolic way, he wasn't making a joke at all.

And I followed Sophia, but glancing back over my shoulder every few seconds at Jan standing still in the kitchen, I was scared. In Sophia's room, I noticed that machete again in the corner. I swallowed slowly as she closed and locked me inside with her where we promptly made love.

I was sweating. I was staring up at the dead bouquet of flowers hanging down from the middle of Sophia's ceiling. "That was the most amazing thing I have ever experienced," she said to me as I rested heavily on top of her. And suddenly, I remembered Michelle.

We made love three more times that day... "*What are you doing to me?*" Sophia would ask me, but I had no idea. We didn't leave her room at all the entire next day.

And the day after that, Sophia had to return to work. I stayed at her home that day, reading *War and Peace*, and that night, again, we made love.

And the day after that, Sophia worked again while I stayed at her home reading *War and Peace* before she returned for us to make love.

Nobody killed me. Nobody put my body in a freezer —

not physically, at least. Although, sometimes, I wish they had.

Because that night, Sophia and I discussed our future together. We decided I should come back to Europe the following summer because I had one more year of school to complete. Sophia would look for a hotel job somewhere in Spain, preferably in Barcelona. She had the skills for it, and with the advent of the EU, she could move to any country on the continent she wanted. I would say goodbye to the idea of graduate school and teach English there. We would begin our lives together. And then, when I made money as a jazz pianist, we could return to the United States...

The next day, after I'd stayed at Sophia's home reading *War and Peace*, after she returned from her day at work, she said to me with her lips trembling and tears in the corners of her eyes, "Christian, I do not think you should stay here any longer."

Somehow, I had known this moment was coming, but still, I robotically asked, "Why's that?"

"Because I work every day, and you should be traveling. You should not be staying here in my home when you have all of Europe to see."

I knew she was right, but still, I asked her, "You're sure that's what you want?"

"No. It is not what I want," she said, "But it is what you should want. I do not know when I will have days off again. You must leave me for now. You must travel. I will see you again in Spain next year."

But, maybe, that wasn't what I should have wanted either. That night, lying in bed, staring up at the bouquet of dead flowers hanging from the middle of Sophia's ceiling, she said to me while we were discussing her family, her past, and our future in the United States, "Christian, I never know if I shall live or if I shall die. Every morning, when I wake up, I make the decision – Will I live today, or will I die today? Every day of my life, I have chosen to live, but someday, I do not know."

I didn't know either. It was something about the way she'd said it. It was something about our future. As she spoke, a heaviness dropped in my stomach. I'd never had such an intense conversation with a girl I was with before. In fact, I'd never had a conversation like that with anyone before. Never had suicide felt so palpable, so real. It was as if I were a serpent tasting death's flavor with the pointed tips of my tongue.

The next day, when we woke up, I packed my bag to go back to the train station. Sophia got dressed to go to work. She wore the costume of a typical Austrian *Fräulein*.

On the bus ride back into the city, we held hands, our fingers caressing one another's palms as Sophia rested her head on my shoulder, and we said goodbye at the station's gate, the same entrance where that man had disappeared into the depths smoking that cigarette I'd wanted an eon ago. Sophia looked into my eyes as she started to cry. She said, "Remember, when you look at the sky, when you see the stars, you will know that I see them too because we are both alive, and as long as we are both alive, I will still believe in us."

"I believe in us, too," I told her.

We embraced, and we kissed. Sophia went off to work while I had three more hours of reading to do before my train to Venice arrived.

Mere inches before my eyes, *War and Peace* was open. Nikolai Rostov was pursuing the wolf, when a real face leaned over 1440 pages and kissed me. I was sitting on a bench at the Salzburg train station.

Sophia told me she'd been so afraid I would already be

gone. She'd told her work she had to go… immediately. In her *Fräulein* costume, she'd run out the front door of her hotel without waiting for them to tell her it was okay. She stood in the middle of the street, stopped a car with her palm, and shouted at the driver: "*Bahnhof!*" He'd driven her as far as he could, but when they were stuck motionless in city traffic, with a mere 10 minutes before my train boarded, Sophia had jumped out of the car, taken off her heels, and run the rest of the way in her dress merely to say goodbye one more time, to caress my face with her palm and touch her lips to mine one more time.

She walked with me out onto the platform. She held onto my fingers slipping from her grasp as I walked up the stairs into the train car, and I waved goodbye to her out the window as we started pulling away. Sophia was crying, and I had no idea what I was feeling. I'd never felt it before, and I've never felt it since.

3.
A Newfound Sadness

"*So you and Sophia are married?*" *Saint Annie longingly* asked of Christian from out the darkness.

Christian didn't answer.

"Are you and Sophia married, Mr. Christian?" Saint Annie asked again.

Christian simply muttered, "Sometimes, Saint Annie, it's best not to know the end."

"But you have to tell me," Annie said. "I need to know how this story ends."

"Okay," he whispered. "I'll tell you. But I honestly don't think you'll like it one bit…"

Coda:
…*And She Banished Me from Heaven*

I was sitting on the patio of a Venetian café, staring out at a canal while nursing a glass of red wine. I remembered my friends from the hostel in Budapest who had been so helpful to me when we'd first gotten to Salzburg: Kristen, Bill, and Gary. And I remembered how a mere week before, I'd planned to rendezvous with them in Venice, but that had been so long ago.

This brunette woman settled into a chair two tables down. She crossed her legs at the knees. When the waiter spoke to her, she responded in Italian. And that single trait led me to believe I needed to present my quandary to her, but I was afraid she'd misread my motivation. So I remained still sitting at my table swirling my fingers around the base of a wine glass.

I wanted to ask her – *Is it possible for a human being to be in love with two different people at the exact same time?*

But I knew what she would say, and I didn't bother to ask.

I'd spent the remainder of my credit card balance on one night in a room at one of the finest hotels in Venice. There were bay windows opening onto a canal. I felt something like a tormented artist from the 1920s. I washed my clothes in the sink that night, and I knew I would be on the streets and homeless for the remainder of the summer. I guess I could have gone back to Sophia's, but I believed that wasn't quite right yet. That was okay, though. I felt like I deserved it. Besides, I had a lot of thinking to do.

When I got back to the States, it didn't take long before Michelle contacted me, terrified that something horrible might have happened, that maybe that was the reason I'd never called her again during my last month and a half in Europe. She was my girlfriend, after all.

"That wasn't it," I told her.

"Why didn't you ever call me, then? We were supposed to meet up in Germany…"

"I know," I said, "But I met somebody else."

"So what?" Michelle said, "We still could have met in Germany."

"Yeah, but I fell in love."

Michelle's whole demeanor changed, "I thought *we* were in love."

"I thought so, too," I said, "But now, I'm not so sure anymore."

"Well, call me when you figure it out," she told me.

I couldn't call her, though. I had absolutely no idea what love meant to me anymore. Because what I felt for Sophia was definitely *not* what I felt for Michelle, and what I felt for Michelle had nothing in common with what I felt for Sophia. But I believed I was in love with both of them. So tell me – *What does love feel like?*

When the semester started up, I had nowhere to live. I'd been in such a hurry to leave the States that summer I hadn't even bothered to secure housing for my return. So I was sleeping on a friend's couch.

He'd sit up with me, smoking cigarettes and drinking whiskey, well into the night, listening to my meditations on love and friendship and lust, and he spoke back sharply to me about his more conservative beliefs – how I needed to forget Sophia and patch things up with Michelle. Sophia was just a fantasy, in his opinion. Michelle was real. But he didn't understand... Sophia *was* real, and I still don't know what the answer was.

I never contacted Giovanni to tell him how my time with Sophia had gone. I guess I was simply too confused about what I might have unleashed. I still feel bad about that today, even while we sit in Malik's darkened room, Saint Annie. Because that wasn't right. He really went out of his way for me, and I never even thanked him. Like I said (it's no excuse), I was just too confused.

Michelle certainly didn't act the way I'd expected her to. She didn't forget about me like I wanted her to, and she didn't hate me like I needed her to, and that meant – I couldn't forget her either.

She reminded me of when we'd make love in the dorm room she'd rented, how we were so afraid her neighbors could hear us through the vents because we could certainly hear them when they spoke. And that fear was because of when she'd driven me to my mother's home that one weekend, and we'd shown up after midnight unannounced, and we'd loudly and drunkenly made love on the bunk beds in my childhood bedroom. And we were so embarrassed the next morning as my mother cooked us breakfast while we realized how we'd taken her by such surprise since she could most definitely hear us the night before and hadn't been expecting anybody in her lonely home – much less me and my girlfriend she'd never heard about. And she reminded me of that day on the phone when I'd told her what our children would look like and how they would rebel against us. And that all meant when Sophia called me from her home in Salzburg once a week, I was too confused to be present for anybody.

But Sophia still called me every week. She would ask me if I looked at the stars at night, and I would tell her I did. And she would say that was "good" because she looked at the stars as well, and that meant – She could still believe in us, and she wanted to know, at the end of every call, if I still believed in us, too. I always told her I did.

Neither Sophia nor I had much money, but the manager of her hotel had faith in Sophia, and her manager *believed* in us. So that same manager bought Sophia a ticket to the United States, to come visit me in November when my birthday was. Sophia told me her manager had never seen her as happy as she was with me, and that's why she wanted to help us be together. Sophia said she couldn't wait to see me and she would bake me a cake for my birthday when she got there.

Something unsettled me about that sentiment and her

statement. Maybe it had something to do with everything I was going through with Michelle. Maybe it was that my friend whose couch I was sleeping on was starting to convince me of his point of view. Maybe it was because baking a cake was simply too domestic and, therefore, brought Sophia's and my relationship out of the realm of fantasy and into cold, hard reality (which may be precisely what everybody wanted from me). Maybe it had to do with my own insecurities – I was afraid when Sophia got to the States, I would appear just an average, American college student to her, nothing special. Maybe it's because I saw her affection as a sign of weakness, and I resented her for that since I was afraid *I* was weak. Or maybe it's because I secretly hate women.

I don't know.

Regardless, I couldn't sit comfortably with the fact that all Sophia wanted to do was bake me a cake for my birthday when she arrived here in the United States. And that's why, when Sophia called me for the last time that one morning, I finally said to her, "Sophia, I don't think you should come here."

"But I should not come there? Why not?" Sophia asked.

And I told her, "This isn't really the best time."

"That is okay," Sophia agreed, "I will change my ticket, and I will come at another time."

"Sophia," I said, "I don't think any time will be a good time."

There was a pause on the other end of the line, and then, Sophia quietly asked, "Is this because of Michelle, Christian?"

I said, "No, Sophia. It's not because of Michelle. It's because of me."

"Because of you?" Sophia wondered. There was a long

pause again, "Does this mean you do not still believe in us, Christian?"

I didn't have a choice. I closed my eyes, and I told her, "No, Sophia. I don't believe in us."

She didn't say anything for a while. Then, she asked, "Do you still look at the stars, Christian?"

I know it was cold, but I just wanted off the phone with her. I really couldn't handle what I was feeling, and I needed a drink… even though it was awfully early in the morning (I don't think I'd ever really drank that early in the morning, at least, not for any reason). So I told her, "No, Sophia. I don't look at the stars anymore. I'm too busy."

And she answered, "But I still look at the stars, Christian, and I still believe in us. Did you hear that? I still believe in us."

"That doesn't mean anything, Sophia," I said.

That's when I heard her subtly choke as she finally admitted, "Then, I guess this is goodbye, Christian."

Which is what, selfishly, I really wanted to hear. "I guess it is," I said quite simply, so succinctly. "Goodbye, Sophia," I said, and I hung up the phone. I didn't even wait for her last words or to hear if her line clicked first.

When I told my friend about that later in the day, he was livid. "You can't just do that," he admonished me.

"Why not?" I said. "It's what you've been telling me to do."

"But you had a responsibility to her, man. You can't just go around treating people that way."

I didn't understand, but that night, my friend told me some guy was on the phone for me, that he had a foreign accent.

"Hello?" I put the receiver to my ear.

"Christian?" the man asked.

"Yes," I said.

"This is Jan from Austria, Christian. Do you remember me?"

"Sure, Jan, I remember you," I said a little confrontationally.

But Jan didn't want to fight. He simply said, "Sophia is dead, Christian."

I choked. Something wasn't registering quite right in my brain. It had to be another prank. "You're kidding me, right?" I tried smiling so he'd let me in on the joke. Because I liked this joke even less than the one he'd played on me when we'd first met.

"No, Christian. Not this time. I wish I was kidding, but I am not kidding this time, Christian."

That didn't make any sense. I'd just spoken to her that morning. I was numb. Finally, I asked, "What happened?" But, somehow, I already knew. I could see her in her bedroom – a bouquet of dead flowers hanging from the middle of her ceiling.

"She swallowed a bottle of pills, Christian. By the time we found her and we could take her to the hospital, she was already dead, Christian." Jan was crying. He begged me, "What happened to Sophia, Christian?"

I hung up the phone.

When Christian finished his story, Saint Annie was crying.

"I'm sorry, Annie," Christian whispered, "I didn't mean to make you sad."

"You didn't make me sad for me, Mr. Christian," Saint Annie said. "You made me sad for you."

"For me? Why?"

"Because you've had to live with so much, Mr. Christian. I don't want you to have to live with so much. You've been so nice to me, Mr. Christian."

Christian didn't have a chance to respond. The door swung open, and Malik was standing in its frame, his massive bulk blocking the pale, artificial light shining in from behind. And Malik did to Saint Annie what he always did to Saint Annie, and Christian felt the emptiness he always felt as he was forced to gaze, once again, upon the suffering Skye like a timid dog tied to a yard post as thunder and lightning roared through the cold rain all around him.

This time, however, as Malik left, he turned to Christian, and he snarled, "I have made a mistake with you, Slave. You suffer watching the Skye, but the Skye does not suffer watching you. In fact, I believe she finds comfort with you here. Next time, she will see what you can endure, and *I* will gaze upon the suffering Skye."

But there was no "next time" for Christian and Malik – not in that capacity, at least. Then again, there's no "next time" for any of us in any of our capacities. For, what did Heraclitus say but that it is impossible to step into the same river twice... to which his student responded it's impossible to step into the same river even once. At which point, that student stopped speaking all together and responded only by moving his finger. But a finger is not really a finger, now, is it? No, not even when talking about whiskey, which Christian didn't have any of at that point in time. His story about Sophia certainly made him crave some, though, but Malik's actions and statements made him wish such fiery flames had never once even graced the sanctity of his lips, which (if we take Heraclitus at face value) it may not have. The world suddenly seemed so pure, and all seemed such a waste. Christian hung his head because he didn't know if he had the strength to endure what Saint Annie already had.

He didn't.

It might have been the next day... it might have been

the day after that… it might even have been the day after that when the door opened once again. Only, this time, Malik didn't block the light. Instead, the bulb's solitary glare streamed around a much smaller, though nearly as tall, shadow with long flowing hair wearing what looked like a dress, which finished her stage entrance with a whisper – "Dear God."

Christian didn't know what to expect in the moment. So long had it been since he'd heard that one word or even thought its existence possible: *God.* He couldn't fathom what fate this newest character brought with her. So he lifted his head slightly from where it hung in place with him chained to the wall. He had no expectations. Certainly not of any relief.

"This is worse than *I* even imagined," the shadow, now obviously female and apparently human, continued as she stepped into the darkened room. She snapped her fingers between long nails, and light appeared. An overhead bulb filtered yellow onto Annie and Christian and our heroine newly entered. Light threw Christian's current predicament out of unconscious darkness and into bleak reality.

It might have been a remnant of his story told Saint Annie, but for a brief second, Christian thought the newest participant in this drama was his beloved Sophia returned to save him. Annie might have thought the same thing. For, in a burst of blinding light, she looked exactly like her. He was wrong.

Once she came into lucid focus, how Christian could have been mistaken, even he wasn't sure. This character had long black hair flowing midway down her chest. Her immaculate jawline and royal nose were both as angular as her long boot heels, and she wore a black dress that, as she turned to close the door, Christian noticed was ribbon-laced up her ivory back. In point of fact, she looked absolutely nothing like Sophia, a little more like Countess Bathory, but looks can be deceiving as Christian had already learned in the afterlife.

"I don't really have time for this," she said. "So we'll get right to the point..." She added almost as an afterthought, "I knew Jafal was up to something, but I had no idea it was this." Then, she looked intently upon Saint Annie. "Did *He* do this to you?"

What the woman meant, Christian had no idea, but Annie almost psychically interpreted her statement either correctly or incorrectly – you and I will never know (who "*He*" was precisely has been lost to the collective unconscious) – as she politely responded, "No, ma'am. Mr. Malik did it."

This newly arrived heroine cast her disapproving glance around the room to settle upon our woebegone hero. At which point, she said, "So that's what he's calling himself these days, is it?"

Christian desired to protest but felt, like a witch survived drowning only to be cast into the fire, too much at stake, and it was.

The woman sauntered across the room and up to Christian. She leaned her face so close to his he could feel her breath upon his lips, something that under almost any other circumstances would have been a welcome sensation. In the present instance, it only made him ache. She said, "I can't unfasten her bonds. So I'll let *you* go, and you can free her. You'll have to do it quickly, though. He could be back at any moment."

All she needed to do was lay a single black fingernail upon his shackles, and the chains fell from Christian's neck, wrists, and ankles. The bonds clanked against the brick wall Christian's back had been plastered to for what seemed eternity. He rubbed his hands upon his bruised and bleeding limbs. Blood coursed back into his nearly severed extremities. How they'd yet to turn leprous and black, Christian, honestly, had no idea in hell. Unbeknownst to him, his mouth opened to say something. Finally, he looked up. But before he could thank the mysterious woman, she'd disappeared. He hadn't even heard her boot heels click away.

Christian wondered, but, for his part, he was finally free. And just in time… Even without the woman, the bulb still burned overhead. Malik could be anywhere. Christian didn't know. Amid the clanks of link upon link, Annie was struggling like a fish drowning in air. "Could you help me, Mr. Christian?" she begged. "Help me get out of this place."

He didn't have the key, though, and he didn't know what to do. As if he were that child still visiting those boxes abandoned in that dark room inside his mother's home, Christian's stomach plummeted deep into his gut. "I don't know how to," he dumbly admitted. Then, he mumbled almost to himself (though, he never would have *admitted* it even to himself) without even looking in Annie's direction, "I'm gonna go find help." And he left Saint Annie alone as she had always been – as we always are – in actuality in Malik's chamber.

Barefoot across Malik's cold, hard floor, overwhelmed by his current master's decay, Christian breathed deep the demon's noxious odor of rank sweat and rotting food as Saint Annie's lonely tears (*Chriiiiiistian*) receded into the universal backdrop. The exiting hallway was darkened by closed doors and thick draperies on either side. Christian simultaneously walked both faster and slower than he desired. Unobstructed still, all he prayed, at the moment, was the front door could somehow be opened.

Light burst in from the street outside. The door wasn't

locked. It appeared midday. Christian still wasn't wearing any clothes, but that wasn't the first thought in his gut as he stepped out of Malik's small apartment onto the sidewalk where a shard of glass, as piercing as a viper's fangs, struck Christian's heel in retribution for some past digression.

A drop of blood following each footstep, enkindled panic straining his empty bowels, Christian limped, as if he had a clubfoot, hustling along the sidewalk to discover an alleyway where he could hide, a dumpster where there might be something to cover his body. Suddenly struck by his blatant nakedness, nothing assuaged his steadily building terror at being accosted, at being discovered for his nudity. He'd dreamt all this before. Although, he couldn't remember that at the moment. He'd had the dream over and over again since college. He was still in elementary school, at recess, where he took off his clothing along with everybody else, but when playtime was over, somehow his clothes went missing while everybody else redressed themselves. He had to return to the classroom, amid jeering schoolmates, completely disrobed. Luckily for him, at the moment (it must have been the middle of the workday), Malik's decrepit residential street appeared completely empty. His classmates had all disappeared.

The familiarity of an alleyway broke off the sidewalk in the distance. Despite his fear of what waited for him there, Christian determined to explore since he certainly knew he couldn't stay on the street without any clothes. Officer Ygg might be upon him at any moment – pointing his pistol right between his eyes. Although, he didn't *necessarily* know there weren't any laws against public nudity in Pandemonium *per se*. Like a city's scavenging rat, Christian glanced furtively from side to side. The serpent had yet to materialize.

Christian ducked down the alleyway. A sole dumpster

sat alone at its end. Nobody was sleeping beside it, and Christian was reminded of...

He threw the black top back. Plastic crashed on green metal. A man jumped out of the mess. Christian jumped in place, and if there'd been anything in his bladder, it would have been released.

With mozzarella strands of pepperoni pizza matted into his black hair and beard, Evius, chewing a piece of green molded crust, stood knee-deep in the mess, his black eyes staring down on Christian. And although Christian knew it was his long-lost guide, the man appeared even more different and wild than he had the last time Christian had encountered him so long ago as he swooned off a can of simple dog food.

Maybe it was because of his upward angle, but Evius stood so much taller than Christian ever remembered him. His hair had grown from a hipster's into a metal head's, and his five-o'clock shadow completely turned to midnight. His eyes, always deep set with bags, now cratered a full suitcase. But he held his hand over his heart as if he were saying America's pledge of allegiance, and he smiled his dark eyes lighting upon Christian. "Holy shit, man. You scared the bogeyman out of me. I never thought to see you again!" And still wearing his own heavy boots, Evius leaped out of the dumpster to embrace our hero in his birthday suit.

Christian was too dumbfounded to respond, but true to character, Evius prattled on and on in his manic manner, "Holy shit. Holy shit! So true. So true... Where in the hell you been? I swear I left you and you disappeared. I thought... I had no idea what happened. We ate that crazy old man's dog food, and you took a nap, but he totally freaked out, man. It was like he was some sort of jealous god, which if you think about it... I had to... I'll tell you, man, Pandemonium's changed. It's gentrification, man.

Total bull shit. What in hell you gonna do?"

Evius cocked his head to the side. Stepping back, he took in Christian's naked form. "Hey, wait a second. Where you been? You aren't... Were you at a party? While I was sleeping in this fucking trash can, man? That's cold, brother. That's real fucking cold. I thought we were friends. I thought we were... After everything I did for you? You left me alone with that crazy old man, while you went and... While I was homeless! That's bull shit, brother. Who the fuck do you think you are?"

For a moment, Evius appeared ready to slap Christian as if they were lovers. For his part, Christian stared back blankly at his former guide. Evius shrugged, "Whatever. I guess you don't really want to talk about it. I hope it was a good party, at least. The devil knows I can't find any. Hold on. What in the hell are you doing? We need to get you some clothes, man. I don't know what the laws are anymore about public nudity here in Pandemonium. What with how everything's changed since the white devils moved in and all. Where in the hell they came from... They've totally fucking... I guess, though, maybe you know more than I do these days. You may be totally cool. Maybe not. Hey. You got friends in high places, brother. And when I say high, I mean *high*. I don't know. Have you seen any of them yet? Not 'them', but *them*. I wish they'd go back to the other side, man, but don't tell *them* that. I mean, everybody's welcome, I guess. Thanks for coming back for a poor, old beggar like me. I just wish I was more presentable to somebody like you now. Pandemonium's supposed to be free and all that blah, blah, blah. Shit."

A theory of recognition registered in Evius' eye. "Hey. I know," he said, and he leaped back into the bin where he threw up a rain of garbage behind him and disappeared beneath layer upon layer of mushy refuse.

Christian was as adamant as a set of sardonic gargoyles, though, he was nowhere near as animate when Evius dramatically reappeared and said, "Now, don't worry. It's not like there's a dead body down here beneath all this garbage, which looks exactly like you by the way, that I took all these clothes off of. Because that would just be too weird, now, wouldn't it?" He threw out a white dress shirt (with a light yellow stain on it – who knew what that shit was), a pair of jeans, and brown boots – nothing like Christian's previous outfit… no socks or undershirt this time, though.

Suddenly, and quite miraculously, Christian found himself dressed yet again for the first time in forever as Evius asked, "Now, what were you saying we had to do next?"

Nothing, Christian thought, but he knew, even though Evius must have read his mind, that wasn't true. They had to…

"HEY!"

Annie…

"Uh-oh," Evius said, and he whispered to Christian who hadn't turned around yet to see who or *what* was shouting at them. The voice did sound familiar, though, but Christian couldn't quite place it. "I've been dodging that crazy copper since you and I first showed up here. I don't know where in the hell *he* came from. I swear, this current reign of terror has to come to an end…"

"That's right, boys, I'm talking to *you*." Christian turned to see Officer Ygg, his uniform still slightly out of place, approaching our two travelers with his hand lightly caressing the butt of the gun he'd yet to draw. "Just take it easy there, faster pussycat, these L.A. guns are a real zodiac mindwarp. So don't you fuck with me, now, okay?"

Evius whispered to Christian, "I think you'd better get

out of here, killer. I'll distract him."

At which point, Evius stepped in front of Christian as if he were a mother throwing her arm protectively in front of her only son during a high-speed near collision. "Now, just listen here, Officer. I don't think…" Evius began.

But Officer Ygg wasn't having any of it, "Judas priest! Morbid angel, what in Samhain's hell you say to me?" Then, Officer Ygg's gun was drawn, and before Christian could say anything, he screamed, "Deicide!"

A sharp crack broke the alleyway's silence. It echoed across the buildings entombing the trio. Evius' head jerked back as if the hand of God had taken that moment to grab him by the hair. A cool breeze splattered Christian's face, but before our hero could begin wiping the blood from his eyes, Evius collapsed to his knees. Then, our illustrious guide through the afterlife smacked facedown onto the cement. That sure as hell looked like it must have hurt as a sticky river of red pooled in the concrete grooves beside that familiar rat's nest of dirty black hair. Christian's breath cooled where it was trapped inside his chest.

Evius must have finally gotten his wish.

2.
De Mysteriis Dom Sathanas

Awake in the holding cell was hard. All Christian could envision was Evius, gnawed upon by the rats he had never seen, growing stiff on the cold concrete. Officer Ygg had left Christian's only friend (yes, Christian finally thought of Evius as his friend – how our world changes with death (which, in fact Christian knew already... sometimes the realization is simply arrived at too little, too late, which, in fact, Christian already knew, as well)) where he lay as our hero was shackled from wrists to neck once more amid myriad admonishments of how, "Boy, is your carcass in *real* trouble this time, Mr. Big. The bolt thrower's going to stick the anvil to you now. Lizzy Borden'll be reading *your* obituary."

If only he could wish. The terror itself was insurmountable. Starting in your toes, it creeps up your thighs, through your groin, into your stomach, shocks your chest cold as the concrete slab you're sitting upon, and settles static in your brain. The wish he'd made on that long-ago day at the fountain in Salzburg with Sophia still had yet to come true (but I won't tell *you* what it is... for that very reason – there's still time to come).

The cast of characters had grown more motley as time devolved, which it most definitely does. Despite the desired wish yet to materialize. Evius, for all intents and purposes, was most definitely gone. Ghosts filled Christian's cell along with him. *They* materialized, shimmered between memory, fantasy, and reality. A girl he'd seen as a child… a woman he'd known by name… a man he'd wished to fight… a bully who'd dogged his youth… a character from TV — appeared and disappeared: corporeal, static, ephemeral. A demon, complete with horns and fangs, shadowed the left-hand corner, licked his drooling lips. Christian was truly haunted now. By shadows, shades, and bodies. In reality, in fantasy. For better, for worse. In sickness *and* in health. Until death, we all do part. Mother Mary, in blue nun's habit, occupies this bench on the right…

"Hey…" was whispered from somewhere amid the shadows before him, "Whatchou here for?"

Christian shook his head. His shackles rattled like Saint Annie's as she'd pleaded with him to help her escape while he just left her all alone in Malik's lair.

"Cuz I don't know what in the hell I did. Do you?"

Christian didn't respond.

"I asked you a question!" the voice screamed from out the darkness. It seemed real enough, but Christian couldn't be too sure anymore.

Then, Joshua's haggard face, shocking Christian out of his stupor, appeared inches before his gaze. The old man was wrapped tight in a straitjacket. He gummed his scruffy lips. His bare feet were shackled together at swollen ankles. Christian thought he smelled like the Great Beast must have in his cage. It was the scent made Christian realize all this was *really* happening.

And he screamed.

Joshua simply laughed as a hidden key clinked a missing lock. The non-existent door clanked. Light streamed into the empty cell occupied quite simply by Joshua, Christian, and the silent nun in her blue habit.

Malik, his bulk blocking the light as it always did in the darkness of his apartment-palace, appeared like a nightmare's wish materialized in the frame. The devil smiled. "*Now it's time for some real fun and games.*"

In two strides, he was upon them. With a growl, Malik grabbed Christian by the chain connecting his wrists to his neck. He held Joshua by the padlock on the back of his jacket as he turned to the cell's final occupant and told her, "I'll be back for you later." But she didn't respond as Malik weightlessly dragged Joshua and Christian together out the door. In some strange sober moment, Christian thought it so odd – the nun didn't even flinch.

Outside the cell, blood-spattered stone walls lit by flickering shadows from a distant fire glowed eerie and cold. Christian stumbled against them jerked forward by Malik pushing Joshua ahead of himself. "Who you think you're shoving?" the old man grumbled.

"SILENCE!" Malik bellowed, which Joshua refused to heed. Instead, he continued his protestations.

From before, much like through the first tunnel Christian and Evius had traversed after leaving Machpelah, screams echoed, but this terror *felt* more tangible now. There was no freezing breath through open pores. Rather, physical heat radiated out the distance. Previously, there had only been the unknown to fear ahead. Now, reality had grown fantasy's vampire fangs. Gears cranked. Chains rattled. Grunts sounded, and the screams bore on and on through Christian's skull. This was, truly, hell.

They were underground. Christian already knew that. Officer Ygg had pushed him through a manhole's open

cover in the middle of the crossroads of two busy city
streets (Ave. Σ and א St. to be precise) to get here. His gun
in the small of Christian's back (right where Kundalini
could have uncoiled from), Officer Ygg had forced him
through Pandemonium's hidden sewer system – complete
with roiling pythons and yawning alligators – long before
this tunnel we're walking down now came to an end, finally,
which it did, and Christian gazed upon a wasteland: the
open abyss.

Flies, rubbing their hairy forelimbs atop unearthed
jewels fleshy beneath the beetles burrowing under
Christian's boots, buzzed everywhere through the darkness.
Barring the trio's way, a rusted iron trident dripping torn
meat descended behind Joshua in front of Malik in front of
Christian. Joshua stared dead-on ahead. Malik, even at his
towering height, looked up. A massive leathered hand with
long, broken nails flexed hard as it held tight the metal rod,
and a tired voice. Persuasive, deep – pointed out in front of
them to the left, "There's no exit. What was, is, and always
will be is us, my friend." The trident ascended. The trio
continued their trip as Christian passed underneath the
stone statue of a man with a serpent's face, his forked
tongue breathing down upon them on Christian's left as he
moved into the ossified screams of a roasting, oblique
plane.

The third of three in this haunted house, now, that
would make *him* the Holy Spirit: Christian, that is – despite
his earlier misgivings. Evius' gargoyle koan had come full
circle to fruition like the flies in front of Christian's eyes
right at that very moment creating a pointillist's blur of the
world envisioned. Just as he had predicted in his earlier
delirium, he didn't like being the last in line one bit. With
every passing moment, he glanced over his shoulder to see
what might be about to appear in the darkness behind him,

what amorphous figure's nails might be ready to slice through his white shirt with the yellow stain on it and grab him by his slick sweating skin. All Christian saw in the darkness, though – nothing but the stone statue of that man with the lizard gaze's glare, a red glow emanating from nothing below igniting him, turned upon Malik (seemingly safe and content in the warm middle of two others) and his awkwardly struggling train.

Joshua was the first to notice them. "Goddamnit!" he screamed, and Christian thought he'd fallen. He hadn't, but the plane veered down to the left. Ascending it from out the flames, with what seemed to be their robes burning away, two leprous monks carrying sickles in opposite hands appeared. They didn't stop walking as they approached the trio, but they barred their blades in the direction of the wanderers. Before Christian could close his eyes, duck, or turn, the duo, skin and hair now catching their clothing's flames, had sliced the blades through either side of Joshua's straitjacket without a hitch in their steps as they kept walking. To Christian, it appeared the first through the haunted house was perhaps in the most dangerous predicament, then.

"You…" Malik, apparently confused as to whether to drop his burdens and pursue or to ensure his damaged goods were safe, bellowed before Christian realized Joshua was somehow free. The straitjacket's buckles clanked against the ground's stones as those malformed monks simultaneously ascended into the deeper darkness.

Much quicker than he had when attempting to attack Christian on the subway train midway through his previous journey, Joshua turned on Malik. None of his aged weight apparent in his current agility, mimicking a dog's snarling grin, Joshua flashed his teeth. He brought his fingers up as if they had claws. "Stand down!" Malik shouted with his usual presumed authority to the old man. Whether or not Joshua heard him, though, was anybody's guess. The old man leapt off the ground. In mid-air, he clamped his teeth deep into the flesh of their captor's neck, raked his nails down Malik's cheeks. Blood spraying, Malik – so different than his previous airs had always made him appear – screamed shrilly.

Christian was too taken aback by the Master's apparent weakness to respond in any way whatsoever. He blinked but didn't think about running as Malik dropped Christian's chain to the ground while he fell like a body bag of so many rocks. Joshua – his eyes crazed from bloodlust, his mouth and hands dripping red – looked up from his newfound prey. "Bite?" he asked Christian.

Not even because of the last time he had offered him a meal, the dead man felt he might vomit at the thought of a morsel from Malik's throat. He was no baby sparrow receiving a regurgitated last supper from its long-dead mother. Not any more, at least.

When, up from the earth, as if hidden beneath a mechanized trap door underneath the stage, a shuddering rumble began. The ground cracked apart beside Christian's feet as he wobbled in place – both from his knees and from the *force*. The entire world flickered in and out like bad reception on a rabbit-eared TV set from Christian's early childhood development, like his vision when he took the inopportune moment to mix too much alcohol with weed. The *Deus ex machina* emerged.

This creature was, sincerely, Beelzebub: The Lord of the Flies.

A spider, more specifically. A black widow more magnificent and sublime than any Christian had ever encountered before, which he knew by the red hour glass as if Death Himself were timing Malik's blood draining through the sands of time. For a second, he recalled Saint Annie's story of Israfel, the horse. Then, he forgot... everything as the spider's 8 legs (each, easily, as long and lanky as Christian's entire body – a foot fetishist's fantastic dream) began moving mechanistically towards Joshua still clamped down on Malik's throat as if he were fulfilling his first threat to Christian on that deserted desert's subway train – *You'd think I was a vampire saying something like that: I remember that neck. I can assure you I'm not.* Although, at that very moment, if he could speak from his open throat gurgling blood whistling in the wind, Malik would surely have disagreed.

With the spider towering above him in the smoky darkness, casting her shadow before her over him as she was lit from behind by the pit's flames, Joshua started up from his disturbed meal. "I see we have a real connoisseur on our hands," the old man said as he wiped the blood from his lips and hands and smeared it down his shirt with a flourish and a bow towards the giant arachnid.

The spider didn't waste any time. She set one hind leg on either side astride Malik, and she shot a long web from out the back of her abdomen with which she began twisting and turning her scavenged prize along the ground, wrapping him up in her gossamer to die in her embrace.

"I already did the hard part for you," Joshua shouted above the sound of the black widow scrambling her prey along the earthen floor. Malik's moans muffled beneath his webbed sarcophagus, which Joshua became exceedingly aware of. "The least you could do is give me a piece..." he begged. But with the last bits of web trailing out her anus, the spider drew her newest mate up to her bosom, and with a many-eyed glance at Joshua (totally ignoring Christian), she began to walk slowly away.

"Wait a second, lady. Where you think you're going?"

Joshua growled. He grabbed Christian's chain from where it lay twisted on the ground, and the old man began dragging our hero along behind him as the two of them followed the spider carrying her burden deeper down Pandemonium's trail.

Christian trundled along, kicking over rocks and bones, stumbling behind Joshua who kept shouting at the spider to – *Give me back my damned meal!* as he picked stones and skulls and femurs off the ground to throw at the spider's armored hide, which, of course, terrified Christian the old man might draw the widow's ire down upon the two of them defenseless against her massive natural weaponry.

Where the spider eventually stopped, Christian had no idea, but he was right behind her. It didn't seem she'd come home since there was no sticky web to stand upon – simply the same earth scorched as if the Soviets here were retreating from Nazi pursuers, as well.

There was a reason for her current hesitation, however. In front of them stood, oddly enough, a toll booth as if our triumvirate plus their spider (like the world's original triumvirate plus Cleopatra) were trying to flee the United States for Mexico. But Christian wasn't aware of that. All he knew right now was the gate was down, and although, Christian and Joshua could easily have slid under it while the black widow could just as easily have stepped over it, they waited.

The toll booth window slid open, and a face peered out its smoky gloom. The man in the booth smiled. He had dripping fangs hanging over his bottom lip, and poking through his flat cap were two red horns. Christian remembered something, but he wasn't sure what it was. Just as in life, trauma had damaged his memories.

"Now, what do we have here?" the thing in the toll booth asked. "It looks like you may be carrying contraband of some sort or other." Christian wasn't sure if this were true or not, but he thought he saw the spider subtly shake her head, *No.* "Well, let me see, then," the thing in the toll booth went on, and the black widow dropped her burden, with a dull thud, to the ground.

The booth's door opened, and the toll collector – his back hunched over, his hands hanging down to his knees – appeared with a pair of shears that could only have been the same shears that had cut Christian's clothes off his body before he had been sold into Malik's custody. The collector dug straight into the spider's web mummifying Christian's former captor.

Malik again revealed beneath the web's sticky remnants smeared across his face and chest, the toll collector set his arms akimbo. "Well, this is no good at all," he said. "What's your name, sir?"

Malik, somehow still alive and aware, croaked from his chewed-out neck, "*Malik...*"

"Is that what you're known as?" the toll collector asked Christian and Joshua.

"Well, I never..." Joshua began while Christian simply nodded.

And the toll collector shrieked, "That is NOT true! I know you... You are a nothing, a nobody, a small, little demon. *You* are NOT Malik. You are *Jafal.* To claim that name, Malik, for yourself, Jafal... Well, that is.... That's..." the toll collector looked again at Joshua and Christian. His eyes were aflame. If he'd been closer, their heat would have blistered Christian's skin. "You two may go," the toll collector said. "*They* must stay," he nodded at Malik and the black widow.

Without any further hesitation, Joshua dragged Christian underneath the toll gate. After standing straight on the other side, not paying attention to where he was going, Christian stared back over his left shoulder. He was lucky he didn't get turned to a pillar of salt. Not that he really had any recollection of such a myth. As far as *he* could tell, there was nothing of The Lord in that place. So there was no reason not to look back. In fact, there was every reason *only* to look back. Given the past, his future was simply too terrifying to imagine. Only he and Joshua were left in that haunted house. Their syllogism's middle term had already been removed. The Truth behind Evius' koan.

The toll collector disappeared and reappeared from his booth carrying a hacksaw in his right hand and a Mason jar in his left. The black widow, to Christian's amazement, appeared to be smiling and rubbing one set of her limbs together as if excited for the coming scene. How does a bug, even a gigantic one, display the possibility of *emotion*? That's what Christian found himself immediately wondering, but she did. For, the world is everything that is the case. Regardless of what Christian believed.

The toll collector dropped to his knees and began sawing through the flesh encasing Malik's skull. Christian's former master screamed a blood-curdling cry like Christian had never heard, not even in the darkest depths of a crack house's horrors. The demon obviously wasn't dead, and the toll collector (even from Christian's distance) appeared to be grinning like The Joker from ear to ear. The spider leaped up and down in excitement in place.

The top quarter of Malik's head was removed. As if by some sort of magic, Christian was able to make out in intricate detail every single one of the killer bees swarming through the collector's Mason jar – their furry abdomens, their sharp stingers. He could hear their buzzing wings. The toll collector removed the bottom part of Malik's brain with a silver spoon. The jar was opened, and the bees were dumped into Christian's former tormentor's empty skull cavity. The toll collector mashed Malik's brain, mingled with earthen dirt, back into his head. The bloody top of his skull was sloppily replaced and stapled into place via an industrial stapler produced from the collector's pocket to entomb the hive alive in Malik's head.

"Voila!" the collector screamed an excited squeal.

A bee crawled out of Malik's nose and flew away. With a guttural shriek, the demon leaped to his feet. Slamming his palms against the sides of his head so hard what was left of his brain must have bruised, Malik ran circles over the scorched earth. But he couldn't escape what was trapped inside himself. He slammed into a mountainous stone wall, and the toll collector exploded in guffaws. His teeth chattering, his eyes wild, blood and bees dripped out of Malik's nose and mouth and buzzed from his ears as Christian, now sick to his stomach, finally turned away from the torturous scene.

He felt no resolution, no restitution. In fact, he felt an emotion he had become quite unaccustomed to over his years of concern about only his own suffering – *sympathy*. For the devil was in so much pain. Beating his head against the scorched earth, Malik writhed and cried and tore at his scalp. Something like this must have happened time and time again to Christian's former tormentor (the scar running down the demon's cheek... How had *that* come to be?). Malik's madness might not even have been his own fault. It might have been a result of his *world*. Christian wanted to cry – for Sophia, for Annie, for Evius, for Malik, for everybody on this abandoned planet who never fulfills their dreams... But even after everything he'd been through, the world still wasn't a place for tears. That fact made Christian want to cry even more. An infinite regression; a logical absurdity – one among many.

Joshua dragged him along the non-Euclidean plane, which it shouldn't have been at such close proximity. Every few steps, Christian would stumble, unsure of how to walk in a world not adhering to the geometrical laws he was accustomed to. *He* was still a three-dimensional man, or so he believed. But still, Joshua dragged him on as if they had some place to be, some secret assignation to keep. Which they did, Christian simply didn't know that fact yet. Joshua did, though, or so it seemed, at least. The old man ran his hand along the scorched stone wall beside which they walked while he mumbled, "I know it's here somewhere... That's not it... That's not it..." Until he turned, looked at Christian, smiled raggedly, and said, "Here it is."

Christian didn't know what to make of the old man's pronouncement. He was sweating. He didn't know where it was or *what* it was. In his chains, he swallowed in hesitation and wiped his brow with his cuffed together hands – unsure what the future would bring. Not that he ever was. It's simply how the world is. Certain only he would be dragged into whatever abyss the old man contemplated while Joshua, once again, *seemed* to know.

Whether or not the old man pressed a button or something of the like, Christian never did and never could know. The rock wall slid back, revealing the stones themselves to be false, a manmade façade, something Christian had never even imagined as he stumbled along beside them. Which meant the workmanship was actually quite sound given the amount of rocks Christian had broken during his career as a stone mason. He had an eye for such falsities. Behind the stones, a red door studded with black metal dots was revealed as if it were the entrance point to some sort of heavy metal tribunal.

"Well, I guess we'd better go in," Joshua said as he turned the doorknob before Christian could even protest, which he knew already was in vain. The old man stepped inside and dragged Christian along behind him.

1.
Closing Argument

Initially, the room they entered appeared familiar as a witch's black cat. Even though a blood red curtain blocked the stage directly opposite them. Whether or not this false proscenium was only for show was anybody's guess. But something, if Pandemonium proved true, was most definitely hidden behind the veil. The floor sloped down to the right. A hole in the ceiling, revealing 2x8 girders, supported whatever roof this strange cell had atop it. There was a broken down table in the middle of the room that, for some strange reason, reminded Christian of an altar for rites of black magic somebody might imagine themselves to perform. For the life of himself, Christian couldn't imagine *why*. A lingering odor of rat piss came up from the cobwebbed corners. But it was the chains attached to either wall making Christian shiver.

"Where are we?" he wondered.

Joshua didn't say anything. The old man simply stared at the curtain as if awaiting some sort of sign from the netherworld. His intensity didn't fade until... with a metallic rattling of gears, the curtain began drawing back. The wizard was about to be revealed, and Joshua hopped to attention. He ran circles around Christian with much more force than his aged body had previously appeared capable of mustering – at least, previous to his vicious attack on Malik. Crowing like a cock, Joshua kicked Christian behind the knees. His cries turned into a howl. Then, a bellow, "Kneel!"

Not of his own volition but just as he was commanded, Christian fell to his knees. Joshua grabbed him by the hair, and as if our hero were a dog who'd pissed the floor, he forced his nose into the ground. Approaching the earth, Christian noticed the labyrinth etched into the ground beneath him, and he vaguely recalled the cathedrals of Europe. The old man growled, "And bow before your Lord…"

Joshua was so much stronger than he appeared. (*You know, I killed a man once.*) The cranking gears stopped, and a cold wind brushed over Christian. Within the wind, voices could be felt. Christian already knew what they said. Unsure whether the final voice was real or imagined, Christian heard – or, rather, felt – the words, "Let him go, my friend."

The pressure released from the back of Christian's head. First, he turned to his left. He remembered a wooden floor. Even though it should have been, it wasn't Joshua standing beside him. Instead, next to him was a human body, but it wasn't old. This body had the fully muscled legs and torso of a man grown well into his thirties while wearing golden sandals and nothing more than a loin cloth over burnishing skin. A dog's black head took the place of Joshua's face. The Joshua creature licked its nose with a long, canine tongue. It held a staff topped by a metallic bird, wings spread to fly away. The only imperfection in the wood was a crack that extended through the staff's top four inches. Christian remembered the sparrow dead upon his floor starting this journey. The pinnacle of this staff was, somehow, that same bird gilded and reborn. Then, the golden bird atop the staff came to life. With a cry, it ruffled its feathers and flew away into whatever eternity lay beyond that hole in the ceiling.

Christian wished...

"Silence!" the Joshua dog creature screamed.

Christian thought, *But I didn't...*

"Silence!"

"It's okay, friend, let him..." the other's voice soothingly went on, "... look now."

It was as if he didn't have a choice. Hesitantly, Christian glanced forward. Center stage, on a golden throne of red velvet with a cobra's snakeskin hood ascending the back, a man's carved face screaming off of either arm, sat (as imperfectly manicured as when they'd first met) Evius... Life after death after life after death. Something like the eternal transmigration of souls, the wheel of samsara – Christian couldn't believe his eyes. His eternal guide appeared as if nothing had ever happened... as if this whole comedy had been nothing more than a split-second's dream.

On stage left, right next to Evius, an empty throne was placed. To Christian's left, on Evius' right side, were six more thrones. The empty thrones' backs were embroidered in black symbols Christian simply couldn't understand: ל ו ה י
נ ו (Evius) א

"I thought you were dead..." Christian said.

"I am," Evius responded. "But so are you."

"Who are you?"

Evius shook his head. With a dismissive flourish, he said, "It doesn't matter." He leaned forward to point a long nail at Christian's chest, "What does matter is the weight of your heart, Christian..." At which words, one of the sparrow's many feathers, previously caught on the ceiling's holey edge, fell out of the sky. Like a dog lapping a fly, the Joshua dog monster caught it tight between his fingers. Only to let it go. The feather twittered through the air, landed to tickle Christian's nose where he blew it back up into the atmosphere. Whether or not it eventually landed, Christian never knew.

"Now, we have a real problem here," Evius said. "We need to assess the reality of your situation – as unreal as *that* may be."

"What does that *mean*?" Christian begged.

Evius looked to his right. In one of the chairs (ה), the air began vibrating as if the fabric of the universe itself were splitting apart to reveal the strings composing it. Out of the madness, a funnel cloud swirled. In some sort of strange inversion, Christian felt himself Dorothy beginning her colorless journey to Oz. Even the Wicked Witch's cackle could be heard/felt... But there was no broomstick, only the woman who had liberated Christian from Malik's imprisonment, seated with one hand gripping either arm of her throne. Her immaculate jawline and royal nose still as angular as her long boot heels, she wore the same black dress she'd had on when appearing to Christian in Saint Annie's cell...

"I don't think he deserves it," she was *in medias res*. "As far as I'm concerned, he had his chance. That poor little girl... Guilty as charged."

"Duly noted," Evius said. "Next..."

What the hell's happening?

The air between the arms of the chair labeled   ' shivered. A lightning bolt crashed, and Saint Annie was there. At the sight of her, a lump rose from Christian's heart to his throat. She was clothed, finally, in what she was probably wearing on the day she never knew she died – a black tee shirt tucked into cutoff shorts. Her backpack appeared beside her. She *was* a child. Christian could taste the guilt the woman in black had charged him with. But he wasn't going to cry. Saint Annie was saying, "But Israfel, Mr. Christian was so nice to me. He told me the story, the story about him and Sophia, and it was so real, so sad. He doesn't deserve it, everything he's been through. He doesn't deserve it. He's so innocent, Israfel, I can't believe it. Is that okay?" She glanced to her left across the woman in black at Evius. What she saw in him, Christian didn't know.

Evius nodded. "Point taken," he admitted.

Christian counted the number of chairs. His saliva stuck in his throat. That whole time, Evius must have been…

To the immediate left of the woman in black, a fire scorched the 1 chair. Out of the smoke and flames, Vesper appeared. Christian's heart stopped. She crossed one serpentine leathered leg over the other as she said, "I don't know what the child's talking about. We gave him a chance with the game, but he couldn't answer any of our questions, not a single one. I don't know what you can do with him, but I know what you can do *to* him." She stared Christian dead in his eyes as she ended with the simple word: "Guilty." A coldness nobody could save him from coursed out of Christian's brain through his entire body. If he'd known, things would have been different.

His soul felt as cold as the water beginning to bubble up on the 1 seat. Those bubbles solidified like so many drops of mercury as they sprouted hips and a torso and legs and arms and feet. Before Christian knew what was happening, Belle was sitting there in all her aqueous glory. "I agree. I gave him a present, but instead of simply accepting it, he tried to steal my dust from me. There's only one thing I can say for him, and I think you know what that is…"

Evius nodded and grinned. "Of course, I do, my dear. I'll note it in the record." But he wasn't writing anything down.

Christian felt no hope of escape. The trial was fixed. Whoever Evius actually was, once upon a time, Christian had thought him a friend. But as far as he could tell, right now, he was down three to one, and if the number of chairs were right, it would only take one additional guilty vote to send him to the devil knew where.

When on the 1 chair furthest from Evius, Zoe appeared. Christian dropped his head in despair as she said, "I don't know what to think about the defendant. He came on real strong the first time he met me, and then, he was terrified whenever I tried playing with him later. To tell the truth, I feel kind of sorry for him. He has no idea what he wants and even less of an idea how to get it. How could he? He's like a child. So... No, I don't think he's guilty to tell the truth. I think he's more misguided. Yeah, that's what I think about him. He's misguided, but still, I want to know – Why are we spending so much time talking about somebody who hasn't even done anything special so far as I can tell? Forget about him. It feels like we've been on this subject for years. Unless you can finally convince me *why* I should even begin paying attention..."

"We're getting to that," Evius interjected. "It's the *dénouement* we may never get beyond. Witness!"

Christian looked up. From Evius' immediate right... "Hello, Christian," Sophia's sonorous accent rang through the makeshift courtroom. The tears building behind Christian's eyes in anticipation of his own imminent anguish gushed forth, but for once, not for himself. He was speechless. She was everything he'd dreamed in that brief moment when he'd truly contemplated the hole in his original ceiling. The only words he could choke out of his throat were – "Are you real?"

"As real as you are," Sophia said.

There she was, again. Her short, black hair still cropped to her neck, still parted boyishly to one side. As fashionably European as ever. Still, after all these years. There was so much Christian wanted to say. He sobbed, "I'm sorry." It was so little, but it was all that came to him in the moment, "I'm so sorry…"

"I know, Christian. I know you are. I am, too." Her accent was too beautiful to even hear.

"For what?"

"For everything. Like you."

"You were so young…"

"So were you."

"I know, but I…"

"It's okay," Sophia said. "I forgive you." That was all Christian had ever needed to hear. Finally, he felt he could live. He was no longer that baby bird, dead as soon as it had hatched. He wiped his eyes. He felt his wings. If only it weren't too late…

"But let's not get too far ahead of ourselves," Evius said. "There's still one chair left. Whose could it possibly be?" He looked at the one chair to his left while Christian realized, in that precise moment, the jury was hung.

So much older than the last time he had ever seen her, Christian's mother appeared there. Wringing her hands, a tear came to her aged eye as she stared at her only son on his knees in that disheveled throne room, his hands and feet shackled together while a beast loomed over his left shoulder. "Mom?" Christian asked in disbelief, "What are you doing here?"

"I just wanted to see you one last time," she said, "To put my hands on your innocent face…"

Christian's mouth dried out. He remembered when he'd

first met Evius, when he'd tried to leave right before his former guide had pulled out that joint, and he thought...

"So it's decided, then..." Evius said.

Christian's mother wiped her eyes, sniffled, and nodded, "Of course, it is."

"Exactly," Evius said, and he stood up. His boots clicked as he hopped off the stage and approached Christian. He nodded, and the Joshua beast lifted our hero to his feet.

"Well," Evius said, "Looks like it comes down to me to be the tiebreaker again."

"But..." Christian said, "How could there be a tie? It was an odd number. You heard them. I'm innocent. Four to three." He glanced across the faces of all the women on stage. He didn't really know any of them other than the two who were crying. "Can I go back to Machpelah, now?"

"You don't get it, do you, Christian?"

"No," Christian said, "I don't think I do..."

Evius produced a gun from out his pocket. Christian needed to run, but the Joshua beast held him tight in place. Evius pointed the gun straight into Christian's face.

Christian tried straining out of the barrel's gaze. He cried, "Why are you doing this to me?"

Evius shrugged, "What else am I going to do?"

The Joshua beast knocked Christian in the back of the legs. He fell to his knees once more. From behind a veil of tears, Christian looked up at Evius who said, "Remember, One has all power..." He leveled the gun at Christian's temple. He squeezed the trigger. An explosion blasted through Christian's mind. And darkness *was* upon the face of the deep.

Portrait by PJ Adams

About the Author

Michael Anthony Adams, Jr. is originally from Whittier, CA. He holds a master's degree in Philosophy from the New School for Social Research in New York City. As a teenager, he was the lead vocalist and lyricist for Richmond, VA-based hardcore band Broken Chains of Segregation. In 2012, he began publishing his collected works under the pen name Israfel Sivad. He's the founder of Ursprung Collective, a spoken word/music project referred to as "fantastic brain food" on ReverbNation. He was the primary lyricist on indie rock group One & the Many's first two albums, *Forms* and *Hours*. His writing has appeared in the *Santa Fe Literary Review*, *The Stray Branch*, *Badlands Literary Journal*, and more. He currently lives with his partner and collaborator, artist PJ Adams, and their children in Baltimore, MD.

www.MichaelAnthonyAdamsJr.com